Predator and prey...

FANGS OF FATE

REBECCA PARCHA

A UNTISH SERIES NOVEL

To the dreamers, the storytellers, and the inspired.
To the brave, the bold, and the beautiful.
None can write your story, none but you.
Only you can determine your course, only you.
Choose the courageous path of hope, chase your aspirations, and love your deficiencies—you're more powerful than you know, and perfect just the way you are.

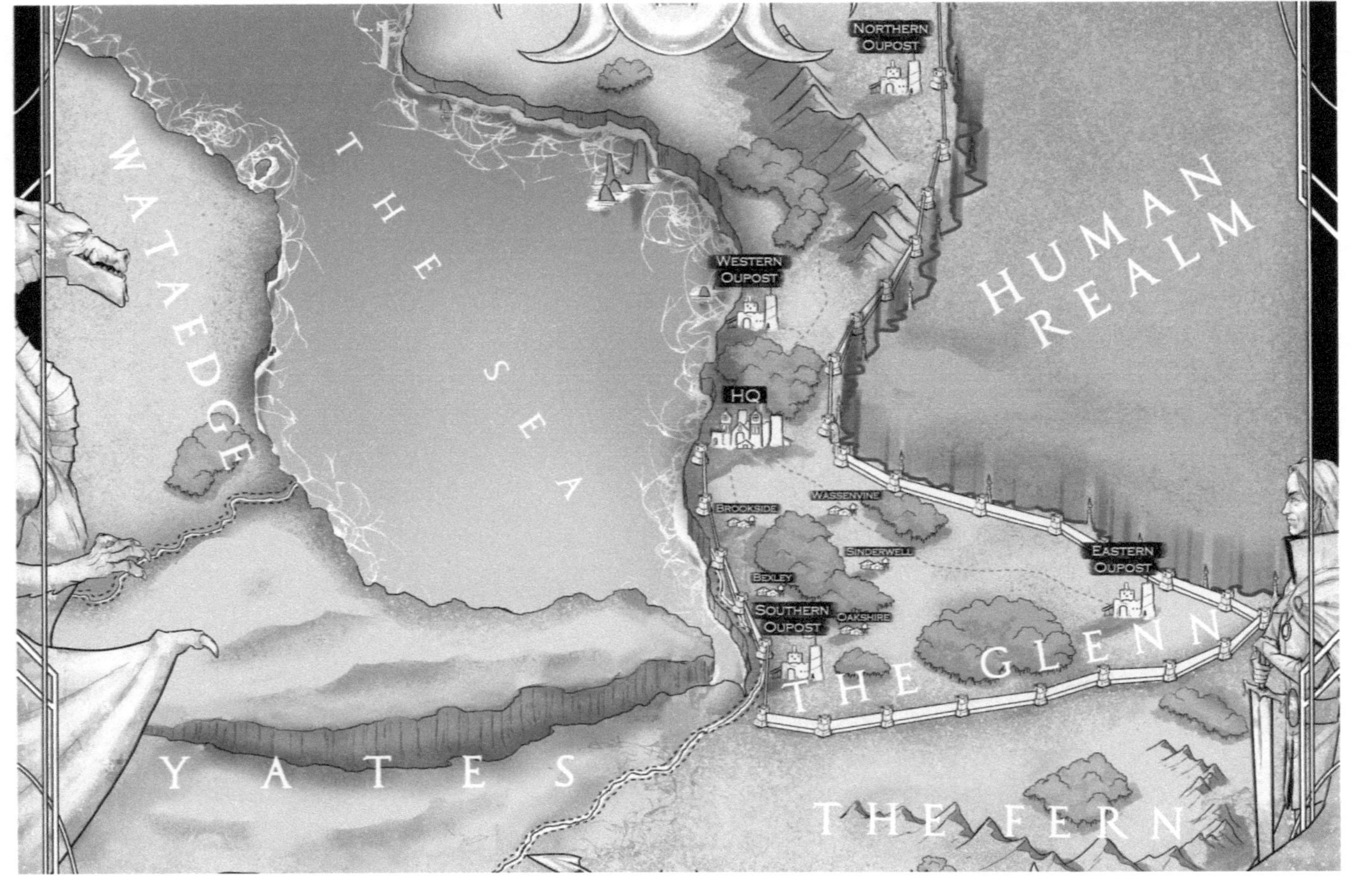

HUMAN REALM
NORTHERN OUPOST
WESTERN OUPOST
HQ
WASSENVINE
BROOKSIDE
SINDERWELL
BEXLEY
EASTERN OUPOST
SOUTHERN OUPOST
OAKSHIRE
THE GLENN
THE FERN
THE SEA
WATAEDGE
YATES

CHAPTER 1
TATE

The heat from the flames was getting closer. I needed to leave. He laid there, pinned against the floor by my body, my wrist at his throat. I dug the tip of my thumb in, pricking his skin. Blood bloomed where I squeezed. I leaned down and licked it up. It tasted remarkably good for a spoiled bag of blood like this man.

Ten innocents. He killed ten kids when he burned down the last apartment complex. Five of those children belonged to a foster family. He was an abomination to mankind and any death would be too kind for him.

His eyes were fully dilated, fear filled the air. I could taste it, a symphony to the iron on my tongue. He whimpered and I knew he'd beg for his life if I released enough pressure from his throat. I wouldn't though. I smiled icily. Bending over, I brushed my lips next to his ear, slowly exhaling.

"Judith. Amy. Kyle. Roy. Trever. Nancy." The names of the children he murdered. The ones he killed in cold blood. He shuddered and squirmed, trying to break free.

"Claire. Benny. Natalie. Hannah." I looked into his eyes—a window to a dark soul. "You took their lives. Consider this justice."

I lowered my mouth to his jugular and then clamped down. My fangs sank in slowly, lengthening the painful puncture. He screamed and it competed with the sound of the flames in the next room. The building would crumble, and his body would be the only one in the rubble. I had sounded the alarm and screamed 'fire' when the flames were but mere sparks.

The building was practically empty to begin with. He lived in a dump. The complex likely violated every regulation code there was, and anyone here was likely a convict and doped up on drugs like this bag of shit. I pulled deeply and filled my throat with his blood. It had been too long since I'd last fed. Feeding has always felt a bit at odds with my personality. In childhood, it had been rainbows and pink everything. *Then*, I'd had the warm embrace of my mother, the shelter of a safe home, and no concern as to whose blood I'd need to consume next. I was young. Now, all the warm safety of my childhood had been stripped, leaving me to deal with the steel of the world. Now, I was both predator and prey.

Feeding was what my nature demanded. And grotesque as I once saw it, it felt right. Especially when I was feasting from a degenerate like the man beneath me. I needed to release him. I could start to feel the heat creeping up from below. This room would be engulfed in flames soon. I couldn't drain his life force—it was against the rules of the Glenn. One more draw, then I'd release him and leave him to burn alive.

Images of those tiny corpses filled my mind. He had left them to burn, to die. He had been their foster dad and *he* had started the fire and left. He was a vile man. The pictures from Tim's computer wouldn't soon disappear. I still saw them when I laid awake at night. The small, charred teddy bear beside the body of an innocent soul—a mark that would forever scar my heart. They were human, I knew this. I shouldn't care. I wasn't *supposed* to care. Yet, some part of my DNA couldn't leave it alone—I couldn't feed from humans if I didn't think they deserved it. It would be a fatal flaw had I not found a route around my conscience four years ago when I completed my turn. I was sixteen then; like all vampires, it was time to either transition or choose to live the life of a human...forever. Naturally, I chose the longer existence. My first mistake.

I drew again and began to withdraw but the flow down my throat was too sweet, it beckoned me further.

Sweat began to drip down my back, my forehead. Warm, very warm. The flames would be visible any minute.

Fire was fatal for my kind—a similarity we shared with humans. I should leave, should have already left, as I have no intention of going up in flames with him. But...the sweet iron liquid called to me. One more draw, just a *little* more. The cherry note to his blood was intoxicating.

I had been overfeeding lately; the past month I'd had an increase in both hunger and vengeance. It made sense. Or at least I believed so, given the date. One year ago today, my mother was taken from me. There would be no justice for her.

I could feel his body go limp beneath me. *Crack!* The sound of embers, of wood being swallowed whole by flames climbing the walls. Time was up. Closing my eyes, I drank. I pulled. I swallowed. His blood was almost gone, just a few drops remained. Two more drags and there was hardly anything left. But...I couldn't stop. The high from draining took over. My head swam, and adrenaline swallowed my senses. Power filled my veins; I squeezed his throat tighter and heard a *snap*, distantly aware that his jaw was no longer pressed against my cheek, that he made no other noises. He was gone. I pulled again, but this time no blood came. I had emptied him.

My energy doubled, strength flooding my system, and a comforting warmth flowed through my veins. My limbs tingled and my head felt light. There really wasn't anything like a blood-drain high.

Retracting my fangs from his throat, I let him fall to the floor in an unnatural heap. The room was on fire. I looked toward where the window was and only saw a wall of flames.

I could have just made a fatal mistake. I stood, angling my body to where I knew the window was. Blood help me. With a deep breath, I lunged through the flames, bright orange and hints of blue filled my vision. Heat swallowed me with intensity and drew the breath from my lungs.

I broke free from the fire and was falling in the crisp night air from the second story. I landed on the ground twenty feet below and tumbled. The glamour may hide my bone discrepancy, but gravity couldn't be fooled.

Deep breath in, steady.

Slowly, I rose from a crouch and shook out my legs. The old pain returned, but I blocked it out—easier to do on a blood-high. My skin itched but didn't hurt. Odd considering my contact with the flames.

Sirens sounded remarkably close, but no first responders. *Yet.* I rose from my crouched position and set into a jog, slow at first to allow my body time to recover from the trauma of the impact. I ran around the block, past the chain-link fence, down an alley, and then up another. After thirty minutes I approached my apartment. If I was ever thankful for my version of jogging, which rivaled most human athletes, it was in times like these. The high from feeding was still present, my head still abuzz.

The fire in my chest had been ignited.

This was likely why they outlawed draining our vessels. Not only did it cause a supply issue, but it made the hunger increase. Well, mental hunger, I physically felt sated.

Entering the apartment, I shut the door and headed for the shower. I turned toward the full-length mirror and paused. My clothes were practically nonexistent. The once solid leather jacket and leggings, my favorite pair, had been so badly burned they were in patches. There was more visible skin than my 'clothing' covered. How had I not noticed that sooner? Looking closer, I expected to see welts, burns, third degree or worse, but my skin was just pink with a strange black tint. Odd. I poked at it tentatively, but it didn't hurt.

I shook my head; this made no sense. None. Perhaps it was an illusion from my draining high. I hadn't drained someone fully in three years. Tonight, I'd lost control. Thankfully the body would be nothing but charred remains and no one would know what had happened. Specifically, President Dale and the guara wouldn't know I violated the ethics code this side of the veil.

I stepped out of my boots and set them to the side before stripping out of my clothes and tossing them into the bin. It was time for new clothes anyway. I pulled back the rose gold shower curtain and hobbled into the steaming water. My left leg throbbed a bit, as it sometimes did when I overexerted myself. I've only ever known what the world is like with two different-sized femurs, injured as a baby, and so specialty shoes had been my way of life. Other than the uneven footing when barefoot, I really didn't notice it much.

The water pressure was glorious, soothing my aching muscles. I got away with it tonight, but I needed to rein myself in; this couldn't happen again. I scrubbed at my dry skin, noting the red patches. Even in a blood-high, the insistent itching was notable. Turning off the tap, I stepped out and grabbed my hot pink robe and threw it on, before shuffling into my fluffy white slippers.

Thank blood no one from the Glenn could see me here.

I smiled as I made my way to my room and grabbed my healing lotion. I rubbed it in slow circles on my arms where the burns were the worst. Five hours. I needed to be back to the Glenn in just five hours. I smiled, enough time for a catnap. I pulled back the furry cream comforter and climbed inside. Setting my neon green alarm clock for four hours, I rested my head back on the salmon satin pillowcase and allowed my tingling limbs to lull me to sleep.

CHAPTER 2
TATE

Pressing through the veil was never pleasant. Today, in particular, the guara seemed to be enjoying themselves as it took all my strength to push through and then all my stealth to catch myself before careening into the ground. Jackasses. I looked up at the laughing guara, sneers on their faces, and flipped them the bird.

Straightening the strap of my tote bag, I headed for the Glenn's headquarters. High Lordship Lee had a strict policy, first complete the blood drop *then* enjoy access to the rest of the Glenn. One of President Dale's many annoying rules: feed others, then yourself. As if he lived by that standard. Prick.

Sauntering in, I squared my shoulders and moved past the main gate—fifty feet high and made of solid iron. It was an enormous eyesore and one that was built in the last fifty years; supposedly, it provided protection from other Vamps—as if we needed it. We've been living in peace for the last several decades, since the Great War a century ago. A large shadow formed in my peripheral, and I surged left, ducked, and was met hand-to-hand by Chance.

"Ah, a pleasure as always, Tate."

"Chance. Let go of my fucking hand."

His grip tightened as he smirked, that stupid smirk that had several female vampires dropping their pants. Not me, never again. Never mind his dreamy blue eyes, the color of glaciers barely submerged in crisp water. Forget his curly blond hair that waved perfectly over his left eyebrow in a way that suggested he knew just how hot he was.

An enigma, that's what he was. Vampires were not attractive—we were mediocre at best. Somehow, Chance seemed to be an exception to that rule; he'd bedded nearly every female in the Glenn. I returned his smirk and inched to my fullest height with a straight spine. Still several inches shorter, but I didn't care—after my recent feeding, I felt formidable.

His left eyebrow raised. "You better than anyone should know I have an exceptional sense of smell." He lowered his head and sniffed. Actually sniffed. "You want me. Just admit it, TK," he said the last word in challenge, while pulling me closer to him. Much too close.

I snarled at him even as my stupid, stupid heart betrayed me by beating faster. The luck of a twenty-year-old female. His familiar scent of spicy bergamot filled my nostrils, beckoning me back to a year before. No, I refused to remember. Things were very different now and for good reason. He was unforgivable. *He* was responsible for Irene.

"No, *Chance*," I said as I poked my finger into his chest. "And in case you missed it, it's called a pun. Your name is the same as your answer, just add a 'no' in front. And if you need any other help," I inched even closer, never to be outdone in a challenge, "you can go ask your daddy. In fact, you can come with me, and I can explain your total lack of scruples." I yanked my arm free and took three steps back.

His nostrils were flaring. Ah yes, the big bad Chance had his feelings hurt. Good.

"You're not even supposed to be here," I forged on. "I thought all the trash stayed in the S.O." I savored the way his face blanched as my jab landed.

"Really?" His jaw ticked.

I simply crossed my arms and held his stare. He thought his dick did all the talking but forgot that intelligence is a prerequisite for many areas of life, sex included.

"My men in the Southern Outpost are well trained and the best in our military," he began. "Disrespect me all you want, Tate, but watch what you say about the soldiers who *risk* their lives for their country, and for spoiled brats like yourself."

Without an ounce of apparent effort, he jumped twelve feet up to the battlement's staircase, and then jogged up the final steps to where the rest of the guara remained. Just like him to show off his unique gifts of agility. He barked out several orders and then stormed off for the tower. Oh yes, I'd gotten under his skin, just not how he wanted.

CHAPTER 3
CHANCE

Tate was always trouble. I couldn't blame her for her hostility toward me, but I often wished she'd return to the female she once was. That was a female I could get on board with, one I had, in fact, spent many cold nights with. But that was before, she'd moved on and frankly so had I—bitterness was time-consuming and unwelcome.

I headed back toward the boardroom and took my seat toward the head of the table. I had been promoted to dux, that put me in a position of power here at the Glenn's HQ. I outranked the majority—arches and dokimoses answered to me.

Dux Rusty Richards sat down across from me as the other board members filed in and took their seats. "This had better be good, I was in the middle of helping a dokimos find his brain." Rusty huffed, his fist coated in dried blood. I bet he was helping the recruit by beating his brain out of him, or as *he* considered it, breaking the dokimos's will.

"Anax Graf would only call this meeting if it mattered. Believe me, I had to leave my position in the Northern Outpost to come down here for this meeting," Arche O'Connell grumbled as he sat his overly large self down.

A round of agreement sounded as the door to the room swung open and Anax Graf entered. She sat down smoothly; her black coat buttoned all the way from collarbone down to her waist, meeting perfectly pressed trousers.

"Duxes, thank you for coming. We don't have much time and I know many of you aren't for pleasantries, so I'll get right down to it," she began. "We've had a breach in both the Southern and Eastern Outposts. It appears some of our *own* allowed members of enemy Vamps to enter."

The room collectively gasped, our attention solely on Anax Graf.

"Both sustained damages." She opened her disk and projected an image of the two outposts, before and after the attack. They looked relatively intact, not much physical damage.

"We lost a total of twelve arches and one anax at the Southern Outpost and eight arches at the Eastern Outpost." A list of names and photos appeared next to each Outpost.

"That's hardly an attack," Rusty spat, his fury radiating from him. "Are we sure it wasn't just a squabble? You know, youths these days have absolutely zero restraint. Have to beat it in 'em." He flexed his now bruising hand.

"Dux Richards," Dux Phillips, a young dux like me, spoke up, addressing Rusty. "We don't attack our own, not then and certainly not now." He leveled a look at the old male that embodied the way I'd felt about Rusty my entire life.

"Quite right." Anax Graf motioned back to the projection. "We've ascertained the bodies of two soldiers from the Eastern attack, but we were unable to gather any identifications. However, our techs believe them to be members of the Fern Vamp based on a few identifiable symbols on the unburnt portion of their uniforms."

Shit. This was serious. The Fern Vamp was supposed to be aligned with peace; we weren't allies, but we certainly weren't enemies. Or rather, we hadn't been.

"With such a low body count can it be assumed they were after something? Scouting perhaps?" I asked, it was the only logical reason why we didn't have more bodies.

"Yes, we believe they were after intel on the Glenn and our military defenses."

"Shit," Dux George spoke up from the other end of the table.

"Yes, Dux George, *shit*," Anax Graf said, making the expletive sound infantile. "We don't know what they stole, but we do know that our II database was breached as four of the dead arches were from Internal Intelligence." She swiped and the screen dropped to the four arche's photos—all appeared highly intelligent.

"It is believed," she continued, "that they succeeded in hacking the mainframe and accessed data on classified military maneuvers. Our techs are still working to identify what exactly was taken." She lowered the projection for a moment before looking down at the table and then back to meet our collective gaze. "In the meantime, we need to interrogate the suspected personnel involved in this treason and ensure our borders remain tight." She paused—her black eyes seemed almost soulless. "It may be a hard truth to swallow, but some of our own were clearly involved."

The whole room fell silent. Nothing but stale, suffocating air.

"You all know the state of our last Peace Treaty Conference," she forged on like she hadn't just accused an unknown number of guaramen of treason. "Only three of the four Vamps showed up, the Fern attended but it appears they are no longer aligned with peace. This, in addition to the *gifts* we've been receiving, leads us to believe war is possible. We must ensure we are at our strongest and the intel that was stolen must be recovered."

The severity of the situation hit me. My soldiers, good males and females who have served under my leadership for the last two years, were likely to go to war. Worse, some young arches who had sworn allegiance to the Glenn were *traitors*. My stomach soured. Those bastards deserved to pay.

"Dux Richards, Dux Dale, Dux Holland, and Dux Phillips, you will be conducting the interrogations at the Southern and Eastern Outposts."

The murmuring silenced.

"May I ask why this is given to us rather than the duxes of the Southern and Eastern Outposts?" Dux Holland, a rather meek female asked. She was a surprising choice for a dux in the Western Outpost. Small. Young too.

"You may. We are not sure how high up the conspirators go. And while we believe this to have been the acts of arches, as there weren't any retina scans of the upper ranks that day near the intelligence center, we cannot be too careful." She waved a hand, highlighting the leadership photos from each base. "We have no enemies alive," she spoke quietly, but her tone was firm. "We must find the defectors. This must be handled with discretion and dealt with swiftly."

"We'll get 'em. Don't worry about that, I know a thing or two about instilling fear and justice," Rusty spat the last word, literally. His saliva speckled across the table as his overgrown eyebrows furrowed even deeper over crimson eyes.

"I will have additional details sent to each of you before you depart in thirty-six hours."

"We're not leaving now?" Dux Phillips asked, his black eyebrows arching with the question—he was very easy to read.

"No, there's a council meeting tomorrow night you will *all* need to attend. Presently, there is a certain issue that needs to be dealt with— one that involves the recent attacks. President Dale is requesting the presence of Dux Dale and Dux Richards in the interrogation room, immediately."

With that, the meeting adjourned, and I headed down to the basement. If there was an interrogation that was connected to the recent breaches at the outposts, it meant we had a prisoner and that meant we had a lead. I cracked my knuckles. Anticipation filled me as I thought of all the possibilities this prisoner posed. We could oust the mole and put an end to a war before it began. Or at the very least, we would have a tactical advantage if we could understand what the Fern Vamp was after.

CHAPTER 4
TATE

The Glenn had been my home since I could remember. Not that I liked it much with its oppressive, ugly walls and pristine buildings. Most of which were made of glass, trimmed with bright, shiny metal: cold, calculated, sterile.

I headed to the collection office and entered the cataloging room. I needed to drop the bag of blood before heading back to the clinic. I hated these types of shifts. The nightly drop-only shift was given to me twice a week. Two days on, two days off. The 'on' days meant I had to make the blood drop by six AM before heading back for my eight AM shift at the clinic, and then back again by six AM the next day. It utterly sucked. But at least I had my world-walking pass. Not all young vampires my age were granted it; we had to earn it by age or job, and I chose the latter. The labor was much better than waiting until I was fifty.

Glenda took the bag and began indexing it, cross-checking my list with her system. This process was remarkably fast considering the amount of blood I brought each time. She approved the list and sent it back for testing, after all, we didn't want any diseases. That was one bonus of testing blood *before* partaking. Within five minutes, I was on my way out.

"Hey, TK, wait up!" a familiar voice called from behind.

"Blood, what were they thinking letting *you* back in?" I teased as my blue-haired bestie engulfed me in a bear-hug. Her thin body smashed my cushy one as her arms locked around my back. Skin, bone, and muscle—that was Shae, through and through.

"Annnnd...what do you think?" She pulled back and spun in a circle, showing off her new pixie cut. The black and blue tattoo of a dragon crawled up the back of her neck, poking out from underneath her black T-shirt, and danced with her movement. "I just got it done, human side of course cause let's face it, vampires suck at cutting hair." She blew a stray lock out of her eyes. "They always take too much and leave me with a nick, something about the predator in them," she nudged me as she spoke.

"It looks like you, Shae, although I'm surprised you let anyone touch it since the last debacle." Six months ago, she had elbow-length brown hair with purple highlights framing her face. That is, until a *newer* stylist, human side, lightened her hair and totally fried it— Shae had to have someone else cut it shoulder length just to remove the dead ends.

"Yeah, you know what they say, get back on the horse and all." She linked her arm through mine and strolled with me toward the business sector of the city.

"Sooo...suck on anyone *hot* recently?" She wagged her eyebrows as she side-eyed me, bumping me with her bony hip.

"Oh, you know, new perp every now and then. I love a good vessel," I shot back, ignoring the obvious innuendo in her question.

"While I do find your certain *delicacies* interesting, and deserving of being your meals, I was inquiring about a certain rookie detective, you know, what's his name...Bob or Richard? Or does he just go by Dick?"

"For corn Shae, it's *Tim* and you know it." I elbowed her in the ribs, earning me a yelp directly followed by a chuckle. She unlinked her arm from mine and jumped in front of me, walking backwards.

"Corn, yes, do tell me, TK, did he ever succeed in finding the hole?" For the love of blood, she knew how to really go for the jugular.

"Say it any louder and the whole Glenn might know I'm having *sex* problems," I whispered the last two words. Red bloomed across my cheeks; surely it was from the temperature, I was warm that was all. When I was challenged by a male, I held my cool, but for some reason *girl talk* made me uncomfortable, nervous—perhaps it was the vulnerability of it all.

"So, you *are* still having sex problems."

I rolled my eyes; she always wanted the deep and dirty. "I wouldn't say problems exactly, he's just...uninspired." We turned down toward Perry's Coffee and each ordered a large blood latte before heading to a nearby metal bench with chipped paint.

"So, the uninspired man-child," Shae began, never one to let an interesting topic drop, especially if it meant she got to poke fun at me. "Tell me, does that affect his ability for his teeny weeny to salute or is it just bland vanilla when he does rise to the occasion?" She took a sip of her latte, red foam forming a mustache across her upper lip. The girl loved her puns.

"He rises, and by human standards it is good, it's just not exciting with him. Not like it was with—"

I stopped myself, I wasn't going there. From the look in Shae's light blue eyes, she knew exactly what I was thinking.

"He's grown you know?" She paused, swirling her coffee. "He's been a dux since last year I, uh, just ran into him. He really does seem to care about his soldiers, so much so that he says he misses the arches at the Southern Outpost now that he's stationed here. He seems...well. And I know he misses you."

A dux since last year? The timing was *too* conspicuous. It couldn't be a coincidence, could it? I willed the pounding in my head to stop.

"He should have thought about that before he hid the truth from me, before he defended his father's actions. You of all people should understand that. My mother was a second mom to you." I bit down on my tongue before I lashed out at her any further, this conversation never went well.

Years ago, Chance, Shae, Nora, and I were besties. But things changed, paths diverged.

"I heard from Nora," Shae chirped. The change in topic was welcome. Shae knew when to push and when to let things go, it was part of why we were both so close even with all the dynamics constantly changing.

"Oh, how's she enjoying freezing her butt off in the Northern Outpost?"

"Well, she swears her ass is rock hard now and honestly, it looked it." Shae's eyes gleamed a bit with mischief. "But her personality is *perky* as ever, annoyingly so, and that's a lot coming from me."

I wonder how close of a look Shae got. "Perky, eh?" It was my turn to tease. "Doesn't surprise me."

"Yeah, yeah." Shae rolled her eyes. She was ever one to dish but did not receive it well. "She's back for a few days. Dux Phillip's summoned her last week. She uh," Shae cleared her throat, "misses you, Tate." She dropped her grey-blue eyes down to the paper cup.

"I miss her too, but she *chose* to leave."

Shae huffed. "It really wasn't much of a choice. You know we are all required to support the Glenn at twenty-one. She doesn't *like* the human realms and her gifts align better with enlistment."

"Well, she could have world-walked with us. Even if she has little self-control, she could have just been a transporter like you. She *could* have stayed."

Shae's eyes filled with hurt, widening at the corners. Shit. "I didn't mean it like that. It's just a hard topic for me."

"I know." Her smile was sad. Thank blood Shae saw more to me than my temper and quick tongue. "We all make choices, TK, and we don't always have the luxury of a bird's-eye view."

The comment jarred me. Even with our closeness, I'd never confided in Shae about certain abilities.

"Well, hopefully she makes the most of her time here before

heading back to being a popsicle." I glanced at the clock; it was about time to head back to the clinic. I stood and threw my cup in the trash bin nearby. "You coming?"

"I don't world-walk anymore, Tate. Last night was my last shift at the clinic." Shae focused intently on her barely touched coffee, guilt smothering her face.

I stood there dumbfounded. "What?"

"I joined the Internal Intelligence Team. They're sending me to the Southern Outpost for training, to learn from their IIC."

The world suddenly was too cold, the streets too full, my brain too fuzzy. My reality was about to shift again.

"You did what! Why? You have another three months before they assigned you somewhere. I thought you'd stay here, with me." Hurt began to claim my heart, my soul. Stars shimmered in my eyes as my vision blurred.

Another one, gone.

Shae yanked up her sleeve and showed me the tattoo on her shoulder. Blue, periwinkle-blue covered her shoulder in a diamond symbol with a sword and fangs through it. The symbol of the guara.

"I got tired of just drawing blood and carting it around," she started. "You knew I was weary of spending so much time human side. I crave a good challenge and I'm a wiz with coding." Her eyes pleaded with me to understand. Willed me to hear her out. But the thrumming in my ears made it hard to focus, to feel anything but betrayal. "Tate, we both knew they'd enlist me to join the Internal Intelligence Team. This way I got to choose a location and picked the SO instead of the WO for its training center." She gulped. "Plus, the location is closer to my family."

"Bullshit. You and your family never get along, and besides, they're desert people. They're stationed closer to the Eastern Outpost, not Southern. Why the hell would you join the guara?"

"TK..." She reached for my hand, but I pulled away.

"No! You don't get to pretend to be my friend after you just stabbed me in the back!"

"I know you feel that way, Tate, and I've *really* tried to talk to you about this when I chose this path months ago—"

"Months!" I exploded.

"—but you've been human side so much, and when you're here you never let me broach the topic and—"

"You've known about this for months and have pretended to still care about me when you chose them! Chose to leave me, knowing that I would never follow." My head spun.

Joining the guara was my nightmare, plus they'd made it clear when I turned that my uneven footing would be an issue—it would take intense training to make up for my 'deficiency'. Even if that weren't the case, I'd never want to be a part of the unjust system. Murdering and fighting for sport wasn't my scene.

I exhaled. This was all too much. "We had a plan. We were both going to *stay* here. You could have opted to join the HQ Education Allegiant Team like we talked about. The guara was never something we discussed."

"Tate—"

"No!" I spun around, not caring that I was raising my voice and making a scene. "You're worse than Nora." I kept my back to her. "She was at least up front about it. She's always been violently inclined. She chose *before* these monsters destroyed my mom without so much as a trial. But you?" I scoffed. "You could have followed our plan, the one *you* came up with, or hell, you could have run away, and I would have followed." I glanced over my shoulder, locking eyes with grey ones that seemed suddenly so cold. So foreign. "You voluntarily joined the fricking guara."

The look in her eyes saddened. "There's so much I wish I could tell you...I wish I could make you understand."

"Don't bother. If you are going to throw your life away, leave me out of it." I focused my eyes on the crowded sidewalk in front of me.

"I leave on the next transit to the Southern Outpost. It could be any day. Please don't leave things like this."

But her pleading fell on deaf ears. I was already halfway down the block.

"TK! I'm going to be at Frankie's tonight, please come! I really would like to explain this to you!"

Her voice faded as I pounded the cement and sped for the veil. My chest hurt, it constricted. Betrayed. I'd been betrayed again. I couldn't leave the Glenn soon enough.

CHAPTER 5
TATE

It was a rough day at the clinic. I may have aggressively stabbed a few too many patients—on purpose. As a result, Dr. Ferrari sent me to the back to do indexing and begin preparing the bags to transport via the couriers. After several hours of it, five o'clock finally came. I couldn't wait to leave. My chest was still tight from my interaction with Shae. My one friend who hadn't left for the adventure of the guara, who still made time to hang out with me and binge-watch trashy TV, had *chosen* to leave. Shae was the only friend I'd ever tandem fed with. And she was abandoning me while insulting my mother at the same time.

We were a part of a society, I understood that. We had jobs and choices, I also got that. But the guara were a bunch of hunger crazy individuals who had no restraint. They were the ones often sent to Disciplinary Hearings for overfeeding and killing; they were the ones to start bar fights; it was their world-walking passes that were often restricted because they were too volatile. And she chose them. I felt sick.

I filled the last duffle bag for transport and then grabbed the four bags I was responsible for, more tonight than normal after a higher collection day—the weekends were always prime days. The Glenn would be well fed this week. The clinic was a necessary evil, the blood draw saved lives—human and vampirical. The service I provided was vital; I had self-restraint where others succumbed to bloodlust. It was wired within me to protect them, even if they were just human. One more reason I hated the guara—they had no value for life, save for themselves.

Of course, we harvested blood from *within* the veil too, but I was far less interested in working at a processing or harvesting plant. The human side offered something simple, a comfortable environment to take blood from willing vessels, even if it was a fragile facade. Here, I wasn't the weakest. No one noted my limp or fangs thanks to my glamour. Here, I was one of the elites.

The door creaked as it opened, and Dr. Ferrari walked in; fan-fricking-tastic. She was tall, nearly six and a half feet. Vampirical females rarely surpassed six feet, but six and half? It was an anomaly. She had always bothered me, her appearance set me on edge. She wore a doctor's lab coat with scrubs underneath. Her gold hair was beautiful, loosely falling off her shoulders in perfect full curls. Her green eyes were...mesmerizing. I froze, transfixed on her beauty. No one should be that beautiful.

Why had she chosen that glamour? Vampires were notoriously common, plain, but this female—this creature—strode toward the cabinet next to me with long, confident steps. She wanted attention, clearly. Her skin was pale, so very pale and it almost glistened. She nearly walked through me to reach the cabinet to my left. I guess I was practically invisible to her, well unless she needed me, and even then, it was usually for an unpleasant task.

"Can I help you, Tate?" she said the last word sweetly. Pure venom. Buy into it and you wouldn't realize what it was until you were paralyzed, and your blood was being drained.

"No, no. I was just...uh, just lost in thought I suppose." I paused, raising a brow in silent challenge. "It's been a long day."

"Indeed." The blonde smiled, a smile that I could almost taste.

"Perhaps you should get some rest. Have you finished cataloging all the samples from today?" Her scent was odd and ancient, like that of cinnamon—even that bothered me.

"Yes, they're cataloged and packed for transport."

"Good. Then that will be all, enjoy your evening." She reached into the cabinet and pulled out a large chart. "Oh, and dear, do make sure you feed. You're looking a little ashen and I don't need any incidents on my watch."

I shook my head in response.

She turned, file in hand and headed for the door, pausing before pushing it open. "You know, your pallor really does look sickly. Want me to draw your blood and run some tests?" She tsked, shaking her head. "I wouldn't want you sick and infecting the rest of the staff."

Naturally she wouldn't. "No, I just need food and rest. Thanks for the offer." I saluted her and turned my attention back to the computer in front of me.

My blood boiled. Of course, I needed to feed, I hadn't since yesterday and even though that was an *extremely* filling feed, I couldn't halt the cravings. A blood-drain and blood-high was fun until it wore off and then cravings started. I supposed it was one reason President Dale enacted the no-kill law. It preserved a precious balance.

Working with blood had been particularly challenging today when my self-control was slipping. Only thinking of Shae and her utterly shitty decision kept me distracted enough to not seriously consider syphoning some of the blood. I cracked my knuckles; I needed a feed, and I knew just the vessel I wanted to feed from.

Roy Mackalst had been on my list since last week. He only lasted this long because I was hunting the pyro perp—killing children placed you at the top of my list. Beating them? Well, that ranked you as next. Yes, he had this coming. I yanked harder on the grip I had on his shoulder, lifting his body further in the air. My heart raced; air seemed to escape my chest. Liquid beads slid down my cheek and chin as deep red covered the front of my shirt, my arm, my hand.

The scent of iron filled the air, and the floor began to stick. My maroon footprints covered the beige rug. It was the color of rubies, so deep and full of meaning—full of heart. It was a sign of life, a sign of passion, a sign of love. Now, it was also a sign of death. How many times had Roy himself been covered in the blood of innocents?

My hand shook, the adrenaline from the feed was still racing through my system. I could feel the strength pulsating through my body. I needed to stop; if I continued, it would be another blood-drain. I could feel it, he was almost there—just a few more draws, and the drain would be complete.

Until recently, I'd never had this problem. I'd feed from my target and then ensure they met justice, via the human police. But lately, enacting my own justice and emptying them had been calling to me, a siren beckoning ships to the rocks.

Rage fueled my movements, rage at the loss of life, the abuse of sweet innocence. Anger at the betrayal of those we trusted. Justice, that's what this was. I closed my eyes and drew again. Euphoric. That's what I felt. It never felt like this with those first few feeds from vessels. Transitioning had been difficult. The guilt that accompanied my transition kill was smothering and isolating. No one, aside from my mother and Fletch, could relate. This, however, was easy.

Rich, sticky iron filled my internal wounds. Only one more, then I'll stop. On my third attempt, I was met with nothing. He was dead. My body tingled and my head felt light; the high from this was even stronger than the last drain. If I wasn't careful, I'd be an addict. I should be worried about the Glenn finding out; about violating President Dale's no drain law, enforceable with a Disciplinary Hearing, punishments that could entail death. But all I could think about were the children this monster harmed.

"It hurts, Mommy!" Maroon eyes looked up at green ones shadowed by sandy blonde hair.

"I know, it's going to be ok, Tatealia. Just hang in there," Mama whis-

pered, rubbing my tiny back and looking at my mangled leg. It was red and swelling quickly. The pain from it was sharp and felt severing.

"Make it stop!" I cried, leaning into her touch. I didn't know what had happened, I only wanted relief.

A door down the hall opened and then shut, jarring me from my thoughts. The giant lay before me, cold and lifeless. His face still held hues of shock, fear, and pain. The blue eyes staring up at me were cold, icy. He would no longer be a threat lurking in their little shadows, bruising tiny faces, and filling their heads with nightmares.

I bent over to pick him up. Grabbing his wrist, I pulled as I hoisted him across my back. *Snap!* His arm fell to the floor. *Damn it!* This needed to be cleaned up, no more questions. That's what the Glenn required for our cover story to succeed—the virus needed to stay contained. If mortals thought it was spreading again, if corpses were popping up everywhere, then the clinic would lose its tight hold on the human population.

My heart rate increased; it became erratic. I could clean this up, the mess could be remedied, and the body discarded—no one needed to know. I just needed to calm down, take a few breaths. The song sung to little vamplings filled my synapses:

Sweet, sweet birdy. She came and fed her nest,

She came and got some rest,

She came and put her chicks to the test.

One by one she pushed, she nudged, until at long last, each little birdy was thrown from the nest.

Some flew, some struggled, some didn't make it. This is the way we learn sweet, sweet bird.

This was the song they sang to us at infancy; the song that was played during our first feed, our first kill. This was the melody that made us killers, transitioned us into our vampirical nature. Only fitting that it would be my anthem as I cleaned up the mess that my *nature* created. Not my fault. Fletch would agree. After all, did we punish a wolf for hunting and devouring a deer? Roy was no deer—he was a predator himself.

New strength filled my veins. The world would understand if they knew. They would thank me, or at the very least, his children would no longer be at the end of his butcher's mallet. That dead bird needed to flop. I was no monster, I was the hero in this story—and if my actions did, by some accounts, make me a horror, then I'd gladly take up that mantle if only to protect the defenseless.

Looking around, I surveyed the room. The cherrywood executive desk had splatters of blood across it. I wiped it clean. The papers, once neat and stacked atop the desk, now lay scattered across the orange tile. What a stupid choice for an office, but then again, he was a stupid, stupid man. I threw the papers out.

The modern black lamp in the corner lay on the floor, the shade surprisingly intact after his silly struggle—as if he stood a chance. I picked it up and positioned it near the desk. The two chairs in front of the desk were overturned, thankfully not marred by the man's odious blood. An easy fix. The shag rug he lay lifeless atop would be the perfect thing to transport him.

I bent over and rolled the body up, throwing the busted arm on top of his nearly severed neck—a fitting coffin for such a man. The look on his face when he saw me lurking in the shadows, such shock and horror. When I dropped my glamour and he spotted my fangs, he sucked in such a deep breath and let out a high-pitched scream. Who would've thought this bird could sing?

Humming the tune, I surveyed the room: it was bland, but clean. Throwing the rug filled with the maimed man over my shoulder, I walked out onto the balcony I'd come in through—its mere existence a testament to his ego—and jumped off toward the ground below. Thankfully, it was only a couple of stories down to where the truck I'd 'borrowed' waited. My feet hit the ground and I rolled. Not my best, not my worst. Twisting my left ankle in a circle, I released the building tension and willed my left leg to stop throbbing. These jumps were a lot for me; even in this world, I had limitations.

Dropping his body in the truck with a sickly *'thump,'* I winced. Did something snap off? Whatever. I shrugged as I climbed in the driver's seat and moved it back further to fully stretch out my legs and then drove miles outside of town to a large cliff. The roads were empty this time of night; ever since the virus became widespread, people were more fearful to be out at night. I reached a pull-off that was rarely used and put the truck in park.

I threw open the door and hopped out. The cool night air was a welcome reprieve from my internal temperature. I reached for the shag rug and hoisted him over my shoulder, then began walking to the cliff edge. Even bloodless, this man still weighed an astronomic amount. A large root from a nearby tree caught my foot and—*oof!* My speed only hastened my impact with the ground—I hit hard. The corpse in the rug flew from my grasp toward the edge. *Pop!* The rug unraveled, and the corpse rolled out as it plunged down into the ravine. The head snapped off and caught on a bush, eyes wide and mouth open. His severed arm caught on a root sticking out from the cliff while the rest of the corpse fell about twenty feet below before getting caught on a tree branch. Damn it!

He almost went all the way over. Judging the distance, I didn't have the desire or fitness to scale the cliff and knock him all the way over. Somehow his final posture seemed fitting.

I stretched my leg out and shook it, trying to loosen the ache taking root. My vision was beginning to halo—a weird effect from a blood-drain. One more reason we weren't supposed to kill—a breach to nature's balance could mean unintended consequences. I looked around, no one used this road often even in the day. It was unlikely he'd be discovered, and even if he were, his decapitation would hide my fang marks—at least I hoped it would. I was tired, the high from feeding was messing with my senses. I needed to get the tote bags of blood back to the Glenn before my protective coating wore off and I fried in this atmosphere. Turning around, I hopped in the truck and headed for the veil. I hummed the nursery rhyme as I commanded the roads before me, a lone vigilante.

CHAPTER 6
TATE

The antechamber to High Lordship Lee's office was as offensive as the male himself. Draped in crimson and black, the entire room was excessive and yet, felt lacking. It was pure posturing. Lee liked to feel strong, powerful, untouchable—he liked his décor to speak for him, to put every visitor on their toes. I scoffed, such a typical power tactic from a male who clearly has his own daddy issues. Males.

The arche in the corner of the room hadn't moved an inch since we arrived here twenty minutes prior. I hadn't been expecting to be sent here upon entering the Glenn, but the guara informed me my pass had been flagged and I was *escorted* straight here. As if I couldn't follow orders. Perhaps they thought I'd skip this summons? I exhaled through clenched teeth. Like I'd be stupid enough to do something like that. Anyone who didn't appear for a summons to the Chief was immediately detained and usually severely punished or even killed. He was the High Lordship of the Guara, head of corrections, governing our city— not to mention, scary as hell. I chewed on my freshly manicured thumbnail, a bad habit. The neon blue polish chipped off, a tell-tale sign of my nerves.

I settled back on the black leather sofa, willing myself to calm. This was likely nothing. It would be alright; this was nothing to be nervous about. Lie. I was lying to myself and even I couldn't buy the shit I was trying to sell. Something was wrong. My mother had often come home telling me of the way office visits like these went; they usually ended in imprisonment or a scheduled Disciplinary Hearing. I bit the inside of my lip trying to simultaneously slow my breath and thoughts. Breathe, just breathe.

The skin on my right wrist itched, I needed to stop scratching it, but stress caused it to flare up. So completely annoying. I just needed to focus on something else aside from my fate lurking behind the obscene cherrywood door framed in red velvet curtains. The interior design was glaringly bad—red on red on red, and in every shade. It truly was hideous. The high from my feed last night was wearing off and left me craving more. More blood, more vengeance, more power. Ever since the fire perp from a couple nights back, the bloodlust was growing. This was what they warned about in school—what led to the human mortality crisis.

The door cracked open with a loud creak, the narcissistic asshole, and then a cool gust filled the room. It was stale, like that of dusty books, and held a note of mildew to it. I swore he had some unnatural power at controlling the air around others, but he never listed that as a gift—and of course, according to his own rules, all abilities must be listed on our personnel profiles, save if you have a confidentiality clause issued by the council. To fail to do so was an infraction and possible trial. That rarely happened, but, last time it did, the vampire who was caught using undeclared magic was condemned. Swift execution followed.

"Tate." My name on his tongue was both a command and a greeting from High Lordship Lee. I sat up, gathered my bag, and headed for his office.

This male had betrayed my mother, handed her over to President Dale without so much as a council trial. Her case was restricted along with the supposedly closed notes that alleged her guilt. I hated him and hated that I had to play his games, follow his rules, live in the Glenn. I stalked into the office, my back as tall as I could muster. I refused to let him see my fear, to taste my hate. I willed my face into a neutral expression, a mask of boredom. The door abruptly shut with a slam behind me. I jumped, in spite of my posturing. Asshole.

He was definitely holding back on what his abilities could do. With a scarred hand, he gestured for me to sit, never looking up from the sheet in front of him. His long, crooked nose stemmed from a large space between his beady eyes that appeared to sink halfway into his obtusely large head. He was the father of ugly, scary, and the content of nightmares.

"Anything you'd like to report?" he spoke calmly, quietly, without so much as glancing in my direction.

I could sense the danger in his demeanor. "I have a duffle bag of one hundred and ten blood bags, Sir."

"That's all you have?" He looked at me then and the air in the room seemed to ice over, to freeze.

"I'm not sure what you mean, Sir."

"Let me refresh your memory." He pulled out a grotesquely decapitated head and thumped it on the desk. Mouth open in horror, blue eyes glazed over in death. Roy.

"I..."

"Save it." His words silenced any excuse I had. I could deny it, but something told me there was no use.

"You know, Aaralyn," a slow, sharp voice spoke from the back corner of the room. "I have been very lenient with you given your relative's history."

"President Dale." I tried to conceal my utter shock and unease.

I'd only ever seen the male up close twice before, and not once had his attention been directed to me. He was in a military suit and held his cane, for show of course, in one hand while leaning against the blood-red wall. His grey eyes were piercing and at odds with the smile pulling at his lips. An expression that promised violence.

"I take my no-kill policy very seriously. Do you know why the law was put in place?" He took a towering step toward me, his cane clicking as he did so. "The Glenn was in danger. Our food source was being exterminated." He paused, balancing the cane in front of him on a finger before letting it fall and catching it. The dragon emblem at the top of it was gauche.

I said nothing. Clearly his question was rhetorical.

"We had just survived the Great War," President Dale continued, his focus now locked on me. "The Four Houses were formed, and we had been overfeeding for a hundred and fifty years. Humans were going extinct."

"I didn't think you cared for humans," the words were out before I could stop them. His High Lordship's strike hit my face before I could even blink or correct myself. I flew back from my chair and landed on my ass. The whole room was spinning.

"You will address the president only when appropriate and never with that tone." Lee spat a glob of spit in my direction. I could hear footsteps approaching, the fine clip of dress shoes. The president came into my peripheral.

"Where was I?" he spoke, clearly enjoying himself. "Oh yes, discussing those disgusting *parasites* we feed from. Humans only exist because *I* protect them. *I* outlawed overfeeding to ensure the human population stays plentiful for our future generations. Their lives are a mere breath compared to ours. I saved our race." He pointed to his chest with the cane. "The Glenn is *stable* because of me. I will not tolerate rule breakers and those who cannot control their own compulsions." He tapped his cane on the floor. Once, twice, three times.

His High Lordship was on me before I could respond. He pinned me down and punched my face. Once. My left cheekbone was surely fractured. Twice. My nose was broken, blood began to spray everywhere. Thrice. My right eye would sport quite the shiner. The intense weight left my chest as Lee crawled off of me.

My entire head felt like it was splitting. I couldn't open my right eye; the swelling had already taken over. The president pulled out his white pocket square and wiped speckles of maroon blood from his cheeks. He wiped my blood droplets off his left hand before neatly folding it and placing it back in his jacket pocket.

"I wasn't careful enough with her mother. I will not make that mistake again. Schedule her Disciplinary Hearing, book her as a third offense." The president turned to leave taking three swift strides to the door. "Oh, and Aaralyn," he cooed. "One more misstep and I'll have your head the same way I had Irene Aaralyn's." With that he opened the door and left.

"Clean yourself off and get the hell out of my office. You'll be notified when your hearing is scheduled." His High Lordship heaved his large body behind his desk.

Fury began to pound in my system. Just the mere mention of my mother coming from *his* lips had hate radiating through me. He was the one who took her from me. If I could have focused better without the world tilting, I very well may have lunged at him—a crime of death, but worth it.

"I said get out," Lee's voice promised more *lessons* if I didn't immediately move.

I tried to rise, but the room kept spinning. I inhaled and willed myself to stand, the contents of my stomach threatening to empty.

"Don't forget the bag. Take it to be cataloged and then head over to medical."

I reached down for the bag and gripped its strap before turning toward the door. My steps wavered, but my vision was clearing enough for me to make out the path to the door, dragging the bag behind me. My leg was throbbing again, as it often did when my body experienced shock, trauma, or high levels of pain. It sucked.

"And Aaralyn," his lordship started, "make sure next time you're outside the veil you do the damn job right and keep your bloodlust under control." A wind followed his command and slammed the door shut.

I hastened my movements even as my anxiety heightened. I would never be trapped or killed. My anxious fingers dug into my free hand, biting my palm as I entered the hallway.

CHAPTER 7

CHANCE

By the time I made it to the interrogation room located deep in the belly of the HQ building, I was two-parts enraged that our borders were breached, and one-part disgusted with Rusty. I refused to think of him as Dux Richards in my mind. The male was quickly angered, old-school, and ruthless. Good qualities in a warrior but questionable in a leader. Even at my 'youthful' age of twenty-six I knew that.

The interrogation room was cold, everything down here was inhumane and lifeless; from the stainless-steel walls, tables, and chairs to the florescent lights that were used, everything was sterile. Fire, while threatening, also was a symbol of comfort—a reminder of our past, our strength—as such, it was forbidden in the prisons, dungeons, and interrogation rooms. Personally, I thought fire would be effective down here—a symbol of death. But according to my father, President Dale, it was also an honorable way to go ... not like the recently discovered ways of death.

President Dale faced the one-way glass, arms folded behind his back. He didn't even glance up as we entered. Rusty went to his one side and I to the other, both focused ahead on the interrogation room behind the glass wall.

A young male sat with his arms bound in steel and cobalt to the chair—a chair that was bolted to the floor. He didn't look older than seventeen. He was pathetically built, likely a scholar or computer geek, *not* a warrior.

"What is he being held for?" I voiced the question, using a firm tone—one of a leader. I refused to look weak in front of the powerful male, to let my father make me cower.

"Treason. We believe he was an accomplice to the attack on the SO," President Dale said. "A currier to be exact."

Was he my father? Yes, but I preferred to think of him as commander first and father second. There was no room for nepotism in the military.

"Have we ascertained how he helped? What intel he has?" I asked, anxious to get to the bottom of the most recent attack; my stomach acid was rising.

"Not yet, that's why you are here." He smirked as he narrowed his eyes in challenge at me. "Dux Dale," he prodded my shoulder with his finger, "you'll be assisting myself and Dux Richards in the interrogation."

Rusty let out a huff and cracked all his knuckles, on both hands. "We'll break the truth from him," he spat the words coating the floor in his saliva.

"After you." President Dale motioned to the door with his head.

I moved and Rusty followed as I pushed through the heavy glass door and entered the room. The stench of piss and body odor filled the room. The bound male looked even younger up close. How could he have gotten things so wrong at such a young age? I steeled myself, age didn't matter in war. If he was so much as complicit in the attack on the Southern Outpost, he deserved what was coming to him. Thirteen lives. Thirteen were lost at the Southern Outpost. Good soldiers who served the Glenn were now gone because of a traitor; it was an outright act of war.

No. I shook my head, straightening to my full height. No mercy would be given, none was deserved.

"Dux Dale, if you'd like to start the line of questioning," President Dale commanded rather than requested—as was expected of a superior—and handed me a manila folder. I opened it and scanned through the documents prior to approaching the boy, Lucas. He was nineteen.

"Lucas, what intel did you hand over to the Fern Vamp?" I circled him, waiting. Nothing. No response. "Answer me!" I demanded, but he sat there, pale, refusing to cooperate.

The president tapped his cane. I grabbed Lucas's left pinky finger and snapped it. The break was a sickening sound, but it didn't bother me. Neither did the ensuing scream. He deserved this.

Thirteen lives, twelve arches and one anax died *because* of him.

"I will break every bone in your pathetic excuse of a body. Answer me and you'll be expedited to your execution." I leaned in, inhaling the scent of fear. "Let me let you in on a little secret. You will die. It is just a matter of *how* and when." I tipped his chin up with my finger, forcing his brown eyes to lock on me. No fear shone there. "I can break every bone, let Dux Richards skin you alive, strip your nerves from your exposed flesh—which let me assure you, is possible and hurts like hell —or you can answer my questions and have a timely, albeit painful death." He flinched, white spreading over his already ghostly pale face, but he didn't respond.

Fine, I wasn't one to make shallow promises. I grabbed his index finger and pulled, *snap!* I grabbed his next finger and pushed, *crunch!* I grabbed his thumb and paused.

"Who were you working with? What intel was passed along?"

He didn't answer. Even with his face contorted in pain, he remained silent. Three more taps sounded in the room. So be it. I yanked, and his thumb popped off—I chucked it across the room as crimson painted the floor and covered the front of my uniform.

"TELL ME WHAT INTEL WAS ACCESSED!" I shouted. Usually, soldiers would flinch or piss themselves with this type of questioning, but this boy didn't so much as look at me. If he weren't the enemy, I'd be impressed by his resolve. But he was the enemy. Thirteen lives, he killed good soldiers.

There was no excuse.

Tap. I grabbed his forearm and squeezed; I could feel the ulna breaking, black and blue blossomed, the blood clotting and building beneath his translucent skin. His screams filled the room, even still, he wouldn't look at me. My stomach roiled.

"Allow me, Dux Dale," President Dale spoke, his voice lethally calm. He outstretched his hand toward the boy and Lucas's body began to rearrange itself. The 'healing' gift my father possessed could be used to cure, but given his rank in the military and history, it was usually used as a means of torture. Lucas screamed, his voice growing raspy as his cries escalated. His bones rearranged and became whole. About one minute later, his arm looked good as new, aside from the now faint bruising.

"Begin again, Dux Dale."

And so, I did. Now was not the time to be weak. *Tap.* I broke every finger and his forearm three times. *Tap!* I started on the other side.

Still, he would not speak. He would not answer.

TAP! I gripped his collarbone and pushed, snapping it inward. He screamed and then passed out. President Dale outstretched his hand and the boy's eyelids fluttered open and he began to scream again.

"Dux Richards, I believe it's your turn," the president commanded.

I stepped back, chest heaving. I had interrogated many prisoners, none as pathetic looking as Lucas, and yet, none had withstood me—ever. Aggravated, I stepped aside cursing myself for my inadequacy as Dux Richards approached, cracking his knuckles.

Tap, Tap, TAP!

"Son, you're going to wish you were dead," Rusty spoke as he grabbed a knife from the nearby tray. He approached Lucas and pressed the blade to his forearm. He slipped it under the layer of skin and shaved upwards. Lucas's cries were deafening. Rusty lifted the blade to his face and sniffed.

"You know why my name is Rusty?" He paused, his eyes dilating until his entire irises were black. "I love the taste of blood." He licked the blade—black veins began to spread from his eyes. It was forbidden to drink the blood of vampires, even in sexual context it was punishable, but Rusty didn't care.

I glanced at my father, he was unfazed—bored, even. *Tap!* Rusty then lowered himself to Lucas's arm and sunk his teeth into the bare, exposed flesh. Lucas's scream became unintelligible, and he passed out as Rusty drank deeply. The flesh on Lucas's arm turned bright red as the rest of his body paled. Rusty's face became darker, the veins spreading until his skin was more purple-black than it was pale.

"That's enough, Dux Richards. We need him alive," President Dale spoke, placing a hand on Rusty's back. Rusty stiffened, released a growl, and then released Lucas's arm and stood upwards.

The motion caused a spray of blood to coat the floor. Lucas's body slumped, he almost looked dead. Even the flesh on his arm looked pink but not red. President Dale reached an arm toward Lucas's body causing it to twitch, then shake, as a gold aura surrounded him. Lucas's arm began to brighten, redden, and then darken to purple as his veins turned dark red, then maroon, then deep purple. His eyes bulged open, and his once brown eyes were now red, dark red.

"Begin again Dux Richards."

And Rusty did, he took the blade to the other arm and Lucas's screams became white noise.

Tap, tap, TAP!

Still, he would not answer.

CHAPTER 8

TATE

I had dropped the blood bags off to be cataloged and then headed straight for medical. The looks and blatant judgment from everyone were beginning to grind on me. I had my ass handed to me, but to be fair, it was by his High Lordship, and I hadn't been expecting the attack. I also had zero military training, and while I was the hunter outside the veil, in the Glenn it was painfully obvious that I was prey.

The medic had just finished applying balm to my face, a cold compress to my right eye, and gave me a healing tonic to ingest before abruptly leaving me on the gurney. Bloody gauze covered the tray. I knew from experience the tonic would make me either vomit or have diarrhea in about twenty minutes. Good news was that the headache was gone, the numbing sensation alleviating the pain from the shiner I was sporting, which should be healed within the next six to eight hours. If only I could avoid everyone for the next eight hours. But alas, that would be impossible.

I got off the gurney, swaying a bit before finding my balance, and left the clinic. The air outside was cool and crisp, the perfect fall evening. This close to the ocean, the air was moist.

Exiting the city district, I headed toward the village just outside the city limits. I was grateful that my residence was outside of all the towering cement and metal buildings, far from the ugly guara wall. I was doubly thankful that I couldn't see the hideous HQ skyscraper from the village thanks to all the weeping willows and maples.

Fletch was under my favorite maple tree with a circle of young vamplings surrounding him. He loved to teach, and from the looks on their faces, they adored him. He had several books and posters sprawled out in front of him that he would lift with his mind and show the whole class the different points of interest. Today it seemed he was teaching geography.

I always loved that subject; it promised such freedom. The little vamplings seemed to as well, as they were 'oohing' and 'ahhing' over Fletch's poster and the places he pointed to on it. One chubby vampling boldly declared he planned to visit the Fae land, the rest looked at him wide-eyed before sharing where they planned to visit— much more practical locations, like one of the outposts or the rainforest. At twelve, I'd also been determined to visit every place and unlike most, I *actually* made it out of the Glenn.

"What is that symbol?" a little girl with lots of freckles and large glasses asked Fletch.

"Ahh, Rita, this is the Untish Dragon symbol. They're mythical warriors thought to have protected the land and maintained nature's balance," Fletch answered and then began to redirect the class to the final territory on the chart.

"What happened to them?" Rita asked, shoving her too thick glasses up her pudgy nose. This was dangerous territory, even I knew that, but Fletch being Fletch humored the girl rather than simply dismissing it—as all vampires were instructed to do whenever the Untish warriors were brought up.

"Well, myth has it that they left this world when they felt it no longer deserved their protection. Others posture that perhaps our world is better now and their services are no longer needed; as such, they've simply evolved and are now the birds in the sky. And still..." He paused, meeting my eyes from across the way. No, Fletch, just keep it to yourself. But he ignored the begging in my eyes. "And yet some suggest that they are, perhaps, hiding in plain sight: by interbreeding within different Vamps, lurking in the human realm, or fortifying the Fae land." Crap. He did it, he took the girl's already inappropriate question one step further—he broke the law, a minor law, but still, if it gets back to President Dale, Fletch will be fined for this.

"Interbreeding!" Rita exclaimed. "That's impossible. My parents say that vampires can only mate with other vampires or humans," she finished the word with a scrunched nose. The Fae were *taboo* and humans are considered vermin by many; prejudices still flared.

"Ahh, yes. Well, much of what I just said is merely speculation. And..." Fletch glanced down at his watch, "a topic for another day. Class dismissed." With that, all the little vamplings rose in a flurry and went bounding off toward the softly lit village.

For being around so long, we still lived simply here in the Glenn— especially in the village. Most homes were simple structures with minimal electricity and plumbing; our roads were lit with fires everywhere, even though they were unnerving, they brought a certain comfort. A reminder that death could occur, life was fragile, and yet we survived. We moved forward. The juxtaposition of it all, the perfect symbol of her existence.

Because fire was the easiest way to kill a vampire, most feared it and gave it wide berth. Even the guara seemed to disdain tending to the fires. But it was better than the obnoxious florescent lights of the city district. Better yet, it reminded us of our own fragility.

"I was wondering when the little rabbit would venture back to her burrow," Fletch said by way of greeting, his eyes bracketed in new wrinkles—he was worried.

My bruised face was likely the cause. The swelling had thankfully gone down, but my right eye was still black and blue.

"I always come back. This time I got caught up with a perp, but uh, I made it back." I pulled him into a hug and embraced the older male. At eighty-seven, Fletch was considered a mature adult who was nearly old enough to be placed on the inner council. The average vampire lived for about two hundred years, with the exception of President Dale who was over three hundred years old—though no one quite knew how that was possible. President Dale claimed the Blood Mother had blessed him, but it seemed odd to say the least.

"Ahh my Tate, another mess?" Fletch's gaze was piercing. He grabbed my chin and studied my face. "How bad is it?"

I couldn't lie to him if I wanted to, he was like a father to me. "Nothing I can't handle. Just a little dismemberment from an overfeed."

His eyes sharpened with the last word.

"Really, it's fine. High Lordship Lee was in a piss-poor mood, likely aggravated by the president's presence, but—" Fletch's grip tightened on my shoulders. "—Lee is always a piece of work. I took care of it and will be more careful next time."

An iciness took over Fletch's face. I'd never seen this look on him before. "What was the president doing there?"

"I'm honestly not sure. He went on a rant about the history of the no-kill law and insulted my mother." Hate, deep and strong, bloomed in my heart as I thought of the way *he* spoke of my mother.

"Tate, you must be careful. Now more than ever. Things are...complicated," he spoke softly. "Rumors are spreading, devotion is being questioned." He looked around, ensuring no one was nearby.

"What are you saying, Fletch?"

"Just...be careful. Don't give the guara any reason to focus closely on you." With that, his eyes softened and he released me. "Come, let's go get dinner and you can tell me of your latest target." He turned and headed toward the south end of the village.

An uneasiness fell over me. Whatever Fletch wouldn't say couldn't be good. Something was off, more so than usual. If he wouldn't tell me, I'd make it my mission to find out.

.   .   .

AFTER HOURS of grilling Fletch and getting absolutely *nowhere*, I finally caved and told him about my latest perp. He listened intently, laughed when I told him about the head *popping* off, and then sobered up again when I told how I'd left the body.

"I know, I need to be more careful. Blah, blah, blah. But Fletch, he had it coming and part of me, the savage part, reveled in the way his limbs fell off. It felt like he was being mutilated by justice. Like he got what he deserved." My passion for justice was one thing Fletch had always inspired in me and was proud of—no matter how gruesome some considered my methods, Fletch never judged.

"Tate, you may have served justice, but you exposed yourself. I'm not sure you going outside the Glenn is a good idea," he said. "I may speak with the council about reassigning you for a bit, remind you of the good you can do *here*."

"Reassign me! Are you fucking kidding me? You know I *need* to leave. I cannot be trapped here. I *will* be more careful Fletch, but don't you dare speak a word of reassignment to the council." My rage quadrupled and my hands began to shake; my bodily responses were beginning to concern me—they were almost foreign. I was usually better at holding my emotions in check. Something was wrong.

"Fletcher," he stiffened at my use of his full name, "what the fuck is going on?" My eyes pierced his and a fire deep in my belly began to fill my blood with heat—I was angry.

"Calm down, Tate. I just want to protect you. I promised your mother."

"Protect me from what?" I demanded.

"From yourself!" He gestured to me with his hand. "You're stubborn and thick-headed and are *gone* so much you don't know *what* is coming. I don't even know all that's coming, but the council is on edge. The president is on edge. We have a trial tonight following the assembly. *Another* trial. This is the third assembly in a row where we've had a trail. Things are unbalanced right now, Tate, and you drawing attention only puts *you* in danger!" His entire chest was heaving. "I can't let you end up in a trial. You will not die like your mother!" Fletch's blanched face was taut with grief. His final words sunk in. He was afraid *I'd* be put on trial? For what?

"Fletch, I'm not going anywhere. I'll be more careful. I promise."

His grief was palpable.

"Worst case, they pull my world-walking permit for a bit. You wouldn't mind me being around more, now would you?" I teased, trying to lighten the mood.

"Stranger things have happened Tate. I shouldn't tell you this," he started, "but two more outer council members went missing. We don't know where they are. Suspicions are rising, words of traitors and spies are being rashly spoken, and the council is considering *all* courses of action to take."

Two more missing? That makes *eleven* this year, and it was only August.

"I'll be careful, I promise." And in that moment, I meant it. I didn't want to concern Fletch with my suspicions or escalate our conversation any further. More than likely, he was just being an overprotective, grouchy bear like normal.

CHAPTER 9

TATE

The assembly was a bleak affair. The seating was colosseum style in the shape of a bowl; we found ourselves near the top. The outer members of the council filled the nearest three rings while the inner members sat in twelve chairs facing the podium. The place where the newest convict would be tried. Fletch's golden head was barely visible to me from up top—he sat in the row closest to the bowl. Thankfully, my face had healed enough where there was just the faintest visible swelling; I only had some discoloration splotching my face. Two more hours and I should look like new. Yay for me. *Not*. This whole thing should never have happened, but then again, shit that shouldn't happen surrounded me.

I sat there trying to focus on something other than my nerves. I hated assemblies. Hated that I kept waiting for *my* damn notification of the Disciplinary Hearing. After Meed, the council chairman, went through the debriefing of new rules, broken rules, fines, penalties, and upcoming events, the president took the stage. His sharp chin was noticeable even from where I stood. It seemed to grow pointier with every meeting. It was at odds with his puggy nose and round glasses.

"Councilmen. It is with great heaviness that I approach you with sobering news. Wayne Mets, an outer Councilman—" one I'd never heard of "—disappeared early Saturday morning. We've recently recovered his remains and believe it had been a hostile event performed by one of our *own*." He paused and nodded to Hoseff, head of cabinet security, who walked to the atrium door and reappeared a moment later with a bound man, head covered with a black sack. Hoseff escorted the individual to the seat directly in front of the podium.

"As you know, feeding from another vampire is strictly forbidden. It upsets nature's balance and is barbaric. It is and always has been met with a zero-tolerance policy," the president continued. "The guara have apprehended who we believe to be responsible. It is, at this time, to be determined if our perp did indeed feed from and murder Mr. Mets. His trial starts now."

Hoseff pulled the hood off the vampire, revealing a young, sickly-looking male. His scrawny arms looked like he'd barely worked a day in his life, hardly strong enough to lift a bag of blood. But to *overpower* an old vampire? President Dale had to be kidding, he looked barely able to lift a coffee cup let alone attack a vampire long enough to feed from him.

Something *felt* off. His color didn't seem right, either. Even from way up here, I noted a purple tint to his skin and his eyes...they only glanced up once, but I could have sworn they held a hint of red—that wasn't natural. Goosebumps began to coat my skin; the young male had been dabbling in something he shouldn't have been.

"Luina, if you please." Chairman Meed motioned for the Truth Seeker to approach.

Luina was a spindly female who resembled a spider closer than anything else; she'd always creeped me out. She was one of the few who held power *without* a rank. Even now, she stalked as she approached the stage. Her black coat was crisp, not a single wrinkle, and flowed from her neck down to her knees, just above her perfectly crisp black trousers. Her black hair was pulled up into a tight bun and her black eyes began to focus on the young vampire. She creeped me out more than any other vampire in the Glenn, and it wasn't just her looks. Her particular *skill* set always put me on edge.

"In proceeding with the Glenn rules," Chairman Meed spoke as Hoseff secured the vampire in question to the chair on the platform, "we will begin with some questions to which Luina will confirm the honesty of the answers."

Luina outstretched her hands toward the young vampire and took a deep breath. Even from here, I could see her pupils dilating to almost the entire size of the iris.

"Lucas Meitch, you are accused of breaking one of the most sacred rules of the Glenn—feeding from another vampire and murdering them. How do you reply?" Chairman Meed spoke loudly and firmly—surprisingly so, given how frail he appeared. At two-hundred and ten, he was by far the oldest councilman. "Answer the question."

"This house will soon learn what the president did and—" Lucas's voice was cut off suddenly and he began to convulse.

The kid was just out of puberty, he couldn't be older than eighteen. He stopped shaking and his head hung. Surely, I wasn't the only one who saw this and thought it was odd. The purple tint to his skin darkened and even from way up in the stands, it was clear that something was wrong with Lucas' physiologically.

President Dale nodded to Luina who cleared her throat and then waved her hands. A golden hologram appeared, hovering over Lucas's head. It flashed red in the corner; Luina pinched the corner and pulled it up—a memory.

"I warn you, this may not be pretty," she spoke, her voice like shards of glass. She released the memory and gruesome couldn't describe it. Blood everywhere, Wayne's screams in the background. The image focused in on a bloody heap in the middle of a cement room —Wayne's body. His face came into focus, it was heavily bruised and looked oddly pale at the same time. "Please, stop. No! You can't! This isn't right, it's not natural!" The image cut.

"Is there anymore to the memory?" Chairman Meed asked Luina as she pinched her head in concentration.

"There...appears to be more but it's...blocked. I cannot access anymore. It would appear Lucas has been practicing his mental wall skills and I'm afraid he's very adept at it. I can only see the portion of the memory I just played," she spoke every word as if it pained her that she couldn't dissect Lucas's mind further. Her brows furrowed. "Perhaps, if I were to get in contact with his blood, I could form a stronger connection." What she was suggesting was forbidden. Vampire blood was *supposed* to be sacred, not even used for interrogation unless it was approved by the council—something that hasn't been approved in over two hundred years.

"Luina, you know what you propose cannot be done," President Dale answered. His tone indicated what she suggested was the whim of a naughty child, not that of a hardened war anax who proposed breaking one of the Glenn's sacred laws. "However," he continued, "I believe your intel has more than proved that Lucas is responsible for Wayne's death. Council, I now turn to you for your judgment."

One by one, each of the twelve inner council members voted guilty. Half of the inner council was newer, they've only served for the past twenty years or less, with two of them having just been instated this past year. The older council members hesitated before condemning the boy—looking as if they regretted their decision but couldn't see a way around it. The memory was damning.

I found myself simmering with rage—this was wrong, I felt it in my bones. Wayne deserved justice and the memory was evidence, and yet I *felt* something off. It felt corrupt.

I scoffed, then coughed in my arm to cover up the action. My mother wasn't even given a trial. She was interrogated and condemned within the private bounds of the inner council's authority at President Dale's direction. No trial, no public evidence. Espionage. That was what she was convicted of and killed over—what they came home and told a nineteen-year-old girl. I was told her memories betrayed her and that the council chairman and President Dale didn't bat an eye before issuing her execution. I was too young then to witness any of it. Instead, Fletch held me when I fell apart as the guara delivered the news. I had been *with* Chance, in the most intimate way, while my mother was being slaughtered.

"Given the unanimous vote, I now sentence you, Lucas, to death by enthrawment," President Dale's voice cut through my thoughts. The room audibly gasped. Normally, death sentences were carried out by the prison anax the following day via a poison vial. But enthrawment was a death of *magic* followed by the death of the individual. It was said to be incredibly painful and as such was reserved for rare circumstances.

"If I may," Fletch's voice cut through the auditorium's murmurs, "the boy is young, I believe he's barely eighteen. Perhaps we could simply offer him the death of a vial instead?"

"Ahh, Fletcher. Always the romantic. I'm afraid we take killing one of our own very personally and will hand out justice in the strongest sense. Or have you no morality?" The president's glare intensified as his eyes narrowed on Fletch. "Do you not care that he slayed one of our own, a councilman such as yourself? Do we need to replay the clip?" Each one of Collin's questions got more and more severe.

Fletch sat back down in his seat, silent.

"Perhaps we should question your loyalty to your own? Do we need to be concerned about your obvious ignorance of the law?" No one moved or said a word as the president stared down Fletch—his eyes had increased in their blackness with dark veins stretching out from each eye, swallowing his face whole. The enthrawment was about to begin.

"No, I thought not. Now, if there are no other *misguided* thoughts, we shall begin," President Dale's final words died off as the room went black.

Lucas's screams began a moment later as wind whipped through the room. It felt wrong, like magic was screaming through the air as it was pulled from Lucas. His screams heightened at the same time I felt a tug at my own senses. I felt pressure everywhere, the magic within me rearing back, begging for this pull to stop. Lucas's screams escalated with each second, my ears hallowed out, until his screams suddenly stopped.

With a burst of blinding light, the room returned to its normal shade and Lucas lay on the stage in a heap—he looked more like a husk than a person. His entire small body was shriveled up and unnaturally purple. Suddenly it wasn't a young man with blond hair shriveled up, but a female with honey brown hair and piercing green eyes. My mother. Her body, a dried-out husk before President Dale's feet.

I shook my head. No, this was not her. This could *not* have happened to her. Her fate must've been better. But hadn't the unsealed portion of her records shown she was executed via the highest level of punishment, such as enthrawment?

President Dale dabbed his head with a handkerchief and waved to Hoseff and the guara to remove the body. As they carried out the husk, a certain wrongness lingered. The image of my mother as a husk assaulted me. My dinner threatened to expel. I needed air.

As the corpse was taken from the room, I looked away; I couldn't see my mother like that, I refused to. The assembly was dismissed, and everyone quietly began to make their way outside. I'd never experienced an enthrawment before, and from the shocked look on so many faces around me, neither had most of the Glenn. It was unsettling at best and had my own magic clawing at my skin. I needed to get out of here and stretch my limbs. A bob of blue hair was cutting through the crowd. Shae. I couldn't handle this, not now. I turned abruptly and made my way to a back alley that led to a path out of city limits—far from the blue-haired pixie and the grey husk just inside the building.

CHAPTER 10

CHANCE

The assembly had been a rough one. Lucas was barely alive when we dragged him up to the podium for his sentencing. The fact that he also was responsible for a councilman's death had my teeth on edge. My gut said I was missing something. This young vampire withstood all the torture and not once relented any viable information; he walked, miraculously, to his death sentence —head high.

I've only ever seen that with soldiers who believed in their cause. That was what felt so wrong. If Lucas was willing to die for his cause, then the impending Vamp war was going to be a bloodbath, and not the kind I enjoyed.

I cleared my way through the crowded city streets and headed toward the nearest human district. It was only a twenty-minute walk for a vampire, but given my increased gift of speed, it took me less than ten. The outside of the human district resembled that of modern cities. Skyscrapers, suburbia, the modern sprawl of life. The humans who resided within the Glenn were guaranteed certain rights and were paid for their blood 'donations'.

I pushed my way down a notably crowded street and headed for my favorite pub. I passed Patty's on the right; the noise from within was nothing short of sex-crazed, drunken revelry. I wasn't in the mood for a *live* feeding that ended in sensual pleasure. Glancing in, I noted several members of the guara engaged in feeding—their blood vessels perched on their laps with either their wrist or neck extended to their user. They'd better have their heads about them, even though *I* was leaving tomorrow evening, *their* drills were just about to double down. With war coming, they needed to be prepared, not drunk and horny.

I continued down the street until I saw Donavan's. This was the closest thing to a pub the human district had to offer. Most places near the capitol highlighted their *live* feedings, but Donavan's specialized in bloodwine and bloodbeer. Just the right amount of nourishment and liquor to calm my nerves tonight. I stepped into the dim lighting. The wooden floor was worn from use and matched the beams on the ceiling that were cast in a warm glow from the torches on the walls. That was another thing that made Donavan's unique, they were permitted to have fire. This was, as most knew, because Donavan's was actually owned and run by some local vampires who commuted to the human district to run their business.

I headed to a solitary chair and table in the back when a whistle caught my attention. Turning to the left, I noted Dux Holland and Dux Phillips, the latter with his finger between his fangs as he finished his call to me. Like I'm a damn dog. Fuck 'em.

I sighed; I supposed I needed to engage with them since they spotted me. I changed trajectories and took the last remaining seat at their table. It was still secluded, but closer to the stage currently occupied by a human girl and her guitar. She was painfully off-key.

"Didn't expect to see you here tonight, Dale?" Phillips raised an eyebrow in question.

"Even the best of us need a break, Phillips. What are you drinking?"

"Help yourself," Holland responded as she pushed her cup over to me, the pitcher in the middle of the table followed next. It smelled like mulled wine and was warm. I lifted it to my lips; the fresh taste of iron and berries hit my lips. Mmm, they splurged for the good stuff.

"So, what do you think we're going to find in the Southern Outpost?" Holland asked, her stern face at odds with her stature. She was small, petite even, but evidently was gifted enough in skill or magic that she landed the rank of dux.

"The traitorous bastards I hope," I replied, stating the obvious.

"Shouldn't be hard. I've heard you're the one who they call in to *break* the tough cases." Phillips winked, his words starting to slur. Clearly, he'd been here long enough to get drunk.

"We'll see. Traitors can be difficult to sniff out and even when caught, if they believe in their cause, they may never break." The image of Lucas passing out from pain only to be reawakened to a new nightmare as Rusty skinned him filled my mind.

He was willing to die rather than give up any information. That was as scary as an approaching army. "If you are devoted to your mission, no amount of pain can break you. If you believe in the 'why', then the suffering you endure doesn't matter." I downed the glass of wine and refilled it from the pitcher. It was a thick sludge, and slowly filled the cup.

"You think Lucas had something to do with the recent breach in the Outposts?" Holland asked, her light brown eyes far keener than I liked.

"That's classified," I responded, finishing my cup in three long swigs before refilling it again. Phillips motioned to the serving girl for another round.

"*Mmm*. Classified." Holland's eyes pierced through me. "I know you don't know me well Dale, but if we're supposed to work together in the Southern Outpost's breach investigation, I hope we can learn to trust one another." What she didn't say, her face told me. She *would* learn my secrets whether I wanted her to or not. I felt compelled to tell her my deep dark secrets, to talk and spill my guts. My tongue began to loosen.

"I—"

The pressuring sensation abruptly vanished as the server appeared. Magic. Holland undoubtedly possessed magic.

"Here's another pitcher. We do have some *fresher* selections tonight, duxes, if you are interested." She inclined her head to the door right behind the stage. The VIP lounge, with live vessels no doubt.

"Don't mind if I do," Phillips said as he got up and sauntered over toward the door, his path anything but straight. A small twinge of pity passed through me for the vessel—vampires were not gentle feeders when drunk.

"Place is pretty busy tonight." I nodded to the packed tables. Normally Donavan's was a bit less crowded as most vampires preferred live feeds if they came to the human district, and unless you had stature, the VIP lounge here was inaccessible.

"Yeah, Monty's closed down recently due to...uh, staffing issues," Joanne, the server, responded. Her face was taut and hand shaky as she picked up the empty pitcher.

"Staffing issues?" Holland asked, her eyebrow raising. A gentle intrinsic pressure flitted past me and smothered Joanne.

"Y-yes," Joanne stammered. "People have gone missing. Monty's lost all its servers in the past month." Her eyes bugged out and the sensation ended. She backed from the table hastily and excused herself.

"Was that really necessary?" I asked, seeking to understand Holland more than question her use of magic on a human.

"I like to know what I'm dealing with." She shrugged. "And if my favorite bagged blood establishment is getting crowded, that's a threat to *my* leisure. I like to eliminate threats." Her words were weighted in meaning.

New respect filled me for Holland. She may be small, but she certainly wasn't afraid of me and didn't give a damn about my connection to President Dale. It was refreshing.

"So, Dux Dale, are we going to be able to effectively partner on this mission?"

"I believe so, *Dux Holland*," I said her name with finesse and gave her a wink which apparently startled her as she moved back an inch.

A smile pulled at my mouth. So she did get shy, but it had nothing to do with war or espionage. No, something told me Dux Holland was reserved in her personal life and perhaps hasn't had much experience in the bedroom. "Dating anyone?"

That earned an uncomfortable gulp from Holland. "I don't see how that's relevant." She shifted in her chair before downing the rest of her bloodwine.

"Well, if we are to trust one another when trying to find our mole, I think personal relations can be important information." While I meant what I said, in truth, I enjoyed toying with her.

"I see. Then to answer your question, no, I'm not currently engaged in any such relations." She poured more wine before tucking a honey-golden stray piece of hair behind her ear.

"Why not? You're not bad looking, even if you're a bit...stiff." I noted her shoulder-length dishwater light brown hair, square face, and strong jaw. Not the most feminine features, and yet they worked for her. Her light brown eyes bore through me in a way few did...it was oddly attractive. As was her small stature that seemed to soften her harsh jawline, even if her nose did seem a bit puggy for her otherwise taut face.

"I'll ask you to leave my personal appearance out of the equation," she spat, bloody saliva landing on the table to the left of my hand. Charming.

"*Mmm*, I think I see your problem," I smirked.

Her hand reached across the table and grabbed my jacket, while her other palm held a razor to my throat. She was impossibly fast, or I was drunk, either way it was a *turn-on*.

"You don't see anything. I've been underestimated my entire life, but I will not be made to feel inadequate." She released me with a shove before settling back down across the table.

"You know, I find violence rather attractive." I tilted the glass to the side in my hand, swirling the wine.

"*Pfft*. Of course, you do." She shook her head and crossed her arms, but she didn't retract her blade.

"You know, we have four hours until curfew. I can think of some fun ways to pass it..." I was half joking, but if she was open to it, who was I to stop fate?

"I'd rather have glass in my eyes." I guess that was a no. "Besides," she continued, "I heard you had a thing for unhealthy females like Tate." Hearing Tate's name always elicited an unwelcome throbbing.

"Nope, I've finally cleared my system of her."

"I doubt that's true, but for your sake, I hope it is." Her tone changed from sharp to a serious deadpan.

"What do you mean?"

"Nothing really, just rumors."

"Such as?" I wasn't one to play this game. I may not have magic, but I sure as hell got my answers.

"Just that her guardian, a Fletcher Backshy, has been speaking of the Untish and breaking the law by discussing forbidden topics, myths really. Such a stupid thing to do if you ask me, it just gets you listed on the guara's watchlist."

"He's not on the list." I was certain I would have heard of it if he was.

"As of this afternoon, he *is*."

Shit, I'd been so preoccupied by the interrogation I hadn't noticed the updated list. "Well, like I said, I'm not affiliated with Tate anymore so whatever nonsense Fletcher is spreading is of no concern to me. Let the guara do their job."

"Right." She snorted. "You know, Dale, I do hope we can learn to be honest in the future, our lives may come down to it." She stood up and grabbed her coat from the chair, the shoulders making her small frame look boxy. "I'm calling it a night. I'll see you tomorrow for the trip debriefing. Please, do me the honor of keeping me updated on any *relevant* changes." With that, she strode out of the pub.

I sat there alone, Tate and Fletcher on my mind. I shouldn't concern myself with Tate or her business. Still, if Fletcher was in trouble, it could reflect poorly on Tate, and given our history, I owed it to her to at least give her a heads-up. Or did I? The wine was making my thoughts a bit murky.

I either needed to order another or head back to the VIP lounge. After a moment of hesitation, I dropped several coins on the table, and headed for the black door that promised a blissful distraction.

TATE

Outside, night had fully settled in. I took several breaths to steady myself and then peeled off from the crowd before emptying my stomach. Honey brown hair, green eyes, grey skin with a certain wrongness to it—the lifeless body, a husk. The image wouldn't leave me even as my stomach contents did.

I needed the sea. I needed to remember her as alive, not picture what she may have looked like in death. I veered off from the main avenue leading from the city to the settlement and took a path further into the trees. Their branches began to canopy over the trail and led the way to the cliffs—my favorite part about the pathway, it overlooked the sea. Mom had always loved this route and took me down it many nights, usually after a bad dream or hard day at school.

I trailed along the coastline deeper into the forest. The trees got thicker the further I went, and fog had begun to settle in over the foaming waves below. I had just two hours until curfew. Another lovely rule President Dale had started enforcing within the last ten years. Apparently, we were less likely to give into blood-rage if we were safely inside before night truly fell—or some political rhetoric like that. Bullshit if you asked me, but no one ever did.

The cliffs curved and carved out their path against the roaring ocean below; you could see the torch lights in the far distance, the southern tower of HQ, the heart of the Glenn. Home of the guara. It was at odds with the freedom the sea offered. One was a cage, the other an open expanse. It was the latter that called me.

The forest seemed oddly comforting and the crashing waves were like a lullaby. My mother had told me that nature could be rejuvenating and help us center ourselves. Since she passed, I had often disappeared down this path, seeking the warmth of its embrace.

I closed my eyes, and I could still see her as I did the last time. She was strong, one of the best warriors in the guara. She was a dux and the best spy our Glenn had ever seen. She was free, fun, ruthless, and yet, tender. She told me to seek autonomy as much as justice, and taught me the importance of love. I was still searching for the freedom she embodied. It teased me, hovering closely, but just out of reach. A secret I didn't know how to unveil. Like so many things in my life, I was always focusing on the wrong thing, only seeing the trees and not the forest.

My temperature began to spike, the tingling in my limbs increased even as my left leg started throbbing with every step. My stomach ached and demanded food, itched for the psychological high as much as the physical. These cravings were getting out of hand. I needed to feel air, to get in touch with *my* truth.

I continued to hike for another thirty minutes until the southern tower's lights were merely a dim haze in the distance. The Human District was about another twenty minutes south. That's where *most* teens went for a night of debauchery. Human vessels, wine, sex—it was party city. I never felt comfortable there; the way they *served* humans by *humans* at those restaurants felt too grotesque. I suppose I wasn't one to see how my drink was prepared.

I never understood *why* the humans who resided there chose to remain. The Glenn offered many shelters and places where they could live and donate blood with more decency. But who was I to judge?

A snort escaped my lips.

At least they now had a better mortality rate thanks to the blood bags from veil side, bags that *I* carted through the veil practically daily. That and President Dale's no-kill law offered the humans inside the veil life, opportunity, and limited protection. How odd that he should value human lives? It was the antithesis of who he was as a leader—he was no saint and seemed to revel in taking lives, just as he did when he stole Lucas's soul today.

A shudder coursed through me.

At last, I reached the outcropping that jutted out over the sea. The only sound was my breath and the waves below. No one behind or in front. This spot had always been my haven. I climbed down the hill until I located the rope I had secured over the cliff's edge. Slowly, I lowered myself forty feet down the side, using the rope to steady myself until I found the natural footings along the edge of the cliff. Releasing the rope to descend the final ten feet always gave me an adrenaline rush. I landed in a crouch and then removed my boots and set them securely next to the rough stone wall.

The edge was small and cut out from the side of the cliff; it gave me just enough room to lie down in either direction. Small, but secure. It was tucked in enough to provide a wall against the wind. *This* was my place. The one spot no one ever found me or thought to look. The one place I could fully be myself. And it was here that I allowed myself to breathe. Here, I could release the inner tension from holding *it* together. Here, I could stop hiding *that* piece of myself.

I looked toward that intrinsic thread. It wasn't always easy to find and often was camouflaged from disuse, but it was there waiting for me—the piece of myself I rarely acknowledged. Begging me to free it.

I internally pulled once, almost a gentle caress. *'Hello friend'* it seemed to say. I tugged again, but the thread remained coiled. I gave it a bigger yank, but it still refused to release.

Damn, stubborn self.

I sighed. Fletch always said I only did what *I* wanted, I guess that applied to all sides of me. So be it.

Taking a deep breath, I turned to my last resort: I threw myself over the cliff edge.

The free fall always drew a scream from me—a certain desperation. I used this energy to pull on the cord with more stamina than before. It budged; I began to feel the tell-tale tingle but not the burn that accompanied the shift. The waves were becoming dangerously close...

I could start to make out individual swells. This had to work, or this would be it—not the worst way to go, but too soon for my taste. I tugged on the thread one more time, pulling it with all my defiance, and finally, it released and fully uncoiled. My body began to tingle, then burn as fire filled my veins. I rearranged before my internal temperature rapidly cooled. With a final snap, I opened my eyes—the eyes of a raven.

CHAPTER 12

TATE

Being a bird shifter was a gift that I was both lucky and unlucky to have. Aside from gifts of agility, magic was incredibly *rare* in vampires, shifters were rarer. Some considered shifting a violation of natural law, but others simply thought it was freaky—all understood it required an underlying access to a large quantity of raw magic.

I wouldn't really care what they thought if it wasn't illegal to shift. No one in the Glenn knew I could shift except for my mother and Fletch. I was—to my knowledge—the only vampire who could shift into a bird within the Glenn. There had been a few other shifters, mostly into things like cats, and they had disappeared or had been executed for either *defying* nature's laws or for *conspiring* with the Shifting Vamp—a rogue group who refused to join any of the Four Houses after the Great War. They were outcasts, biologically wrong beings and dangerous to society—or at least that's what the Glenn tried to indoctrinate. I wonder how Principal Predi would respond if he knew that one of the school's Blood Queens was, in fact, a shifter. He'd probably lose his puny mind.

It always felt odd to me. How could being a shifter be classified as 'unnatural' when it was, in fact, natural? I'd heard other Vamps accepted those known for their shifting abilities. But those were just rumors. As a child, I loved stories of magic, dragons, and shifters. And once I discovered my ability to shift, a year after I transitioned, my mother smuggled me into the HQ Library and got me access to the database so I could research *everything* there was about shifters.

In a nutshell, there wasn't much data. Mostly folklore and a recent history of the known shifters over the last century, along with their fates. A fate I'd like to escape.

My mother made sure I knew the Fern Vamp allowed shifters to live, even if they weren't tolerant of vampires who originated from outside their borders. My fail-safe if I should ever look to leave the Glenn.

I banked left and let the breeze lift me higher. Nothing compared to the freedom of flying. How could something so natural and right be evil? I was alone in this. It was just me, my thoughts, and the clouds. Not even my mother understood the feeling of shifting. A gift I'd apparently inherited from the male who sired me.

According to Fletch, my mother came from a line that had shifters sprinkled throughout; although, no one had the ability within the last seven generations—save for me. My father was a shifter, or at least that's what I gathered from the hushed mentions of him I'd managed to scrape from my mother before her death.

Fletch, ever the historian, told me shifting used to be more common than it is now—that as we've evolved over the last couple of centuries, shifters slowly stopped appearing. Well, that or they hid it like I did.

I stretched out my wings and reveled in how the constant ache in my left leg wasn't present. In this form, I suffered no injury, had no ailment. Thank blood that I was never discovered.

The Glenn tested our DNA at birth and again in early adulthood, seventeen to be exact, right after we fully transitioned to determine any irregularities as well as gene markers of special abilities. They claimed this was to determine how we could best serve the Glenn, but really, it was a witch hunt. Thankfully, my last test didn't show my shifting trait, though I never knew *how*. I'd often suspected my mother hid it from them.

A weight pushed my wings down and made inhaling hard: guilt. I highly doubted my mother committed treason. No, it was far more likely she died because of me. Was she working with the Shifting Vamp to secure me a place and got caught? There were so many missing pieces.

I began to circle down, letting the air buff my descent as my adrenaline picked up at the thought of plummeting. I had only been able to shift for three years, give or take, and had only shifted a handful of times due to the inherent risk of being spotted. Once I realized this cliff existed, it was a game changer. I had a haven to shift where I couldn't be seen. I tried telling Fletch that, but the old worry-wort 'forbade' me from it—as if he could. He was always the pessimist. He also had the nerve of regularly trying to *ship* me off to outer settlements where there was the least amount of oversight from the guara, not to mention I'd be far away from President Dale.

But the idea of simply monitoring a small human village just north of one of our smaller vampire villages shouted *boring*. It was like being sentenced to watch cattle graze and make sure the wolves behaved. No thank you. I was and always would be a wolf, even if I didn't like to feed from most vessels.

I adjusted my course and continued to fly over the bellowing sea below. The wind blew through my feathers, raven blue with rose gold tips that were translucent against the stark black of the night. Each breeze, a song welcoming me back. Beckoning me forward. I flew higher, above the clouds blanketing the sea. Above the oppressive surf and the sheltered tree-lined coast. I flew up until the air was too thin and even then, I pushed further. Something about limitations always bade me to test them. There was a fire in my belly, especially when I shifted, that was intense and insatiable. I could see the expanse before me, clouds that just appeared to be a cottony fairyland of promise and freedom.

I opened my beak and released a cry—it came out strained and almost restricted, as always it felt like a half measure. Unlike what President Dale did to Lucas. There were no half-measures there. There weren't any half-measures with what they did to my mother either.

She was gone, as was my father. The infamous 'he' in my life, the male who would forever haunt me. The dad I never knew and likely would never meet. My mother didn't give me answers and now, in her death, I wouldn't find them. I often wondered if maybe he were ancient and old, dead by now. If he could shift, perhaps he was at the end of his life when he sired me. I shivered at the thought.

Is that why I've been cursed with the shifter gene, nature's balance?

These questions always circled my mind, especially up where I was completely alone with my thoughts. As always, there were no answers, just more questions asked into an ominous void.

Fire burned in my chest, flowing through my veins. I began to climb again, my wings beating faster and harder than before. The thinning air burned my chest.

I could feel that thread, coiled, glistening, beckoning me forward; internally, it seemed to disappear into a darkness, a latent murkiness. I could never seem to break beyond that wall. I could sense more, glimpse the power turning, but then when I tried to focus it just... vanished.

I was tired of the unknown. Tired of limitations and rules. I rose higher, even as my lungs protested. Even with my head buzzing, the oxygen getting too thin, I pressed on. The wall began to fade, I could glimpse the raw magic begging to uncoil, dancing in golden-pink flames.

Flash. The image of the vampire husk on the floor.

No, I would not focus on that. Higher, I needed to go higher.

Flash. Screams from the auditorium filled my ears along with pain, magical pressure, a sense of wrongness.

I yanked on the string, willing it to break free from the wall and release the tension in my chest.

Flash! The memory from a night a little over a year ago...Fletch, pale-faced telling me of my mother's death. Her body never recovered.

I pulled harder on the string—I was tired of pain and half-measures. My mother had been taken from me.

FLASH! The husk on the floor appeared again, but this time it was my mother, her honey-golden hair now tinted purple with her green eyes no longer green, but a sickly red.

Rage, so deep and raw filled my belly; pain so intense took over my nerves. I opened my mouth and roared.

Fire erupted from my mouth and engulfed the sea of clouds. My vision went hazy, my body throbbed from the internal pressure begging for release. I screamed and more fire erupted. What the hell was this?

I'd never done this before. I searched for that string, and it no longer was in a dark pool but seemed to flow into a pool of *fire*.

The thought was numbing, panic began to fill my mind. This couldn't be happening. I couldn't be breathing fire.

Doubt began to take over, my flaps became unsure. Dizziness and then blackness began to cloud my ability to think, to process. I was falling. Wind rushed past my face, through feathers that no longer felt secure. I needed to right myself, but the mechanics of flying escaped me. The sea began to rise as I descended to meet it.

The cliff, I needed to get back to the cliff. I willed myself toward it, trying desperately to adjust my course. A little more to the right, a little more—

The sea was clear now and the white foam became distinct swells. I had moments to land before the sweet song of the sea became my eulogy. The cliff was just ahead, I had to get there.

Haze began to overtake my vision; my eyelids were heavy. So very heavy.

No! I needed to open my eyes, focus. But the welcoming warmth of oblivion enveloped me. The cliff was just ahead, I could make it. I could—

Darkness welcomed me in a warm embrace, and everything faded.

CHAPTER 13
TATE

I opened my eyes, I was alive. My mahogany eyes slowly adjusted to the dark lighting. Rough, jagged grey blobs surrounded me. The ground I was on was hard, dirty. The gritty texture of the cliff dug into my bare skin—my clothes were long gone from shifting. Squinting, the grey shapes became rocks. I was on the cliff. The realization of what just happened hit me. Hard. I had *breathed* fire. Something had changed, but I wasn't sure *what* exactly. What I did know was that I needed to talk to Fletch. He would have some answers, and that tight-lipped male *would* talk.

He would give me answers this time.

I stood and my head began to swim. Slow, I needed to take this slow.

Inhale. Exhale. Stand. I could do this.

Carefully, I began to rise until my feet were under me and the world stopped spinning. There, one step in the right direction. I located the brown satchel tucked into a small crevice in the stone and yanked it free, nearly losing my balance. I closed my eyes as I allowed my head to steady and the world to stop spinning. Slowly, the dizziness faded, and I pulled out a spare change of clothing I kept in the bag for exactly this reason. I grimaced as I realized I had been wearing one of my favorite shirts *before* shifting. Now it was gone…like so much in my life.

After stuffing the bag back into its hiding place, I slowly stepped into the black leggings and then pulled on a loose V-neck shirt. Its soft material was comforting, warming my now frenzied soul. I felt…better. I picked up my boots and stepped into them, cinching the laces tight before turning to climb the cliff. I lifted my gaze to the thirty-foot stone wall. It was in times like these that I wished I'd found a *less* remote place to shift, to hide.

It took me twenty minutes to make it to the top. It was a relatively short scale, and I fell three times. Three. Now my ass was sore in addition to the splitting migraine I was sporting. I reached the top just as the first drop of rain landed on my head. Great, I'd be wet *and* late when I finally made it back to Fletch. Curfew was hours ago—but what was another broken rule?

The path back to the Glenn was soothing, it acted as a good 'cool down' from my exercise in the sky. Especially now when my adrenaline was in overdrive.

A snap from behind had me looking over my shoulder and told me I may soon be wet for a whole different reason. I saw no one, nothing. The path was vacant.

The forest was quiet aside from the calming symphony of the rain pelting the forest floor. Perhaps it was a rabbit. I began to continue forward when my back began to tingle—the air felt slightly different. I was no longer alone. I didn't have to turn around to know who was behind me. I could always feel when *he* was here.

"Hello, Chance."

He stood there with his arms folded across his chest. His black T-shirt's sleeves boasted two insignias that highlighted his position in the guara: dux. Of course, he naturally wore the black cargo pants that were standard issue and had weapons strapped to his hips. Bulky, ugly, oppressive. Since the guara took over the justice system one hundred years ago, their uniforms hadn't improved much.

"Care to tell me what you're doing out here, Tate?" he spoke, voice dripping sex even as his body threatened violence.

"Nope," I simply said and began to turn around only to be stopped by his hand at my shoulder. He was so damn fast. I had thought my gift of speed was fast, but it was nothing compared to his.

"Tate, I know you too well to believe you forgot about curfew and just happened to be traveling this path *alone*." His blue eyes were piercing in a very uncomfortable way. I often felt they saw much more than I wished.

"You don't know shit," I spoke in calm succinct words. More venom laced my smile than honey.

He chuckled and lifted his other hand to cup my cheek, caressing my face slowly with his thumb. "You and I both know that's not true. What are you doing out here? Looking for someone?"

The implication in his question was clear, as was my answer. Not him, never again.

"If I was, it certainly wouldn't be you," I snarled. "I've found that loyalty and intelligence are prerequisites for *any* form of intimacy." I removed my face from his grasp. "So, as you can see, you do *not* fit that bill. Perhaps, I was looking for someone who could *actually* satisfy and offer a promising future; what, uh, what's your du-arche's name again?"

His eyes flared at last.

"I think you've forgotten how amiable I can be." He leaned in, the scent of sea and mint was overwhelming. It was just as seductive as I remembered. "Try me, Tate, ask me for anything."

Images of silken sheets, tan skin, and the warm embrace of bodies intertwined assaulted me. Pleasure pure and deep, better than anything else I've ever known; the comfort of his body holding mine, the familiarity in each movement—

No, those times were over. Long over and would not come back. I took a step away.

"See, that's what I thought. Tate, you used to be a fireball unafraid of any challenge, but now you are all bark and no bite," he spoke, disappointment etched in every word. "Not to mention, you're being stupid. Sneaking out past curfew, and on the night of a trial? What are you thinking?" His eyes intensified, concern and anger warring in them. He sucked on his one fang.

The act had my traitorous body responding with warmth spreading through my core.

"I don't think you want to know what I'm thinking..." I muttered.

His eyes brightened a bit and I swear he was scenting the air. He inhaled deeply and remained frozen—a statue. My body acted on its own accord, and I ran a hand up his chest. Damn, he was built. His muscles contracted at my touch, and I could sense his pulse increasing. His eyes ignited, the glacier blue brightening with each stroke of my finger. I paused as our gazes locked, the power of the surf with the strength of redwoods—icy blue and mahogany.

Blue sea eyes beckoning me further, promising pleasure. Just like before. My breath quickened as I moved my gaze down to his mouth. It was inviting and his full lips twitched, curving up. This was a dumb idea. I was playing with fire and he knew it.

"Tate." He grabbed my hand gently in his and pulled it away from his touch. "As much as I would like this, I think we both know you're not ready."

How dare he. I yanked my hand back as if his mere touch burned. He had no right to tell me what I could and couldn't handle. If he thought he broke me, he was wrong. Damn wrong. I reacted.

I reached up and cupped the back of his neck pulling him down toward me and took his lips savagely. Oh, Blood Mother. This was a mistake. He tasted like home. Fire in my core ignited as his tongue swept in and began to devour me with equal savagery. I met him stroke for stroke, exploring every inch of his mouth. His hands moved down to my hip, and he cupped my butt along with the back of my shoulders. He lifted me up and pressed my back against a tree, pausing only a moment before he tilted my head back further and intensified the kiss. There was nothing gentle about it. It was a kiss that consumed.

I wrapped my legs around him and dug my fingers deeper into his hair, eliciting a groan from him. This was so much...so, so much. I could feel the length of him getting hard, the sheer size of it was intimidating and a reminder of everything I was missing. I could palm him, I wanted to, but the position I was in made it hard to do that. He broke the kiss and began to work his way down my neck, kissing and sucking as he went. His golden curls tickled my collarbone and offered the most salacious sensations.

My core began to ache with need. I wanted him...desperately. I needed him to fill every crevice, to make me sing. I wanted his length gliding inside me, the pleasant friction leading to a glorious release.

I moaned, begging for more. His fangs grazed the sensitive side of my neck, sending pure pleasure shooting through me. He met the mark on my neck, the lover's mark he'd made when I was just seventeen. He wore a twin mark on the left side of his throat. We'd given them to each other back when we'd thought we were in love. Back when I trusted him, but that was before—

The thought was enough to jar me from my sex stupor. I didn't need him. Didn't truly want him. No, this was Chance. This was the male whose father, President Collin Dale, killed my mother in the name of justice for her supposed treason. The son of the Glenn's leader who just publicly killed a young boy in an act of twisted violence that even magic repelled. No, this was not someone I would find pleasure with.

He found my mouth again and this time when his tongue swept in, I bit down. Hard. He pulled back with a yelp and dropped me at the same time. His blood dripped from my mouth, and I licked it up, slowly —watching him the entire time.

"Damn it, Tate! What the fuck was that?"

"Which fucking reason should I give you?" I practically shouted. Control, I needed to control my anger before I said something really stupid and ended up on the end of Collin's court proceedings.

"What the hell does that mean?"

"Nothing. Just leave me alone. I'm not interested, OK? It may be hard for the great 'Chance,'" I used air quotes, mocking him, "to understand, but not every female wants you in her pants. So why don't you just turn around and head back to your buddies at the guara and go harass some other poor female?" I lifted my chin as I punctuated the last few words. "Maybe one who's drunk or desperate enough to be satisfied by *you*." I turned to leave but then he was in front of me.

"Not so fast, Tate." He heaved, clearly trying to catch his breath. "You may be a good kisser, but it wasn't enough of a distraction to make me forget my initial question. Why were you out here?"

The insufferable prick. Just like him to go from kissing to interrogating. Same mouth, very different expressions.

"I just wanted some space and air especially—"

I couldn't finish the sentence.

"Especially what?" His gaze was relentless.

"After what your father did to that boy!" I spat in his face and tried to shove past him.

"That boy *murdered* one of our own and deserved his punishment," Chance's voice dropped to a lethal calm. It was a warning, and one I knew I should heed.

"Oh yes, with a punishment so cruel it's only been publicly witnessed a dozen times in the past century and reserved for the worst of the worst. And by the way, how did a scrawny, barely developed *boy* take down a fully matured councilman? By all counts, council members are supposed to be the elite, the wisest and strongest of us; the most developed. And yet, somehow this boy killed him and instilled so much fear that Wayne was begging for death?" I was venturing into dangerous territory, and I knew it. But the image of the husk was still too fresh.

"You saw the memory. There's no way around it." He paused, running a hand through his ruffled curls. "I don't know how Lucas got the drop on Wayne, but once a feeding begins, we become unpredictable, and you know this. Damn it, Tate!" He sighed.

"I don't know what I saw. What I know is that his body was a husk. And that is what they did to my mother," my voice broke with the last word, and I hated it. I hated showing this weakness, especially to him. "Did you know that?" I lifted my tear-filled eyes to his. "Her file lists her execution as 'Enthrawment'. Did you even bother to check or to learn what became of the female who viewed you as a son, the one who welcomed you into her home and trusted you with her daughter? Or did you just go gallivanting off to the Southern Outpost, washing your hands of her blood?"

He closed his eyes for a moment. The energy in the air shifted, the violence lessened and instead, an empty void of sadness swept in. "Tate...I'm sorry for what happened to your mother. But this," he gestured out to the expanse and then to me, "this needs to end. The constant defiance, breaking Glenn curfew, questioning leadership."

"Oh, because you've never questioned leadership? My bad. That's right, you're the golden boy who was handed a dux's position because of who his daddy is."

"Careful, TK." His eyes snapped to mine. Any gentle mourning was now gone, replaced by the narrow gaze of a predator.

"No, you lost the right to call me TK when you withheld information about my mom's questioning." I shoved him. "You know, when you bedded me while they took her life. Don't you ever call me TK again."

He gulped, a sign of guilt.

"Don't you dare do that," I snapped, a different heat filling my veins. "You don't deserve to feel better about yourself by expressing remorse or have the audacity to feign regret. No, you don't get to play 'nice' or pretend to be the good guy. You're not. You. Are. Not. Good." I spoke each word with a finger digging deeper into his chest. He grabbed my hand and held me there.

"I can help you, Tate. Just, let me help you get into the guara. It will help assuage any questions that people may have."

"Questions? What could the council, or rather your father, possibly have to question me about?"

"Nothing, I misspoke."

"Misspoke or lost your nerve?"

"Use your brain, Tate. Do you really think Fletcher's defiance today went unnoticed? Already the guara have been asked to up surveillance on *his* class. Word has it he was speaking about the Untish. You know that's forbidden. After the war, the council decided it was best to silence any murmurs of the myth, and now of all times, we can't have rumors of the Untish circulating."

"What the hell does that mean?" My pulse quickened. *"Now of all times,"* I mocked.

I couldn't stand the thought of Fletch being in trouble. I knew speaking of the Untish was taboo, but dear blood, to be put on additional guara surveillance? That was extreme, well unless we were seeing increased enemy activity, then perhaps it would be considered as *possible* treason, but even so, the Untish would have to be real— something I'd never really allowed myself to consider.

"Fucking-A Tate, stop asking questions that can get you in trouble, and start following the Glenn's rules."

"Stop lying to me. What the hell do you mean by 'especially now'?"

He stood there, unmoving, refusing to answer. But I saw it, the twitch in his eyes, the subtle tightening of his forehead; he was worried.

"Please, Chance, just tell me. I can't help Fletch or myself if I don't understand the situation. Basics of assessing, our training, remember?" I pulled on the past as my eyes softened in the way I knew he could never resist. His gulp was visual confirmation that I had indeed struck a nerve.

"I...I can't. Let's just say that Fletcher needs to stop talking about the Untish and you need to be a good world-walker who doesn't stir anything up, doesn't stay out past curfew, and who doesn't give the guara *any* reason to question your allegiance."

The fact that he hadn't mentioned my impending Disciplinary Hearing meant he wasn't aware, and I for one was not about to bring that up. Instead, I wanted to focus on why he was so uptight. He *definitely* wasn't telling me something.

"Is that what's been putting the council on edge? Do we have another war to prepare for?" The possibility made me sick. I wasn't alive when the Glenn went to war a century ago, but the damage still existed today. It was a burn, forever fragmenting our world.

The Glenn was split into four sects over the political differences in fighting the Fae armies of Mydant and nearly half the population was killed. I didn't want to see that, to see my friends, innocents die for some stupid political gain.

"I don't know. But you need to get back to your home and village limits, now Tate." The finality in his words and expression told me I would get no further with him, he was always the good soldier. I turned and began to stroll away, frustration brimming beneath the surface of my blank expression.

"And Tate," his voice called after me, "I won't be able to cover for you again. If you are caught outside city limits past curfew, I will have to write you up. Please, don't make me do that." The softening of his voice almost felt like concern.

I almost pitied him, but the image of Fletch in danger…the look on his face when he told me about the loss of my mother…

Never again.

My brilliant mom had been turned into a husk, just like Lucas was. That was something I wouldn't forget—ever. I continued to walk away without another word.

CHAPTER 14

CHANCE

ate was an agitating female. Immature—she wasn't one to forgive and forget. But I cleared my conscience. I warned her and now I needed to get her off my mind. The feeding from earlier should still be fresh in my memory, but all I could taste was Tate. Her soft butterscotch flavor still filled my mouth, my tongue, it plagued my memories at night and now my old cravings returned. I'd been reacquainted with my old drug: Tate.

They say when vampires mate, we can bond or simply fuck. Tate was the former—to my total annoyance. Why couldn't she just have been a fuckbuddy like the other females I've bedded; a one-night stand with no ramifications? I needed a kick in the balls, I needed to wake up to reality. Tate and I were done, I owed her nothing. I had a mole to oust and a mission to prepare for, not fornication in the woods. Besides, there are other females, and after toying with Holland tonight, perhaps she'd be the perfect conquest when I needed a bit of stress release.

The barracks in the outer tower to HQ were filled with rich body odor and the floors were covered in mud. Whoever was on sanitation was about to have their balls handed to them—and not in a pleasant way. I made it past the cafeteria and the training center, heading through the leadership office wing toward my chambers when familiar breathing—heaving really—accompanied by loud footsteps sounded behind me. Du-Arche Pinely. This night just kept getting better.

"Dux Dale, I was informed you will be leaving us in less than twenty-four hours. I have the debriefing from today's disturbance as well as the updated guara watchlist. Can I assume I'll be taking over operations here upon your leave?" Naturally, Du-Arche Pinely would inquire about his new rank.

I extended my hand for the folder. A power play on my part, I'll admit. I didn't need a paper version of any of this as I could access it on the database via my disk, but I liked to keep Pinely on his toes and remind him who is in charge, even if I would soon be physically absent. He placed the folders in my hand, his jaw flexing.

"Yes, I'll have a list of updated drills and operational changes to be instituted starting tomorrow. You will ensure they are incorporated in my absence and keep me updated with any changes or news of importance." He stood there, a new shade of red beginning to crawl up his neck. His oversized gut bounced with each heave from his lungs. Apparently, the short walk from the other side of this wing was a bit too much cardio for him. I'd never particularly cared for the male, but his clear lack of self-control or attention to personal health grated me. A crumb, likely from a cookie, and some red splotches dotted his lower right beard; his hygiene was as lacking as his willpower. With Tate irritating my nerves still, I had zero tolerance for him. "That will be all, Du-Arche." With that, I turned and headed for my chambers.

Sleep, I knew, was not an option—I was too amped up. Instead of heading to bed for a frustrating attempt at sleep, I crouched over the maple desk and thumbed through the folder. Basic additional information pertaining to the impending travel was the first thing listed. We would take the underground circuit, the most common method of cross-country traveling, and stop at two minor settlements on the way —a check-in as much as it was a break from the stale confines of the tin can.

The whole trip would take three days. Not bad considering the large distance we'd be covering. The Southern Outpost wasn't as far as the Eastern, considering that HQ was essentially neighbors with the Western Outpost. Still, it would be a long trip through heavily forested, dense land with lots of elevation changes. The circuit made travel comfortable.

In a way, heading back to the SO felt like heading home. It was forest and sea, fog and mystery. The training facility there had prepared me to become the male I was now and still held a certain whimsical element.

My thumb slipped on a sharp edge, drawing a bit of blood. Fuck. I wiped it on my pants before focusing on the next page: Dux Holland. She would, of course, be accompanying me. I flipped through her file. I had asked to see it this morning when I'd been informed I would be working with her. I needed to know if I could count on her. After tonight, my gut said yes, but still, I needed more information.

She was top of her class, graduated ten years prior, and was awarded the medal of honor for an undercover mission that was listed as confidential from three years back. She became a dux two years ago. Still fresh. At least we had that in common. I'd only held my dux position for the past three years. It would have been nice to be paired with someone with more experience and a long-standing position, but I suppose the one good thing about her newness to the position was that she was clean—unlikely to be tainted or perverted by whoever was a part of the rebel group responsible for the recent attacks. I knew many of the members of the Southern Outpost from my work there last year. It was hard to picture any of them betraying the Glenn, but I knew that at least *one* had, and that son of a bitch would pay.

I flipped to her skills and wasn't surprised that she was top of her class for tactical maneuvers, hand-to-hand combat, and an expert marksman with daggers. I scanned the page to locate her magical giftings and was surprised to see it only listed one outside of the usual prowess and agility: Emo-Tasting. That didn't line up with what I'd witnessed tonight. If she was an Emo-Taster, then she'd be able to feel our emotions and taste them as her own. But she had compelled me tonight, that was an extremely rare gifting and one that wasn't in her folder. Why would she openly show me this? If she did secretly possess the power of compulsion, it was highly coveted and may not have been listed as a magical gifting by orders from the council. I understood they did that for espionage or tactical advantage, so why show me?

Shaking my head, I pulled up my disk and opened the digital hologram pulling up the most recent copy of the guara watchlist. There were currently forty-eight individuals in the capital that ranked as a level one threat. Scrolling to the bottom I spotted Fletcher's name. I hated my job sometimes.

Sighing, I opened the new orders page and began to update them. Anyone considered perfidious and all those who've had recent travel to the Eastern or Southern Outposts would be brought in for questioning first thing in the morning. Starting at noon tomorrow, all individuals listed as level one threats would be surveyed by the guara at all times. Travel would be eliminated.

We would need to double down security, specifically at the veil and all external watch towers of the capital. Additionally, I would need to assign Research to do full background checks on any ties the level one threat personnel had to Lucas Meitch, the Fern Vamp, or any soldiers posted at either of the breached outposts. My head began to throb; yeah, sometimes I really hated my job.

By tomorrow night, all these changes will be in full force, and I'll be leaving HQ to go on a snake hunt. This time tomorrow, everything would be different.

CHAPTER 15
TATE

Fletch was reclining by the fire, a glass of bloodwine in his hand. His usual tranquil expression was mottled with worry. I was likely the cause of it. I shut the door and strode over to the overstuffed chair opposite him. He didn't even look up...he was pissed.

"I uh...need to talk to you," I broke the silence. His gaze stayed transfixed on the flames. Stubborn mule. "Fletch, something strange happened, and I...I don't know what to make of it." At last, he met my eyes, and for once I couldn't read his expression.

"Did you know, Tate, that your mother loved the sea. She said it was full of power and mystery—that she could draw her strength from it. Funny, isn't it?" He tapped his fingers on the glass of wine.

I didn't answer, he rarely chose to speak of my mother.

"She was a free soul, a rule follower, the best warrior my generation had seen, and yet, it was the sea that made her nervous while simultaneously brave. The sea. A place she wanted her remains to be scattered and a place she will never see again because of *him*," he spat the last word. The earlier vision of President Dale standing over the husk came to mind. Except it was my mother this time, my sweet brave mother, who was reduced to a dried-out bag of skin because of the monster who ruled our Glenn.

"I hate him," I spoke without thinking.

"And yet...you smell like his son." His words were an unexpected blow.

"I...I didn't invite that attention from Chance."

"Didn't you? Don't you always?"

"That's not fair Fletch, and you know it. We were close once and now we're enemies."

"Tate, I believe I've always given you reasons to trust me. A truth for a truth. I believe I've garnered honesty from you."

"I am being honest." I adjusted in my seat, the springs whining with my movement.

He wouldn't respond, just kept staring at the flames. How could I tell him about what happened when he was in this kind of mood? I stood; we'd have this conversation later. Before I could make it to the edge of the rug, he reached out and gently grabbed my wrist.

"The trial today brought back a *lot* of unpleasant memories. Memories of your mother," his voice was a mere whisper. "I'm sorry for lashing out." He looked so tired and suddenly so much older. Fragile even.

Chance's warning filled my ears. The guara was watching Fletch and he suddenly looked so small, so vulnerable. I squatted down in front of him, cupping his hand in mine.

"Fletch, you need to be more careful. Chance said that the guara is watching you because of your speaking about mythical creatures, like the Untish, in class. I heard you today. And...I got the impression that things are stirring up. Chance alluded to another war coming."

"Hmm. President Dale would like that," he said, pausing to empty his glass. "He wants an ignorant generation. Do you know what's more dangerous and powerful than any skill or magical gift? Knowledge. President Dale wants to strip it from you and from these kids. I'd rather die than let him do that."

The thought terrified me. I couldn't lose Fletch too. "It's just a fairytale, Fletch. The Untish aren't real. Why are you so selfish?" I rubbed my forehead; this was not how I wanted this to go. "Just...just stop spreading tales and follow the rules in school. I don't like the idea of your allegiance being questioned."

He pulled his hand from mine and lifted the bottle of wine to his lips. He tipped it back and took another long swig, draining it before picking up a new bottle of wine from the floor next to two other empty bottles. He grabbed the cork with his teeth and popped it before putting the bottle straight to his lips. Odd for Fletch to forgo a glass. He loved to be a snob about following etiquette.

"Tate, the Untish aren't mythical. They were real. They are real." Now I knew the wine was getting to him. No one had ever seen a Untish. In school, we'd been taught that they never existed and there weren't any articles about them in the Village Capitol Library. I stood and grabbed his elbows, lifting him with me. He needed to sleep this off.

"Fletch, you've had too much. Get some sleep. I have to be at the clinic tomorrow morning for my shift, but when I come back, we can—"

He brushed my hands off and stopped moving. Locking eyes with mine, his gaze boring into my soul. Even with his gaze focused, he faltered a bit, the bottle sloshing red over the dark wood floor.

"Tate, I've been so wrong. I thought that protecting you and not exposing everything was right, but—"

He stumbled over the ottoman, nearly falling. I reached out and steadied him. I hadn't seen him this hammered...ever.

"Ok, hush now. You've always taken good care of me Fletch, let's just get you to bed." His weight was bearing down on me and keeping him upright was beginning to get difficult.

"No, Tate listen to me!" He dropped the bottle to the floor, red liquid gushing all over the floor, and gripped my shoulders. "There's much we need to speak of. And soon, we don't have much time."

What was he talking about? I didn't have time to respond before

Fletch crumbled to the floor, slipping through my grip, and began laughing like a lunatic.

"Gods Fletch, how much did you have?"

"What does it matter? We're all on borrowed time." He sat there sitting in a puddle of bloodwine. It was the most unsophisticated I'd ever seen him.

He was incoherent. I needed him sober to talk about what had happened. He needed to heed my warning from Chance. I shook my head. Tomorrow. I'd talk to him tomorrow. In the meantime, I should be making him coffee and cleaning the floor. But this was the first time I'd heard Fletch laugh, really laugh, in over a year. So, I sat down next to him and grabbed the bottle. It was practically empty but thank blood the wine was thick and about a quarter of it remained in the bottle. After taking a long swig I decided to heed sage wisdom: if you can't beat 'em, join 'em. With that, I took another swig and kicked off my shoes. Time to let go a bit.

CHAPTER 16

TATE

Being back at work was a refreshing reprieve from the pressures of the Glenn. Normally, I'd stay here as long as I could withstand this world's limitations. Two days. After that, the sun would begin to burn my skin and all those human stereotypes for vampires in daylight would become true. Unfortunately for me, I had to go back to the guara sooner than I'd like—as the guara informed me at my departure this morning, my world-walking pass now required a check-in every twenty-four hours. No doubt Chance's work at trying to 'mitigate' my potential damage. Insufferable jackass.

Furthermore, my Disciplinary Hearing was scheduled for tomorrow, in the late morning. Things really couldn't get worse.

Cody, my supervisor at the World Draw Organization (WDO), was in a particularly bad mood today. He had scheduled me for blood draws *knowing* I haven't fed in over twenty-four hours. My guess was that Chance ripped into him, and Cody, the ever-loving altruistic person that he is, was now taking it out on me. Talk about projection.

Most of my patients were the standard citizens getting blood drawn to 'help fight the disease' and test for contamination. Mostly college students today. Well meaning, but stupid kids who never questioned the why behind the WDO. Not that many did. It was established fifty years ago as a means of attaining blood for the Glenn and preventing overfeeding on the human population. It had been installed by President Valley, President Dale's predecessor, and was, oddly enough, something that Collin had fought at the House meetings with the other Vamps—back when we were still speaking to them—but he'd been outvoted by the inner councilman from each Vamp.

Now, I leave one corpse with a missing head and his High Lordship sends me to corrections? Hypocrites. But it didn't matter, not really.

Hunger gnawed at me. I could choose to feed from the blood bags, as I was allotted two pretested bags a day while serving at the clinic, but the cold taste along with the innocence behind the source never agreed with me. I much preferred my vigilante methods. Call me a junky, but I had developed a palette for fresh warm iron from assholes who don't deserve to have it circulating in their systems.

After cleaning up the rest of my station, I headed to the back of the clinic and punched out. Another eight-hour day served. I began to walk toward the door when an unwelcome head of gold walked through—Ferrari.

"Oh Tate, I see here that you drew eighty patients today but only logged seventy-nine bags. May I ask why?" Her voice had the cadence of ice shards, tearing through your ears in an oddly impeccable way— it was the perfection of it that I hated. The beauty that exuded from her was, quite frankly, unnatural. I still hadn't determined what she *was*, only that she seemed odd, and I just couldn't picture her being a vampire like she claimed to be. I'd never once seen her feed on blood. She was also too pretty to be human. Her glamour was strange if she wore glamour at all. A conundrum, that's what she was.

"Yes, one patient passed out as the draw began and so I rescheduled her draw for next week."

"You know standard procedure requires you to report this. She could be contaminated, and her draw needs to occur on schedule."

What a load of crap. Everyone here knew, well at least all the vampires here knew, that the virus was pure myth. There was no viral pandemic. *We* were the pandemic fifty years ago. Before world-walking became more regulated in order to maintain the veil between the realms and prevent another multidimensional war like we had a century ago.

"I forgot. I'll fill out a report first thing tomorrow." I approached the door when an odd sensation filled the room. My energy rapidly depleted and my head felt light—my thoughts blurring.

"Tate, you don't look well. Here, let me help you." Ferrari reached for my shoulder and moved me to a nearby chair. The room began to spin a bit and my vision became hazy. Pressure. I felt pressure. "Perhaps you should have a blood draw yourself to make sure you're not infected. Working with blood carries many risks, as you know," she said, adding an ingenuine 'tsk'. "When was your last draw?" She pulled out her tablet and quickly punched in my ID number which was swiftly followed by another series of 'tsks'. "It looks like you're outside of protocol. You need them every three months since you work with blood and it's been nine. *Nine* months, Tate. Not good. I'll do it right now." She reached for a nearby supply cabinet. Like hell she would.

"Nooo—I'm, I'm fine, really." But I wasn't. I could barely string together a sentence. My limbs felt latent, heavy even, and my head was foggy.

"You don't look it. This will just take a minute and then we'll get it tested ASAP to ensure you're not a liability to the clinic." Of course, that was her concern. Assuming she was human and bought into the whole pandemic bullshit, she wouldn't care for me, only her own ass.

Her skin nearly glowed, it looked translucent. Which of course was impossible; another symptom of my sudden illness. Maybe this was a severe case of blood withdrawal after a blood-drain followed by no feedings. Or the aftermath from an excessive use of energy. I had drained myself yesterday by simply shifting. This was likely the result from that.

A cold needle pressed to my skin, it was more painful than necessary but then again, Ferrari didn't seem like the gentle type, despite her appearance. She also didn't take 'no' for an answer. My blood began to flow into the bag, and she sat there with a cold smile plastered to her perfectly symmetrical face. Her ivory skin was flawless, and her blue eyes shone with iciness. My skin began to pebble, the room felt noticeably cooler.

"Almost there," a snake said to a mouse—Ferrari's mouth moving as she spoke.

I glanced at the bag, it was two-thirds of the way full, she'd used the largest needle. Of course, why use bedside manner when you can use a sledgehammer? But the fullness wasn't what gave me pause; no, it was the color of my blood. It didn't appear wholly red. It looked maroon with streaks of gold dancing throughout it. Clearly, I was experiencing vision problems too. The pounding in my head began to intensify, and I forced my eyes shut. I felt a sharp sting in my arm and let out a yelp. I tried to focus on the cause of the pain, but I couldn't get the room to stop spinning.

Just as my head began to swim from pulsating pressure, the tingling of my skin stopped. The tension in my head disappeared all at once, leaving an even worse dizzying aftermath. The room felt sweltering, and my stomach roiled.

"There, all done," Ferrari said as she yanked the needle out, taking her time to inspect the blood while slickness coated my arm—I was leaking everywhere. A moment later, my arm was wrapped in gauze and medical tape, and she was gone, my blood bag already placed inside a transport container.

I began to stand, but the room went out of focus. The ground came careening toward me and impacted with absolutely zero grace. I laid there on my back, staring at the iridescent lighting as the ceiling spun. I'll just lie here for a minute. Just a minute...

CHAPTER 17

TATE

My phone buzzed, the ringtone blaring through the room. Blearily, I opened my eyes and realized I was on a gurney in the break room of the clinic. A glance at the wall told me it was two AM. I'd been out for over eight hours. Shit. I had mere hours until I needed to check back in at the Glenn. I really should give Chance a piece of my mind. But right now, it hurt too much; that was the weirdest blood withdrawal I'd *ever* experienced.

I reached for my phone just as it stopped ringing. Ten missed calls, seven of which were from Tim. Fan-fricking-tastic. I'd missed our date. He was going to be all insecure on me again, and I needed him focused. I needed intel.

He was a rookie detective and often assigned the rougher cases, or the ones where the greased hands of law enforcement wanted the case dropped. Better give it to a newbie who didn't have the connections or experience to close the case. Law enforcement at its finest.

He *had* rescued a victim or two, but the perps got off on technicalities...

Not enough evidence. Those bastards were always my personal favorites. Well, that and the domestic violence cases where the victim refused to press charges. Those really bothered Tim; they bothered me too, so much so that I wouldn't be able to think of anything else until the monster's blood was flowing nicely down my throat like a glass of rich merlot.

I punched Tim's name and hit redial. He answered on the second ring.

"Tate?"

"Hey Tim, I'm so sorry I missed our date."

"Are you ok?" He was always the Good Samaritan with his first area of concern for me.

"I'm fine, I just passed out last night. I think I've been working too hard and haven't eaten enough. But I just woke up on a cot in the break room here at the clinic." I willed my voice to sound calm even though my nerves were on edge. I still hadn't fed for close to thirty-six hours and the hunger pains were gnawing at me. I needed a meal—warm and fresh.

"When's the last time you ate? Did you have a doctor look at you?"

"I don't remember. And yes, Ferrari took my blood last night when I started feeling ill, just to be safe..."

"Thank God. Keep me posted, there's still so much we don't know about the VOFS virus and if you have it, we'll need to get you treated right away."

Ah yes, the VOFS virus. Humans still believed their missing population from a little over fifty years ago were slaughtered by a blood-borne virus, i.e., vampires. It was said that if you had two fang marks on your body, you needed to be tested right away as those were the first symptoms of the 'virus'. After the no-kill law was put into effect along with blood bags, vampires stopped the slaughter and humans recovered... well relatively recovered. There were still human lines missing.

"I know, I really don't think it's that though," I assuaged him.

If he only knew.

"But you work with blood, Tate, you know I wish you'd quit there. It's not safe and they don't pay you *nearly* enough."

I massaged my aching temples. Not this again. "Tim, we've had this conversation before. I like where I work. I'll be fine, I promise. Can we reschedule for tonight?" A long pause on the phone told me he was worried about the virus and getting infected. "That is, if my results come back negative."

"Of course, I'd love to. Keep me posted and let me know if there's anything I can do."

"I will. How's work going? Anything crazy?"

"Not really, just the usual."

"Any news about Tony Gari?"

Tim sighed heavily into the phone. "He was released yesterday; can you believe it? Judge let him out on bail. His trial date is set for two months from now. Two months." I could hear him grinding his teeth. "Sometimes I wonder what the point is in our justice system. I mean, I'm likely to be sent on another call, dragging another body out of the river that we all know Gari is behind, and yet I can't do anything about it. I mean, what's the point?" His tender heart would get him killed one of these days. And yet, I shared his sentiment.

"Any idea if he'll skip town? Or is he stuck under observation?" I needed an address. Taking down a mobster was on my list, but it had many risks. Too many moving parts for me to tackle as hungry as I currently was. I needed to think clearly.

"No idea. I mean, technically he's supposed to stay in city limits, but with his underground system, it's impossible to make sure. I just can't believe the judge released him. If I didn't know better, I'd say..." He heaved another long sigh into the phone. I could practically hear his heart pumping blood into his enlarged neck veins that were likely bulging.

"Say what?"

"I shouldn't say it."

"Tim, it's me you're talking to. If you can't share what's weighing on you with your girlfriend, why have one?"

"Damn, I love you."

I cringed at his use of the 'L' word.

"I mean it, Tate, you know me so well."

"As you do me." I tried to sound sweet and hide the strain I felt in just saying the words. I really didn't want to string him along, but the system worked. He unknowingly provided me with my perps and he definitely reaped perks from this relationship.

"Yeah, I know my little cold case hunter." He laughed a dry chuckle. "I suspect Judge Rollins is in Gari's pocket. He let him out on a criminally low bail and then set a delayed court date. No required surveillance, no ankle monitor, nothing. He's treating him like he's a first-time offender, not the known crime lord that he is. It makes me sick, Tate."

And just like that, I had my next target.

Glancing at the clock, I had just two hours before I was expected back at the Glenn. It was early, but Judge Rollins was an early bird who liked to stop at Raised Roasters for his morning donut and coffee before heading to the courthouse. I just hoped today was no exception.

Naturally, he lived in the nice part of town. His house cost just over one-point-five million dollars. After an in-depth search on the black web using my encryption disk, thank you Shae, I could tell he just bought a two-million-dollar vacation home in the Bahamas—last week. Following the recent transfer of funds to his account, I located an offshore account that was, to my delight, connected to none other than Tony Gari. That was all the proof I needed.

I parked around the corner and then jogged down the block to his home. After jumping the ten-foot fence, I slunk into the shadows and waited. My left leg throbbed from the landing, if only gravity could be fooled. I waited behind the detached four-car garage for thirty minutes in the crisp morning air. It was getting bright out, but thankfully the large willow tree still offered me enough coverage and shadows to hide in. At last, I heard the screen door slam shut. Show time.

The judge was a stout, fat man and quite frankly, delicious looking. The perfect butterball. I waited for him to approach his vehicle and pull out his keys before I struck from behind. One arm wrapped around his swelling mid-section and the other yanked his shoulder to my mouth. I sank my fangs into his jugular and began a quick draw. He struggled, but I pinned him to the ground, using leverage to keep him in place. He thrashed and bucked, dug his nails into my forearm, breaking the skin, until at last, he stilled—paralyzed by my venom.

I pulled and pulled, savoring each drag of blood while simultaneously desiring more. The hunger was more intense than I could remember. It was almost as bad as the first time I fed when I was a teen—the need beckoned me to continue, to drain his life force and then some. I was lost in the melody of his blood, the thumping of his heart as it pumped the rich iron into my mouth.

It held the sweetness of a dessert wine and was slightly fatty—not my ideal flavor, but right now it didn't matter. His blood coated my tongue and my throat, floating within as my body began to hum. My vision intensified and I didn't just see the individual drops of sweat dripping from his fattened throat, but I could see a glow...slowly exuding from his body and being drawn into my hand. Flowing in an odd gold-tinted river. It was enough to startle me from my euphoria.

I released my fangs from his throat and removed my hand. The body lay unmoving on the ground, but the gold aura flowing from him didn't stop, it continued to get pulled from his corpse and was flowing into my hand—my now shining hand. What the hell?

I jumped backwards but it didn't stop the flow or the building sensation I could feel under my skin. It burnt, but pleasantly so; this was something I'd *never* experienced before. The tingle in my limbs intensified even as I could feel pressure building and then releasing in me, like an adjustment at the chiropractor. I waved my hands, willing the pull to stop, but nothing stilled. The golden aura just continued to flow, increasing in strength even as my distance from the body increased. *Snap!* The body seemed to sink in on itself. The judge was long gone.

I was in way over my head.

Panic began to seize my mind as my entire arm glowed brightly, blinding me temporarily, and then abruptly stopped. The corpse before me was dried out, almost husk-like, and my hand was just a hand. What the hell just happened? The corpse looked different from enthrawment, it wasn't purple or shriveled in a series of wrinkles, but...it looked similar. All the moisture had evaporated, and the muscle left was little to nothing. The skin appeared to be suctioned onto the bone—no visible fat remained.

I closed my eyes and exhaled. This would all make sense. Fletch would fill in the dots, I was certain of it. First, however, I needed to deal with this body. Quickly.

I threw his body in the driver's seat, strapped his seat belt on, and then turned the engine over. Shutting the door, I drew out my gun, added the silencer, and began firing rounds into the car's gas tank until, at last, it exploded, and fire erupted, consuming the car. That'll do.

Leaving the scene of the crime, the smoky haze followed me, clouding my mind. Whatever was happening to me needed to be sorted out ASAP. President Dale could never know.

I hopped the fence and began jogging down the street. A certain eeriness settled in—I wasn't alone. I could feel eyes on me but couldn't see them. I was used to being the predator this side of the Veil, not the prey. I looked around, scanning the nearby houses, cars, yards. Nothing. Just an overactive imagination I assured myself...

And yet, deep down I knew it was a sugarcoated lie that I'd have to deal with eventually. I just hoped I'd have time to figure out my shit before whatever or whoever was watching me became an issue.

CHAPTER 18

TATE

The Glenn was abnormally quiet. I had just pushed through the veil and had to do a double-take of the wall. Security had been increased, significantly. Where two or three guards once stood at the perch, there were now seven or eight. The entrance that was usually manned by two guara, was now manned by six on the outside of the gate and six on the inside. I'd never seen the veil so heavily manned, and certainly never the *exit* so thoroughly monitored. A chill crawled down my back as Chance's warning echoed through my mind. Something was off, or worse, something was *coming*.

"Tate Aaralyn, you're late to check-in," the guard informed me as I approached the archway to the city, his shadow flickering in the torches' light. It was just past dawn this side of the veil.

"Give me a break, I'm three minutes late."

"Protocol. Search her." Two other guards approached and quickly patted me down, emptied my bag on the table—fingered my vibrator, bastards—before nodding to the lead guard.

"Reason for your delay?" He motioned for me to collect my items, now strewn about in the metal tray.

"I fell in love." His eyes snapped up to mine. "He's human, tastes delicious…and his blood tastes good too." I winked at him. His complexion darkened as his eyes narrowed. Males.

"Relax, I just slept in this morning. Lots of traffic getting through the veil you know, those semi's really back things up." His eyes were dead. Pfft. My humor was wasted on him.

"Wait here." He walked away, leaving the other two guards to watch me while he made a call. A moment later he returned, looking oddly tense.

"When is the last time you spoke with Fletcher Backshy?" His question threw me. Was Fletch in trouble? Was Chance messing with me because I rejected him?

"The night before I left for my shift at the clinic. Why?" My pulse quickened.

He didn't respond and instead stepped away again and began speaking into his shoulder, likely speaking directly to Chance or whoever was currently in charge of wall operations.

"You may enter, but if you are late again, we will be revoking your world-walking pass. I am also to inform you this is your second strike. A third will result in sentencing with possible forced conscription to the guara. I recommend not missing your Disciplinary Hearing." He stepped aside, as did the other guards, and I passed through the arch.

Tension was blooming everywhere, my chest included. Why did they ask about Fletch? Was this really because of his myths? Or had someone spotted me shifting the other night?

My head was buzzing with questions. The high from my recent feed was still strong, heightening all emotions, including my anxiety. I clenched and unclenched my fingers. Likely, Fletch would know the answers. He usually had the inside scoop on these things and there was so, so much I wanted to discuss with him. The extra guards were honestly the least of my concerns.

Self-consciously, I pulled down my jacket sleeve further to cover my hand. It had stopped glowing a while ago, but I didn't know the cause, and I didn't want it to start shining again. Not for one minute. Certainly not around the guara.

The streets were beginning to get more populated as the blood sun was cresting the sky in the east. I always found it amusing how the time veil side and here didn't align perfectly. Roughly, it was nearly nine AM human time and five AM vampirical Glenn time.

The tingling sensation I'd felt earlier had returned and I wasn't sure what to make of it; I felt oddly stronger and yet, more vulnerable than ever. Is that what power was?

Making a left down Main Street I headed for the outskirts of the village. Not long ago I was breathing fire. Fire. I didn't know how that was possible and wasn't sure it had actually happened. Perhaps, it was a hallucination of my overactive mind and remnants of a blood-drain. That spoiled skin-bag could have been doing drugs, maybe it just passed into my system.

Something strange was going on and while the logical part of my brain assured me I was just tired, it also suggested something was wrong and a visit to medical could be helpful. But doing so also meant President Dale would find out and *that* was the last thing I wanted. Especially given my shifting gene. Thankfully, the blood draw at the clinics were for show and vampire blood, once this side of the veil, was to be dumped, as feeding from one another was strictly prohibited.

I inhaled the sweetness of the air. A defining trait of the Glenn's atmosphere as opposed to the human realm. The light was just beginning to color the sky—streaks of red, orange, and yellow danced across the auburn clouds. Our home appeared up ahead, nestled into the side of a hill, the grass backlit from nearby torches, highlighting its browning color and the dead leaves that dotted the hill. The oversized maple tree that sheltered the house was beginning to transition to fall.

This was home. It had always felt like home, even now with Mom gone and Fletch living in her stead, I still felt the warmth of its embrace. I reached the door and turned the handle. Locked. Odd, Fletch usually left it open for me since he was disturbingly aware of my schedule. Perhaps he'd forgotten or had gotten wasted again?

He should be home; classes wouldn't commence for three more

hours, around eight-thirty. I pulled out my keys and unlocked the door, then entered the home.

"Fletch?"

No response came. The place was dark with the window coverings pulled close. I shuffled through the kitchen, setting my bag on the stone counter, before grabbing the lighter and reaching for the torches. One by one, I lit all four in the main room, their light casting the room in a cozy glow. Empty. He wasn't in the living room. I padded down the hall to his room and found the door ajar. He wasn't home. Frustrated, I heaved a sigh and made my way back to the living room. It was cast in a comforting orange glow.

Fire was such an odd thing; it could kill us and yet it brought comfort. A juxtaposition my mother had loved dearly; the thing that gave us a comfortable existence could also take life. I headed toward the couch and kicked off my shoes.

Fletch's bag sat beside the chair across from me, contents sprawled across the linen cushion. He would never leave for school without his bag; he rarely went anywhere without it, so where was he?

Exhaustion pulled at my senses. I needed sleep. Thank blood I had some time before my next shift at the clinic. After being up all night and the weird withdrawal or shifting aftermath, my body demanded sleep. A bottle of wine sat at the foot of the couch, a staple where Fletch was concerned. I picked it up and popped off the cork before taking a long drag. Bloodwine, always the good stuff. From the taste I could tell this was vintage—the wine was thicker than normal, meaning a higher blood to liquor ratio. Just the way Fletch liked it. More nourishment and less buzz.

Pulling an oversized pink blanket, one of the few frilly things I still owned, up over my lap I nestled into the couch's brown leather, savoring its warm embrace. The wine began to heat my belly and calm my fears. This was good, I'd just relax here like this until Fletch got back—surely, he'd be home before classes began to gather his bag. And when he did, we'd talk. Then I'd have answers before the den of wolves tried to devour me with *their* questions. I took another long drag and let my mind begin to numb.

I stayed like that for a couple of hours. The numbing bliss was quieting the anxiety. The clock showed it was seven forty-five. Fletch still had not come home. Old nerves returned. Where was he? My phone dinged, startling me. I threw back the blanket and made my way to the counter where my bag sat. Digging out my enhanced rectangular device, I squinted against the bright blue light of it.

Hey babe, what you up to? Just got off my night shift—went late, again. Thanks, boss. Anyway, I still have some energy, want to come over?

I knew what Tim wanted and perhaps he'd make the perfect distraction. I pushed back some stray golden-blonde hair and shot back a quick response.

Yes, a visit to Tim would be the perfect distraction and provide me intel for my next feed. Screw Fletch for not being here. I wasn't going to stay here waiting all day. No, I had a life to live. I jotted down a quick note to Fletch, letting him know I was pissed and needed to chat, then turned out the torches. I opened the door and left; the blush blanket crumpled on the wine-stained floor next to the half-empty bottle.

THE BED creaked as Tim thrusted from behind. He was getting on my nerves—again. At least this way I didn't have to look at him. I could hide some of the cringes breaking out across my face. This sweet detective was utterly clueless when it came to the female anatomy. I could give him points for one thing though, he'd taken my mind off of Fletch and the guara—well, he had until now.

He grunted as he pushed forward again, my core heating with the friction. He really enjoyed sex. Not that I minded much, but sometimes the routine of it all was unrousing. The sex was tolerable, good even by human standards, but painfully bland. His moves never changed; it had become very routine. In about one minute, he'd climax with the most obnoxious grunt and then roll me over to pull me into a sweaty hug. I sighed, audibly.

Oops.

"Everything ok?" he asked, his voice strained as he paused his movement. Shit, I needed to fix this quickly.

"Great, don't stop," I said.

"Tate, if this isn't good for you, we can try something else?"

"No, no. It *is* great." I tried to keep the panic from my voice. Tim couldn't handle what I really wanted, what I craved. I was too strong for him and the kind of mind-blowing orgasm I wanted would break him, quite possibly, literally. But he didn't need to know that. He was my distraction and my informant. I needed him in more ways than to merely sate the physical.

"Really, this is amazing. I was just about to climax." I tried to sound flirty, but it came off irritated. He pulled out. Not good.

"Tate, what's going on? Did I do something to hurt you?"

"No, really, I'm fine. It's just been a hard week and I'm still feeling a little lightheaded." At that he climbed off me completely. I turned around to meet his eyes. His hairy chest was gleaming with sweat and his erection instantly shrank as he settled back onto his knees. It was a respectable size when it was fully enlarged, but still only by human standards. There were certain vampire traits that were true gifts, and the reproductive organs were one of them. Well, that and an increased sex drive coupled with passion that Tim could only ever imagine. I was the best he'd ever had; he'd told me that and I wouldn't be surprised if it were true. Who could compete with vampirical prowess?

"You're not feeling ill still? Maybe we should take you back to the clinic?"

"Tim, the results were negative and just showed I was dehydrated and needed to up my potassium. Stop worrying about me and how about we finish what you started."

Men liked that, to feel in control. Even *this* boy scout's ego appreciated feeling sexually macho. I climbed up onto his lap and settled down, hovering just over his now erecting manhood.

"Tate, I don't know. If you're not feeling well, I wouldn't want to

—" But his protests were cut off as I settled down onto him, squeezing as I went, eliciting a moan from his lips.

"Oh heavens, you are amazing."

Naturally, I was. But it was time to get a little pleasure out of this encounter and perhaps I could push him a *tiny* bit further than normal. I let out a little whimper and then pushed myself up, using my hands on his shoulders, before slamming myself back down. The friction was divine, and I began to feel the tingling sensation of pure pleasure. I repeated this motion, building on the desire burning within. Harder, faster, better.

I ignored the insane amount of body hair that began to brush my bare breasts and instead relished the way his warmth teased my taut buds. He groaned and it was all the encouragement I needed to bury my hands in his hair and lower us to the mattress. I closed my mouth over his and slipped my tongue inside. I sucked and pulled at his tongue, groaning as I did so. This was actually good. Perhaps I'd learn something new.

I continued to rotate my hips and impale myself on him, up then down, and repeat. He began to meet me thrust for thrust and reached even deeper within. His hands settled on my hips, and he began to move even faster. Good, but fast. Too fast, at this rate he wouldn't last. I stiffened my arms attempting to slow him down, but it was too late.

He tensed and grunted out loud. It was over. He pulled out and then pulled me onto his now gleaming chest.

"So good." He yawned.

Clearly, I'd just worn him out. With a peck to the head, he closed his eyes and dozed off, completely sated while I burned with desire. This was never going to last. I *really* needed to find a better informant.

Climbing out of bed I went to the kitchen to get my purse, the vibrator inside saw more action and gave me more pleasure than Tim likely would in his lifetime. My bag sat on the chair just inside the kitchen nook; the old yellow table's paint was chipping. It, like this apartment, had seen better days. They really didn't pay law enforcement enough.

Tim's laptop sat on the table next to a stack of manila folders. I hesitated. The point of this whole thing with Tim was to get info, find my targets, and make the city safer for women and those who were vulnerable. The one good part about sex with him was that he was a heavy sleeper and usually passed out for a bit after a good orgasm—especially when he completed a late-night shift like he just had.

Sucking on my fang, I set my bag down and opened his laptop. Entering the password I'd figured out months ago, his mom's name and birthday, I opened the police database. He had several open tabs in the browser. I scanned over them. All searches for people with the same last name: Johnstain. Allie Johnstain, Ben Johnstain, Carter Johnstain, the list was long. They were all listed as missing.

Allie Johnstain's file caught my attention. I enlarged it. She was pretty with bright red hair that was bluntly cut at her shoulders. Pale skin scattered with heavy freckles and brown eyes that were incredibly striking given her complexion and hair color. A rare combination. A beauty. Was that why she was taken? I began to read the notes, scrolling through the general data and timeline. She disappeared three weeks ago. She was nineteen and went to OCU, a freshman majoring in marine biology. Smart.

She was last seen on campus heading to the dorms. This could be a good case; if I could find the perp responsible, I could feed, leave him alive with two puncture marks, a new public case of the virus. He'd become a leper and never hurt another woman again. Did one of the Johnstains take her? I clicked on Ben's file. When females went missing, often a boyfriend or family member was responsible. He disappeared three months ago, which meant he likely wasn't the one responsible for Allie. Unless...he was the master planner?

I bit my lip as I clicked on the next file, Carter Johnstain. He too had shocking red hair, pale skin, and splashes of freckles. Clearly, they were related, likely a sibling. Only, while Allie had breathtaking brown eyes, Carter's were rather boring and common. I glanced through his case file's main notes. He's been missing since last year. Odd. Reading further, I saw what I was looking for. Carter was Allie's brother, and Ben was their uncle. Bingo.

What were the odds of three people who were related to each other going missing over the span of a year? Were they all disappearing of their own free will, or was someone systematically targeting them?

I glanced down to the paper on the table and noticed Tim's handwriting. He had jotted several notes but two in particular caught my attention.

Family lines disappearing. Johnstain line is vanishing, could it be like the Culbecks? If so, why?

And the other note was a bit more alarming.

Why the sudden uptick in missing persons? Gari connection? Targeting certain blood. Could it be related to the virus? Willa and Norman Johnstain, 143 Julber Street.

My pulse quickened, of course the virus wasn't to blame...but a nagging feeling began to set in. Could we be overfeeding again? Was there a stray serial vampire who was out there selecting bloodlines and eliminating them? We had a case like that fifty years ago, it was dealt with via public execution in the Glenn. Could it be happening again? Was I now hunting one of my own? Or worse, was this somehow connected to Chance's warning and the increased guara?

I pulled up the missing persons from the last month in the system. The number on the screen couldn't be right. Seven hundred people? Looking at last month, the number was just over four hundred. I expanded my search to the past six months. Nearly two thousand missing persons had been reported, from this small city alone. The population here was just over five hundred thousand.

Clicking on the data from this time last year, I selected a span of six months. The number was significantly less. It was just shy of nine hundred. Going back five years, the numbers showed about three hundred missing persons in that span; ten years, and the number plummeted to about two hundred. Over the course of six months, ten years ago, only two hundred people were reported as missing. And now, the same stretch nearly reached two thousand?

The pit of my stomach soured. How many of these people were related? I entered Johnstain and hit search over the span of five years in the missing person's database. Nearly forty-eight Johnstains had been reported missing. My mouth went dry. I typed in Culbec and hit search. Seventy-eight Culbecs went missing in the same five-year span fifty years ago. That wasn't normal.

Was there something special about the Johnstains and Culbecs? If they came from a line of unturned vampires, they could, in theory, have magic and their blood which, according to myths, could enhance that of the vampire who drains them—or damn them. But where were the bodies? I reselected all Johnstain missing persons and clicked on 'closed'.

None. The search field was empty. A sigh escaped me. I searched next for any corpses within the files, maybe bodies were recovered but their murderers never caught. The computer froze, the icon in the middle spinning; I tapped my fingers on the wooden table, patience was never my strong suit. Finally, it loaded. Again, it showed none. Not one single body from the missing Johnstains was recovered. That seemed impossible. With the last serial vamp, he left a trail of bodies. Where were all the missing Johnstains?

The questions were pulsing through my head. I needed a distraction. Glancing at my bag, I knew the perfect one and it had five settings. I smiled as I grabbed my vibrator and headed for the shower.

CHAPTER 19
TATE

The smell of bacon welcomed me as I emerged from the mist in the bathroom wrapped in a thin white towel. I smirked as I sauntered out. Tim's eyes swallowed me whole, focused on the snug towel that barely covered my assets. He was humming, his black hair still a mess from bed, and was already dressed in his uniform of choice: loose dress pants with an oversized button-down sloppily tucked into them. The brown belt holding the too-big pants up was worn and had seen better days. I could see the vague imprint of his wallet in his back pocket. Funny that his dress pants *had* a back pocket.

"Want some?" He held the pan with the sizzling bacon up in the air. Grease splattered the front of his shirt and coated the square tiled counter.

"Smells amazing. I'm surprised you're up." I winked. He'd just had a huge workout a couple of hours ago. But I suppose he was hungry, even if he'd just had me not long ago...

"Yeah, Chief called twenty minutes ago. We have a witness who's en route for the missing persons case I'm working. I have to be at the station in the next hour." He pushed a plate of eggs and bacon toward me. I sat down and reached for the coffee pot and grabbed the empty cup near my plate. This man may not know his way around the female 'cuisine,' but he certainly understood food. His mastery in the kitchen was definitely a perk.

"Mmm. This is so good, Tim." I took another bite. For once, the flattery rolling off my tongue was genuine. Vampires may live for centuries, but we still had not perfected coffee or bacon in the Glenn. One of the many reasons I liked being veil side.

"Thanks, I hope you get a chance to enjoy it. I, on the other hand, have to eat on the go."

"What missing person is this?"

"I got assigned a new case two days ago, a young college student just disappeared. No witnesses, her roommates haven't seen her in a week, and she hasn't been to any classes. It's like she just vanished." Jackpot. This could be the perfect perp for me to hunt next and expend some pent-up aggression on.

"Any footage?"

"None. That's why it's so weird. The campus is heavily monitored, but the last footage we have of her is after she left the campus clinic and headed through the park. No footage shows her coming out of the park. It's just like another case I had a month ago." His brows furrowed. "I'm sorry, I get so caught up in my work but I'm sure it's boring to you."

"Not at all." I set my cup down and grabbed his hand across the counter. "You know I'm intrigued by police work. And I care about you, so please don't ever apologize or feel the need to carry any of this alone." His eyes dipped to my lips as he leaned across the counter and grazed them gently with his own. Tender, yet firm.

"What'd I do to get so lucky with you?" I smiled. Tim had a good heart. If he wasn't my informant, he would make a good friend. He chugged his coffee before placing the mug in the sink.

"Well, among other things, you are a great cook." I winked as I stabbed some of the eggs on my plate.

He chuckled in response and then reached for his badge, gun, and phone. I stood and walked to the table where his coat was hanging over the chair back. Picking it up, I intentionally knocked over his stack of folders.

"Oh shit! I'm sorry!" I fumbled to collect them, making them more of a mess so I could clearly see the missing person pictures of Allie and Ben.

"It's ok, just uh, let me do that."

"So many files." I sat back on my heels and looked at all the papers.

"Yeah, it's been a weird month."

"Are they all in reference to missing persons?" I asked as I picked up a picture of Allie Johnstain. She looked young, frail.

"Most of them." He continued to replace the correct files to their folders. Dozens of people, reduced to a manila folder.

Who knew if they were dead or hurting—their poor families. A familiar pang echoed at the thought in my chest. Loss was never easy to move past.

"That's so sad." I sucked on my lower lip for a minute before meeting his gaze. "Do you think they're all connected?"

"I don't know. I have a theory that Gari is involved, but it's hard to say." I needed to push more so I reached for a file also labeled Johnstain.

"Is this another Johnstain?" I asked.

"It is." He reached for the file and added it to the stack on top of Allie's folder.

"Did they go missing at the same time?"

"No. This one belongs to Carter Johnstain, he's her brother and disappeared just over a year ago. It's strange, this family has known so much loss and I have to go question her remaining family—well, the remaining members here in town—again."

"Why would Gari target a family a year apart?"

"That's what I can't figure out. If it is Gari, which I have a hunch it is, then he's attacking a family line at random. I suspect the family does business with him and either these people crossed him or are being absorbed by him and joining his ranks under a new alias." That made sense. He could be growing his network. It was thorough and extensive; he had ears almost everywhere in the city.

"That's just so scary. I mean, from what you've told me, Gari has been arrested for human trafficking right? What if it's that again?" The thought made me angry and simultaneously hungry. I could feast from that asshole. "But you'll get him, right Tim?"

He placed the last file on the stack and then turned and pulled me into a hug. His cologne was a bit strong and barely covered the musk he still had from not showering. "You betcha. In fact, that crooked judge was just found dead. It was listed as an accidental fire, but I actually suspect murder—and I think Gari did it. If Gari can't even keep his people under control, then it won't be long before he slips and I have a real shot at taking him down." His words were full of passion. "Plus, now his case has been moved to Judge Knolen, and she's someone I trust. I think Gari may actually get what's coming to him. So yes, Tate, I'll get him." He released me and pecked my forehead before picking up his coat and heading for the door. We both had work to do.

A glance at the clock told me I needed to head back for my Disciplinary Hearing. Definitely didn't want to be late for that. Pfft.

Plus, hopefully Fletch would be home afterwards and I could finally talk to him about the questions literally burning in my chest. It may have been a couple of nights since I actually exhaled fire, but things were *still* burning. The blood-drains I'd recently committed had escalated the spark in my chest and burned my veins; I still had no idea what had happened when I drained the judge. I'd never seen any aura like that before, let alone been responsible for it; something in my genetic makeup was changing. I could feel it and didn't have the slightest clue how to control it or what it was.

Goose bumps pimpled my arms. I took a deep steadying breath and headed back to the Glenn. One problem at a time. Right now, I needed to look composed and explain why I broke the no-kill law to a committee. I prayed to blood they would be understanding and that they would see my value at the clinic, my peaceful life, and just consider this a youthful indiscretion. If not, it could very well be my life they demand.

Yes, this one problem was certainly enough.

CHAPTER 20

TATE

The metal chair under my legs was cold, pristine. It, like this room, boasted a sterile presence. The room's walls were white, the chrome table in front of me was freshly polished, reflecting the light from the large windows blanketing the southern wall. The other table across from me was a white marble slab with black streaking through it. Three chairs. There were three empty chairs. I knew his High Lordship would be here, likely head of the guara, but who would occupy the third? I sincerely hoped it would not be the president.

I had been waiting in here for the past hour. It was now noon. Just like *them* to keep me waiting. I had practiced what I would say, my sad eyes, and thought of a few faithful things I could say about the guara, President Dale, and Mother Blood. If I could garner their favor, they may treat me like a minor. I wouldn't be twenty-one for two months yet, so they could legally rule and place judgment on me as a minor or adult. I prayed for the former.

The door opened and three figures entered. Finally. The first was, of course, his High Lordship Lee. He was followed by Chairman Meed and Hoseff. It made sense, I supposed, that the council chairman would be present along with security. Still, my nerves were amped. These three could issue a verdict and, short of execution, they could carry anything out. For it to be an execution without a trial, the president would also have to be present and vote accordingly. My fingers dug into my palms. They couldn't kill me. Well, not yet.

They took their seats and pulled out their disks, reviewing the files. The projection was, naturally, one-sided.

"Tate Aaralyn," Meed started after clearing his throat. "I see here you've landed in Disciplinary Hearing for overfeeding and breaking the no-kill law veil side. Is this correct?" Meed looked up from his thick round glasses that somehow stayed perched on his stubby nose.

"Yes, chairman."

"Hmmm, and this is the second adult violation we have on file. The first it appears occurred..." He squinted, looking closer at the screen, the angle of his head making his chin appear to be a banana—sharp and irregularly shaped. "Ahh, yes. It appears you left a corpse to be found veil side a few years back. Is that correct?"

"It is." It had been the first overfeed I'd committed veil side. I'd lost control of myself and couldn't stop. I had just transitioned, and the guy had been a rapist, and even sitting here now, I didn't regret ending him in the least.

"It looks like your minor file is quite large. Minor infraction at thirteen, fifteen, several at sixteen, and well," he looked up from the screen, "it appears you were busy at seventeen. Accessing restricted texts from the library, speaking of forbidden myths, and then this past spring, you've gotten in two bar brawls where your disdain for the guara has been documented." He took off his glasses and tilted his angular head to look me over. "Tell me, why this pattern of rebellion? Are our laws so cumbersome that you had to break several of them?"

It was a rhetorical question. I knew that and yet his gaze made me squirm. I wanted to tell him Irene Aaralyn was why; she inspired curiosity, was accepting of all, and a warrior at heart. And they killed her in cold blood. Not even a council trial, a DH like this with President Dale present, and she never came home. Before that, sure it had been youthful wanderlust and testing of boundaries, learning as my mother encouraged, but now I seethed at the mere presence of the guara in my life.

I bit the inside of my cheek. I could do this. I could get through this; those were just *minor* infractions. I needed to appear as a minor. I cast my face down, staring at my hands that were gripped together so hard they were splotched in white.

"And Lordship Lee, we have evidence of the overfeed?"

"Yes, our security recovered the head hanging from a tree branch."

I cringed. What had I been thinking? Clearly, overfeeding left a weird blood-high and my critical thinking took a hit.

"Bush. It was a bush, and it was on the side of a cliff." I couldn't stop the reply before it was flying out of my mouth.

"You will remain silent unless spoken to." Meed's voice amplified in the small room. Gone was the elderly male and replaced was one who promised violence. I locked my jaw and bit the inside of my cheek. "Since you have spoken as an adult vampire would, and this is not your first infraction or overfeed, you will be tried as an adult."

The room began to spin. This was the worst thing.

"But I'm only—"

My words were stolen from my lungs as the whole room hummed from the power of Meed's judgment magic. He had activated the Judgement Ruling. It was too late.

"Tate Aaralyn, I've seen enough. Second no-kill violation in less than ten years. Criminal juvenile history. Unauthorized, classified documents accessed in our library at seventeen. You are trouble. A second-rate citizen. Tardy for the clinic and the veil check-ins." He looked to High Lordship Lee. "I don't see her doing much good to the Glenn with her presence." He nodded in response.

Meed paused, weighing his words carefully. "It likely would have gone this way in two months' time anyway." He returned eyes of steel to mine, raising his hands as he did so. "Forced guara enlistment." He slammed his hands down on the marble table, the sheer shimmer shining from them pulsed and blanketed my head. It spun before plummeting down, clinging to my skin with enough force to blow my hair up in several directions. Hoseff squinted. Meed sealed his ruling.

The magic began to settle on me, the force of it and its implications were too much. My stomach turned and roiled within. I squirmed, but the force of the magic only intensified.

"Lordship Lee, which outpost needs more soldiers?" Meed's words began to fade. I wasn't sure if I should be concerned or grateful that he didn't seem surprised by my movement.

Enlistment? This couldn't be happening. I couldn't be sent to an outpost. This was a bad dream. I dug my fingers deeper into my palm, willing myself to wake from this nightmare and for my stomach to calm. Pain ached from the pressure of my nails; this was a nightmare, but it was also reality. I could feel the judgment resting on me, clinging to my body, sinking deep into the very essence of who I was. There would be no fighting this, at least not this side of the veil. Magic would confirm the ruling and breaking it would entail taking one's essence from themselves once it was fully bound.

"Eastern Outpost it is. Tate Aaralyn you are hereby sentenced to the guara, effective immediately. You will be on the next circuit to the EO in two days. This is to be your service to the Glenn and shall be from now hence until the council should find a better use for you." He tapped the disk and the blue light faded from the room. "Dismissed."

And just like that, my world changed. The loose tingling from the ruling no longer teased at my skin, it sunk deeply, clawing its way through the barrier that was my flesh and wrapped itself around my core, encasing itself around the tiny bit of magic I possessed. I would be sent to the outpost as a member of the guara.

Hoseff stood up from the judgment table and approached my tiny tin desk. He looked bored, as if he'd seen a Judgment Ruling occur on the regular—his face set in a grimace.

"Worst part of the job." He shook his head. "Come with me." Without so much as giving me a chance to respond, he grabbed my arm and lifted me to my feet. I tried to resist, but the moment I did so, my insides began to scream. Magic would not be put off. I ceased my fight and numbly followed him. All my life, I dreaded the idea of joining the guara. Feared it above all else. And now, I was willfully moving my feet to the very thing that claimed my mother's life. She was a great anax for the guara, she did everything right, and in the end, they thanked her by stripping her of her life, her essence.

Hoseff pushed open a door to what appeared to be a clinic and pushed me toward the gurney. A tall male in a lab coat approached, disk in hand. Next to the bed was a tray of needles. Long and short, all terrifyingly sharp.

"Alright Jim, just another enlistment number. Meed's Judgment Ruling is in place. Indefinite. Forced via Disciplinary Hearing. I just dropped you her file," Hoseff said.

Jim nodded, as he moved his fingers through the air, controlling the holographic screen in front of him. "Yes, yes. Very standard. Secure her."

Before I could react, Hoseff had pinned my left and right arms to the table, while Jim pulled straps up from the table sides and secured them to my wrists. I bucked and tried to break free, but then Hoseff lowered his body to mine, and the pressure became too much. My insides began to shrink; the internal pressure on my lungs and heart was not just from Hoseff's weight, but from my attempt at fighting magic. I couldn't breathe. Jim bound my ankles next and secured me to the gurney. Hoseff removed himself from me, leaving an unpleasant dusting of sweat against my body.

"All yours." With that, he left, and Jim pulled over a rolling stool and sat down next to me. One glance confirmed no one else was in here.

"They always fight and it never makes a difference." He chuckled. "Youths think they can outmuscle magic. It just goes to show the strength of their underdeveloped brains." He tsked.

Who was he talking to?

He loaded a cartridge into a chamber and then selected a rather long needle from the tray and attached it to the gun he was holding. He peered at me momentarily, looking me over with his greasy eyes. "I think silver is a good color for her too."

With that, he pulled back my shirt's sleeve and began to tattoo the guara insignia on my shoulder. The pain was instant. This wasn't just ink; I could feel the magic binding the tattoo in my body. It burned, it consumed, it bonded *to* me. Gone were all thoughts of hate, of the reality I found myself in, I could only think of the pain. Of the smell of my skin burning, the tingling and stabbing pain radiating up and down my arm. I could feel it sinking deeper into me, deeper into my being, mingling with my magic. Like a cat rubbing its back across my magic, trying to understand it. To bind with it. I pulled my magic deep within me. The action angered the force attempting to bind, resulting in a flash of pain, like my nerves were being separated from my body. The magic from the ruling reached up to meet the pen, embracing the ink and showing it around my being—pulling back the shades to my small kernel of magic within.

I tried to fight it, but the needle made contact with my skin again and I relinquished a scream as my lungs seized. I began to shake uncontrollably only to find another strap being applied across my chest, and then another.

After a brief moment of pausing to switch needles, Jim's face came hovering back into view. "There now, the worst is done." He lied. A moment later, the humming from his pen sounded, and then came more pain. I closed my eyes and bit down on the side of my cheek. Blood filled my mouth. I spat it in his direction. I could taste my own blood and it made my stomach turn. I tried to move, to fight, but it was all in vain. The needle came back down, and with it, a whole new wave of pain.

CHAPTER 21

CHANCE

S hit. Fletcher left HQ the morning prior—before I'd increased surveillance and the travel ban was issued. It was likely a coincidence, but the soldier in me was trained to question such things. Nothing was coincidental. I had checked the recent veil departures; Fletcher hadn't scanned his world-walking pass, but another familiar name had, Tate. She was posted at the clinic and was mortal-side until this morning. I had informed the guards to contact me directly with any intel pertaining to Tate or Fletcher. At least she'd come back for her Disciplinary Hearing. I'd also instructed any intel to be sent directly to me following the DH.

After hanging up, I now sat in this overheated can of a train car headed for the Southern Outpost. Most occupants were drowsy or sleeping. Holland was, naturally, awake and currently using her disk to go through personnel files from the Southern Outpost. A look of concentration filled her face, but every now and then, the side of her mouth would tick upwards in a half-grin when she found what she was looking for. It was kind of cute, entertaining even. Still, her silence didn't make for the best company.

I shifted in my seat, sweat dripping down my back. The circuit was probably my least favorite way to travel. It was hot, sweaty, cramped, and full of people who all wanted to eat or fuck each other. I'd spent the better half of a day cooking in here and was more than ready for a hot shower and meal. I spotted Shae upon boarding; her new blue hair suited her. I was initially surprised to see her name listed on the roster. She'd taken an anti-guara stand with Tate last year and had chosen to be a blood courier. Right out of high school. Guess being someone's bitch got old.

I stood and made my way toward the other side of the car and took a seat opposite Shae. She glanced up and gave me a weak smile. The look told me she was in her head again.

"So, did being an errand girl get old?"

"I see being a moron certainly hasn't for you?"

I laughed a genuine laugh for the first time in days. "It's good to have you on board."

"Yeah, well, someone had to come hold your hand 'cause we all know how edgy you get when cooped up in these things."

She had a point, though I'd never admit it out loud.

"So, Dokimos Shae Drew, how does it feel to finally be on your way to becoming a badass?"

"Please, I *am* a badass. Now I'm just going to have more power."

"Don't kid yourself honey, dokimoses get all the grunt work." I tapped my disk and began to scroll through all the training and menial tasks that awaited the new batch of dokimoses.

She groaned as she rested her head back against the wall. "Don't remind me. Nora told me the first year is the hardest, so I'm trying to just have perspective. Visualize the end."

"Visualize the end?" Shae always had the weirdest way of putting things.

"Yes, my therapist said it's helpful when dealing with strong emotions, unknowns, or making decisions. Just picture what I want in the end and then let that guide me." She gestured, forming a river with her hands as they danced in the air.

I rolled my eyes. If anyone would go to therapy, and actually *pay* someone to talk to, it would be Shae. "Therapy? You've got a shrink?"

"Make fun of it all you'd like, but I no longer have authority problems and am working on being decisive. Don't come crying to me with all your daddy issues ten years from now because you thought you were too good for therapy."

"Shae, we may be friends but let's not forget rank." I swallowed back most of the bite from my voice.

"I wouldn't dream of it."

"I'm serious, out here you're Dokimos Drew, I'm Dux Dale." I leveled a look at her.

"See, *you*—" she pointed at my chest "—really could benefit from therapy, Dux Dale." With that, she pulled up her hood and closed her eyes.

Things with Shae had gotten better over the years, but still hadn't returned to how they were before the incident.

"Shae," I started, voice barely above a whisper.

"Yeah?" She opened one eye.

"If you need anything when we get to the outpost, just let me know. I may outrank you, but I'm still your friend. And—"

I shouldn't say more but her nose wrinkled in the way it did when we were kids and she thought frogs were gross.

"I thought you weren't my friend out here." She mocked my voice while moving her arms like a gorilla. Point taken.

"Just watch your back. That's all I'm saying," I said.

"No, you watch my back. I'll be leaving all of you troubled peeps in the dust as I step into my whole self."

I scoffed. "I'll visualize it." I winked and then stood up and strode back to my seat a couple of cars down. I couldn't jeopardize this mission, but I also couldn't not say something to have her more alert. I could only hope it would be enough. She was, in many ways, the sister I never had.

. . .

Ten hours later, we arrived at our first stop; we were finally free, if only for the night. Brookside was a small village nestled in the heart of the forest. It was about one-third of the way from HQ en route to the Southern Outpost. Here, most of the vampires were no longer active military, some elderly, but most had been discharged from the guara and now served in the collection center.

That was the way of life. If you ended your military career early in the Glenn, you needed to find an alternative route to still be useful. Most opted to help monitor the human districts, some worked in the vineyards—tough to grow here but still they managed to produce quality wine—while others worked at collection centers like the one here in Brookside. They were still given the rank of arche, even if only for show.

Of course, there were the transporters who drove the wine back and forth from the outposts, villages, and HQ itself. While it wasn't exactly as valuable as military service, it was still important work. I may be a brute, but I appreciated a smooth full-bodied glass of bloodwine.

The village was small, quaint almost. Well, it would be if it weren't for the constant moaning coming from the blood district. Personally, I was glad I didn't have to get my hands dirty managing the blood collections. It was, after all, necessary for bloodwine and blood bags, but still—I didn't like to get *that* close to my food.

"Gross. It's just gross." Shae had snuck up on me and was staring in the direction of the collection warehouse.

"What, don't like seeing how the sausage is made?"

She wrinkled her freckled nose and glanced up at me. "No, I don't. Besides, they're awfully loud..." She winced as a female cry seemed to echo down the street. The arches of Brookside didn't seem to notice or care. "I mean, how do we know the humans *aren't* being drained?"

"Relax Shae, I'm sure everything here is as it should be. Believe me, if they were breaking laws, the guara would know of it. The circuit makes regular stops here. So, stop worrying and go get some rest and refreshments. We depart at dawn tomorrow."

She gave a curt nod and adjusted her pack before heading off toward the taverns and other newly recruited dokimoses. Forty-three in total this time. I was a bit surprised any were joining us, given our mission, but it also made sense. New blood we could count on to not have been involved in the recent breach. I glanced toward Holland; her back was ramrod straight as she stood speaking with the village dux. He gestured to the blood district. The eeriness of it again poked at me. Beyond the blood district, plumes of smoke dotted the sky from the human villages just behind the hills. It made sense to secure the collection center near the villages, but part of it reminded me of shitting where you eat. It did, as Shae put it, feel gross. Holland turned and began walking over to me, clearly on a mission. I doubt she ever took a day off.

"Dux Bole states all is in order here. Our accommodations are just beyond the blood district."

I nodded. "Thanks." I turned to leave but her hand gripped my arm. I jolted at her touch, both from surprise and at the warmth of her skin. Her speed yet again amazed me.

"Look, I know we don't know each other but we're on our way to locate the inside mole or moles. If that news gets out, we may not be safe here. We don't know who is involved." She lowered her voice and looked around. Was she scared?

"Please, I refuse to be cowed into fear or consumed by paranoia. Our soldiers are good people, and we *will* catch the mole and he *will* pay, but I don't believe it's as widespread as you make it sound." Images of Lucas and his unwavering commitment popped into my mind. Perhaps, there was some cause for worry. And yet, I'd trained many of the Southern Outpost soldiers. Worked with them, ate with them, partied with them; I couldn't conceive that they were rebel spies, growing right under my nose. Could I have been that blind?

"I hope you're right, but still. Watch your back. Something feels off here." She spoke and studied the shadows again.

"Off?"

"Don't you feel *it*?"

All I felt was annoyance, hunger, and the strange sensation of her hand on my arm—evidently, it'd been too long since I'd last enjoyed the touch of another.

"No, no I don't. What I do feel is hunger and I see a tavern that looks welcoming. I plan on being responsible and eating so I don't get cranky and all bloodlusty. Care to join?"

"In a bit, I just need to check a few things." She bit her lower lip. "You really don't feel it?"

I paused and reassessed my other senses. There was a certain charge to the air, it felt sour? Overcharged and rotten. It was odd.

"Maybe it does feel off. But we're only here for one night, and we've been in a tin can literally all day. Take a break, eat, and sleep. If you happen to note anything of suspicion, find me immediately." I adjusted my pack; smaller than the dokimoses' as they did the heavy lifting and carried most of our gear on and off the circuit when needed, but I liked to keep my personal stuff on me at all times.

She nodded as she dropped her hand and I surveyed the village. Small fires, little shops, taverns, and then, of course, the rolling vineyard in the distance. The blood district was fairly loud for just draining vessels, but nothing appeared too out of the ordinary. Where was that strange charge coming from?

My disk pinged, and I pulled it out opening the hologram. Several notifications were there, none urgent. All but one I could ignore. At the top of the list, Tate's name was flagged. I'd set it on priority to send any updates related to her. I stared at the screen numbly. She'd been forced to enlist. She would be joining the Eastern guara. Her freedom had been stripped. My appetite was suddenly gone. Her worst nightmare had come true.

"Damn it, Tate." I shut the device, ignoring the other alerts and headed for the tavern. I needed something strong, and I needed it now.

CHAPTER 22

TATE

I awoke with a start; the blood-orange sunlight began to spill through the windows. Blearily, I opened my eyes and focused on the ceiling. I was lying on a stiff sofa in the waiting room of the judicial building. Blood, I tasted blood. Glancing down at my arm I could see splatters of it. My blood coated my shirt and skin. The tattoo. I yanked back my right shirt sleeve, and I could make out part of the guara insignia. Inked in silver, branded to my flesh.

I leaned over the couch and vomited.

My stomach heaved, again and again, until the floor was covered in red bile, and I could barely breathe. Enlisted. I was now a guaraman. I was a soldier to the very cause I hated. Days. I had mere days of freedom before these bastards would claim my life. I needed Fletch. I stood, not caring that I was standing in my own vomit. They could clean it up. I was done. Done with this place, done with the Glenn, and certainly done with the guara. I could run, but first I needed to say goodbye to Fletch.

It was early evening by the time I walked into the living room. Judging by its current state, Fletch still wasn't home. I began to massage my temple—this was all just too much.

Worry began to gnaw at me. Disappearing like this was *not* something he did. I tried to picture him strung out somewhere, hungover, shirking his responsibilities, but that just wasn't him. Could he be holed up with a female somewhere? Somehow, that also didn't scream Fletch. In the years since I've known him and the past year when he moved in to look after me, not once had I noticed him sleeping over somewhere. Sure, there was evidence that a female friend had recently been in our home, but he never spoke of them. And he never introduced me to any of them.

"Fletch?"

Nothing. Only silence. I walked back to his room to be sure. His bed sat there, unmade just like I saw it last time. Uneasiness began to settle in. I walked over to my room and pushed open the door. I needed a shower and a change of clothes and then I'd leave. I wanted to say goodbye to Fletch. To get answers. But he wasn't here, and I'd be damned if I spent more time than required this side of the veil. I cranked the water to its hottest setting and savored the way it heated my skin. The pain was welcoming. A balm to my anger. If only it could cleanse my soul, wipe away the guara's mark, free my magic...

After soaking in the hot water until it went cold, I stepped out and toweled off. My usual choice of clothes included black leather pants and a black V-neck T-shirt. Today was no different. Consistency. I needed to pretend everything was normal, that I wasn't a flight risk. I threw my blonde hair in a high ponytail and blotted on some pale purple lipstick. Not perfect by any means, but at least I was fresh. I needed to hurry. I'd wasted too much time in the shower and the longer I waited the harder it would be to sneak out of the Glenn. I chewed my bottom lip. What if I never saw Fletch again?

I walked down the hall and paused at Mom's old door. Deep breath, Tate, one foot in front of the other. I needed to leave, but I also wanted to say one last goodbye to her. The female who raised me and died without so much as a grave marker.

Pushing open the door, I stepped inside. Even with years of disuse, I could still smell her: honey lavender. I walked over to her bed and pulled her pillow on my lap, smoothing the wrinkles. Across from me, hanging on the wall, was *Maple*. She was a painting I'd made for my mother when I was ten. I'd taken a piece of an old maple tree and painted our home on it, it wasn't good by any standard, and yet she hung it up in her room with care. She told me she wanted it close to her heart always. Tears began to prick at my eyes, I missed her so much. She would know what to do. She would understand my inner conflict, the bloodlust last night, the fire breathing—she was my haven, and she was gone.

I was all alone.

"What do I do?"

The house just creaked as the wind blew against it. I curled up in a fetal position and allowed myself to cry. Call it self-pity or pathetic, I didn't care. I was tired, alone, and scared. Things I'd never admit to anyone and rarely myself, but here with my mother's ghost, I could be a child and cry.

I would come back to say goodbye to Fletch. No more missing goodbyes.

SNEAKING through the veil was a harder task than normal. It was heavily manned and finding the weak spots had taken an hour of surveillance. I had finally located one exit point with only six guards, four of which were new, and a large group of world-walkers were getting ready to pass through—perfect. I sauntered right through with them, pretended to scan my world-walking pass, and didn't wait for permission. It worked. I was a little shocked, but grateful all the same.

At least one thing went right today.

My blood was boiling, and I needed to exact vengeance. Normally, I would start with the henchman and slowly work my way closer to the kingpin. But seeing as I was about to be shipped off to some blood-forsaken outpost, time wasn't a luxury I had. If I was going to take down Gari, it had to be now. Tonight. And I was ready.

I cracked my knuckles as I squatted in my perch. It looked like six men were guarding the entrance to the warehouse—all heavily armed. From the two hours I'd spent up here, at least six other men entered the warehouse. Gari's Escalade was parked in the driveway. He was here, he had to be. Still, visual confirmation would have been nice. I could do this. I had to, and worst case, I get shot and experience a little more pain. Even so, it wasn't all bad as it would take longer for the guara to hunt me down and bring me back.

Perhaps I could go to the outpost and then make a run for it to another Vamp, maybe that rogue group my mother had spoken of often or possibly the Fern. Would they take me in? My stomach soured further at the thought of betraying the place my mother honored by protecting.

Laughter from below sounded as two of the larger guards popped off some beer caps and took swigs while, apparently, telling stories.

Deep breath, just think of it like a dance.

I assessed each of the henchmen, deciding the big one would be my first target. Take him down, then the large meathead with a buzz cut, and then I'd take the four skinny ones as they came. I'd have to be fast. Even with my increased speed and strength, I couldn't outrun a bullet, and if the guards inside came out before I finished, I'd be toast.

This was it.

I thought of Shae and her voluntary enlistment. I thought of my *forced* enlistment—of the brand now marking my skin. I thought of my mother, killed by the country she spent her life serving...

Fueled by rage, I jumped from the building and began to run right for the big bald one. I was on him before he could react. I grabbed his head and twisted it, *snap!* I twirled and sure enough, buzzcut was right there raising his AR-15. But I was too close for him to fire, and I used my increased speed to kick out his feet from under him before unsheathing my dagger and burying it in his chest. The next moment was a blur. All four skinny guards were shouting and rushing toward me, knives extended, guns raised.

I grabbed the first one's forearm and turned his own knife on him, stabbing his artery. The next one, I snapped his arm and threw him against the wall. A hand landed on my shoulder, and I whirled. Pain erupted in my side. No time to look down and confirm what I already knew to be true; I was bleeding. I grabbed the arm and yanked, it went flying and blood began to spray as the man clenched his stump, trying to stop the bleeding. I yanked the dagger out of its sheath and swiped it across the last guard's throat. Sloppy, this had all been sloppy. They never should have been able to land a strike on me, not with my speed.

I cursed myself for not spending more time sparring when I had the chance. No time to reconsider. Shouts from inside came and I ran through the door before they could come to me. Three men, all in black, running at me. One open fired. I jumped and dodged the bullets, barely making it to the side before the first guard pulled out a razor.

No, I would not get stabbed again.

I landed a foot to his well-built side and struck before he could react. His body crumpled. The next guard, a male with unusual auburn hair, threw a punch. I ducked but couldn't evade his following swipe as he caught my left shoulder. I flew backwards and impacted the wall. There was no way he should have that much strength. Something was not right.

I struggled to my feet, blood oozing from my side. He ran at me, blade extended, and swiped at my head. I ducked and pivoted before burying my blade in his chest. He gasped, clearly surprised, before dropping to his knees. Two down, one to go. I yanked the dagger free and turned on the third guard who was raising his gun from fifty feet away. I lunged.

The fallen guard behind me grunted. I heard the shot before I felt the bullet impact my shoulder. I was thrown forward as red bloomed just below my right clavicle. The floor came closer and closer until I made impact with it.

Pain erupted everywhere.

A bullet should not hurt this much. I'd been shot before, it was painful, but this stung. Poison? I turned my head and saw the guard I'd stabbed stalking toward me. Dark gold blood interlaced with cherry red blood was dripping down his chest from where my blade had been. He wasn't human. How had I missed that? He smiled at me as he planted his foot on my chest and pressed.

"What do we have here?" He raised the butt of his assault rifle and then slammed it down on my skull.

CHAPTER 23

CHANCE

Screams woke me from my sleep. Panicked shouts filled the air, coming from what sounded like the far end of the village near the human district. I was out of bed before Holland came barreling through my door, weapon ready.

"What the hell is going on?" I demanded as I threw my pants on and then slipped into my boots.

"Attack. We're under attack." My pulse quickened at the look on her face. She was concentrating, using magic. "Not human. Not vampire. They're something we can't imagine." Her creamy skin went paler, if that was possible, as her eyes widened.

"Let's go." I threw my tactical vest on as I grabbed my gun leaning against the door.

Holland kept up with my pace as we rushed out into what could only be described as chaos. My blood went cold at the unnatural shrieks coming from all around. The scene out here was devastating. Vampires, new soldiers with no training, were being overwhelmed, gutted by creatures I'd never seen before. Each one seemed different, all appeared to have once been alive—possibly human even. Black and grey scales covered their bodies as their taloned hands—paws, or whatever the fuck they were—scraped against the ground as they ran. They moved with incredible speed on all fours and shrieked animalistic cries. A creature reached for me and before I could react, Holland took him down with six rounds to the chest.

"On your left!" she shouted as she pivoted and began to methodically take one down after another. She was magnificent.

"Wake up, Dale! We've got to fight, NOW! Our men need us!" Her shouts drew me from my stupor, just in time to avoid the black claws coming at me from behind. I pivoted and withdrew a long dagger and sliced the thing's head clean off. Even detached from the core, lying on the muddy ground, it began to scream—deep, disturbing cries.

I looked away from the headless corpse and raced into the mess. I could see vampires' bodies littering the ground. These things crouched over them, eating.

A young guaraman was fighting off two creatures at once, a valiant effort but he wouldn't hold long on his own. One of those *things* reached out and swiped at the young male's face resulting in a spray of blood as the soldier fell. I aimed and shot the creature once, twice, three times until at last, it too fell. The other creature didn't pause, instead, it lunged on top of the male and swiped at his abdomen, pulling and slicing his intestines. No one deserved that type of death.

I aimed and fired at the thing attacking him as I charged. Nothing, it didn't respond in the least. Closer, I just needed to get closer and I could decapitate it. It raised back its claws and swiped again and again, black saliva dripping from its mouth.

I was three feet out—I would end it.

The thing whipped its head at me, and I froze. I knew that face. I'd worked with that face closely this past spring. Arche Shultz. He was a good soldier with promising skills. But that male was gone. Now, all I saw was a bloodthirsty creature. His eyes were pitch black with purple coloring his entire face in deep plum shades. He snarled at me, and his mouth now had not two upper fangs, but four. What happened to him?

My hesitation cost me. I took a hit from the side and was thrown to the ground by another creature. It buried its claws in my gut, and I let out a scream. I reached for my dagger and swiped three times in calculated strikes. I cut clean through its right forearm, causing the black thing to drop. With one final strike, I sliced its throat and it stumbled away from me. My abdomen burned from where its claws had dug, but there was no time to evaluate that. Three more creatures were racing toward me.

I braced my hand on the ground and forced myself up—adrenaline numbing the pain. The whole yard was a battlefield; my men, good soldiers, scattered the mud in heaps, dead. Murdered by evil itself.

The three creatures were about thirty feet away now. Tightening my grip on my dagger, I ran toward them; I was ready for this. The shock that had held me back was now numb and I allowed myself to slip into the tactical maneuvers I'd been practicing and teaching for the better half of ten years. I cut through one creature, slicing it in half, threw a dagger at the second one, the blade landed straight in its eye, while retrieving my pistol with my free hand and opened fire on the third. All three were down, their bodies twitching and their mouths letting out moans and screams. The whole scene was hellish.

Holland was across the field surrounded by a group of moaning, evil corpses. She'd taken down at least a dozen creatures. She could certainly hold her own.

A scream I knew too well drew my attention to the left. There, a blue-haired pixie was fighting off a tall creature. It had dug its claws into her right shoulder even as she used her assault rifle as a barrier, shoving its end into the creature's throat. Shae. She needed help. How had I forgotten about her?

I needed to reach her. I ran, pouring all my strength and increased ability into the motion as I raised my gun, taking down several creatures in my path. She screamed again as she went careening into the side of the blood-processing plant. The creature was on her before she could even move, swiping with its claws and barely missing her. I aimed and fired. Three shots missed but the fourth struck true. The thing fell forward as a quarter-size hole shot blood from its skull. I reached it before it hit the ground and drew my dagger across its throat, one deep motion, decapitating it.

Shae sat there, her blue eyes wide. She looked utterly terrified. I once labeled her a pacifist. Yet, here she was.

"What a time to join?" I tried to connect with her through the shock. No reaction. I reached down and grabbed her arm, helping her up. "You're alive. That's what matters. We'll evaluate and er, *process* later. Take this." I handed her my pistol and showed her how to load and fire the weapon. Blood coated my hand and likely my face. When she lifted her eyes to mine, they bugged out.

"You're hurt." She reached for me, blood coating her own arm— some of it was maroon, hers, and some of it was black as the night. She must've injured one of those things. Good for her. She may just survive this.

"Just point and shoot. Stay near me."

She nodded. I turned and surveyed the rest of the yard. Two creatures fought each other over the corpse of a young vamp, her open eyes displayed nothing short of shock and pain. The processing plant had three creatures guarding it, stoic on all fours as they snarled at the scene in the yard. Why were they staying there? They snapped at the corpses and whined as they saw others feasting on the dead, yet they remained still. Holland was working her way toward the plant, two young guaramen at her side, plowing their way through the throng of *things*.

The plant. I cut through a couple of creatures, attempting to join Holland's course. Shae kept pace with me, firing hopelessly at these creatures. She fired several rounds at a creature charging a nearby vamp. They all missed.

"Damn it!" she snapped.

"Maybe more time at the range and less in the shrink's office would be a good idea in the future." I chuckled a dry laugh as I fired twice, one shot through the head and the other through the creature's black heart. The *thing* stopped mid-leap and collapsed. Dead.

The rest of the yard had maybe a dozen creatures at most. Three of them began to circle around a young guaraman who had a blade drawn and gun raised—he'd obviously had some combat training. But his movements were sloppy, he wouldn't be able to hold three off for long. "Follow me!"

Shae was just a step behind me as we entered a cluster of creatures. I fired multiple times and managed to take down two. Shae nearly hit the soldier who was battling the third creature with his blade. The *thing* managed to evade the young arche's swipe and had reached a clawed hand around his throat. His black talons sunk in, and blood began to flow down the arche's throat.

No, not another one.

I raised my blade and lunged, burying the tip into the back of the creature where I suspected its heart lay. The creature twitched as black blood leaked from my blade, pouring to the ground. It turned, arche in its left hand, and growled at me. Foam dripping from its serpent-like tongue that was barely hidden by rows and rows of black teeth. It raised its free hand and swiped for me; I dodged it—barely.

It smiled, actually smiled at me as it increased its pressure on the young arche's throat—the arche's eyes widened as his face reddened before a sickening *pop* filled the night air. His severed corpse hit the ground. The thing palmed the head and threw it at me. I ducked but a female scream from behind made my stomach drop. Shae, she must've been struck. The creature jumped into the air toward me. I crouched down, weapon extended, and rolled. I expected the thing to be on me, but instead it landed on top of the tavern's roof behind me—a thirty-foot jump at least. A loud burst came from the processing plant to my side. The side of the building was on fire, a gaping hole now claimed its side.

A tall creature jumped through the hole, landing on two feet instead of four like the rest. Its humanoid shape was as disturbing as its massive mouth with protruding fangs. It raised its head and howled once, twice, and then a third time, holding the screech longer than the rest. In one motion, it jumped onto the plant's roof. The three creatures guarding the plant turned and jumped, joining the humanoid creature on the roof. Several other creatures paused and then left their prey and followed the large humanoid thing. They then leapt from building to building, heading for the vineyard that butted up to the forest.

While more than half of the creatures followed, a few creatures remained, their fangs buried deep into corpses. Holland systematically approached them and shot them until they each fell dead. She had it under control.

A swatch of blue caught my attention. Shae was lying lifeless on the ground, face down in the mud. Blood seeped from her side. I rushed to her and checked for a pulse. She was alive, but unmistakably injured. Fuck.

A shriek sounded as a creature threw the body it'd been feeding from into the building and then focused on Shae's body beside mine. It began to run, bent over on all fours, straight for us. Over my dead fucking body.

I raised my gun and fired, emptying my chamber. The thing's body fell to the side and twitched before breaking into moans.

Chest heaving, I bent over and picked Shae up, throwing her over my shoulder. The whole yard was full of corpses. My men, Holland's men, scattered the ground, lying limp. Iron and something notably foul filled the night air. Anax Bole's men were nowhere to be found.

A symphony of animalistic moans filled the yard as the creatures, even the decapitated heads, cried out in death. Holland's eyes met mine and even from a distance it was clear we agreed that something was innately wrong with this. What the hell were those *things*? Turning for the medic building, I carried Shae. Dux Bole had some explaining to do.

CHAPTER 24

TATE

I opened my eyes to see a bright light shining right in my face. My hands were bound behind me; each ankle tied to the legs of the steel chair. Blurry, everything was blurry. I tried to focus on the silhouette in front of me, but it was a painful and useless effort. My left eye was swollen. I could only see through a slit.

I swallowed and the taste of metal filled my mouth.

"The way I see it, you're not a very good spy. I expected more from the president," a gruff voice spoke. I tried to focus, but the spotlight only amplified the pounding in my skull.

"President?" What the hell was he talking about?

"Don't play coy. We both know you're not—" he leaned forward and sniffed, "—human." The cologne he was wearing was smothering my senses.

"And you are?" If this was the same bastard who'd knocked me out, he most certainly wasn't human either.

"Me? Ha," he snorted, "I'm one of the only humans here. Thanks to you." He gripped my chin and squeezed as he dug his other hand into my right shoulder, fingering the bullet hole. Acute pain fired everywhere; my vision darkened, sight eluding me.

He stood there, stoic and unmoving, waiting for my eyes to focus. Gari. This was the monster I'd come here hunting…now I was his prey? Hell no. I had to get out of here.

"So, what? You have an affinity for the supernatural?" I just needed to buy enough time for my strength to return.

"There's nothing super or natural about you, sweetheart. What I don't understand is why the president would send you. I've upheld my side of the deal." He pulled out a knife and pricked it against his thumb, drawing a bit of blood. Bright pink red. He was human, that much was true.

"I don't involve myself in human politics, so I think you've got it all wrong."

"Human?" He huffed and then laughed as he stood upright, releasing my jaw. "Hear that, boys? This brat here thinks I care about human politics." His palm hit my right cheek before I could even blink. Fast for a human, but still weak. I remained sitting upright in the chair.

"You're going to start talking or I'm going to make you wish you were dead."

"How about you start confessing to all the hideous things you've done? You're a monster." I spat a mouthful of bloody saliva, and it landed right on his lapel. His brow arched as he pulled out his maroon pocket square and wiped off my insult.

"Now that wasn't very ladylike. James," he motioned for the tall male in the corner to step forward. The spotlight dimmed. Ah, so James was the beast who'd shot me. His auburn hair was combed back on the sides before lengthening on top to form a stylish pompadour—it was immaculately styled considering the fight we'd just had. There was no doubt, however, that this was the same male I'd fought, for in his hair were splotches of black and red. Blood.

"James here has certain *skills* that I think you'll find particularly interesting. Or at the very least, painful." Gari smiled, a viper if I ever saw one. James approached slowly, dragging a wheeled tray behind him. It had a cloth over it, and I immediately knew I didn't want to know what it was hiding. I pulled against the restraints, biting back the pain from straining my wounded shoulder. I should be able to break free of rope; even average human handcuffs should snap from my strength. But they didn't budge. How much blood had I lost?

"I'd give it a break. It's not human-made nor is it standard," an unidentified voice spoke. His voice dripped with sensual promise, a whisper of pleasure or pain. My skin crawled. His tall shadow approached. He was broad-chested, at least six-three, and his steps were fluid. Whoever this was, I hadn't seen him when I was staking out the warehouse. Everything about his movements were primal. Graceful. I was drawn to him even as I slunk back as far as I could.

"Let me introduce myself. My name is Mardi. I too have certain gifts that Mr. Gari here finds useful." He grabbed a chair and placed it in front of me, straddling it with casual grace. *Clang!* Metal hitting metal. James was getting ready.

"Don't pay him any attention. It's me you need to focus on. Tell me, what's the president's game?" He ran a hand through his shoulder-length dark brown hair. It had a certain matte color to it that screamed bad hair dye.

"I...your hairstylist is the criminal here."

He arched a brow and paused for a moment, apparently taken aback by my forwardness.

"Spare me, Miss Aaralyn. We both know we're talking about President Dale."

Shock flooded my system. Now *I* was off-kilter. How did they know about him? It was forbidden to discuss the Glenn's politics outside the Glenn.

"I see I've surprised you." A smug look took over his tan, symmetrical face. "I like to do that." He winked at me, highlighting the scar his face bore. It started at his center hairline, then jutted to the right through his brow and down his cheekbone toward his ear. Clearly, he's seen combat.

"I don't know what you're talking about." I wouldn't give him anything. Not out of loyalty to President Dale, he could rot for all I cared. No, I wouldn't answer him because he acted like he deserved it; like I wouldn't be able to help myself, like he was *that* good.

"Pity. James, can you refresh her memory?"

"With pleasure." The coldness on James's face was utterly inhuman. He didn't look like any vampire I'd ever seen; our blood was dark red, like that of humans but only in its color. His was the deepest red I'd ever seen—and I could have sworn it held a golden tint. The place where he'd been stabbed bloomed a red-black that I'd only ever heard of in cheap human vampire tales. His eyes were narrower than normal and sported a strange green shade with a yellow hallow around the iris. He was skinny and yet remarkably built. His ears were slightly...*pointed*? I squinted, trying to focus. He couldn't be, could he? They were supposed to be practically extinct in this realm. That or secluded off to their little island, their embassy in this world.

"What does the president do with all the cargo?" Mardi questioned as James grabbed the knife and sparks began to bounce from it. Magic, he was using magic. I couldn't take my eyes off James.

"You're Fae." I sat there in stunned disbelief. I'd been told they'd moved back to Mydant and, aside from their embassy, they'd had no contact with the four Vamps since before the Great War. Yet, here he was...he had to be Fae.

James's face paled as his eyes shot up. He looked uncertain for the first time since I'd seen him; his eyes darted to Mardi. Mardi who seemed unnervingly cool. Unnaturally still.

"The president's cargo. What does he do with them?" Mardi spoke, violence in every smooth syllable.

"You're not surprised he's Fae, which means that possibly you are too."

"What becomes of the people?"

"How the hell should I know?"

He smiled at my question and nodded to James who had seemed to recover from his shock and regain some of his wits. He brought the prong down on my leg and electricity flooded my body. I screamed and then bit down on my lip. They didn't deserve the satisfaction of my cries.

"Tate, what does President Dale *do* to all the humans?"

"You tell me! Gari here is the one murdering and abducting innocents!"

"Gari?" Mardi huffed. "Cute. We both know why Mr. Gari does what he does. Now, what happens to the cargo?"

I refused to answer him. Even if I didn't know what he was referring to, all my instincts screamed at me to keep silent.

"James." Another bolt of electricity hit me, overwhelming my system. I burned from the inside. My blood practically boiled. This much charge could be fatal if it continued.

"We both know what happens to the average vampire if they're exposed to high amounts of voltage. They can be fried from the inside out. Same as they can be cooked from the outside in by fire. Or there's the lovely staking option we could go with. All can be extremely unpleasant and I'm losing patience."

I studied him. He would kill me, his eyes made that extremely clear. But most humans didn't understand the vampirical makeup or *how* to kill us. The idea of staking our hearts was comical. However, something about this male felt off. I looked closer. His cheekbones were defined in an unusual lethal elegance. His lips were full and, wait, I took a double take. Were those fangs?

"You're a vampire." It was a statement, obvious perhaps, but my muddled mind was having a hard time conceiving a Fae and a Vampire working together, let alone for Tony Gari.

"Why did the president send you, Tate?"

"He didn't." My resolve to say nothing was gone. If I was right about him being a vampire, then he knew how to kill me—blood loss and fire were deadly to our kind. His threat about fire and high voltage was real. The stake was a joke he must be patting himself on the back for unless...perhaps he didn't want Gari to know that?

"He didn't? So, what, you just waltz in here straight from the Glenn's HQ building and try to take out Mr. Gari?"

"Who are you?" An eerie feeling fell. The same as the night I murdered the judge. He was the one who'd been watching me.

"What happens to all the humans, Tate?"

"What humans? If you're referring to the ones Gari takes, then ask the monster himself. And stop assuming I'm here on Collin's behalf."

Mardi paused. He was calculating something. I wasn't sure what, but something I'd said made him quiet.

"It's very clear you're an expression of the president's will, doing his bidding and dirty work. Tell me, Tate," he lowered his head as he leaned closer, "as a member of the guara, do you kill *them* for the president, or do you simply watch him drain them for sport?"

Fire erupted in my belly—how dare he. "Collin's agenda is not my own. I am not the guara. I'd die before I killed for him." Anger so deep and true raised within. Mardi looked straight at my now exposed shoulder, eyes squinting. The damn tattoo. I'd been branded and had almost forgotten my impending fate.

"We're done here." He looked at me and had the nerve to appear disgusted. James came closer to me; the knife now shooting sparks two feet high. This would be fatal.

"Not that way, James. Burn her, treat her like the animal she is." He turned and started to walk away.

Burn her?

"You're just as bad as Gari and Collin!" I screamed as James reached for a bottle of lighter fluid and then approached me. He popped off the cap with his teeth and smiled, revealing perfectly straight teeth. I would die.

"Fae don't fear fire like your kind." He squeezed the bottle and liquid shot out all around me. What an ironic statement. Fae avoided my *kind* because we could kill them. The fluid soaked my hair, burned my face. When it hit my shoulder, I screamed. It sank deep into my bullet wound. He continued to douse me until my clothing and skin were covered in it.

"Mardi, don't we need answers from her?" Gari asked, his voice slightly shaken.

"Mr. Gari, she's trash and won't be of any use. Let's dispose of her and send a message to the president that he can't play with you. Sir, you've made a deal with him and have upheld it. I believe it to be in your best interest to incinerate her and all challenges to your authority." Mardi placed a hand on Gari's shoulders, the tension in the taut mobster instantly diminishing.

Gari nodded. "Right, well I'm off then. Take care of her." He turned and left, the repertoire of guards following him. It was just James, Mardi, and me.

"It's a pity. You could've been something great, Tate," Mardi whispered as he nodded to James who held the matchbox. "Now let's see a true burn. Let's see how bright you *will* be."

What the hell was he talking about? I didn't have time to question it. James struck a match and then flung it at me.

I saw the flame, as it rotated in the air toward me, blue and orange dancing through the air with a lethal grace.

I saw my mother's green eyes and dark blonde hair, her smile and bravery. She would not cower, and neither would I.

Fletch's face flashed before me; he would not live ashamed of me. He would continue his scholarly work.

I saw Shae and her perky blue hair; she would become an outstanding soldier and would no doubt keep them all on their toes and laughing, even if it was with the guara. Maybe she'd make it better.

I may be leaving this world, but my friends would continue to do good. They would make it a better place to live, brighter—even as I burned. I smiled. I would finally get to be reunited with my mother. I could leave this messed up place knowing others would carry on my mantle of justice. A strange peace blanketed me, covering my nerves. My soul inside smiled as the match hit the floor in front of me and I was engulfed in flames.

CHAPTER 25

CHANCE

Shae would be okay. Her injuries were minimal, all things considered. She had sustained a broken clavicle, four puncture wounds at her shoulder, and a mild concussion. Other than that, it was just scrapes and bruises. I huffed. Scrapes and bruises, what a mild way of putting it.

I reached the field and found Holland directing the remaining uninjured guaraman to move the bodies of their fellow soldiers into a line so we could catalog the losses. My torso had been wrapped with a bandage. Thankfully, the cuts weren't too deep and the healing tonic the medic gave me was already working.

"Holland." I nodded in greeting.

"Dale." She sighed, the first sign of exhaustion I'd seen from her. "We took quite a hit." She gestured to the rows of bodies already being lined up. "So far, twenty-four of the forty-three dokimoses are dead. They were fine yesterday, and today they're dead. This should never have happened." She leveled a gaze at me and then looked in the direction of the settlement's dux.

He had told us all was in order. He lied. When those things attacked, his men were nowhere to be found. I started toward the asshole. Holland's steps were quick behind me, her small frame visible in my peripheral.

"Hell of a shot, Holland. Where'd you learn to fight?"

"In training, Northern Outpost. My father was an anax there. My mom likes to say I was born with a rifle in hand."

"Well, thank Mother Blood for that. You saved us last night. Kept your cool. I can see why they made you dux."

"You held your own." That was the closest to a compliment I'd ever received from her.

"Where are the creatures' corpses? I want to take a closer look." The yard was covered with piles of black oozing goo, blood if I had to guess, and severed vampire limbs. I noted a few creatures' heads but didn't spot any of their corpses.

"They're all around."

"What are you talking about? Did the dux move them?"

"Dale, they turned to goo." She gestured to a foul-smelling pile next to my feet. "They started decomposing faster than I've seen anything fall apart and now most of them are just syrupy, black goo."

I paused. Only one thing could make things decompose at unnatural levels.

"Magic. Dark magic." She voiced my thoughts for me.

I squatted next to a pile and sniffed. It smelled putrid. Upon closer inspection, I could see lumps in the goo. Bits of purple flesh, a bit of bone, and then just black slimy goo. I went to the next pile. This one contained a claw. I picked up a stick and moved it along. It appeared to be biologically similar to that of human bone structure as it was divided into three segments, and yet, it was a black claw. Sharp. Very, very sharp and scaly. I'd never seen anything like it. I needed something that wasn't decomposed. I surveyed the yard and twenty feet to the right there was a creature's head. I stood up and strode for it, stick in hand.

It was large, larger than vampire or human skulls usually were. It was black and covered in scales, though half of it was all slime, already decomposing. Moving it with the stick, its face came into view. The eyes were sunken in. Deep purple circled the eye sockets that were now filled with black goo. Purple veins jutted out in every direction on unnaturally grey-pallor facial skin—a stark contrast to the black scales. The nose was missing and was just cartilage sporting two holes. The mouth had several rows of teeth, four fangs on the top and four on the bottom.

"It's unnatural. Wrong," Holland's voice jarred me from my thoughts.

"It is. Magic will do that." I looked at her. Studied her movements. Her square face set in a grim expression that somehow made her full lips incredibly thin. Her light brown eyes had darkened to the shade of dark chocolate, delicate and furious; a thing to behold.

"Come on. Time to go talk to Dux Bole." We marched over there, Holland leading the way. Each of her steps was surer than the last.

"Dux Bole. I think you owe us an explanation."

The stocky male sneered at her. "I owe you nothing. I am the dux here, *female*."

"Yes, the dux of a *failed* settlement. Is this the first time you've been attacked by these creatures?" She appeared unfazed by his sexism. Instead, she arched a brow and stepped closer, paying no attention to the foot-and-a-half height difference between them—her confidence was a turn-on.

"I've never—" He stopped mid-sentence, eyes going wide. Magic. She was using her magic on him. I knew from personal experience it wasn't pleasant. "What the hell is this?" His face turned beet red.

"I asked you a question. Was this the first incident like this?"

He turned redder until finally, his mouth opened, and words just poured out. "No! Alright, the answer is no! We were attacked two weeks ago by a small group. We took them out and most of our numbers were intact. Last week we had another assault and lost ten soldiers. It was still a small group, maybe twelve creatures at most. Tonight, was the largest number I've seen. I didn't know there were that many."

"*What* are they?" she demanded. I was perfectly content to stand here and watch her work, it was mesmerizing in its own way. I could practically see the aura surrounding the fat male.

"I don't know. Something unnatural, that much is true."

"You said you lost ten guaramen. Is that why none of your men assisted in the defense of a settlement you swore an oath to protect?"

"Each time they've come they've only been interested in the processing plant. They feasted on the humans or *took* them. My men who fought died and were devoured. So yes, I instructed them to stand down to see if those *things* would simply come for the plant and leave."

Unbelievable. He left us to *die* on a whim.

"How many humans perished in these attacks?"

"Hard to tell. Our warehouse was emptied each time, some corpses were left behind, but mostly they just left it bloody empty." He spat the last word as his eyes darkened.

"Taken?" Holland pushed further, asking my own question.

"That's what I fucking said you b—"

His body spasmed as the aura intensified. Holland released a bit and Bole snarled at her, but I didn't miss the fear in his eyes. "Yes, taken. It's those *human's* fault." He spat on the ground and took a step back from the petite but powerful female.

"How so?" she pried.

"If you ask me, they're playing with magic trying to become the hunter. That's why I've locked them all up, mandatory house arrest for every last one of 'em." He smirked. "I've also increased the blood donations. Didn't you taste the richness of the wine last night?"

"That's a violation of the National Law Agreement of the Four Houses, stature one, bi-law twenty-two of the Blood Donor Compact. Have you received authorization from the president or the district anax?" I asked, speaking for the first time in this entire encounter. I didn't particularly think much of humans, but the law was one thing I'd spent my life upholding. No matter the cost—

An image of sandy blonde hair and mahogany eyes filled my vision; a younger female screaming and crying. One I'd betrayed because I believed in the law, believed in a world ruled by order.

"Answer him," Holland demanded. The male hacked up a loogie, spitting it on the blood-soaked ground before looking at me.

"No, and I don't need some *kid* coming in here and telling me how to run things. Pack up and get the hell out of here."

"As soon as we file an official report, we'll be out of your hair, Dux Bole." Holland nodded to me and then we both looked at the blood processing plant. If illegal magic was being used here, it would take blood to create the creatures we encountered last night.

We left Dux Bole standing there, turning bright red with his fists clenched, and stalked for the processing plant. Dread pooled in my stomach as I pulled back the doors and was assaulted by the scent of rotten iron.

CHAPTER 26

TATE

Light, bright light was everywhere. My senses were overloaded and overwhelmed. I was burning, a living candle. Pain bloomed all over my skin, my toes, my hair. I could see through the flames, the blue-orange fire a lens that encased me. It danced in front of me, tantalizing. If I had been burning for moments or minutes, I wasn't sure.

I should have already started turning to ash, and yet, I didn't.

My blood boiled within and burned. I was being seared. I should already be dead. My heart rate sped up, and I released a scream. Pressure from within erupted and with it my handcuffs snapped. My right shoulder stung, magic clawing its way to the surface, resisting the burn. Refusing the purge. But it was futile. The fire consumed, it continued, it buried itself deep within my core. The pain at my shoulder intensified and I cried out. I needed to stop the burn.

I stood up and noticed the flames clung to me. I began to swat at them, panicking and trying to put them out. What did Tim always say? Stop, drop, and roll? It was worth a shot. I dropped to the ground and began to roll back and forth. Nothing. The light was brighter than ever. I had no idea if Mardi and James were still watching or not, I could only see fire, feel fire, hear fire. I desperately rolled back and forth, harder and faster, and still nothing.

I could hear a melody in the flame, a roar like no other, a strange song that called to my heart. Is this what death felt like? Was my soul passing on? If so, maybe it was time to accept it.

I stopped rolling and laid on my back. The melody grew stronger. I lifted my hands up in the air and stared at them. I could actually see their outline; it was no longer blocked by orange and blue flames, instead my hands *were* the flames—formed and shaped in a strawberry-orange fire.

I moved my arm to the left and the flames followed, momentarily dissipating before actualizing as my hand and arm again. Extraordinary. This must be death's cruel way of messing with my consciousness. The melody grew louder. I could hear it beating and keeping in tune with my heart as it pumped the remaining boiled blood. I no longer felt pain. A calm peace blanketed me as the music grew louder. A figure appeared, highlighted by shadow, the only thing I could see beyond the flame that was my arms. It swayed, moving so it never solidified, a ghost of smoke and ash.

"She won't make it!" a female voice cried, known but not.

"Yes, she will. She has an iron will. She will be strong enough," a male voice spoke, and there was no room for question in the tone he used.

The shadow reached out as if trying to comfort me before vanishing. In its place, the flames grew brighter, darker somehow.

Symbols began to spurt to life in sparks: a stream of fire, a sword, a baby, a female, a dragon.

Rapidly the images changed, forming new ones: song, breeze, rolling waves.

At last, all the small images collided, their sparks forming one undeniable image. A female stood before me. Eyes of flame and hair of fire. I knew her. She smiled at me while pulling out a dagger. She lifted it to her own wrist.

"No!" I screamed. She needed to stop.

But she only smiled sadly as she sliced the blade against her forearm. Liquid flame came pouring out as if gold was in her veins. It pooled, levitating in the air in front of her, before forming a ring with castle-like points. A crown.

The female smiled at me as her blood continued to flow freely from her arm, making the crown larger, more brilliant, until it was on fire and no longer gold. The light from it grew brighter and I could no longer see the female behind it. Instead, the crown hovered in the air and began to spin rapidly, the motion adding to the melody coursing through my very being.

It wouldn't be long now. Death would claim me and these strange moments would be nothing—a hallucination. I recognized the melody, something I hadn't heard in a long time—since I was a baby. I began to hum it out loud.

The crown pulsed, once, twice, three times, and then erupted in a deafening roar. The entire room became blinding white. I could see nothing but light, I could hear nothing but the cry of justice—decided acceptance—in my ears.

The light faded; the female and the crown were gone. Now, the flames I saw only encased my body, moved with my arms; they were strawberry red. Looking beyond them, I could see the warehouse roof. It was metal, manmade, and would likely burn with me.

I hummed louder as I recalled the melody. I wasn't sure if it was my mother humming it in my head or my heart's memory of my father's voice, but I recognized it as home.

I didn't know the lyrics, but what did it matter? I was dying and death was granting me this gift—this piece of my past, my parents. I closed my eyes and surrendered myself to the melody of the flame.

I began to sing the melody's notes. It was nonsense and yet made more sense to my soul than any song, poem, or story ever had. I repeated the melody, my voice straining with the sheer pressure of it. I screeched and I didn't care. It felt so right.

I repeated the melody, louder this time. The last syllable came out a roar. I would face this head-on, unafraid.

My body temperature cooled, the flames no longer boiled my blood. I must be melting now.

"Shut her up!" a strange voice called. It felt distant and disembodied.

"For the love of blood, SHUT HER UP!" Was that James? Who cared, he killed me, he could deal with my death song.

"Coat her, James! Arithi will want to see her."

"Anything to stop the screeching." And suddenly, I felt hyper-cooled. An icy blanket covered me, surrounded me, it didn't quite touch me as much as it encased me. I reached out to touch it and felt resistance. I was in a bubble.

This was the weirdest death ever. Who would've thought you get transported to the afterlife in a bubble? The bubble got tighter, forcing my hand back. It continued shrinking until it was inches from my body. I took one last deep breath as it began to press against my body, the pressure quieting my flames. The strawberry-orange fire flickered, then faded into nothing. All light was gone as the bubble encased my face, pressing to my skin. I tried to inhale, but nothing. I couldn't get any air. My lungs burned; pain filled me everywhere. I tried to breathe again, and this time darkness claimed me.

CHAPTER 27

TATE

A strange buzzing overwhelmed my senses; I tried to move but couldn't. I opened my eyes to see clouds above me. The familiar red tint to the sky confirmed I was within the Glenn's borders, no longer veil side. The sky was just starting to brighten with the light from the pink-orange sun.

How had I gotten here? Strange if this was the afterlife. I sat up, noting my bound ankles and wrists. I was covered in a strange white tunic; it was strapped together with a clip at each of my shoulders and then cinched together at my waist before splitting into two pant legs that flowed down to my ankles, where it was laced with a golden string. I pulled at the cloth; it was rough to the touch and itched. My feet were covered in...fuzzy pink socks? If this was death, it was weird. Who wanted to spend eternity bound in a potato sack?

"Hello?" I called out. Maybe I could make a deal with whoever the afterlife guards were. Angels, I hoped. I had killed, yes, but it was in the name of justice—no reason for a ticket to hell, right?

"She's up," a gruff voice came. Brown-black hair appeared from behind a clump of trees followed by the well-built body of an angel. His white shirt was translucent, revealing an outline of his abs before tucking into deliciously tight black leather pants. I noted the bulge with satisfaction. Perhaps the afterlife wouldn't be so bad. I followed the 'v' near his pants up to his neck to the masculine face. A face that told me I was dead wrong about heaven, this was hell. And this male was the devil.

"No way. No way in hell I'm spending eternity with you."

"I'm flattered and a little offended. You're not my type." He smirked. Was he serious?

"What the actual fuck? Let me go. I'll find myself another tormentor. I've seen more than enough. In fact, where is Mother Blood? I think I ended up here by mistake."

"Mother Blood?" He smiled, his right side curving up more than the left, revealing a ridiculous boyish smile—so at odds with the sharp facial features. "You actually think you're dead?" He seemed genuinely amused.

"I was burning alive for minutes. No one survives that, especially not a vampire. So go get your boss or whoever is in charge so that I can get to where I should be," I snarled as I raised bound wrists, "because, believe me, *you* are hell."

"James, she thinks I'm the devil," he called over his shoulder as the auburn male appeared next to him, dwarfing Mardi by several inches. He too was wearing a loose white shirt that was tucked into black leathers. He wore brown boots that laced up the calf, and his hair, as it was before, was unnervingly perfect.

"She's not wrong. Anna, along with half the females in the tribe, would agree with her."

"Please, let Anna go already." Mardi rolled his eyes.

"Can't, she *chose* you and you were stupid enough to dump her." What the actual fuck?

"You're Fae, does that mean you run the afterlife?" My question jarred them from their verbal sparring.

"Afterlife? She really thinks she's dead?" James chuckled. "You've got your work cut out for you, your darkness." He winked at me. "At least this is cute, unlike her screeching." My face sported a new shade of red; I may not be the best vocalist, but I didn't consider it *screeching*.

"Alright, mistress of fire, let's get one thing straight: you're not dead. And despite what James or any other female may think, I certainly am not the devil." He lowered his brows in a way that told me he most certainly *was* the devil. The things his face elicited in me. I shivered.

"However, you are right about one thing," he continued, "this is hell. But it's hell for both of us. You are the worst person I can imagine myself chained to—demeaned to the role of a babysitter. A living hell." He squatted in front of me, his face mere inches from mine. The overwhelming scent of salt and ash surrounded me. "However, one step out of line and I will make sure you wish you were dead."

I opened my mouth to respond, but nothing came out. I was utterly confused. I needed to speak to someone intelligent, and in charge. Someone who didn't unnerve me the way this male did. I was a complete idiot around him. What was the name I'd heard before I lost consciousness?

"Arithi, take me to Arithi."

His eyes narrowed. "Let's get one thing straight. I give the orders, not you. And as far as any other intel you have, you'll tell me right now or I'll break every single bone in your body with pleasure."

"Or I could break *one* bone in your body." My smile was pure bravado. Where the hell had that come from?

He blinked before leaning in, his breath caressing my cheek, as he licked the side of my jaw. "You could never break me."

A chill ran down my spine, anticipation building. Was I out of my mind? My body apparently had a mind of its own as it responded in the most irrational ways to this male in front of me.

"Using magic to elicit excitement from females is purely manipulative and a sign of SDS."

"SDS?" He spoke slowly as he pulled away from my face, his pupils more dilated than before.

"Small dick syndrome."

The intensity in his eyes deepened as he swallowed, jaw ticking. I couldn't read him. Was he turned on or annoyed? Was it possible for him to be both?

"I assure you, there's nothing small about my build." His voice dropped several decibels as he spoke, eyes lowering to my lips. I licked them in response. Something was seriously wrong with me.

"Aether, Arithi is waiting." James's voice was my savior. Mardi's jaw ticked and his vision cleared.

Leaning over he gripped my arm and yanked me to my feet. I felt dizzy, my awareness flashing in and out. "You are pathetically childish."

He jerked me upright and then pushed me in front where he gripped my arms from behind and steadied me as he shoved forward. I stumbled, my left leg's height discrepancy was, yet again, a thorn in my side. Mardi's grip on me tightened as he steadied my movement and stopped my fall. I could feel the questions arising, but I refused to acknowledge them. I was already vulnerable enough.

I continued to hobble down the path; Mardi's grip was loose but still on my shoulders. We cleared the outcropping and were now on a stone path that led down the hill toward a cliff. I'd never been here before. If we were in the Glenn, then we must be *far* outside the city limits.

We were in the wilderness, so it was unlikely the guara would rescue me. I couldn't believe I was actually hoping to see the guara. How the mighty have fallen. I rolled my eyes.

We approached the cliff, slow but steady thanks to the fact that my boots, wherever they are, were no longer evening my footing. Several small tents appeared in the distance, people milling about. The cliff came closer, and with it, a small unlit fire pit and a single golden chair came into view. We walked closer to the pit, a mere thirty feet from the cliff edge. Rocks crunched beneath my feet as the terrain changed, the stone loosening the closer we got.

Another shove forward had my foot catching on a rock, his grip loosened, and I went careening down. I fumbled, trying and failing to catch myself with my bound hands. My chin hit a rock as my fang sunk into my tongue. Blood and dirt filled my mouth. I looked up in time to see another pair of boots enter my vision. They were small, petite even. I shoved my body upwards to at least get to my knees, ignoring the burning in my mouth and the swelling I was sure was there. A small female, maybe four-ten at most, stood in front of me. She had blonde hair that faded to red. Two thick streaks of white framed her delicate face. Slight wrinkles at her eyes showed her age as weathered hands gripped her waist.

"Really, Aether? You couldn't have delivered her a little less disheveled?" Aether?

"Just be glad she's here at all. I know I've said this before, but she won't be any help," Mardi responded from behind me. So...his first name was Aether?

"That's not for you to decide." Her voice was strong, curt even, she clearly had authority. This must be Arithi.

"Alright, unbind her," she commanded.

"Excuse me?" Mardi's voice was full of indignation.

"Again, not your call, Aether. James, unbind her."

James appeared from behind me and outstretched his hand. The blue plastic-like bonds encasing my feet and wrists disappeared, leaving them blissfully free.

"Much better. Now, Aether go fetch our guest a chair please."

"You've got to be kidding me, she—"

"Now."

Mardi huffed, clearly displeased, before disappearing toward the camp just down the hill.

"I apologize for the measures we had to take to get you here. We had to be sure." She smoothed out her red tunic, highlighting the gold collar, cuff links, and golden embroidery with the movement. Black tattoos crawled out from under the tunic, circling her collarbones, matching the ones on her forearms.

"Be sure of what?" I was more confused now than ever. Were these members of another Vamp? Perhaps the ones Chance was all worked up over? Were they really preparing for battle? If they thought I could help, they were comically *wrong*.

"We'll get to that in a moment dear. First, James, please tell the doctor we're ready for her."

Ok, this was taking a turn for the worse. I scrambled back on my butt and tried to stand as James nodded and disappeared.

I sat there on the ground, dirt covering my once clean tunic, staring at the female in front of me. She sat down in the single chair on the other side of the empty fire pit. She stared at me, red eyes deepening to a molten shade.

Footsteps sounded as James, along with a gorgeous female, approached.

"Dr. Ferrari, if you will," Arithi commanded, nodding toward me.

Ferrari smiled at me, feral and beautiful. The juxtaposition of the two emotions never faded, even Glenn side when my life was apparently in danger.

I scooted back, like hell I'd let her touch me. But my body froze. Blue light surrounded me again. Damn bubble—fucking James.

"Sorry," James spoke as my body was suspended mid-scoot, completely frozen. Ferrari knelt in front of me, brandishing a blade. She reached for my palm, and I was helpless to stop her. With one swipe, she slit my palm.

"There, not so bad." She winked at me and pulled out a glass vial to collect the blood. I stared at her numbly. I always knew something was off with her, that she was *too* beautiful to be a vampire and knew *too* much to be human. Her hair was pulled up in a ponytail, and for the first time, I saw the tell-tale sign: pointed ears. She was Fae.

Drop by drop my blood fell until at last, the vial was full. She stood, nodded at Arithi, and then turned and strode off toward the camp. James reached out and a thin blue plastic covered the wound like a Band-Aid. I was released from my frozen state and just sat there, blinking. What the actual hell? Ferrari and James were Fae! I saw their ears clearly and James's gifts were not that of a vampire. The other Vamp was working with the Fae? To what end?

"Thank you, James. The tests, now, if you would." James nodded at Arithi and then disappeared toward the tents dotting the valley below. He passed Mardi who carried one plastic white chair up the hill toward us.

"I apologize for that too. We just have to take extra measures in times like these."

"I don't understand."

Her eyes sharpened and then softened, almost with...compassion?

"This will one day make sense," she spoke softly. This was the weirdest encounter. Pain, I understood, but kindness from the enemy? Nope, something was wrong. Maybe *she* was the devil. Mardi approached with the chair and sat it facing Arithi's makeshift throne before handing Arithi a brown satchel.

"Thank you, Aether."

He grunted as he backed up a few feet, standing with his arms crossed against his chest, his bulging muscles at odds with his immature demeanor—a child being disciplined. Arithi gestured for me to sit. She was far too calm, kind, and calculated; this had to be a trap.

"Are you the devil?" I blurted out, Arithi's eyes shot up as she struggled to contain a laugh. She sucked both lips in for a moment before composing herself.

"She thinks she's dead. Not the brightest bulb," Aether responded as he rolled his eyes and tapped his forehead.

"It's understandable for someone like her who doesn't know *what* she is. Especially, after just going through a burning."

"Excuse me?"

"Darling, why don't you tell us of your mother." Ok, I was not expecting this. I stood there like a deer in headlights. What were they getting at?

"Please, dear. Do take a seat. We need to have a long chat, and this *can* be a sophisticated conversation." Arithi gestured to the chair behind me.

"I don't think so." But then Aether was stalking toward me, and I'd had enough of his touch for a lifetime. I lifted myself from the ground and then lowered myself to the plastic chair.

"That's better. Now, I know trusting is hard and you have every reason to be skeptical. Unfortunately, I won't be able to offer much comfort as I will be asking the questions and not answering many." She paused and then reached into the brown satchel and pulled out a manila envelope.

"Your mother dear, who was she?"

"Why?"

Arithi sighed and then extended the package to me.

"I see you're not one to trust easily. So similar." She smiled and then nodded at the envelope. I opened it up, and then slowly dumped its contents on my lap. A picture, old and worn, was in it. It was my mother holding a toddler, me. She was young and happy. Her hair was shorter than I'd ever seen it, a pixie cut by all standards, and I was a chubby little thing in her lap. Tears pricked at my eyes. I hadn't seen a picture of her this happy in so long. It was torn down the edge, obviously half of the photo was missing.

"How do you have this?"

"Please, Tate, tell us who your mother was."

"Irene Aaralyn."

Arithi nodded satisfied. Mardi just stood there, watching my face as he remained emotionless.

"She...she was amazing. A legendary fighter, a member of the guara's elite task force. She was kind, she was loving, and she was brave," my voice broke at the end.

Arithi's eyes softened. She nodded. "Yes, I remember that."

"You knew her?" My eyes lifted from the photograph to Arithi's face.

"She was loyal," Arithi said. An undecipherable look crossed her face. "What happened to her, Tate?"

"She was murdered."

"By whom?" Arithi's voice got very still as she leaned forward—hands folded in on themselves.

"President Collin Dale. That bastard killed her." I clenched my jaw, images of Lucas's crushed body filled my mind—images of my mother's body, contorted and purple, crumpled on the floor, lifeforce completely drained of magic and blood. I shook my head. No, I couldn't picture her death like that. Maybe she didn't look like that, perhaps it was a quick death.

"Why? Why was Irene killed?"

"For supposed espionage," I spoke, the words falling lifelessly from my tongue. Arithi looked at Mardi and nodded. He stood there, unmoving. A statue.

"What is all this about?" I gestured to the photo. "Who are you? How did you know my mom?"

"Unfortunately, most of that is classified. For now, let's just say we were friends working toward the same ending, the same goal."

"What goal?"

"Who is your father, Tate?" This was getting so strange.

"My father? I don't know. I never met him. How did you know my mother?"

Arithi paused, unfolded her hands, and gestured at the contents on my lap. I'd forgotten there was more besides the photo. A small golden locket lay there. It had a dragon symbol on it and the back had fire etched into it. I tried to open it, but it was sealed.

"Only once you accept who you are will you be able to open it. And when you do, you'll get many, many answers."

"What kind of bullshit game is this?" I demanded. I was sick of this. I wanted answers. The locket began to warm within my hand, responding to my emotions.

"One you'll have to play if you want answers. I'm sorry. But I'm not the one to offer you answers and there is a way for things like this to be done. Now, tell me, who was your father?"

"I never met him." The admission stung. Abandoned as a baby had left an unhealed wound.

"Did your mother not speak of him? Have you not at least seen a picture?" Arithi prodded.

"No. Apparently, he didn't want a child."

Arithi nodded. "Did you volunteer for the guara?"

"What? Never. I would *never* help them."

"And yet, she bears their tattoo. She's one of them," Mardi's voice cut in; the first time he did anything other than stand there as a sentry. Arithi shot Mardi a silencing look and then refocused on me.

"Why do you bear the symbol of the guara, Tatealia?"

The use of my full name threw me. Very few knew my full name. My mother called me Tate, it was more *human* than the full vampirical name.

"I asked a question, dear."

"Uh, it was forced enlistment. And it's just Tate. I don't go by Tatealia."

"Very well, Tate, why were you forced to enlist?"

I was done with this round of questioning. If they wanted me dead, they'd have killed me already. Then again, they burned me, so perhaps *that* was their failed attempt.

"Answer her." Mardi's voice was closer, too close. My blood began to jump in response.

"I violated the no-kill law veil side," I responded, willing my pulse to slow.

"She's a murderer. No better than the guara." Mardi's accusation stung.

"And you are?" I shot back, focusing on him rather than the matronly female.

"You don't know *what* I am." His face was unreadable.

"Aether, please remove yourself from the circle. Now," Arithi spoke, breaking the trance-like focus he had on me. I could swear I felt his energy increase. Was he affected by me like I was by him?

"Tate, do you know how you survived the burning back in the warehouse?" Arithi waited for an answer. Mardi backed up and I turned back to face Arithi. Was that irritation on her face?

"What?" The locket in my palm remained warm. I pressed it closer between my fingers as if it would somehow shield me from the truth Arithi was revealing.

"How did you not die when burnt alive?" Was that her admission of attempted murder?

I had no idea how I survived, but I wasn't going to tell her that. Information was valuable and if she wasn't going to answer my questions, then I certainly wouldn't answer hers.

"I see. Well, let me *enlighten* you. You are not a normal vampire. You are a rare breed Tate, a legend. Fire cannot kill you. You are, in many ways, one with the flame." What was this nonsense? One with the flame? Was I a fricking fairytale? Nope.

"I can see your skepticism, it's natural for one who's been as sheltered as you've been. But believe me, there will be a day when you will understand. Lean into your heart, into the flame's song, and you will know I speak the truth." She paused and leaned forward. "Tell me, girl, what did you *see* in the flames?"

How did she know I'd seen anything? "Nothing."

"Come now," skepticism filled her face, "do not insult me with a lie. I am a truth decipherer. I can tell when someone is lying. What did you see?"

"Why does it matter?" If she was a truth decipherer, something I had previously believed didn't exist, then I needed to offer her partial truths. I didn't trust her, something in her eyes had me on edge. Or perhaps, it was the fact that she'd just had me burned not long ago.

"They say that what you see in the flames is your destiny, your identity. Some see their past, some the future, and still some, a glimpse of their true being and power."

"What did you see?" I challenged. If she knew so much, she must've gone through a burning herself.

"Smart. I can see why you unnerve Aether so much. I saw despair, a throne that called to me, and a future world dependent on the rightful leader. But you wouldn't know what any of that means." She waved a hand in the air before her face.

"I don't," I answered truthfully. "I simply saw symbols. The sea, streams of fire, a song. Nothing." I gave her selective truths, just like my mother had shown me when the school principal was interrogating me on my abilities after I transitioned.

"Indeed. Streams of fire, a song." She looked to Mardi. "One of us."

"What does that mean?"

"For now, we have more pressing things. Have you seen Fletcher Backshy?" I supposed I would not get any more answers from her.

"Fletch? What does this have to do with him?" Arithi exchanged a glance at Mardi.

"See, I told you she was useless." Mardi shook his head in annoyance.

"We've been in communication with him and recently he's gone silent. He was supposed to check in, but we haven't heard from him. When was the last time you saw him?"

"I don't know, day before yesterday? Or two days ago?" My mind was fuzzy, the timeline a blur. I'd come home and he wasn't there.

"I see. Alright then." Arithi stood. "Hand me the locket."

My fist tightened on it. It was mine, there was no way she would get it back. With a sigh, Arithi motioned to Mardi who was already at my side, prying my fist away from my chest.

"It's mine." I tightened my hold on it, but he was stronger. He forced my fingers open and plucked the golden heart right out of my palm. I snarled at him.

"You can have it back if you light the fire." She gestured to the unlit pit.

"Impossible." I looked around, desperate to spot wood or sticks, flint, or lighter fluid. None. The locket dangled from Mardi's fingers and then he chucked it through the air to Arithi who caught it.

"Someday you will understand." The decision was clear in her eyes and body language as she stood. "You will go back and join the guara and gain their trust. You will be a good soldier and not breathe a word of this to anyone. And above all, you will get in contact with Fletcher and notify us immediately. Aether, you will take her back."

"Wait! Why do you need to hear from Fletcher? What is all this about?" Arithi tucked the locket in her waistband.

"Let's go." Mardi approached me. I sprung up from my seat and darted toward Arithi. She held up a hand and red flames erupted before her, a line in the sand.

"Look, Tate. I knew Irene, and you're right, she was kind and yet brave. I owe her, which is why in part I've been lenient with you. You have promise, and are in some ways, one of our own. However, you are unproven and untrained. Mardi fears your loyalty. We do not have room for risks right now, only assets." She paused, eyes calculating. "There is a war coming. When it arrives, you will have to choose. In the meantime, I'm afraid you must return to your life and move on. Breathe one word of this to anyone and our faith in you will be broken and, friendship with your mother or no, we'll dispose of you." The female before me was hard, ice cold. Nothing like the kind, elderly female I saw a moment ago.

"Please, I can help! I want to. Allow me my necklace as a trinket of trust."

Arithi assessed me, her frame beginning to hide behind the wall of flame she commanded. "Trust is earned. You want to help? Find Fletcher. Once you do, I'll need you to contact us. If you can do this, then perhaps you'll be an asset after all. Understood?"

I still wasn't sure I trusted them, not one bit. But I did know I trusted Fletcher and finding him would be a start. "Yes, I know I can."

"Very well, Aether take her back and instruct her on how to reach us. Tate, contact us the moment you find Fletcher. Should you fail to do so, or speak of this to the guara, we will not hesitate to eliminate you as a threat, Irene's child or not."

"I understand."

"Good. Aether." Arithi waved her hand and the wall of fire disappeared, leaving only a woodless fire in the pit. She turned and began slowly making her way back down the hill.

"Of course, I'd get stuck with babysitting duty, again. Like watching your reckless ass veil side wasn't punishment enough. This way." He turned and led the way, back to where we came, not waiting for me before he began climbing the hill.

"Veil side? I knew it was you!" I called after him, but he just continued his trek up the hill. I hesitated for a moment. Maybe I could get Arithi to talk, follow her to the village and get some answers.

"I wouldn't if you want to live," Mardi called over his shoulder. Asshole. Fine, I'd follow him—for now. I needed to find Fletch anyway. I moved with quick, uneven steps and caught up to him; he didn't slow as he began climbing the hill.

"How will I contact you?" I hated that my breath came out in pants. I was out of shape.

"Let's get one thing straight." He turned abruptly and towered over me more than usual given the hill's advantage. "Arithi may have decided to give you a chance, but not for one second am I willing to trust you. That said, I have eyes everywhere and one step out of line and you will pay for it, do you understand?"

"Got it." I glared at him, leveling my best challenging stare that I could muster. Even at five-seven, I could intimidate. Never mind that he was well over six feet.

"I will take you back and you will act as if nothing has happened. You've been sentenced to the Eastern Outpost. You leave the day after tomorrow. You will need to locate Fletcher before your departure."

"And how do you suppose I do that?"

"Not my problem." Naturally, it wasn't. We continued to walk back to the clearing, his single stride the same as three of mine. Finally, he stopped.

I bent over, hands on my knees. My heart was pounding, too much cardio. Usually this wouldn't faze me, but now, whether it be the weird encounter, the burning, or hunger, I could barely catch my breath.

"Turn," he commanded as he pulled out a blindfold.

"No way, uh-uh." I stepped back into a solid wall of muscle.

"Scared of the dark?" James spoke. Just great, I was now stuck with *both* of them.

"You guys aren't my type and that," I pointed to the scarf, "is not my kink." James loosened a hearty laugh. Some tension eased...at least there was that. Mardi didn't look the least bit impressed or moved, like he was made of steel. Whatever.

"Tate, are we going to have a problem?" Mardi approached me, James still stood behind.

"I don't know, Aether, she seems to have rejected you. Tell me, how many times have you experienced that?" I could hear the amusement in James's voice; a joke that neither Mardi nor I shared.

"No, no problem," I responded, ignoring James.

Mardi reached near my head and then wrapped the fabric around my face. This was absolutely absurd. He secured it to the back of my head and brushed my cheek with his fingertips as he pulled back; warmth exploded over my skin. My heart rate accelerated from his touch.

"James." I felt the muscles behind my back flex as two arms wrapped around me and then suddenly, I was twisting, falling, fading. My existence as I knew it was altered. I felt immaterial and yet my nerves were firing everywhere. The weightlessness ended and my feet touched something solid, allowing the dizzying sensation to pass. I bent over and vomited. I could hear someone else vomiting next to me.

"Looks like you finally have a companion for your weak stomach." James's voice was filled with far too much mirth. I reached up and yanked the blindfold off only to see that instead of grass and rock beneath my knees, I was in a bed of flowers. Bluebells. I knew them well. We had returned to the Glenn.

CHAPTER 28

CHANCE

Bodies on gurneys formed neat rows of death. There had to be hundreds and hundreds of vessels in here. How had I not smelled this from outside? I walked up to each table and noted that the humans were all unconscious. They just lay there; blood being drained into bags. The vampires who worked here all wore green jumpsuits and masks. This was not the usual blood collection protocol. What was strange was the quantity of vessels and lack of soldiers present.

"What's going on here, arche?"

The male didn't even look at me, he just scurried away. His face was dazed.

"Strange." Holland stepped up beside me and pushed some bloody hair behind her ear. Neither of us had a chance to clean up since the battle.

"This is definitely not protocol for blood collection." I walked up to a table and snapped my finger next to a human woman's ear. She didn't so much as flinch. I felt for a pulse to confirm she was alive and then moved to the next gurney. A human male, also unconscious. He had the most extraordinary black hair I've ever seen on a human. It was raven black and reached down to his waist. A purple and blue tattoo of a dragon crawled up his arm and neck; the dragon's head turned into a serpent and somehow gave you the middle finger with its tongue. I bet he was a peach when he was awake. I snapped loudly, nothing. I lowered my fangs to graze his skin and still he did not move. They were comatose. All of them.

I continued down the row and pinched each human vessel's arm. They all remained unconscious, even when I broke their skin and blood began to pool.

"Have you ever seen this before, Dale?" Holland's voice came from beside me. Her shoulders curved in slightly, the day had been tiring.

"Nope. Definitely new. We're going to have to file a report."

"Already on it." Her confirmation added to the list of things I was beginning to like about her.

We continued throughout the warehouse until we reached the back office. Inside, the manager of the processing plant sat, staring at the screen.

"Hello." I shut the door loudly, but like the humans, he remained in a daze. "Dux," I leaned closer to get a look at this badge, "Hoffman. A word please?" He stared at the screen. I moved behind the desk to get a better look at the screen his disk was projecting.

"It's no use. He's been like that since the attack this morning," a new, squeaky voice came from the corner. I looked up and spotted a young vamp, low ranking from his badge details.

"And you are?"

"The only one talking." Smartass.

"Are you insinuating something occurred during the attack this morning, arche?"

"I'm saying that he and all the staff that were in the plant during the attack this morning are unresponsive." The arche looked disheveled. Upon closer inspection, I could see blood on his collar, red and black. He'd been in the fight.

"Where were you during the attack?" Holland asked.

"Outside fighting, just like these cowards should've been. Everyone's been on edge lately, but to remain in here and hide is a disgrace. Even if the dux ordered it. Nah," he spat on the floor, "they deserve what happened to them." His fingers fidgeted in a nervous tic. Clearly, he was unnerved.

"Careful how you speak about your superiors, arche."

"Why? What are they going to do? Lecture me?" He sneered as he stood and strode toward the door.

"Hold up. I am the highest-ranking officer here and as such you will answer to me. What do the numbers on the screen represent?" The arche paused, it wasn't lost on me that he didn't have a name badge and hadn't volunteered his name. My suspicions were already on high alert.

"How should I know?" He lifted his nostrils and sniffed before rubbing at his eyes with his hands. My money was on drugs.

"You said you worked here?" Holland chimed in, walking around the desk to get a closer look at the projection. Her hand casually moved to her weapon. Blood, I loved her instincts.

"I do. But I was just the grunt worker, dragging bodies up from the human district and dumping them back in their hovels. I, as you pointed out, didn't rank high enough to understand the data." The sneer on his face made me want to punch him. He needed an attitude adjustment. Big time.

"Get me someone who can help," I commanded.

"You're looking at him. All frozen and frosty." He gestured to Dux Hoffman.

"Frosty?" Holland squinted focusing on Hoffman.

"I don't know who the hell you think you are arche, but I've had it up to here with your insubordination. Now get us someone who can help or start answering our questions—"

"Dale, look." Holland reached toward Hoffman and a blue aura surrounded him, it became more visible as she projected a bit of her magic at it.

"They're in magicside. Those creatures wielded dark magic here. But none sent any at me? How is any of this possible?"

"Frosty, right?" The arche clapped his hands and laughed, spit flying from his mouth and dribbling on his chin's stubble.

"You saw this before Dux Holland noticed it, how?" I demanded.

"Don't know. Don't care." He continued to laugh, rubbing his hands together nervously, causing his pale skin to redden further. He was thin, probably didn't eat much, and from his appearance and demeanor, I'd guess he was low on the feeding totem pole. Still, he should have been getting rations. He flipped me the bird as he darted for the door.

I was faster. Much, much faster. I grabbed his collar and lifted him off his feet slamming him into the wall. "Answer me now, you lowlife." My voice had gone deadly calm.

His pupils dilated and I could see perspiration dripping at the corners of his scalp down to his mouth. The tint to his teeth was yellow and his left fang was broken.

"You know how." He squirmed as he responded, his clothing stretching in my hands. He was a wielder then.

"What do you wield?"

"Nothing, I—" I cut off his lies with my forearm pressed to his throat, temporarily constricting his airway.

"Holland, want to step in here?"

"Hmm, someone likes having a partner after all, huh?" She smirked as she swaggered from across the desk and looked him up and down. For a small female, she had a way of sizing males up and making us feel so very small and insignificant.

"Answer the question, arche. How did you spot the aura before I did?"

"I'm a reader, OK? Magic speaks to me. I don't always know how to read it, but I can sense it." He wiggled in my arms some more; his body odor was hideous. I looked to Holland, and she nodded in confirmation. The truth. I let him go and he fell to the floor in a heap.

"And you can sense magic on Dux Hoffman?"

"Not just him," he flayed his arms wide, "this whole place reeks of it." He scrambled to his feet and made to bolt for the door, again.

Holland had her rifle's butt in his stomach before I could even react. A smile pulled at my lips; I was really beginning to like working with her.

"Not so fast, why don't you take us to the human district, arche?" she spoke, her hips swaggering as she shoved the arche through the office door.

"Fantastic idea, Dux Holland."

THE HUMAN DISTRICT WAS QUIET. The hovels had seen better days, the roads were broken down, and it appeared the dux here had let the upkeep of common spaces fall between the cracks. Not surprising given his attitude toward humans. We continued down the path, looking for humans to interrogate. The streets were empty.

I approached a larger hovel and knocked on the door. It creaked with the force of my pounding fists.

"They don't like us much," the no-name arche unhelpfully added. He stopped twitching since we left the warehouse, and his color was slowly returning to his face.

"It's not unusual for humans to resent vampires and be uneasy around us, but to be this distrustful reeks of mismanagement on *your* dux's part." Holland shoved past the arche. I really needed to get his name.

"Yeah, well, the ones left really don't like us."

"The ones left?"

"Hello?" Holland spoke at the same time I did.

That was the only distraction needed for the wimpy arche to evade my question. Holland pushed on the door and to my utter surprise, it was unlocked and creaked open. In the human district within HQ the humans interacted with vampires frequently, but they always kept their doors locked when they weren't looking for activity.

Dux Holland took a tentative step inside. No movement, no response.

"They're meek as sheep," the arche beside me grumbled, examining his fingernails.

"Shut up, arche!" I snapped. I grabbed his collar and shoved him inside in front of me. The room was small, furnished with old furniture; a tarnished green couch, worn velvet armchairs, and a fireplace that was roaring with life. Noticeably, the humans here didn't like our kind.

"We just have a few questions," I called out. A creek from the nearby wood floor ousted the tiny human. She looked maybe seventeen. Her clothes were worn and covered in patches, her hair streaked across her gaunt face, and her pallor was paler than snow.

"What do you 'skeets want?" Her voice was laced with anger.

Skeets?

"Just to check and make sure everything is okay here after the events from earlier this morning," Holland reassured.

"Ha, like you care. Don't worry, your sheep are still here. Baaa." She imitated a sheep, revealing uneven, chipped front teeth. "Not like ya be needing more of us."

"Excuse me?" Holland stepped forward. The girl didn't shrink back, instead, she raised her head, hate glaring in her eyes.

"For which part? Takin' my parents last week or my brother last night? Or draining 'em to death?"

"You are protected under the no-kill law," I spoke up, tentatively taking a small step forward. "So is your family. If there has been a violation, please file a report and we will look into it. Are you alone here?"

Her eyes shifted to me. "Alone. All alone." She shuffled closer to the fire and poked at it with a fire stick.

"I gave two nights ago. I still got one more day, so unless you are offerin' me a bonus, you 'skeets need to get the hell out." She then turned her back to me. I've never interacted with a human so utterly terrified and yet stupid enough to turn her back on one vampire. Let alone three.

"Thank you for your time." Dux Holland gestured for me to follow her as we left.

"What the hell has Dux Bole been doing to these humans?" she demanded, grabbing the arche by his arm and yanking him toward her. Despite the fact that he was a good eight inches taller than her, she evidently was in control of the situation.

"Dux Bole doesn't exactly care for the humans. He's a bit old-school in thinking and finds the new laws too..." The arche paused, sucking on his fang for effect. "Lenient."

"Meaning?" I pried. If Dux Bole was violating the no-kill law, amongst others, he would need a full write-up.

"Meaning he follows his own rules here. The strong prey on the weak."

"Dale, we'll need to file a full report."

I nodded to Holland as I surveyed the rest of the small unkept, district. A few humans moved about, even in bright daylight, they all held torches with them. For Dux Bole being so old-school, I was surprised he hadn't confiscated all torches. The arrogant bastard probably didn't think they were a threat even with fire.

"Holland, why don't you go file a report and contact HQ. I'm going to visit another home or two. And you," I pointed to the scrawny male still in Holland's grasp, "what's your name, arche?"

Holland released a wave of her magic at him, I could sense it growing stronger, thickening the air.

"Arche Damaris," he answered, inhaling deeply.

"What did the human mean when she called us 'skeets?" I pressed.

"You been living under a rock?" The charge in the air thickened, he clawed at Holland's hands trying to find release. "Ok! Lay off the magic, lady." He yanked his collar down. "Females," he muttered, earning a glare from Holland. "Skeets' is slang for mosquitos. The humans here view us as bloodsucking parasites."

"They what?" Holland and I spoke in unison.

"Yeah, try as he might, Dux Bole can't seem to stomp out all their spirit. Well, not from the young anyway."

The whole situation violated so many laws. Humans were entitled to certain rights in the Glenn. They also were supposed to respect vampires for our superiority, and that included the way in which we followed the rules and gave honor to the food chain. Something was very, very mismanaged here.

"Stay with Dux Holland," I commanded Arche Damaris and then turned, continuing down the street. The next three homes were all in similar shambles. Two were empty, but in the third, I found three children huddled together near the fire. A very intoxicated man grumbled and sang from a nearby armchair.

"Hello," I spoke quietly, unstrapping my rifle and dropping it to the floor. They didn't need any further reason to fear me.

The children all glared at me. The oldest couldn't be more than ten. Their clothes were either too big or too tight—all in patches and worn colors. Their hair was matted to their faces in knots, and they had the same grey pallor as the first human girl.

"Is there another adult here?"

The man continued to utter unintelligible words, ignorant of my presence. He reeked of beer and piss.

"Where's your mother?" The kids just sunk closer together. I took a step toward them and the younger two ducked behind the oldest boy. He lifted his hand and pointed past me to the processing plant.

"Where are the other adults?"

The child continued to point. No way. No way Dux Bole was stupid enough to process practically *all* the human adult vessels at once. I looked closer at the boy's arm. Puncture marks. These children were being fed from. Another violation.

"Excuse me." I turned and left them huddled by the roaring fire. Holland and I would need to process quite the report; it could take another day or two to install new leadership here prior to heading to the Southern Outpost. I continued through the human district and all I found were pale, scared, mute children.

CHAPTER 29

TATE

I had been in a forest, surrounded by grass, rocks, and pine needles, but now I stood in a field of flowers. How was any of this possible? Mardi wiped his mouth next to me; he still looked sick. Good, at least I wasn't alone.

"What the hell just happened?" I demanded.

"Don't worry about it." Mardi huffed.

"Seriously?"

"Did the blindfold mean nothing to you?" Mardi's remarks were getting weary, winded even. Perhaps the weird traveling we just did drained some of his energy? Or was this James's doing? He was Fae, after all, and I knew very little about what they could and could not do.

"Alright, so about two miles up the path over there, you'll find the main road that leads back to HQ. You have your instructions from Arithi. Once you find Fletcher, you'll notify me."

"And how, pray tell, do I do that?"

"With this." He handed me a small vial on a chain. "When you find him, burn this and I'll find you. Be discreet about it."

I palmed the small metal vial; it was tiny, maybe the size of my pinky fingernail. The chain connected to it was silver and very delicate.

It looked like a crystal some wore for good luck. I clasped it around my neck and tucked it under my shirt.

"Here." Mardi extended a brown bag.

I tentatively opened it. My clothes, not the ones I'd been wearing before, but a new pair of black pants and a black T-shirt. I raised an eyebrow in question.

"Can't go back wearing that."

"And I suppose I'm supposed to just change here," I challenged.

"Be our guest—"

Mardi elbowed James in the ribs mid-sentence.

"I'm sure there's plenty of opportunities to do so before you reach the village. I've already seen enough of you," Mardi sneered before running a hand through his hair.

The air around me intensified. I could have sworn there was a charge to it—a sultry heat. Odd for this time of year.

James muttered something unintelligible under his breath before turning and walking toward the tree line.

Mardi just stood there. Chest rising with every breath. Each breath a call to the wind, to my nerves, to my blood now heating inside—

I shook my head.

"Fine." I eyed the path ahead.

Screw Mardi and whatever mind games he was playing. I needed to get back and find Fletch for my own reasons. I moved forward toward the village. Answers certainly lay ahead.

Mardi's hand snapped out and grabbed my arm. "Tate, if you should speak a word of this to the guara or anyone other than Fletcher, I will make what you endured in that warehouse feel like a cakewalk. Understand?"

I yanked my arm free and ignored him, continuing down to the path—leaving those two atrocities of nature behind. Time to get some answers.

. . .

By the time I made it to the village, it was late afternoon. I'd found a secluded place not far from the two buffoons who'd dropped me off in the valley to change and simply discarded the scratchy linen gown in the shrubs. I was much more comfortable in my standard clothing of choice.

In a minute, I'd be home and hopefully, Fletch would too. He had a lot of explaining to do. The last twenty-four hours were catching up to me. This whole day had been total bullshit. Getting drafted to the guara? Bullshit. Getting jumped on *my* attack, total bullshit. And being literally burned alive? Impossible. Fletch's involvement with another Vamp and complete betrayal of the Glenn along with my mother's legacy? Beyond impossible. Yeah, Fletch better be home and he better be ready to answer some serious questions. Maybe I should even have a drug test done? It was possible this was all a really bad trip.

I crested the hill that led down to my house and paused. The door was ajar. It hung loosely as if forcefully opened, and the hinge appeared broken. I ran down the hill. Heart racing, palms sweating. A strange tingling filled my system, my nerves felt like sparks firing rapidly. I reached the porch and burst through the doorjamb. The whole room was in shambles. The couch cushions had been slashed; cotton coated the floor in maroon clumps. Blood. The whole room had sprays of dark red everywhere. I spotted a broken bottle of bloodwine near the couch next to broken picture frames smashed by the fireplace —a fireplace that now had its embers strewn across the room as if someone had rummaged through it.

My pink blanket had been torn to shreds and was now covered in soot and blood. I turned down the hall, past the ransacked kitchen with broken cabinet doors, toward Fletch's room. I ignored bloody footprints and the clear signs of a struggle. Looked past the broken drywall and odd char marks coating its surface.

I approached the doorframe to my mother's room, and my heart dropped. The door was open, and the room was completely destroyed. The bed had been overturned, mattress cut open, all the wall décor had been smashed and now coated the floor. Destroyed. Utterly ruined.

"Fletch!" I screamed his name.

No answer, but I didn't expect one.

I moved from the room of my shredded childhood innocence as a coldness settled over me. My security blanket had been ripped off. My room, like my mother's, was a disaster. Fletch's room was the worst. I couldn't even recognize a single piece of furniture. The bed had been dismantled, the dresser lay scattered in pieces, and the walls had holes in them to the point the whole room looked like a piece of Swiss cheese.

Arithi's face filled my mind's eye. They were looking for him. Did they do this? Or was he really in trouble with the guara? The questions I'd received the last time I crossed the veil came to mind. They were looking for him too. What the hell was going on?

Footsteps sounded down the hall.

I grabbed a piece of broken wood from the bed frame and pressed my back to a gaping hole in the drywall. The steps got louder and louder. Two guaramen appeared in Fletch's room, weapons drawn. I swung my club at them, catching one off guard. He went flying backwards. The next one ducked and swung his rifle at my club, snapping it in half. He leveled the barrel at me.

"Tate Aaralyn, come with me."

CHAPTER 30

CHANCE

I found Holland storming out of Dux Bole's office. Her normally calm demeanor was replaced with a wild expression.

"We are instructed to stand down," she spoke, the words barely audible through her clenched jaw.

"What?" I placed a hand on her delicate shoulder.

"I contacted HQ and just got off the phone with them following the report I submitted. They granted a waiver for Dux Bole's actions given the current circumstances."

It was understandable but still felt wrong. "They don't want us to change leadership until a hearing?" That was the protocol. Going against protocol was unusual, to say the least.

"Correct. It seems, this wasn't the first attack on a processing plant."

"Is there data on the other attacks?" If we could get a better understanding of where these creatures were coming from, we'd stand a chance at destroying them.

"Apparently they're classified."

"Classified? We're duxes," the words are pouring from my lips, "this is ridiculous. Do they know about the unresponsive vessels and plant processing agents?"

"They don't care, Dale." Her honey-brown eyes locked with mine and I allowed them to bore into my soul in a far too intimate way for our current surroundings.

"I can't believe they're not following standard protocol for infractions." I sucked on my fang. We were facing outside threats, and we did have a mole to hunt down, but still...the idea of leaving this place in such a state felt oddly wrong.

"Dale, if things stay the way they are then this whole settlement will be eviscerated. The humans are practically drained, they're feeding from children, there are hundreds of comatose humans, and we don't know nearly enough about the creatures from last night's attack to leave. I understand we have a mole to hunt down, but doesn't it stand to reason that those things could be sent by the enemy?" She gestured wildly as she shifted on her feet, removing my hand from her shoulder. "We could be missing a very important opportunity to intercept the enemy," her voice raised at the end along with the red now tinting her cheeks. Angry. She was clearly upset.

"Let me call HQ and see if we can persuade them to at least release the previous reports." I pulled out my disk and inserted my earpiece before dialing the head intelligence office.

"Dux Dale for Anax Graf."

"Hold." The line went silent. If I could at least have a better understanding of the dark magic at play, we could have a chance at ending it before it spread. The unconscious humans felt wrong on so many levels.

"Dux Dale," Dux Richards' gruff voice answered.

"Dux Richards? I was calling for Anax Graf."

"You've been rerouted to me. She's not available right now. Are you en route to the Southern Outpost?" Who the hell did he think he was taking Anax Graf's phone calls?

"No sir, we haven't left yet. There's a situation."

"Yes, I've been apprised of the situation. I just spoke to Dux

Holland. Did she not inform you? Dux Bole has received waivers. Leave the settlement immediately and continue on to your assignment." His voice sounded wet, like he'd just fed and hadn't bothered to wipe his mouth or swallow the blood before taking the call.

"Sir, the creatures from last night were boasting dark magic. The settlement here is in disarray. We worry about the extinction of the human district due to Dux Bole's multiple—"

"Let me stop you right there boy. Dux Bole is a fine dux, better than most. He has been granted a waiver and you are to—"

"But protocol dictates—"

"Do not interrupt me. I AM FILLING IN FOR YOUR COMMANDING OFFICER!" Rusty's voice raised, but his excessive spit and gravelly tone made his words barely intelligible. "Do not interrupt me again. You have your orders. We received Dux Holland's report. You are to leave immediately! Do you understand?"

I understood alright. Older generational bullshit. Protecting each other even when it clearly went against the Glenn's guidelines. I would be sure to inform my father about this as soon as I could get a secure audience with him.

I swallowed my pride and the bile rising in my throat. "Yes, sir. I'd like to request the reports from previous attacks to study on our way to the Southern Outpost."

"They're above your pay grade."

"With all due respect, I believe these creatures could be the work of our enemy. An enemy I was *sent* to stop by first ousting a mole. I believe those reports are pertinent to this research and my mission."

"Your objective does not involve the events of last night. Leave it alone, Dale."

The line went dead. I clenched my fists; I *hated* taking orders from that asshole. But orders were orders. It looked like we would be leaving.

Holland looked at me through her brown eyes; she'd heard my end, and her expression told me she understood.

"We leave in fifteen. Tell the arches."

She nodded as I stormed off to gather my belongings. I hated the complete disregard for the *new* laws—the vampirical ways as decided a century ago after the Great War—and I hated the way my father's legacy and legislation was being cast aside to simply 'protect' the backs of less evolved leaders. But most of all, I hated the way Rusty spoke to me. No one speaks to me like that, not even commanding officers. Especially not Rusty.

We were the same rank for blood's sake.

I had a right to all the data about those things from last night—I needed to understand what they were. What if they came back? Did Dux Richards really expect me to just turn a blind eye and carry on like nothing had happened?

I nodded a curt goodbye to Dux Bole and strode for the transport. The human district was quiet when we left. I could still picture the tiny humans huddled together by that fire, almost as lifeless as the vessels in the processing plant. As we boarded, no one said a word. The settlement behind us was bathed in blood and silence.

I could see the bright blue hair, matted in mud, of Shae's head leaning against the back of a seat two cars down. I strode toward her; I needed a friendly face.

"Shae, how are you holding up?" I leaned against the wall of the train car, resting and wishing it could take more than just my physical weight.

"Did you know butterflies only live a few weeks? They go through this metamorphosis and change from these sluggish, little worm-like things, to glorious insects; they sprout wings, becoming gloriously free. But it's short. So short." She blew her bangs out of her face, revealing her grey-blue eyes. Sorrow pooled in them just above freshly healed scrape marks on her face.

"I think I remember learning that in school."

"Yeah, well, I used to think that it was tragic. To live such a short life. I mean, that's the equivalent of seconds for us. But maybe that's nature's way."

She was always one for metaphors. Intrinsic to a fault. "I don't think I understand what you're getting at."

"Those things from last night should *not* exist. They morphed. I knew one of them when they were one of us. He was a year ahead of me in school, interested in internal intelligence like myself. Whatever they became is unnatural. They shouldn't exist for more than mere seconds."

I had no response, so I merely sat down next to her and draped an arm around her. She didn't hesitate to scoot in, resting her head on my chest. Normally when a female snuggled into me, it was preceded by sensual pleasure. Not with Shae. She was always more of a sister to me than anything. We rode like this for several minutes, content in one another's quiet company.

"You know the humans have a nickname for us?" I spoke, breaking the silence.

"They do?" She angled her head up at me.

"Yup, 'Skeets.'"

"Skeets?"

"Short for mosquitos."

She snorted, her eyes narrowing at the sides as the dimples in her cheeks appeared. "Humans are funny."

"Yeah, I suppose they are good for more than just their blood."

"Is the big bad mosquito coming around to realize that other life forms matter?" Shae teased, elbowing me. We both knew there was more truth to her joke than just an offhanded, lighthearted remark.

"Perhaps. Maybe I too am 'sprouting' wings." I winked at her. This didn't need to become a deep conversation.

"I'll visualize that." Her nose wrinkled up as she thought about it. "In fact, I don't think I'll be able to look at you from now on *without* seeing wings on you. Big pink fairy wings." She slapped her knee.

"You amuse yourself," I spoke, shaking my head. I couldn't stop the grin pulling at my lips. This felt good after all that bullshit in Brookside.

The train car continued; the circuit jostled—still my least favorite form of travel. It was metal, thin, the air was stale and putrid. Several soldiers, myself included, still had not showered, which meant the scent of rotting blood filled the air.

But Shae was here. The trauma from last night didn't break her. She would survive.

"Any word on Tate?" Her question jarred me. I hadn't checked in on her since yesterday. She'd been drafted.

"She will be joining the guara."

"What! You waited until now to tell me?" She pulled away, hurt and accusation filling her eyes. So much for light conversation.

"I just heard yesterday. Apparently, she broke the no-kill law veil side and was forced to enlist."

"That's absurd! I mean, that bastard back there was breaking all sorts of laws, and we just left him like nothing ever happened." Shae was always more observant than I gave her credit.

"Think of it this way Shae, with Tate joining the guara, she'll be tactically trained, and with the creatures last night, perhaps it's not the worst thing."

"You think they'll come back?" Her wide eyes couldn't conceal her fear.

"I don't know." I hated the admission. Unknowns and I did not mix.

"I think that's the first time I've heard you say that in ten years."

Punk. Shae was definitely bouncing back after last night. Maybe her therapy was helping. Maybe.

"You know, Dale. You need to make sure Tate is brought to the Southern Outpost. She needs me. She needs…you."

"I have no control over where she goes." Last thing I needed was Tate lingering nearby. Her very scent still messed with my head. "Given our history, I very much doubt she'd want to be anywhere near me while she's being forced to serve in the guara."

"Don't be so proud. She needs us. We're her family. Please try to have her sent to the Southern Outpost. For me?" She gave me the puppy dog look that she's mastered over the years. "Honestly, I wouldn't be surprised if her breaking the no-kill law was a cry for help—an involuntary action intended on bringing her closer to us, forcing her to join."

"That's a stretch."

"Maybe, but you didn't see her face when I told her I was enlisting…"

"I'll think about it, Shae."

She smiled and then snuggled back into my side. I had no intention of bringing Tate to the Southern Outpost, not with these creatures and the mole hunt. No, I'd try to send her to the Western or Northern Outposts. She would be safer freezing her ass off than she would be around me.

I closed my eyes, and for just a second, I wasn't a dux heading to oust one of my own, to condemn a traitor. I was young, an arche on his way to training with his best friend. Try as I might, I couldn't shut out the mahogany eyes from my mind. Tate, damn her, would follow me to my death—of that, I was sure. I just hoped that wouldn't be for several decades.

CHAPTER 31
TATE

The HQ building was colder than normal. My hands wouldn't stop shaking. Something was very, very wrong. I sat in one of the interrogation rooms in the basement of the tower. The metal table was cold and the cuffs around my wrists were too tight, digging into my skin. This was the second time I've been bound in the last day, and it was *really* getting old. The guaramen who escorted me here were mindless goons who didn't say a word the entire time. They dragged me down all three floors and then chained me to the table before leaving. That was at least an hour, maybe two, ago? The room was pristine and blank. Metal walls, black tables, marble floors. The whole thing was modern and crisp. It was a unified horror.

My conversation with Arithi and Mardi kept playing through my mind. They insinuated that Fletch was working with them and so was my mother. Impossible. And yet, my home had been ransacked, Fletch was missing, and as far as I knew, the guara were looking for him. Maybe Arithi wasn't as crazy as I thought. The necklace Mardi gave me dangled against my chest, warmed by my skin. I was surprised they didn't confiscate it.

My dishwater blonde hair was falling out of its ponytail, and it was getting annoying to say the least. I blew at a strand that kept falling in my eye, only for it to lift a few inches and then fall back again. I studied the golden strand. The end of it had a rosy color to it. Were my eyes deceiving me?

The door opened and a spindly figure dressed in all back entered. Luina. The hair on my arms stood as a tapping in the hallway behind her sounded. *Tap, tap, tap.* President Dale's white-blonde head appeared behind Luina's black French twisted bun, and then his face came into view. About four guaramen filed in next. This was quite the audience.

Luina took a seat opposite me as President Dale stood behind her, the guaramen at his back. As if I was a threat to them even *unbound.* I had the least amount of tactical training, and as far as they knew, I possessed no magic uncommon to the average vampire.

"Tate Aaralyn. You just had your Disciplinary Hearing yesterday and now you're back again? *Tsk, tsk.*" Luina's voice was like nails on a chalkboard. High-pitched and shrill.

"Yeah, what can I say, I like the accommodations." I couldn't keep the bite out of my voice, my temper getting the better of me.

"Watch your tongue!" Luina's voice raised before settling down to a deathly calm. "When was the last time you saw Fletcher?"

"I don't know." I was getting really sick of people asking me that question. "A couple of days. Where is he?" I demanded.

Luina looked at Collin who cleared his throat before stepping forward.

"Tatealia, what do you know of your uncle's loyalties and foreign engagements?"

I hated it when he used my given name. That was not who I was. "Nothing. He's loyal to the Glenn, always has been." My pulse quickened as Mardi came to mind, but I quickly squashed that thought.

They didn't look convinced. If only I was here because they heard of my open attack on Gari, that would be easier than discussing Fletch's allegiance.

"One would hope. But that doesn't seem to be the case. The fact is, we believe he's been working with an enemy vamp," Collin voiced as he inspected his manicured nails.

"No, that's impossible. Fletch has been nothing but loyal to you and the Glenn. I swear!" I tried to stand, but the restraints on my wrists yanked me back down to the table.

"Has Fletcher ever discussed the Untish Tribe with you?" Collin asked.

"No. This seriously can't be about a mythical tribe? It's a fairytale, we learned about it in school. Fletch is a teacher. He has taught younglings for decades and they've gone off and served the Glenn fervently. You're mistaken to question his loyalties."

"Watch how you speak to the President!" Luina snapped at me. Her black eyes narrowed as she stepped closer.

"I was hoping you'd be honest with us, Tatealia." Collin sighed. "Luina, if you please."

Luina reached out toward me with her spindly fingers. She was going to do it—she would dig.

Pain exploded in my head; my vision became dizzy. I could feel her sorting through my thoughts, my history. She pulled at one memory, me watching Fletch teach the kids. The mere motion of it drew tears to my eyes from the pressure of her prodding. Momentarily she paused, studying the memory before shoving it back and beginning to shuffle once again through my mind, pulling and prodding.

Lightning shot down my spine, my nerves were rapidly firing as sharp needles stabbed into my skull. I could barely focus, she was saying something, watching something, and then the pressure built again as she shuffled through more memories. My head snapped forward as the pain intensified. Acute pain at the back of my head radiated down my spine before finally releasing.

"Here," Luina's voice began to register, "this is what I've found."

"Tate, the Untish aren't mythical. They were real. They are real," Fletch's voice filtered through the room.

"Fletch, you've had too much. Get some sleep. I have to be at the clinic tomorrow morning to pull my shift, but when I get back, we can talk." My

voice surrounded me and everyone in the room. I'd never heard it like this; utterly disembodied.

"Tate, I've been so wrong. I thought that protecting you and not exposing everything was right, but—"

Fletch's voice stopped as the pain intensified again. I let out a shout as I felt more needles prickling at my mind, digging through my brain like Luina was personally using a knife to cut away memories and split mental files. With a blink of her eyes, the sharp pain left, the pressure was gone, and I no longer felt like my mind was being squeezed.

I inhaled deeply. It did nothing to stop the throbbing in my head or lessen the nausea.

"It would appear that she speaks the truth regarding Fletcher. I searched her mind for any mention of the Untish Tribe in connection to her memories of Fletch, and aside from the one memory I played, I didn't find anything." Luina almost sounded disappointed.

"Well then, at least we know we have one loyal member from Aaralyn's house. I suppose we'll have to proceed to Step Two." Collin nodded at the guaramen. They walked around the desk and grabbed my arms before unlocking the cuffs at the desk. Luina stood, watching, her eyes glistening with anticipation.

On instinct I raised my hands in fists, I wanted to fight. But logic took over, there was no point in it; not only would I lose, but it would be stupid. I wanted to find Fletch and if I cooperated, perhaps they'd help me find him or at least answer a question or two. I lowered my fists.

"Wise move," Luina mocked. The bitch.

The guards escorted me out of the room and led me down a corridor. We made a left turn, then a right, before finally approaching a large hallway. They led me down one hallway and then another for what felt like several minutes before we ended up on a lift that took us *down*. I had no idea how deep into the ground this place went, but apparently it went pretty far.

After a moment, the lift shuddered to a stop, and Luina and President Dale got off first. They scanned their badges, hands, and eyes before a large metal door swung open. Inside it, there were at least a dozen guaramen, all at attention.

We walked past them to the end of the hallway where another metal door stood. President Dale approached it and entered a code before it opened.

The pit of my stomach became even more uneasy and the pounding in my head intensified. Inside the room, there was a large glass window. A couch with a liquor rack sat in front of it with two glasses of wine sitting on a golden coffee table, half drunk. A large black, furry rug sat underneath the couch and coffee table. The place was very bougie. Completely at odds with the rest of HQ. They escorted me past the couch to the window. My breath caught.

Fletch. He was chained to a single chair in an entirely metal room. His face was bruised and covered in several shades of purple and red. His lip was busted open, and his left eye was swollen completely shut. Part of his face was missing skin, exposing his right jaw and several molars. A cry escaped my lips.

He didn't even look alive. His hair was slick and clung to his face and neck, red coated the front of his chest, the floor, and practically every inch of his body was caked in both dried and fresh blood. He had a large knife in his left forearm, pinning him to the chair. Blood seeped from the wound. His stomach had been slashed, and I could see his body was having a hard time self-healing. The fingers on his right hand were broken, jutting out in several unnatural directions.

"Mother Blood. What have you done?" Tears pricked at my eyes. This wasn't happening. This was a bad dream I was about to wake up from.

"As you can see, Fletcher has been interrogated and has yet to provide any useful information," Luina's voice was matter-of-fact. Interrogated?

"He hasn't been interrogated; he's been mutilated!" I began pounding on the window, willing it to budge. It didn't so much as shudder.

"You say tomato, I say tomata," Luina remarked as several guaramen pulled me back from the window. I twisted and fought; I kicked their shins and dug my nails into their forearms, but it was no use. They pulled me away from the window, away from the only male I'd ever known as a father. Tears openly poured down my cheeks, blurring my vision. Was he even alive?

"Enough! Get ahold of yourself Tatealia and be thankful that's not you. At least not *yet*," Luina quipped.

Luina had the nerve to admonish and threaten me? After she'd just stripped away the one male I could always count on; the one male I loved?

I would kill her. I would kill Luina. She would pay for this. The guaramen subdued me, two on each side, they held me bound, and they too would pay. I stared helplessly at Fletch. His chest rose. Thank blood, he was alive. But he was in so much pain.

President Dale sat down on the couch with a sigh. He reached over and poured more wine into his crystal stem and then began to drink as he loosened his belt. The bastard was getting comfortable? He was positioned to see Fletch perfectly. Entertained?

I'd kill him too.

"Luina, please proceed," he commanded. Luina nodded before approaching a door I hadn't seen before at the edge of the room. It was completely made of glass and had no handles or visible markers except for a faint line that highlighted its presence. She pushed on it, and it opened. Stepping inside, she approached Fletch.

The guaramen at my sides dragged me closer to the window. I could practically reach out and touch him.

"Fletcher. You've been rather difficult. I was just informing someone I believe you care about that we've been interrogating you. This will go much smoother if you'd simply answer our questions." Fletcher lifted his head and my heart ached. His right eye was blood-shot. A whimper escaped my mouth. My Fletch, the male who had protected me and raised me since my mother's death, was in pain. He was so strong, but right now he looked broken.

"Where are the Untish Tribe members?" Luina asked.

Had everyone lost their minds? The Untish Tribe were mythical!

"Go. To. Hell." Fletch spat blood at Luina, it landed just short of her feet.

Luina smiled, cruel and full of promise. "Very well." She reached out and gripped the knife in his right forearm. She twisted it and Fletch released a scream.

"Stop it!" I shouted. I pulled at the guards gripping my arms, but their hold only tightened.

"Where are they? What are they planning?" Luina questioned Fletcher again.

Still, he didn't respond. This time she yanked the blade from his right forearm and then stabbed it into his left forearm. His screams radiated throughout the room as blood spurted from both the old and new wounds.

"Please! Stop! Let me ask the questions, please just stop!" I turned to Collin, who was reclining back on the couch, a serpentine smile across his lips.

"I'm afraid that's not going to work my dear." He took another sip from his wine as Fletch's screams resounded again. My heart constricted. I couldn't lose him. I couldn't.

"Please, if he knew something, he would've told you. He's a professor, a teacher. He nurtures life. He doesn't destroy it!" Tears began to fall down my cheeks.

"Fletcher, you've left me no choice," Luina spoke as she looked through the glass and met my eyes. It was one way, I was sure of that, and yet she knew where I was standing. She nodded, and the guaramen holding me moved toward the other corner. Another door, outlined in glass and barely noticeable. They pushed it open and dragged me inside.

I was in an adjoining cell to Fletch. Only a glass wall separated me from him.

"If you'll look in the other room, I think you may find some motivation to start talking."

Fletcher raised his head, his one good eye locking on me.

"Tate!" His voice broke as he spoke my name through his cracked jaw. His good eye widened and I could see panic rooting.

"Fletch! I'll get you out, this is all just a misunderstanding!" I wasn't sure if he could hear me, but I prayed he could. We may be separated, but we were not alone.

The guaramen holding me threw me forward with enough force to bring me to my knees, the impact breaking my skin. I didn't care. Fletch could see me, he was aware and hadn't been mutilated beyond repair. We could work with this.

"I'll ask you one more time Fletcher, where are the Untish and what are they planning next?"

Fletch's eye looked at me and filled with tears. I could see it, the apology. Reality struck me deeply. This wasn't a mistake. He knew something, he actually knew something, and from his face, I could tell he wasn't about to break.

"Fletch?" I asked, my voice cracking. I stood up and rushed the glass wall, pressing my hands to its smooth surface. This couldn't be happening. I knew Fletch; I trusted him. He was a good male. Not a traitor.

Had Arithi and Mardi actually been right? Had they been working with Fletch and did they know about this Untish Tribe? I didn't know much about the myth, but what I did know suggested they were shifters or dragon riders. I couldn't exactly recall because it was absurd. And yet...was it possible Arithi was a part of the Untish Tribe?

The dragon symbol I saw in flames when I was burning came to mind. Dear Blood. The reality began to sink in.

"I'm sorry." Fletch's voice broke as he looked at me.

Those two words crushed me. President Dale's accusations were right, and now they knew that. There was no misunderstanding here. Fletch was an enemy of the Glenn.

"So be it. Perhaps this will change your mind." Luina looked at me, and for the first time I saw an expression of regret. The guaramen shuffled out of the room quickly and the door shut with a click.

I stared at Fletch. I didn't know the male in front of me. Even if he did betray the Glenn, would he really betray me? Did my mother really commit the treason she was executed over? Was my life full of lies?

Before I had time to ponder it further, a clicking sounded, and the room began to hum. The vents overhead began to pump air into the room. An ugly green fog began to seep in. Fletch's eyes widened as the gas hit the floor and began to rise, reaching out for me. I pounded on the glass, willing it to break. To be with Fletch one last time, if even for a moment. Willing him to deny the charges, to plead not guilty, to spare me.

"I'm so, so sorry." Fletch's broken voice would not spare me. No, he'd sacrifice me too.

I wasn't sure if it was the agony from my breaking heart or the gas, but my body dropped to the ground and began to convulse in pain.

CHAPTER 32
TATE

Green was a funny color. The color of sickness, mold, and death. It figured that the green gas would be toxic and incredibly painful.

"Tate!" Fletch? Was that his voice? What'd he want?

Screaming filled my ears, so loud it hurt. Who was screaming?

My throat hurt, it was sore and felt strained. It burned. My skin burned, my lungs burned—everything burned. And that incessant female wouldn't stop screaming. Where was she anyway? My eyes, they're shut. Why can't I open them?

Realization dawned on me. I was the female screaming. It was my voice echoing back to me. Pain, I was in such great pain. Delirious pain. The gas must have a hallucinatory effect.

"Stop! Please, she's just a kid! She has so much life ahead of her! She is NOT involved!" Fletch's voice sounded wet, like he was screaming through tears or blood. Which one, I didn't know. Perhaps it was both. An interesting combination to say the least. Why was he screaming?

"Tell us what the Untish want," a female voice spoke, cold and uninterested. I could hear her voice. It was quiet for a moment. Where was the female who had been screaming?

"They, they..." Fletch's voice was cut off by loud screams of female agony. Where was that female? And why couldn't I see?

"They are seeking information on a top-class weapon they believe the Glenn is forming. I don't know where they are, but I know they mentioned the Southern Outpost. They don't give me specifics; I'm just an intel source for them!" Fletch's voice faded out. What nonsense was he was speaking? Who were the 'they' he spoke of?

"What intel?" that cool voice screeched.

Pain seared through me again; I opened my eyes and instantly regretted it. Female screams became my everything, overwhelming every sense.

I was nothing and everything. I was at home and not; I was here but unaware. I shook my head, focus. Something important was happening, but what?

"Nothing important! Schedules, recent enlistments, access to the library records digitally—" Fletch's voice ended in a grunt of pain. Why was Fletch here?

I dug my hands into the ground, cold tile, wet and sharp, met my fingers. I raked my fingers over my body as I rolled, trying to rip my skin off—to end this pain.

"Stop! I swear that's all I know!"

"What intel from the library?"

"Genealogy records. I don't know why they wanted it."

Female whimpers and shrieks engulfed me. Someone needed to shut her up. I clawed at the thing crawling over me, my skin was not my own. No, it was a foreign body, an alien attacking me, trying to eat me from the outside. I just needed to break its grip. I sliced at myself, over and over, trying to get the creature off of me.

"What date range for the records?" that calculated voice asked. What were they speaking of?

"The last hundred years, since the Great War. Please, END IT!" a familiar voice cried out, his words were sluggish and hard to hear.

My body twisted and jerked, the thing encasing me refused to let me go.

"Very well."

Snap! The spraying hum surrounding me shut off. Then a fan turned on, a sucking sound, and the air around me began to twirl. My nerves were firing rapidly—pain, I was in acute pain. How had I gotten here?

I opened my eyes. I needed to free myself of the thing attacking me, slicing me open. But everything was blurry. After several painful blinks, the pus in my eyes cleared enough for me to see my body. It was cut and torn, blood oozing from several cuts with greenish pus surrounding it. My skin was shredded.

If this wasn't hell, then it was a hellish place. Funny, I was funny. That female laughed. Where was she?

"Fletcher Backshy, I hereby sentence you to death by fire," a shrill voice proclaimed. I knew that voice, who was it?

Everything was still blurry. My right eyelid wouldn't open all the way, it was stuck, and it was gooey. I tried again, this time both eyes opened most of the way. Bright orange air danced with a hint of blue. It reflected off of glass. Fire. I saw fire.

"Tate, no matter what, know that my love for you was true. You... you always were my firecracker in life. Shine bright from your heart, only it knows the truth!" Fletch's voice broke.

He was here. He was speaking to me.

I tried to focus, but the light was too bright. I could make out a silhouette in the flames. A male from the looks of it. Screams filled the room. Male screams. They were familiar?

He was in pain. He was the male in the fire.

My brain was trying desperately to compute what was happening. Random facts. What was the correlation and where had Fletch gone?

The sucking noise in the room stopped and this time mist fell. Little drops all over my skin. Each drop felt like needles digging in my skin. That female was screaming again. I looked around but I could not spot her.

The male's screams harmonized with hers.

Fletch? Flames, I saw flames on the other side of the glass. A figure was in them.

Horror, pure and undiluted, overtook me. Someone was being burned alive. I tried to stand, but my legs wouldn't cooperate. More fluid fell and began to coat my skin.

"Tate, you're going to start to feel some relief soon. The fluid will help, it's the antidote for the gas. Just be patient. You should lose consciousness soon." That horrible voice was croaking again. I knew I knew the voice, but I couldn't put it together.

Frustrated. I was angry.

A peaceful sensation began to fall over my skin, the pinpricks stopped, and the fluid became a welcome blanket to my core. The room fell silent. The female screams stopped, and the male ones apparently ended as well.

I heard only mist, drops of water, and the distant crackle of flame. My eyelids were heavy—ever so slowly, my eyes began to close. Numb, I was blissfully numb. I felt a nagging at the back of my mind. Something important was happening. Or was it? It didn't matter; nothing did as the welcome embrace of oblivion claimed me.

CHAPTER 33
TATE

I opened my eyes slowly. I was lying on a red velvet couch. A glass wall was in front of me with a coffee table nearby that held a freshly filled crystal stem of bloodwine.

"She's up," a female spoke. I followed the voice to the corner where a tall female in black stood. She was thin with black eyes and matching hair. Luina. What was she doing here? In fact, where *was* here?

I tried to sit up and immediately regretted it. Pain and nausea claimed me, sending me straight back to the cushioned couch.

"Medics, please," President Dale's voice registered next. He stood next to Luina, gazing into the glass wall. "Try not to move Tatealia, it will hurt until the drugs kick in." He was speaking to me, but why?

A male dressed in all blue scrubs approached me, kit in hand. He reached out and took my arm, then with his other, he pulled out a syringe. I pulled back; my skin was screaming at me. It was torn; cuts covered my entire arm. Looking down, I could see my black tank was torn and bloody. My flesh below was covered in crisscrossing slashes. The stench was nearly unbearable.

"Hold still, miss." The medic retrieved my arm, more delicately, and this time I allowed him. The pieces felt so close but so far. Nothing made sense.

The medic plunged the needle into my flesh with searing pain. He retracted the needle, leaving a cannula in my arm, and then pulled out another syringe.

"Wha...what," every syllable hurt, "is that?"

"It is a healing agent. It should have your skin good as new in the next eight to twelve hours." He paused, looking at me. He was waiting, I realized, for my approval. I nodded, unable to respond.

Something important had happened, I knew that. But what?

"It will come back. Memory disruption, hallucination, and cognitive impairment are all common side effects of the nitrous gas. I apologize for the requirement of it, however, given the situation, I'm sure you understand," Luina's cold voice triggered something. Panic began to seize my chest.

"Nitrous gas?" My voice was hoarse, and my throat felt raw.

"Yes. Your memory will return. In the meantime, have a glass of wine and when you feel well enough to move, the guards on the other side of the door will escort you out. Your convoy leaves first thing in the morning, approximately ten hours from now."

Convoy? They were speaking as if I were in the guara. I wasn't, I would never—

Flashes, memories began to assault me. I had been enlisted, assigned to the Eastern Outpost.

"Ahh, I see. I know you had registered at the clinic veil side, but given your infractions, I was informed you were scheduled for enlistment," President Dale spoke, turning from the window to focus on me. "My boy, Chance, was a good lad; but the guara made him a man. Taught him responsibility, maturity, and hard work. He's a good soldier now, a dux even. Someone I can be proud of. Just think of how you can serve the guara in years to come." He tapped his cane once before picking it up in his hand. "I'm off, please ensure Tatealia is given a room in the guara quarters tonight prior to her departure." The unspoken threat in his voice was there: the guaramen were my escorts, and they would ensure I was on board the circuit the following morning.

President Dale walked out of the room, Luina followed, neither bothering to look back. It wasn't lost on me that she didn't answer my question. I still had no idea why they'd used nitrous gas on me. Something was very wrong.

I sat up on the couch, taking a moment to steady myself. I could feel the medication working, my mind becoming less hazy. I reached out and grabbed the glass, my stomach felt empty; the drugs were making me nauseous. Hopefully, the wine would help it subside. I took a long gulp and nearly spat it out; my throat burned. I forced it down and then placed the stem back on the table, still half full.

The glass window stood there mocking me. I stood up, my head wavering. One minute. I would stand for one minute and then approach the wall. My shoes were missing, which meant the walk would also be uneven. Nothing new, and yet, dread began to pool in my stomach. My heart rate increased. I knew something ominous lay beyond the glass; somehow, I knew it was terrible.

Flashes began to return, green gas, a metal chair, blood...so much blood. Screams, female screams. Male screams. I couldn't stand still any longer. I began to approach the window. The room turned sideways as I started to fall. Putting my hand out, I caught myself on the coffee table and then forced myself upright again. I just needed to move slowly. One foot at a time. I would face this, see what lay behind the sheer wall.

The glass was just ahead now, and I could see a metal chair with black charred clumps on the ground. Organic matter. It was burnt flesh, black and red scorched blood everywhere. A scream escaped me.

Images came back. Fletch's eyes, his bloodied arm, the knife, his screams...the fire. No, no, no, this couldn't be true. I pounded my fists against the glass.

"FLETCH!" The glass wouldn't give.

His apology replayed in my mind. I was gassed because of him. He didn't stop it, not right away.

"No! Blood no! Please, not you too!" I limped quickly to the end of the room and pushed open the glass door. The entire chamber reeked of charred flesh. Smoke clung to the air. I rushed to the clumps on the floor. His remains. They were burnt to a crisp and completely unrecognizable.

They surrounded the chair, scattered across the floor. President Dale and Luina just left him like garbage.

A sob escaped me. This couldn't be real. I dropped to my knees before the remains and my hands began to shake. No, this was a bad dream and I'd wake soon. I had to. Fletch was the only family I had left.

Blood still boiled in a small puddle near the chair. They must've used a chemical fire.

Pure hate claimed me. I threw my head back and released a scream that came from the depths of my soul.

Fletch. My Fletch was gone.

Tears began to spatter across the floor, pouring down my face next to two streams of snot. I reached out and tenderly began scooping the clumps together, wincing as they broke apart at my touch. He was scattered. I desperately scooped chunks into my hands and scooted them closer together, as if I could somehow undo this whole thing. Bring him back.

The clumps kept crumbling at my touch. I was only making it worse.

I released another scream—the glass shook, and my body convulsed. I poured my pain and energy into the cry, willing time to rewind and for Fletch to come back to life.

But nothing happened.

Bitterly, I stopped scooping and sat there, unable to move. My vision was beginning to blur with tears as my breaths came in quick uneven pants. My nails were covered in his blood and charcoal. Fletch. I cried out his name again as I dug my fingers into the sides of my face and relinquished a sob that shook me to my core.

He was gone.

I could hear steps behind me, the guaramen were in the chamber.

"Why?" I wailed as I gripped the chair with my hands and squeezed. It dented from my touch. Cold, lifeless. This was the instrument that held my Fletch while he burned alive.

The chair was the last thing Fletch had contact with. He was so strong and withstood so much torture and pain. Then he caved...for me. I was his downfall. The reason he was no longer here. Perhaps had he not given them the info, he'd still be alive, and I'd be able to get him out, rescue him.

It was my fault.

"Grab her," one of the guards spoke from behind me.

Numbness settled in; I felt nothing as they surrounded me and yanked me to my feet. I stared at the charred clumps on the floor, the pool of blood. This was all that was left of him, of the male who was like a father to me.

Slaughtered.

The floor passed me by, but my eyes stayed locked on the spot where I last saw Fletch. Tears streamed down my face as I could feel my heart cracking inside my chest. I was broken. I was responsible. I had failed him.

As they escorted me from the room, despair began to claw at me—I hadn't even managed to bury him or give him any dignity. I'd only made it worse.

The guaramen escorted me down a long hallway. I had no idea where they were taking me, and I didn't care. All I could think of was Fletch. Tied to a chair. The male in the flames.

He died and gave up his cause because of me.

I didn't want to remember him that way. Didn't want to see his remains, the shadow in the flame, his beaten body...but the images would not leave.

"My love for you was true."

His voice haunted me. Everything about our relationship had been a lie. He betrayed the Glenn and never told me. He helped an enemy Vamp and never explained anything to me. He sat there while I was gassed and waited. I closed my eyes, letting the guards drag me.

Anger and betrayal battled with sorrow and guilt.

Happy memories of him from my childhood combated the bad. My mind was a battlefield of emotion, and yet, somehow everything was numb. They placed me in a small room with a cot and adjoining bathroom, the standard issue for a dokimos in the guara, before leaving.

I was alone, physically yes, but also in every way that counted; I was utterly alone. I sank to my knees and wailed. My Fletch was gone.

CHAPTER 34
TATE

There wasn't any window in my room. No way to tell the time. I'd laid on the floor in a fetal position for hours. Fletch was gone. My only father figure, the male who'd raised me, was no more. Everyone in my life that mattered had been taken from me, first my mother and now Fletch.

The guara was to blame. They executed both of them. But why?

Fletch had apologized, although I wasn't sure for what exactly. It sounded to me like he was admitting to conspiring with the enemy. Another Vamp. With individuals like Mardi, James, and Arithi, if I were to guess.

They did this to him. *They* put him in a position where he was gathering intel and betraying the Glenn and my mother—unless what they said about her was true and she too was a traitor. If that was the case, nothing in my life was what I thought.

President Dale's immaculate suit and cold, lifeless eyes came to mind. He'd stood there, calm and collected. Right along with Luina. Those bastards just stood there smug, knowing what I'd discover. What I'd be forced to live through...again.

He had been staring at Fletch's remains, speaking calmly to me about all I could learn from the guara. About what I could *be* for the guara.

I hated him, hated this whole damned world. Hated the *guara*.

A knock on my door sounded before a guaraman entered with a tray, a biscuit, and a carafe of blood. Breakfast.

"You have thirty minutes until we will escort you to the circuit. Shower if you'd like, but ready or not, you will be on the train at six am sharp. If I were you, I'd be in uniform unless you want to join the rest of the dokimoses, naked." He sneered at me and then turned and left.

Click! The door locked.

I stared dumbly at the tray on the bed; there was a folded uniform sitting next to it, sporting the standard issue black and blue. The blood next to it wafted through the air, it was warm. The scent of it sent my stomach turning. Vomit came from my lips, spraying across the floor and my legs. I heaved again, but it was dry. There was nothing left in my stomach. Cramping claimed my abdomen, my soul. At least I felt this pain.

For the first time since last night, I *felt*.

I sat there, marinating in my own bile. The stench was a welcome relief to my senses, overwhelming the memory of Fletch's charred remains and their odor. I sat there, rocking back and forth, my arms wrapped around my body. I began to tremble, shaking. My breaths came in rapid inhales, sharp exhales.

Not enough. Not enough oxygen, time, life.

My skin began to tingle as the vomit started to sink deeper into the still-raw flesh. Even with the healing, you could see the shadow of claw marks. Perhaps they'd scar. What did it matter? My soul was already marked by last night's events—I would forever bear *that* wound internally. I should bear what I'd done—what I'd caused Fletch to confess—on my skin externally, forever. A reminder of what occurred. What was taken. What I caused.

Water. If I set the marks in hot water, it may actually scar.

I stripped out of my clothes, noting for the first time *how* shredded they were. Good, more injuries to worsen. To ensure I forever bore the external scars that mirrored my broken heart, I cranked the shower water to its hottest setting and waited. Steam began to fill the air. Perfect. I stepped into the shower.

My skin was pink and pale, with crisscrossed slashes scattered across my arms, legs, and stomach. Bloody water began pooling at my feet as the water cleansed my skin. My blood. Fletch's blood. Mixing together in one last moment of solidarity.

Silent tears began to stream down my face in a river of pain. The heat from the water felt oddly good. It shouldn't, since vampires hated heat, and yet I found it comforting. I pressed the handle further, but it wouldn't budge.

Not hot enough.

I pushed harder and it snapped off, the heat increasing. I winced and then smiled. Maybe I was psychotic and enjoyed pain. I grabbed a bar of soap and began to scrub at my skin. The patches of blood stained me; they wouldn't remove easily. I scrubbed and scrubbed until my skin felt raw, until my gashes were bleeding fresh blood, and the old blood was finally gone, washed down the drain.

A knock sounded from the door; it was time to go. I stepped out of the shower and dried off before slipping into the uniform. My fresh wounds were starting to clot but undoubtedly staining the inside of my clothes.

I couldn't look at myself in the mirror. I couldn't face any of what had happened. Something was very wrong with me. I should be fighting this, running, screaming. But I didn't deserve life outside the guara.

Fletch was dead, in part, *because* of me. I deserved the painful reminder the uniform would bring. To spend my days in self-loathing. I should have been more aware. Should have listened to Fletch that night when he opened up rather than dismissing it for an old, drunk male's babbling.

Yes, comfort was not something I deserved. The door opened. Time for my sentencing.

I couldn't bring myself to exert any energy beyond basic mechanics. Everything was numb.

"You really should have eaten," one guard mumbled as the two guaramen escorted me, one on each side, down a large corridor and to the elevator. I was being led to the circuit, but somehow that didn't matter. Nothing did, because Fletch was gone.

CHAPTER 35

CHANCE

I appreciated the sponge bath, even if it was quick and not the long soak I wished for. Thank blood the circuit had a latrine with a bathing station. It had been purely practical to get most of the grit off, easier to focus. No, I wasn't trying to rid myself of the anxiety that plagued me from the last attack. I certainly wasn't trying to cleanse myself, there was no cleansing one's soul of that type of grime.

Holland and I had been reviewing our case files for hours. We'd gone over the personnel at the Southern Outpost until the roster practically bled. We'd run a cross-check on any family ties to other Vamps from the personnel along with any behavior indicating discontent or lack of allegiance. Each soldier was a good man. Each one had a long history within the Glenn.

A few had infractions, there were of course those who were forced to enlist, but none had a glaringly obvious reason to defect, to betray. The mere thought of it made my stomach turn. I was mentally accusing males and females, my men, of the worst crime possible. Each time I ruled one out as an obvious candidate, I felt relief and dread. I still wasn't any closer to ousting our mole and our resources were fairly limited by remaining afar.

The report from the Outpost concerning the attack was short. It listed the eight casualties along with the details of the damage. I recognized two soldiers: O'Conner and Leiner. I'd worked with them closely last year. Their deaths were a true tragedy.

I searched the database for images of the corpses, but they weren't there. So incredibly frustrating. Apparently, no one followed protocol anymore.

"I recognized one of them you know," I spoke for the first time in an hour. We'd been in this tin can all day poring over everything available to us while the circuit carried on toward the next settlement.

"One of who?" Holland's voice was fragile. Fatigued.

"The creatures."

She didn't respond. She just stared at me, waiting for me to offer more.

"He was a good male. His name was Shultz. I worked with him briefly last spring in the Eastern Outpost before I moved over to train at the Southern Outpost. He had a bright future. I don't even recognize what he's become."

"Dark magic can do that," she spoke softly. "Did he ever give any inclination of dabbling or breaking nature's laws? Sometimes it just starts out as a curiosity, and it can just go so wrong so fast."

"No, he never struck me as the magic-wielding type. He had no giftings that I knew of."

"Do you think he's involved with our mole?"

I hated that she voiced the question I'd been avoiding asking myself. The creatures were enemy-made, that we had taken for granted. No one could get away with creating dozens of those things in the Glenn without oversight noticing. Arche Shultz was a creature. Did that make him a traitor?

"I don't know. People change. The male I knew would have never betrayed his country. But, like I said, people change. Metamorphosis and all that shit."

She placed a delicate hand on my shoulder, each finger far too fragile to be capable of violence. And yet, she held her own. More than that really, she'd single-handedly shot and destroyed at least two dozen creatures. She was remarkable.

I reached up and cupped her hand with mine. The warmth from her creamy skin seeped into my calloused fingers. Her nails were filed to a short square, feminine yet practical. So much like this female.

I looked up over my shoulder and found her staring at our hands. I didn't think as I wrapped my hands around her waist and pulled her onto my lap. She smelled of lavender even after being stuck in a sweat box, pouring over papers. Astounding. She looked straight into my eyes with her brown ones, piercing me with a stare. I cupped her jaw with my left hand and tilted her head up further to mine, meeting her in the middle with my lips. I swallowed her small features with my obtuse ones. My right hand found its way to her formidable hip. Her curves were glorious—

She pulled back and placed a hand on my chest.

"What are you doing, Dale?" I could feel magic beginning to prickle at my skin.

"Oh no, this is an even playing field, Holland. No magic."

"But—"

I placed a finger to her lips, at which she arched an eyebrow. She was getting ready to pounce with a response no doubt.

"I think you're remarkable, Holland. Exquisite."

She studied me for a moment before adjusting on my lap and straddling me. One hand ran through my loose, wavy curls, scattered across my shoulders, as her other hand drew circles across my chest.

"Exquisite, huh?"

"Absolutely delicious."

"You've barely tasted." She leaned forward and placed a gentle kiss on my jaw. "How do you know I'm exquisite with a mere sample?" She kissed my cheekbone. "I mean, I appreciate the flattery, but it feels a bit half-hearted seeing as you've barely seen me as more than a soldier. Seems you've formed an opinion with very little research." She kissed my chin, then my jaw all the way up to my ear where she leaned in and whispered, "Not very protocol of you."

"Research, huh?"

"Yes. I appreciate a soldier who is more...thorough."

The last word sent shivers down my spine as her breath was hot on my neck. Desire was already burning, and I was hard. I was ready to more than taste.

"Let me be very, very thorough. Trust me, I never disappoint." I pulled her closer to my chest, practically crushing her in my embrace, and claimed her mouth with my own. She met me stroke for stroke with her tongue; she too was tasting. What a saucy little thing.

I cupped her ass with my hands and then dug one into her hair as the other climbed up her shirt. She let out a breathy moan, and I released her mouth and began to kiss her neck, starting at her ear and working my way down her delicate spine. I found her collarbone with my mouth and grazed it with my fangs, teasing. Testing.

She moaned again, but this time it was demanding as she began to grind on my lap. My cock got even harder. I wanted her, right here, right now, in this tin car as hot and stuffy as it was. No, I didn't just want her, I needed her.

I reached for her bra in the back and unclipped it, gently massaging her skin in tiny circles with my thumb. Her hair was soft in my hands as I moved her head back so I could continue my pursuit. She arched backwards into my hand as my mouth returned to her collarbone. I extended my tongue and licked the column of her chest down to her shirt. I unbuttoned the top one with my mouth, then licked the skin underneath.

She began to tremble underneath me. She'd see how thorough I could be.

My hand lowered on her back to the base of her spine and stopped, stroking lazy circles. Her breaths sped up, and she lurched even further back into my touch.

"Holland, you sure you're okay with this?" I asked, hating every moment my lips spent apart from her flesh.

"Yes," her answer was breathless.

That was all I needed. I lowered her to the floor and straddled her.

Slowly I moved my mouth to the next button and undid it, then made my way to the next, tasting her all the way.

"Thank Blood, because I intend to taste every part of you." I slid my hand up to cup her breast. Her nipples were peaked, ready. Practically as hard as I was.

"Oh blood, this is…"

"Exquisite?" I finished for her as I intended to do *in* her as soon as I could get my pants off. I reached the last button just below her belly button and took my time with it. I licked the inside of it, around it, and then finally popped the last button open. Now for the pants. She reached up, stopping me, hands on my shoulders, before she yanked at my shirt and pulled it off.

"Couldn't let you have all the fun, could I?" She pulled her hands over my chest slowly as she kissed each of my pecs before lowering herself backwards and yanking off her bra. She lay there half-naked, the most beautiful sight I'd seen all day. Her breaths were coming in short pants as she grabbed my arm and pulled me onto her. Her pink nipples were hard even as she lowered to her back.

"I thought you wanted a taste?" She turned her head at me as she opened her legs. Blood, I loved a challenge.

"You have no idea." I leaned over and yanked her pants zipper all the way down. Then with my hands I slowly, teasingly, pulled it off, getting a good grip of her ass as I did so. I pulled the last of the material off, revealing a hot red, lacy thong. Who would've thought this practical soldier wore something so frivolous? I leaned over and grabbed her panties with my teeth, scraping her inner thigh with my fangs. She let out a moan, and I repeated the movement as my right hand traveled up and grabbed her breast. I circled her nipple with my thumb before yanking again on her panties. Her moans escalated.

The train car jostled. We'd soon be at our destination, and I had no intention of leaving this business unfinished. I pulled her red panties all the way down to her knees before dragging them off the rest of the way with my hand. I put my tongue to her thigh and licked all the way up to her apex before dragging my tongue down her center.

Delicious.

She shivered as I repeated the motion, beginning to explore the inside as I teased the sensitive bud with my hand. She moaned as I pulled back and found the bud with my mouth and pulled. I slid one finger in, then two, and began to pump until I was knuckles deep in her warmth. I pulled out and resituated, getting ready to explore more with my tongue, when she pulled back.

"Uh-uh," she wagged a finger, "just a taste this time."

"You have to be fucking kidding me; this is my best stuff." The beast inside me roared.

The car jostled again as overhead beeping began signaling our approach.

"I'd like to try out the merchandise before this tin can stops, if you know what I mean." She pointedly looked at my engorged cock. I was nearly bursting from my pants with a massive erection. I smiled—I most certainly could oblige. I reached down to unzip my pants, but she stopped me with her hand.

"Allow me." She pulled at the zipper with her delicate fingers and paused, cupping me. Her face reddened as she did so, nearly to the shade of her panties now strewn on the floor. She yanked down and they dropped to my ankles. I stepped out of them as she slid her hand down the back of my underwear, cupping my ass.

"Not bad."

Was she kidding me? My ass was rock hard, nearly as firm as my manhood. I sat back down on the chair and pulled her with me. She straddled me.

"Well, since you wanted to test the 'merchandise' out, why don't you take point?"

"Don't mind if I do." She wasn't fazed in the slightest as she lowered herself onto me. Slowly, so painfully slowly, her core enveloped me until she reached the base of my shaft. Heaven, that's what this was. Pure warm, wet bliss. Satisfaction filled me.

She moved up and down, the friction was too much—I moaned as I dug one hand into her hair and the other to her butt. She continued moving, her scent was all I could think of—she was all I could see.

Lavender, she smelled of lavender. Hell, she tasted of lavender.

The friction from her motion was glorious. She picked up the pace as she dug her hands into my shoulders, scratching with the most pleasant pain I'd ever felt. I moved my hips to meet her move for move, thrusting and tightening my grip on her as I did so. She claimed my mouth with hers and yanked on my tongue as she came slamming down on me.

Too much, this was too much. I sucked her tongue back as I thrusted, once, twice, three times, and then with all-consuming pleasure, I came. She moaned and sunk deeper into my chest, grazing her fangs against my collarbone and then my neck, doubling the sensation I was feeling.

It was a release of power.

My vision filled with stars, and for a moment every nerve was hyperaware as endorphins flooded my system. Blood, I loved a good orgasm.

She panted as I held her there, our bodies slick with sweat. Slowly our breaths leveled off as we sat there holding each other, swaying with the motion from the train.

"I approve," she said before lowering her head to my shoulder and snuggling in. A smile pulled at the left side of my mouth; she truly was remarkable.

"Exquisite."

CHAPTER 36

CHANCE

exley was empty. Well, practically empty. The village's dux who met us, Dux Carran, seemed unfazed by the fact that the soldiers with us were barely outnumbered by the number of guaramen he currently had in the village.

"Where are all your men?" Holland asked, her short hair pulled back into an adorable and yet sexy pony at the base of her skull. I could still smell her; the after-sex breeze, as I called it, was very potent. From the look on Dux Carran's face, he could smell it too. I could feel myself enlarging in pride.

"It's a harvesting village. We manage a vineyard. We don't need many men."

I arched a brow.

"Maybe so, but since we arrived an hour ago and were taken to our quarters for the night, we haven't seen more than a couple dozen men here. Care to explain where the rest went?"

He glared at me, clearly not loving the challenge. His barrel chest rose with each breath, brushing the bottom of his long, ruddy beard.

"We are understaffed. Thank blood for you, we've grown tired of each other's company!" He clapped me on the back and let out a laugh. Was this guy serious?

"So, you're telling me that you haven't lost any men to uh, any strange events?" Holland asked. I could see her prepping to use magic.

"Business, business, business, eh? That's all anyone wants to discuss anymore! Tell me, how's ol' Bole doing? He still got a stick up his arse?" His accent accentuated the last word while he simultaneously threw his head back and laughed. "I can't imagine he was happy 'bout you two and all your *business*." He wagged his brows as he threw his arm around my and Holland's shoulders before starting toward the pub. "Aye, it's rude to talk all business before even having a drink with your host."

"You're not our host, so much as a *fellow* member of the guara, and it is your duty to see to our accommodations, as it is also your duty to apprise us of any irregular events." Holland's voice was rising as her footsteps sounded faster, attempting to keep up with Carran's large footsteps.

Dux Carran was actually fairly large for a vampire. So much so that I had a hard time keeping up with his strides, even with his arm around me, propelling me forward.

"And I shall, but first let me *see* to your thirst." He thrust open the door to the pub. "Aye!" He raised our hands in his in victory, the few unknown patrons raising their glasses to him in cheers. "Please, enjoy Bexley's finest, the best wine in the Glenn."

The pub smelled remarkably refined. No sweat or hoppy scents could be found. Instead, it was elegant, small tables with black cloths were scattered about. Candles lit the place and wine glasses graced every place setting. So at odds with our 'host'.

I'd be lying if I said I didn't want to partake.

"Helga! Some of our finest fer our guests." Carran led us to a table and gestured for us to sit. A large and rather busty vampire came swaying out from behind the counter, her standard-issue uniform was covered with a black apron. She poured liquid gold from the decanter and filled each of our glasses before winking at me and venturing back behind the counter. The place was glaringly empty. So incredibly odd.

"Where, Dux Carran, are your men?" I demanded. Enough of this show.

"Ach! Can't you have a drink and then talk business? You kids are all the same, business this, HQ this, protocol this. For the love of blood, have a drink with a fella before hounding him with bureaucratic bullshit!" He grabbed his goblet and threw the contents back, some dribbling down his beard, before reaching for the decanter and refilling his glass. His demeanor sorely lacked grace.

"Dux Carran, thank you for your er, hospitality, but really you must answer our questions. There have been some *concerning* events," Holland tried again to get an answer from him.

"Aye! Dire indeed. But first, take a sip lass! *Then* we'll talk." He downed the glass again before refilling, white wine continuing to wet his beard.

"White usually isn't what I drink." She sniffed the glass. It was abnormally white. Where was the blood?

"You never know until you try!" He filled Holland's glass, spilling some on the tablecloth, before pushing the glass closer to her.

Holland looked irritated. She was not used to this lack of coherence from another soldier, especially one of equal rank. The air began to tighten but I shook my head. She shouldn't use magic on him. She'd used it too much already, and with the potential mole and their network, we really shouldn't be showing our hand just yet. She seemed to understand and the pressure in the air dissipated.

I lifted the glass to my mouth and took a drink. Fruity flavors assaulted my pallet in robust energy. Crisp and light.

"Delicious." I took another sip and Holland followed suit. The wine was actually very good, it tasted aged, but it also lacked a certain iron flavor. "But I must ask, where's the blood?"

"Ach! Youth always has to mix what shouldn't be mixed. Tell me, have you ever tasted wine this pure?" He swirled his glass before downing it.

"Can't say that I have, mostly because I prefer it to have nourishment to it. You know, *blood*. The thing we need to live," I replied dryly. Dux Carran was beginning to get on my nerves.

"Tell me, Dux Carran, where are all the humans in this settlement?" Holland asked, taking another sip; she apparently liked the flavor.

"In the cafeteria." He snorted.

"The what?" Holland choked on some of the wine and then proceeded to cough, trying to catch her breath.

"Aye, the place where we feed from livestock, if you know what I mean." He winked at us before reaching for the bottle, but I reacted faster and grabbed it first, holding it out of his reach. If he wanted to play, fine. I was all game.

"How many guaramen are at this settlement? I need a number."

"You're messing with the wrong dux, boy," he growled as his eyes squinted. Good, let him be pissed.

"Boy or not, I hold the wine and if you want another glass, you'll answer a very basic question. What is your headcount?"

He studied me for a minute before taking a hand up to his unruly beard and pulling on a single strand that was braided, beads hanging from the end.

"Not that I answer to you, but we have just shy of a hundred, last I counted."

"A hundred? That's a skeleton crew!"

"According to documentation, you should have at least five times that amount. Where did all the personnel go?" Holland's eyes were wider than I'd ever seen them—the light brown shade lightening to almost pure gold.

"Ach. We've had some incidents." He reached across the table and yanked the bottle from my hands before putting it straight to his mouth and downing the remaining contents, spilling a good portion of the wine.

"Incidents? Care to expand?" Holland pried. I could see her physically restraining the magic begging to be released. To speed up this painful process.

"Aye." He dropped the decanter and it clanged to the floor. "Creatures have been attacking us for the past month. We've lost a lot of men." His voice was slightly slurred as he pulled the back of his hairy hand across his mouth, wiping away the remnant of wine.

"When was the last attack? Why wasn't it reported? What measures have you taken to prevent future loss?" Holland's questions peppered him.

"Lass, let's get one thing straight. I'm the dux here. This is my village. I take any loss personally. I have filed reports and oversight has simply instructed me to continue harvesting grapes and report any future problems. I've filed three reports."

"But I didn't see any—"

"Ach! They probably wouldn't be there."

"That's not protocol. If there's an attack, you should be receiving reinforcements and investigators from Oversight," I spoke. Surely Dux Carran was just covering his ass; oversight would never let multiple attacks simply slide.

"You're cute, kid. And you're green, it shows." He pushed back from the table and stood up. "I'll be going to get a meal now. You're welcome to join, but I'll warn you to be polite. My men are hungry and even with our limited personnel, there's a supply issue, as I'm sure you've seen with the last settlement. Bole's correspondence certainly has made that clear." He sauntered to the door.

Holland looked at me, questions shooting from her eyes. Vessels, he had to be referring to vessels. I didn't particularly mind feeding from them, but it also wasn't something I frequently did. I often just drank from blood bags or bloodwine; vessel feeding often turned intimate which clouded my judgment. Plus, too few vessels meant it could turn violent.

In prasinos, vessel feeding wasn't allowed; only high-ranking officers could partake in a direct feed. The rest of us got cold blood. Even with my new status as dux, it felt strange to feed from vessels while away from HQ.

"Don't get me wrong, I understand the need to feed from uh, vessels, but I'm not sure I'm comfortable doing it," Holland said. For the first time since I'd met Holland, her vulnerability was shining.

"I know, but we need to feed Holland or else we may not be strong enough if another attack should come…"

She gulped in response, eyes lowering to my lips. Yes, feeding certainly could turn intimate.

I grabbed her hand and led her out of the pub, following in the direction our friendly giant went. I could see him up ahead entering a B&B. We followed him inside. It, like the pub, was surprisingly elegant. Fine cushions adorned the occupied couches, the chandelier appeared to be gold and crystal, the floor a fine marble. Each couch had at least three vampires feeding from a vessel. Some clamped around the neck, others the arms, and some chose the more intimate feeding of the thigh. Holland took a step back, uncertainty filling her eyes. I stopped her with a hand to her shoulder.

"Trust me?"

She bit her lip and then nodded. I needed to find an available vessel. That would appear to be a problem. I glanced around the full room, every vessel already appeared to be in use. Looking toward the back, I noticed a door, so similar to those at the outposts designed for high-ranking officials.

Pushing it open, I found a large conference room filled with chaises, rugs, and candles. Ah, as I guessed, this would be where the more intimate feeding would occur. In the back, I spotted Arche Damaris feeding with two other arches from our group. They all appeared to be in a blood haze. That vessel looked pretty close to dry. I began heading that way and walked past several sensual scenes. Two vampires going at it while feeding from the same wrist of a vessel; a vessel and a vampire enjoying the sensual high that came from feeding; a group of naked males and females all engaging in some type of post-feed orgy with at least one human.

Holland gripped my hand tighter. She was clearly uncomfortable with the scene around us.

"Holland, have you ever group fed before?"

"I don't see how that's any of your business." But the red in her cheeks was answer enough. I refocused ahead of us; this would be a *very* public group feed. But with no bloodwine or bags and a limited supply, I didn't see any other choice. We needed our strength.

"I'll make it as smooth as possible. You don't have to do anything you're not comfortable with."

We reached Arche Damaris, and I yanked him up from his feed. He was blood-drunk. Naturally, he'd lack self-control.

"Damaris. Get your act together. Get outside and stand watch, and for blood's sake, pull your pants up." He barely registered what I said, the haze was still too thick. I slapped him across his face and he went flying backwards, careening into the wall. I probably shouldn't be enjoying this as much as I was, but the punk was getting on my nerves. My very hungry nerves.

"Get outside now."

He blinked at me and shook his head. He was responding much quicker than I would've guessed. "Damaris, grab some men and take them with you. I want a group of at least five outside. Got it?" I turned, spotting an open vessel at the back. She looked plump, hopefully she was juicy.

"Dale." He reached for my arm and turned me back.

"Dux Dale to you, arche," I growled at him. Hunger mixed with the scent of blood was beginning to make me irritable.

"Dux Dale, something's off here. Magic, I can sense it."

"What type of magic?"

"Like at my last settlement but different. Stronger somehow. It just feels off. Dark."

I didn't like this. We needed to leave, but first we needed to eat. What a fucking mess.

"Find Dokimos Drew, blue-haired female, all intrinsic like, and stay with her. Get a group of at least ten men who are at least partially fed and be prepared to depart at any minute. Notify any of our soldiers who haven't fed that they need to do so immediately as we won't be staying here long." I paused, dread pooling in my gut. "And Damaris, if anything occurs, I want you to notify us immediately. Take Dokimos Drew and get her to safety. Do you understand?"

He nodded, grabbing the two blood-drunk arches nearby and escorting them to the door. The vessel I had spotted was now in use. Damn it!

Another vessel lay before us, lifeless. I checked and found a very weak pulse. This wouldn't do at all; if we fed, we'd drain her completely and then be responsible for breaking the no-kill law.

"Perhaps, I can assist." Dux Carran approached, a brunette male in hand. His eyes were sharp, and he appeared flushed—human and very ripe.

"Very kind of you." I grabbed the vessel and lowered him to the couch, more aggressively than necessary, but I was done taking things slow. I pushed the existing vessel off and she landed on the floor with a rather loud thump.

Turning to Holland, I offered her his wrist. She hesitated.

"What's wrong lass, don't tell me you're one of those human-loving pacifists?" Carran let out a loud rumbling laugh, it nearly drowned out the surrounding sensual moaning.

"A bit of privacy would be appreciated, dux," I spoke, winking at him. I didn't care what I was implying; I needed him gone.

"I bet it would. Lucky bloke." He made a scene of eyeing Holland up and down before wagging his brows at me and lumbering away.

"Dale, I don't know about this. I mean, maybe we should just leave now. I heard Arche Damaris, and this seems like an unwise use of time."

"Holland, can you trust me?"

Her eyes shone with hesitant trust. Enough, it would be enough.

I led her closer to the vessel; he was clearly high on something. Hopefully it wouldn't cross through the feed. I knelt to one side of the chaise with Holland opposite me. I lifted his arm, gesturing for her to do the same, and then clamped down on his wrist. Warm, iron-rich blood assaulted my tongue. It was delicious. It tasted of raspberries and grapes. I hadn't had pure blood like this in far too long.

A moan ripped from Holland as she dug deeper into his wrist, blood leaking around her mouth. Pleasure roared through my system; I could feel my energy stores refilling. I took another deep drag and savored the taste. There was something underneath the blood, something I hadn't tasted before. I couldn't place it; it was elusive yet familiar. Another moan from Holland had me reaching over with my free hand to cradle her neck. Her eyes were shut, and she seemed to be enjoying herself.

I stroked her neck with my thumb and gently dug my fingers into her scalp. I took several more drags as I focused my senses on Holland. Her pale skin was glowing, blood sensually dripped from the corners of her mouth. She was blissfully oblivious to the crowded room around us. Amazing.

I closed my eyes and adjusted my fangs on the vessel. I could feel his supply running low, I would need to finish soon, as would Holland. I felt a petite hand reach over and caress my chest. Holland. She suddenly pulled me back from the vessel and walked around the chaise to straddle my lap. Her face was speckled with blood and her eyes were hazed. She had more restraint than I did. I reluctantly let the vessel go and grabbed Holland around her waist. I was hungry, but for something *other* than human blood.

She claimed my mouth with hers before I could even move. The taste of iron and her sweet saliva claimed my senses. I pushed the vessel off the chaise, he too fell to the floor with a thump next to the woman, and then I lowered Holland to the couch. I dug my hand into her light brown hair, undoing the tie that held it in place. Her short locks fell over her shoulders, just dusting them with their ends. My other hand found her lower back and began to stroke her skin in tiny circles, slowly moving lower. She moaned into my mouth and reached behind me, sliding her hands into my pants. She stroked a line up my ass to my back.

Energy erupted through me. I needed her now.

I pulled back and yanked off my shirt as she ripped hers open and then yanked down my pants. I was blood-drunk, I knew that, but still I found my bulge impressive. She moved her pants down too, revealing a turquoise thong that contrasted her delicate skin tone so perfectly. It hugged her generous hips and accentuated her curves. Fuck me; she never stopped surprising me.

I lowered myself to her, kissing her belly button and then slowly worked my way up. I unclamped her bra, a perfect match for the thong, and yanked it off with my teeth before claiming her left breast. I pulled at her nipple with my mouth as I swirled my tongue around it. The sweet taste of her sweat filled my mouth; a salty iron that was incredibly intoxicating.

Her hand gripped my shaft and I nearly lost control at the contact. I could feel the pressure building, demanding release. Not yet, the pleasure of the pain was such a huge part of euphoria.

I moved my mouth from her now peaked nipple and licked slow, lazy circles around her breast as I worked my way up to her collarbone and found the delicate spot, perfect for fangs. If it weren't illegal or I were an irresponsible kid, I would engage in that pleasure too; but I still had enough wits about me to resist. Her grip tightened on my shaft, and I bucked. The motion she began had every nerve ending begging for more. She worked her way up and down the length of me, the perfect pressure and slickness from my sweat, her sweat, and precum made her motions slick.

Slowly, she guided me to her entrance, and I didn't hesitate. I thrusted inside and the pure warmth encased me. I found her mouth with mine and began to explore it. She rocked her hips in pace with mine and met me thrust for thrust. Pressure kept building and she released a moan as her hands dragged down my back, fingernails digging in and no doubt leaving marks. Ones I'd proudly bear.

Release exploded through me, and my body trembled, trying to contain the effort, pleasure overwhelming my senses. She shuddered in turn, tightening around me and then releasing.

We lay there for a minute, breaths heavy, blood-haze thick. The whole room felt numb and quiet. Yes, it was common for group feedings to turn intimate, but with Holland, it was more. I hadn't had a high like this since Tate.

CHAPTER 37
TATE

My hands were still numb and clammy. I took several shallow, rapid breaths trying to get as much oxygen as possible. I was moving. They led me down a hallway, a turn here, a turn there. It was a labyrinth. My feet were moving but I wasn't really sure where I was going or where I'd been. Someone said something—instructions? The circuit was just ahead. I was shoved inside and numbly searched for a seat.

The train car was packed. Excitement stirred on many young faces. Only a few looked unsure or regretful. None mirrored my expression.

I moved toward the next connecting car, also full. This one noisier than the last and mostly full of males who were quite literally arm wrestling over the seat cushions. I continued on through the testosterone-filled air and worked my way to the exit door. Perhaps normally I'd have minded the ogling eyes, the jeers, the whispers. Now? I felt nothing; no annoyance, anger, or indignity. I was empty.

After moving through five cars that held roughly a hundred and fifty dokimoses and arches, I finally found a half-full one and took an available seat at the back in an empty row. I fumbled with the seat belt, trying to close it.

Soft brown eyes filled with pain: Fletch's eyes.

"I'm so sorry." Some of his final words.

They changed everything.

They meant that he had in fact betrayed the Glenn. That in some twisted way, Luina was in fact exercising justice. It didn't *feel* right though. Fletch wasn't a bad guy, and I knew if he truly had betrayed the Glenn, there had to have been a good reason. I just wish I knew what it was. The car jostled and I swayed with the movement. We were moving. I could see several other dokimoses across from me, some sat next to me, all strapped down in their seats. My peripheral told me this too had become a full car.

"I can't believe we're here. I mean, I knew today would come, but damn it's actually here!" a female voice squealed, getting higher pitched with every word. "We're *finally* doing something important, making a difference, protecting the future!" So much for being left alone to my thoughts.

"Please, I knew I'd end up here. It's what *I* was made for," a male answered.

"Well, *I* wasn't sure. But I'm glad I did. My brother joined the cause last year and my sister several years prior. My father and mother are both still serving, high-ranking officers and all."

"You don't say?" the male sarcastically replied.

Fantastic, these two *knew* each other.

"Yeah, yeah. I've said it before but come on! It's so different to live *this* reality. I mean, we all knew serving was required and I always wanted to er...guard, protect. I just never pictured it being like this, so raw and exposed. So thrilling! I thought I'd be stuck within the confines of the sacred, but here I am." She sighed. "Still, I'm surprised since I don't have that much self-restraint."

"You don't say," the male repeated, his voice dry but also offering a note of fondness. Gross. Just get a room already.

"I know, I look all put-together with my pristine braids and no makeup motto, but deep down I *love* adventure. The idea of being a traveling guardian—" she coughed, as if embarrassed by her words.

Traveling guardian?

"I mean, guaraman, it's just something I've dreamed of. A real-life protector. No dusty books for me!" The chatterbox continued. "I mean, I love research and learning, but have you ever spent that much time in a library? *Boring*," she drew out the last word and then ended with a snort. The male grunted in response. Her polar opposite in every way.

"What about you?"

"Vala, she may not—"

"No one wants to be alone, not truly," she cut him off.

They were talking to me I realized.

I pulled my eyes up from the floor and assessed these two for the first time. A female, nearly six feet tall, sat across from me. Her dark skin complemented the blue-black uniform. Her hair was, as she had said, divided into several delicate braids, its dark color highlighting the blue undertones of the shirt she wore. Even without makeup, her face was feminine and delicate. A rhinestone nose ring sporting a diamond graced her left nostril. She raised her brows at me, clearly waiting for an answer. What had she asked?

"You do know how to speak, don't you? Or are you just not much of a talker? See you would be *perrrfect* for research. I mean those librarians are all like, 'shhhh' and 'no talking' and oh my gosh, it would just be impossible for me to do well there."

"You don't say," the male next to her spoke. His tan skin was accented by sandy red-brown hair that was buzzed, giving him a stern appearance. A standard issue guaraman if I'd ever met one.

"*Ha-ha*," she side-eyed the male. "I know I talk a lot but why not? We have hours of traveling before we get to our destination and I'm all about the chitchat and expressing myself. So much better than thinking about how we're in a tin can buried underground with a bunch of vampires and like, no food," Vala—I gathered—finished before visibly shuddering. "So, why'd you join, honey?" She was talking to me again.

She reminded me of Shae. Pain blossomed in my chest. So much had changed.

"I uh, was enlisted after a correction hearing." To my utter surprise, Vala looked speechless. It didn't last long though.

"So, you mean you *didn't* want to join? They like forced you on here? They can actually do that!"

"I just had other plans." I owed her nothing, no explanation or friendly conversation. I leaned back against the seat and tried to close my eyes. My head was pounding, and the bright lights were aggravating the pain.

"I don't understand you. I mean, my parents are always going on and on about what an honor serving is. I mean, we're like living in *thee* era. The Vamps are getting more and more sophisticated. My mother is a scientist, she's been telling me that President Dale is really making some breakthroughs and is pushing forward, challenging nature. I mean, now of all times to be a guardian and protect the whole, I'm honored."

"Vala." The male gave her a stern look. He fidgeted, looking unnerved.

"OK, Jared, message received." Vala rolled her eyes. "My mother is an inspiration. Nothing wrong with speaking about her." She leveled a challenging look at Jared.

"You know," her attention returned to me as she spoke, "she started out just like us and then moved up through the ranks. She then found her passion in science and turns out she's like *really* smart. So, she's a head scientist for—"

"Uh-hem," Jared cleared his throat. "You look really nice today."

Vala blushed a bit before grabbing a stray braid and twisting it around her finger. "Say more." She lowered her face to her palm, resting her elbow on her lap. Ever the lovesick puppy.

I tried to tune them both out. I didn't need to know the personal history of these two.

"Oh, you find me entertaining alright, Jared darling."

"I do?"

"Hmmm. We both know I'm the most fun you've had and will ever have."

Great, now they were openly flirting. I tried to focus on the hum of the circuit. It would be eighteen hours before we stopped at a settlement for the night; I guess they don't like the idea of hungry vampires taking desperate measures while contained in a tin can. I could survive it. Besides, what did it matter? Whether or not I had to listen to this childish flirting or sit here in the quiet. This was my punishment. Perhaps I deserved to have happiness rubbed in my face. Perhaps it would teach me to listen.

And so, I sat there, quiet and listening. For hours.

I'd managed to sleep for some of it, how much I wasn't sure. Vala and Jared talked, flirted, and made out the rest of the time. I'd learned that Vala was twenty, she'd chosen to join early by a year. She'd gotten straight A's in high school English but she struggled in math. Her mother sounded like a classic control freak who insisted she follow in her steps, just like her older sister, Jane, had—Jane, who was now serving at the research institute. I also learned that, even though I found Vala's insistent chattering annoying, I liked her spirit. She seemed upbeat even though her childhood home sounded more like a competitive performance-based boot camp. She apparently was good with an arrow and had good aim with a rifle. She'd taken karate religiously and had extensive swordsmanship training. All things the guara loved, which is why her father put her in those activities since she was *three*. Way too young if you ask me, but somehow Vala seemed to be thriving.

Jared, on the other hand, only contributed a few sentences here or there and mostly communicated with grunts or sighs. He reminded me a bit of Tim when he did speak.

The thought sent a pang of regret through me. Tim would never know what became of me. He wouldn't know I didn't willingly just dump him. Or had I? I didn't fight as I was dragged onto the circuit. I could've thrown a punch or tried running.

Then again, what did it matter? Lately, the only actions that mattered were the ones I made without knowing. Going home to look for Fletch. Being brought in for questioning. Hell, losing my mother and accepting Fletch's guardianship. Perhaps if I had insisted that I'd be alright on my own at nineteen, Fletch would have traveled to the EO like he had planned and become a professor over there. He could have been safe. So much of this was unknowingly my fault.

I clenched my jaw. This whole life seemed like a cruel joke. Like somehow in my infancy, I pissed Mother Blood off and was paying for it with my life and those I cared for.

Perhaps I was being vain in thinking I was the reason for their deaths, that I had that big of an impact, and yet, I felt the guilt of it all. They were gone. And I was here. A guaraman.

All I ever wanted was to make a difference. Now I wish I'd never touched a single life, never altered anyone's path.

My life was an utter shit show. Everything I believed in and thought I knew was wrong. Gari claimed to be taking humans *to* President Dale, which violated the guara's own laws. Unlikely. Fletch and my mother were alleged traitors. Unthinkable.

Fletcher was gone. This was the largest impossibility of them all. My fingers were twitching and my stomach felt like it was about to start eating my insides. I should have eaten this morning, but I couldn't stand the thought of putting anything down my throat.

Jared and Vala continued their bantering, mostly composed of Jared's grunting and Vala's interpreting his meaning and then rambling on more. If we didn't get there soon, I might actually throw up. The car jolted a little bit as the brakes sounded. We were slowing down.

"Alright, everyone listen up." A large male stood at the front of the car, projecting his voice in an amplifier. "I'm Dux Harder."

Vala snickered and Jared rolled his eyes. They both were very mature. Not.

"Quiet please, *children*." Dux Harder leveled a glare in our direction. "We will be at the Wassenvine settlement soon. Upon arrival, we will be meeting up with Dux Shaully and his team. They will continue with you onto the Eastern Outpost as your commanding officers. When we reach the settlement, you will behave according to the guara rules. You may enjoy food, shelter, and consensual sex if you'd like, however, you will not fight or act in any manner that disgraces the tattoo in which you bear. You will be departing tomorrow morning. This means you need to ensure you take your packs and weapons with you upon departure. We'll be there soon," Dux Harder finished before sauntering back toward the front where the duxes' quarters were. I bet they had luxurious chairs and better airflow up there.

"We'll be there soon, Jared!" Vala squealed. "And as long as it's 'consensual'," she mocked Dux Harder, "it should be fun. And for my sake, I do hope it's long."

Jared blushed at this. For all his tough male persona, he apparently was a bit of a prude. Figures.

The circuit slowed further and then stopped completely. The circuit hummed with mechanical sounds as steam was released, and everyone began to unclip their harnesses and stand. They stretched out their long limbs, Vala pretending to lose her balance and falling into Jared's arms. It was my turn to roll my eyes. The doors opened and the personnel began spilling out into the evening air. It was crisp and refreshing compared to the stuffy train car.

"You coming?" Vala looked at me pointedly. I hadn't moved since the circuit had stopped and our car was now practically empty.

"Yes." I stood and then reached above in the compartment. A standard-issue backpack was there along with a rifle. Just great, now I was supposed to carry this ridiculous pack and symbol of the guara. The symbol of death.

I sighed and slung the pack over my back before shouldering the rifle. Vala and Jared stepped out of the circuit first, and to my surprise, they paused waiting for me to catch up. Vala hooked her left arm through mine and placed a hand on Jared's shoulder, linking the three of us.

"Well, you two, we're here and I don't know about you, but I'm ready to have some fun. Once we're at the EO it will all be prasinos and rules blah, blah, blah. Let's party!" She launched us forward in the direction of a pub.

"I uh, think I might just go find a room and a cot." I tried to carefully pry myself from her, but her arm tightened.

"Uh-uh, nope. Not after you listened to me share my soul and learned all my secrets. All I know about you is that you're in a bad mood, don't want to be here, and apparently have no social skills. That or you don't like to talk."

"Val," Jared spoke, using his pet name for her, "maybe she just doesn't like us. Besides, I thought you wanted to have some alone time?" He cleared his throat at the end of his sentence.

"Hush, Jared. My sister told me that if you want to do more than just survive prasinos, you need friends. And what can I say, I'm a sucker for a charity case." Vala dragged us both behind her in the direction of the pub. We entered through a double sliding glass door and found the room packed.

"I don't think there's any room, so I think I'll just—"

"Oh no," Vala cut me off, "no chickening out now." She stood on her tiptoes, surveying the room "There! I see an empty table, let's move, gang."

Gang? Who did she think we were?

I sighed heavily; I suppose sitting with these idiots would help pass the time more than lying awake on a cot would.

She secured a small table, more of a barrel really, with stools around it and plopped down. She patted the ones next to her and Jared took a seat. I followed suit. A server dropped off a bottle of wine and three glasses.

"So, sweet cheeks, what's your name?" Vala asked, pouring herself a full glass.

"Excuse me?" This girl was something else.

Jared filled his cup and began to drink.

"Yeah, I mean I'm sure you've gathered my name is Vala, this oaf here is Jared—I've yet to ascertain his value in a certain area, if you know what I mean." She winked at me as Jared choked on his wine, spattering it across the table, some landing on Vala's lap. She shot him a glare before returning her focus to me.

"I, uh, my name is Tate."

"Tate, nice name. Tell me about yourself, Tate." She placed one elbow on the table and leaned into it.

"Well, as you know I'm here not by choice, I'm an only child and..." Both my parents are dead. That made for great table conversation, not. "Pass me the wine."

Jared obliged. I lifted the bottle straight to my lips and began to pull deep drags from it. Decorum be damned.

"Woah, slow down there, cowgirl. There's plenty for all." Vala reached for the bottle, but I stopped her outstretched hand with my free one.

"Nice reflexes! See Jared, she'll be a nice addition to our party." I emptied the bottle and dropped it to the floor. It shattered upon impact.

"If not a messy addition..." Jared clearly was disgruntled. I guess *he* wanted more.

"Noted, you're not into any messy kinks." Vala winked at him.

Jared's jaw dropped before immediately shaking his head and standing up. "I'll, uh, go get more," he mumbled under his breath.

"I'm not sure I understand the dynamics of you two." I turned to focus on Vala. The bloodwine started to fill my stomach and give me a nice buzz.

"What's to understand? He's trying to get me to go to bed with him and I might, but until then, I find you can learn a lot about a person by just talking and testing the boundaries with diction, and then analyzing their responses." She leaned in. "Not to mention, it makes for good foreplay."

I looked at her, really looked into her chocolate eyes. They were so similar to the color of Fletch's eyes. "You remind me of someone."

Fletch's eyes were soft when he laughed, a flashback to him on the couch, drunk on aged bloodwine and rambling on about the Untish Tribe. The charred remains clumped on the floor...

I shook my head. "I need more wine."

Jared returned in perfect time with three full pitchers, not bottles. As if that'd stop me. I grabbed a pitcher.

"Thank you, Jared." Lifting it to my lips, I began to gulp it down. I needed to lose consciousness. I couldn't think about Fletch or what happened in the glass room for another moment. Bloodwine began to drip down both sides of my cheeks and coat my shirt.

"Slow down there, girl. There's plenty, I promise," Vala's voice began to cut through the sound of my gulping.

"Val, if she wants to down it, let her. Maybe we'll actually learn more about this lost cause that way."

"Shut up, Jared. Good to note you don't consider a drunk female a compromised one and plan to take advantage."

"That is not what I—"

"Just shut it."

The pitcher finally ran dry. I placed it on the table with a thud and used my sleeve to wipe at my face. Both Vala and Jared were staring at me, eyes wide.

"What?"

"Nothing, you just, uh, must be hungry." Vala noticed the spatters of bloodwine coating the barrel.

"Something like that."

"You were telling us about you. You mentioned I reminded you of someone?" Even through the lightheaded haze taking over, Fletch's agonizing cries haunted me. His last apology and weird goodbye played through my head. I needed more wine; I needed to forget.

"Nope. Pass me the pitcher." I reached for it, but Vala's hand shot out and stopped me.

"You know, I get drinking to numb and that you don't want to be here, and don't get me wrong, I'm a party girl through and through—"

"Good to know," Jared mumbled.

"Shut up, Jared." She gave him a side glare before refocusing on me. "But I also firmly believe that talking is a better method of coping than just drowning yourself in wine."

Now she reminded me of Shae. Too much, it was all too much, and the haze of the wine was barely dampening the pain tangled inside.

"That's nice. But if we're going to be friends, Vala, let me make one thing perfectly clear, I set my own limits. I, and only I, decide how I want to cope, and quite frankly, you don't know shit about what I've been through."

"Why don't you tell me?"

"Nope. Now I'm either going to down another pitcher here or head to the bar and down one there. What will it be, *friend*?" I elongated the last word, drawing on it and all it implied.

She looked at me; I could see judgment laced with concern in her eyes. Screw her. I placed both hands on the table and began to stand, but she grabbed my wrist.

"Here." She handed me a pitcher and I drank.

CHAPTER 38

CHANCE

I could've laid there with her cradled beneath my body all day, but screams coming from outside made it clear that would not be an option. We were up in an instant, throwing on our clothes. I could see the clarity coming back as her eyes sharpened out of the blood haze.

"Where are my weapons?"

I pointed to underneath the chaise where I'd kicked them earlier. She reached down and quickly strapped her holstered pistol to her waist and grabbed the rifle. We made quick work of getting dressed and headed for the door. I slapped a few vampires on the way out and called out orders for the rest to get dressed and follow.

Outside, the scene was chaos. Guaramen were rapidly firing at an onslaught of creatures. Unlike the last settlement, where the creatures were mostly on all fours, the majority here were on *two* feet. Long, sharp talons came from their fingers. They were fast, far too fast for natural law. I leveled my rifle at a beast roaring toward a group of cowardly guaramen who were fleeing with no sense of discipline or sobriety. I fired once, twice, three times. All straight to its chest. It stumbled back, black blood oozing from its chest, before righting itself and looking at me. It smiled as it healed itself, scales covering its open wound in a matter of seconds. It roared and began to race toward me.

I fired again, aiming for its head and missed. It jumped and landed a foot in front of me. Its left hand swiped for me and I lunged right, but its right talons managed to graze my shoulder before sinking deeper into my abdomen. Blood seeped in its wake. I could feel its talons digging deeper as it looked straight into my eyes. Its irises were fully dilated, and all thoughts became murky. I was staring at a pool of black blood, and somehow, I was not afraid. My body was relaxing, my muscles slowing down and my adrenaline dissipating.

Holland screamed and lunged for the monster. She was atop the thing; her left arm gripped its throat for balance as she stabbed its brain with her dagger. Repeatedly, she buried the blade into the creature.

My senses came rushing back, pain raged from my side. I fell to the ground as the creature roared and began thrashing, trying to dismantle Holland. I needed to help her, but my wounds were deep. I looked around the yard for my rifle; it lay ten feet away. I began to crawl toward it, demanding my body not give out. I was built for this. I trained for this. I would not fail.

I grabbed the firearm and aimed up at the creature, finger just about to pull the trigger when it fell, lifeless. Holland jumped off its back as it crumbled and swiped black blood from her face.

"Dale, we are not prepared to take them. They aren't dying when shot. We need to evacuate. Now."

I looked around the yard and saw swarms of these creatures taking down armed guaramen left and right. Our few men were doing a good job of keeping the vast majority at bay while they backed up to the pub, but the creatures were overwhelming. It was a slaughter. A series of cries came from the vineyard as hundreds of black and grey bodies jumped and ran through the vines. We needed to leave, and we needed to do so now.

"Retreat!" I shouted as I stumbled to my feet, adrenaline once again coursing through my body. Holland kept up with me, step for step. We headed for our men.

A loud lumbering scream erupted as dozens of armed guaramen poured from the B&B with Dux Carran at the head. He had a spiked club and let out a battle cry as he ran straight for a creature and swung at its head. Black blood sprayed everywhere. He laughed as he turned to the next, decapitating that one as well.

"Like squashing spiders!" he shouted at me as he threw me his sheathed sword. I unsheathed it and ran into the fray. I sliced at a creature, removing its arm, and then its leg, and continued forward. The pain from my gut became numb as I surrendered myself to the battle.

More and more creatures poured into the settlement. Even with Dux Carran's additional prepared men, we were overwhelmed.

"We need to evacuate now!" I shouted to my men and Dux Carran.

"Ach! Sissy, we can take 'em all!" Carran shouted back as he swung his club haphazardly, nearly taking out one of his men, before taking down three creatures in one large swing. Animalistic screams sounded in the near distance. The vineyard. One glance told me hundreds would be on us in moments. Dux Carran seemed to make the same observation.

"Fall back to the circuit! Defend and retreat!" he called to his men.

We reached my group of men and I cut through two creatures' abdomens before turning to take down a third.

"This way! Head for the circuit!" Holland shouted to our men. I could see blue hair out of my peripheral and was thankful that Shae was still upright. A creature lunged at me and met its swing with a strike of the sword. It caught my blade in its talons and squeezed. My blade snapped and it opened its mouth to reveal several rows of sharp black fangs. I yanked my blade free from its grasp and buried its jagged end in its gut. It roared and stumbled back, swiping at me with its talons. I ducked and yanked my broken blade back before striking its throat.

Black blood blanketed my face, temporarily blinding me. It took advantage of this and swiped at me, sending me backwards. I tumbled to the ground. Wiping the blood from my eyes, I could see the creature jumping toward me, blood streaking behind it. This was it. I searched for my blade, but I no longer had it. The creature was beginning to lower; I would be dead in seconds.

A sickly thud sounded as the creature's projectile altered and it fell in a pile just inches from my body. A club was lodged in its back. Carran stood behind it, heaving heavily.

"Get to the circuit!" he shouted as he picked up my fallen, broken blade and dug it into the jugular of a beast nearby. I tried to get to my feet, but the pain in my stomach was too deep. I stumbled. Dux Carran ran over, yanked his club free, and then scooped me up, throwing me over his shoulder like a damn child.

He swung at beasts, taking one after another down, clearing our path to the circuit. All the while, I dangled helplessly from his shoulder like a fucking rag doll. I could see the circuit approaching. We were almost there. Dux Carran made a run for it. As I swung from his back, I could see swarms of black and grey blurs engulfing the settlement, grabbing the dead vampire bodies and feasting. Some were even throwing the dead over their shoulders and *returning* back to the vineyard.

A large humanoid creature jumped atop the pub, just like the other settlement, and howled. An eerie return of screeches and howls followed. Several creatures were charging us. They weren't more than a hundred yards behind. One unlucky soldier fell, disappearing in the herd of creatures. We were the last ones, the furthest back, and the next target for these things.

Carran huffed. "Hold on, kid!"

Before I could respond, he jumped, and we were airborne before landing inside a metal can; we made it to the circuit. The doors screeched shut as the train shuddered before jolting forward. Creatures screamed in the distance, their cries marking the beginning of something terrifying.

CHAPTER 39

CHANCE

My chest was heaving with heavy breaths. I could barely maintain a sitting position and was half leaning on a wall, bracing myself to stay upright.

"They got you good." Holland's light brown eyebrows knitted together in concern. "I thought you wouldn't make it..." her voice trailed off in uncertainty.

I understood it. Being emotionally vulnerable sucked. Perhaps the blood-haze sex had been a bad idea. I wasn't sure I wanted to be emotionally responsible for someone else.

"Yeah, well, they'll have to do better than this." I winked and tried to straighten. Immediately, I regretted it; stabbing pain filled my stomach and shot up to my chest. The wound was bad.

Dux Carran snorted as he towered behind Holland. "I'd say those claw marks *are* just about enough to take you down, boy."

Saving my life or no, he was getting on my nerves.

"How did you know?" I'd been thinking about it since the circuit started cruising and we were a safe distance from the now decimated settlement. "The clubs. You were prepared."

"Ach, yes. They come into my settlement and think they can treat us like prey? Ha." He snorted. "I dunno know what they are, but bullets didn't stop many last time." He puffed his chest, red chest hairs popping out from underneath his unbuttoned guara shirt that was now half-shredded and completely covered in dried blood. "One thing you'll learn as you age, boy: a club can kill most anything." He winked at Holland. "If you're ever open to some new tricks, I'd be happy to share my sizable knowledge with you."

Holland's face turned a brighter shade of red than I'd ever seen.

"So, you knew that bullets wouldn't stop them and didn't say anything?" Rage began to fill my veins. We could've been prepared. We could have fought them off better, maybe even won. I looked around the train car. We had left with maybe seventy men combined.

"I donno owe you anything. I saved your arse back there, don't ya forget it." Dux Carran lowered his brows. Was he really threatening me?

"According to the Glenn's Code of Conduct, you *did* owe me that knowledge." I tried to stand and couldn't—I crumpled even further into the wall. I needed a medic.

"Dale, just take it easy. We should be at the outpost in an hour or two. You need to refrain from moving if you don't want to bleed out." Holland gently adjusted me, bracing the wound.

"Listen to the lass, boy. I did not save your life so your pride could kill you."

"How long have they been upright?" I wanted to strangle him. But if I couldn't physically manage that, I could at least use my brain to gather intel.

"Since the first attack. Though the swarm this last time was far larger than I've seen before." This time, Dux Carran had the decency to look perturbed. Maybe there was more to this meathead than just sex, blood, and wine.

"They were on all fours at the last settlement," Holland whispered, clearly thinking the same thing I was.

"They're evolving."

. . .

WE REACHED the Southern Outpost an hour later. To my utter humiliation, Dux Carran hoisted me on his shoulders and carried me into the Medic Lounge to be seen. I protested, of course, but Holland's pleading look—and the fact that I couldn't even stand—demanded I find a way to cope. I may not be able to walk, but at least I could say *I'd* had Holland. Twice. And despite Carran's relentless flirting, Holland didn't appear to be interested. Which, to my great entertainment, bothered the giant greatly. As it should.

I'd been lying in bed for the past six hours, connected to IVs and having all sorts of medications pushed. The sheets were scratchy. Guess not much had changed. The door opened and a familiar frame filled the door.

"Glad to see you're up," Holland said as she entered.

"Yeah, I bet you are." I winked at her, and her face started to flush. I fucking loved that about her. "I think I'm about ready to yank this IV out. Tell me the bag's almost empty?"

She walked over to the stand behind me and checked the bag. "Almost. I'd say another twenty minutes and you should be all done."

"Good. We have a lot to do."

"About that, we need to talk." She sat on the edge of my bed and began playing with a frayed piece of fabric from her black pants. "These attacks are getting worse. We've survived two of them thus far, but I can't imagine we're the only ones. I've reached out to HQ and filed reports and they've simply accepted my reports and then classified them. I've tried to reach Dux Rusty and Dux Phillips, but they haven't answered. What if..." She left the question hanging in the air.

"They'll be alright. As much as I'd personally like to see Rusty bite the bucket, he's too annoying to allow us the peace of his absence. Phillips is strong and smart. For all we know, these were isolated events."

"Really?" She leveled a look at me. "I'm not stupid, Dale. Dark magic is at play here and that likely means there are obscene amounts of magic being expended. The results would likely be larger than just two attacks. This Outpost hasn't seen any attacks since the one last week. And as far as I can tell, they haven't witnessed the creatures," she lowered her voice with the last word.

"What are you saying?"

"These attacks are within *our* borders, Dale."

She couldn't be seriously insinuating we were responsible for their creation, could she? My father, as messed up as he was, wouldn't violate natural law.

"No. We don't have all the facts."

"But Dale, I can't even access security footage from the attack last week. It's been deleted. And HQ—"

"HQ has their hands full. We are under enemy attack, remember?" I couldn't keep the snap out of my voice. "Look, Holland, I've served my entire life under the Glenn's protective covering. I've watched my father enact laws to protect our way of life. There's simply no way that HQ or my father has anything to do with this." I placed my hand on hers and gave it a gentle squeeze.

She bit down on her tongue and averted her gaze. Fine, if she didn't believe me, then I'd prove it to her.

"Holland. We know the enemy has infiltrated our borders. These creatures are just another weapon, and we will defeat them."

"You knew one of them," her voice was barely above a whisper.

I clenched my jaw. She had me there. I don't know how Arche Shultz became a creature, but he was listed as a casualty of the Eastern border attack last week.

"I don't know how he became that...that thing." I ran a hand through my hair as I spoke. "But I do know he was murdered by the enemy and that means his body was likely taken when they escaped. I don't understand why or how, but we know dark magic is capable of many things."

Her pale brown eyes pierced my ice-blue ones. She wasn't fully buying it.

"Here, let's just go to the command center and start compiling reports from the recent attack, personnel, and any missing persons.

Then we can contact HQ about any discrepancies, and I'll request an immediate meeting with leadership for guidance on next steps."

She nodded at me but didn't seem convinced.

I gritted my teeth.

"There is a reason for procedure, Holland. We live in a civilized society because of law and order. Don't forget that."

CHAPTER 40

TATE

Vala was steadying me as we left the pub—I was pretty sure Jared had helped direct me through the maze of barrel tables in the overcrowded room. Outside, the night air was fresh. It was exhilarating. Finally, the numbness was slowly being erased. Dizzying freeness took its place.

"Guys, look at the stars!" I threw my head back as I spoke. I used to love to stargaze with my mother and Fletch. Guess I'm on my own now. Perhaps they're in the heavens twinkling down on me. Fletch wanted me to be a firecracker, to be free. I would be.

"Woah, steady there." Vala reached down and pulled me upright. "Let's get you to bed and you can sleep it off."

"Sleep? Are you kidding me? For the first time in weeks, I feel *alive*! No sleep for me." I spotted some vines and tiny grapes in the vineyard. "Look! How cute are these?" I pulled Vala with me as we went into the vineyard. I was pretty sure my words were slurring, but I didn't care. They understood me clearly enough to follow.

"Val, this is nuts. We're going to get in trouble. *This* wasn't supposed to happen," Jared's voice was low, like he was trying to speak to Vala without me hearing.

"Hush, it's fine. She wants to check out the vineyard and the air will do her good. Plus," she reached out and cupped a cluster of grapes, "they are cute."

"He specifically said to stay out of the vineyard."

"Mhmm, and you always do what you're told?" Vala retorted, eyebrow raised.

"Yeah, man up, Jared and grow a pair," my last word was slurred beyond recognition.

"You two are relentless."

"What? Does this motion make you uncomfortable?" Vala squeezed the cluster of grapes as she spoke.

"Eww. Ok, you t-t-two get a room already. I'mmma...I'mma going for a walk!" I broke free from her grip and made it all of ten feet before I began to stumble, laughter overtaking me as the ground approached. Two large solid hands stopped me.

The smell of salt and ash surrounded me. Even in my drunken state, I recognized that scent. Like it was somehow a part of me, darkness to my light. Freedom to my pain.

But...it couldn't be, could it? I looked up into a pair of dark eyes shadowed by wisps of black hair falling into his face, caressing some grown stubble shadowing his jawline.

"What in the hell are you doing out here?" Mardi held me steady even as his voice was that of thundering ice chips.

"I...uh, we were just following her and making sure she was safe, and she wanted to see the grapes, cause...uh, cause they're cute. And actually, they really are cute, and you know she *may have* had a bit to drink." Vala tilted her head as she spoke. "And we thought air would be good. Fresh air that is." Vala's rambling had grown on me.

"Enough, dokimoses!"

"Sorry, Ae—" Vala grunted as Jared elbowed her. "Sorry, sir," she finished speaking barely above a whisper as she massaged her abdomen.

"And you." He leaned in closer to me, the scent of smoked ash was intoxicating and strangely welcoming. There were hints of something

I couldn't quite place, but it beckoned me closer. If a person could smell like sexy ash, he certainly did. He sniffed in my direction. "You reek."

Rage roiled up. How dare he? I shoved against him, but he didn't budge, and instead, I pushed myself backwards only to be stopped by his hands—again.

"Letta meee go." I began to smack him.

"Dokimoses, return to your rooms, now."

"Are you kidding me? Yo-you're an imposterrr!" I shouted and this time he covered my mouth with his hand and pushed me deeper into the vineyard, my back brushing the vines.

"You two head back, I've got this," he commanded Vala and Jared without taking his eyes from me.

"But—"

"Now!"

Footsteps retreated. Vala and Jared had left me with this male.

"Tate, I need you to keep calm and shut the hell up about anything that could get us in trouble." His body was warm as he pulled me close to him. Sweet blood, my body responded to his warmth. His mere presence had my heart rate increasing.

"I bettt you woulda liked thattt." Mother Blood, I couldn't even speak.

"You clearly lack restraint. You're useless." He shook his head, even as his eyes bore deeper into my soul.

How dare he? I may be intoxicated, but I wasn't stupid. I knew when I was being demeaned.

"Let. Me. Goooo." I pulled, and this time he released. I went careening back in the vines; vines that then threw me forward to my knees and hands.

"You basstharddd." I pushed up and was now in a seated position, bracing myself with my hands.

"You never signaled." His eyes bore through me before landing on my neck. The necklace. I was supposed to let him know when I found Fletch. Well, I found him and thanks to him, Fletch was gone.

"It's your fault!" I snarled as I raised my voice, finding clear words for the first time since I entered the vineyard. "You killed him!"

He appeared unfazed. A wall of stone. He bent over and yanked me up. His speed was so incredibly fast. He placed his hands on my shoulders, giving me a gentle shake. A shake that excited and frustrated me at the same time. Stupid hormones. Stupid drunk mind. Stupid, stupid, stupid—

I shook my head.

"Don't you touch me!" I struggled to keep my voice even. The air was clearing my head, but the anger in my belly was the sobering factor. Mardi was responsible.

"Tate, listen to me. You need to get your head screwed on right and be quiet. We're risking a lot for *you* and even if I think you're a complete and utter waste of effort, certain people disagree. So, prove me wrong, damn it, and shut the hell up."

"Is there a problem, Anax Mardi?" Dux Harder came into view.

"Yesss—"

My voice was muffled as Mardi managed to pull me closer, my face warmed by his chest. The look in his eyes promised violence. For the first time since we'd gotten here, I was actually scared. That made me angry.

I could feel sparks flowing through my veins, and maybe it was the alcohol, but I could swear I began to see through flames that haloed my vision. Mardi's eyes widened before he leaned in and cupped my face with both hands.

His lips were on mine before I could respond.

They were large, warm, and wet. All-encompassing. My anger fizzled and suddenly I couldn't think clearly. My pulse quickened as I deepened the kiss.

Tasting. Wanting. More.

I pulled his tongue into my mouth further, savoring the way he stroked mine with his own. His grip on my cheeks altered and one hand lifted my chin up further while the other swept back behind my neck and dug into my hair. A new high began to take over my system. My nerves were firing relentlessly, sparking even.

I was kissing him. Had I lost my mind? Somehow his mouth felt safe, known even. Like we were dancing a dance we'd rehearsed a million times. His grip loosened and his tongue's movement slowed. I could feel him slowly searching me, gently, before pulling back and then breaking the kiss.

"Nope, no trouble Dux Harder. Is there Dokimos Aaralyn?" He was speaking to me like he hadn't just kissed me. Like my body wasn't just all nerves firing rapidly from one stupid kiss with a male I should *never* have engaged with.

"Right," I replied dumbly. Dux Harder surveyed us for a minute before nodding his head in confirmation.

"Well then, I'm off. Let me know if you need anything before your departure at dawn, Anax Mardi."

"Will do, thank you."

Dux Harder nodded at Mardi and then disappeared back toward the settlement.

I stared at the male before me, wrapped in shadows and mystery. Who was he? "What was that for?"

"Ah, she finds her tongue and is finally sober enough to be intelligible."

"Jackass."

"You nearly got us killed."

"You kissed me."

"So?"

Was he kidding? That kiss wasn't just a kiss, it was a *kiss*. One like I'd never had before—one that scrambled my senses. Surely, he'd felt it too.

"Who the hell do you think you are?" I tried to raise my righteous indignation, but oddly, I just wanted to lean into him and kiss him again. The alcohol was still clearly impairing my judgment; perhaps I wasn't as sober as I thought.

"You have to make everything so damn difficult." He leaned in closer to me and I didn't back away. Chest heaving, he paused; emotions flickering so fast in his eyes I couldn't read them. His jaw ticked before he wordlessly picked me up and cradled me in his arms, close to his chest. I could feel his heart beating, his pulse quickening. Thank Blood, I wasn't the only one who was responding to our proximity. My body begged for more of his touch.

What the hell was in that bloodwine?

He walked toward the settlement, weaving behind different buildings before entering a fancy-looking inn. The duxes' quarters. I couldn't say I minded the idea of having more of his touch, but *he* didn't even consider asking if I was interested. Didn't have the *right* to ask.

"Put me down," I demanded.

"Not a chance." He stalked through the doors and went up a set of stairs.

"Now." I straightened my spine, trying to get free of his grip.

He paused and had the gall to smirk at me. His palms tightened, fingers digging in slightly to my curves. "As if."

"You asshole!"

He remained wordless as he stalked up the stairs and then made a left down a hallway. I squirmed as he kicked a door open and then shut it behind us. The heat in my cheeks and core doubled at the sight of the bed.

How could I possibly desire *this* male?

The space was smaller than I expected. Only a small parlor and then an adjoining bedroom with a large bed. He approached the bed and opened his arms, dumping me on it like he couldn't wait to be rid of my touch.

"I can't believe you." I glared up at him.

"Look, don't get the wrong idea with the kiss. I just needed everyone else to *think* we were a thing for the night so I can make sure you don't do something that could cost us all our lives."

His words stung, proved by the hurt burning in my chest. "I'm not staying here." I began to rise, but he blocked the doorway with his body.

"Like it or not, this is the safest place for you right now. Arithi thinks you're worth it. I'm not so sure, but for tonight, you'll stay here where I can ensure your safety."

My safety? I was safer away from him and Arithi. She was the one asking about Fletch. The one seeking Fletch. The one who tasked me with finding him. *They* were responsible for putting him in danger.

"You killed him!" I lunged at him and began yanking on his hair. His yelp brought me so much satisfaction. I yanked again on the black strands, harder this time.

"You ended Fletch!"

He stood there, allowing me to pound on his chest. He remained unmoving as I pounded again and again, pouring out my rage, my pain. He took it without defense, without question—he just allowed me to mourn.

Moments later, I stilled, my energy depleted. Fletch was gone, and with him my sense of home, my belonging, my past, and my future. I was alone.

As if in answer, Mardi pulled me into a hug and stroked my back.

Not alone.

I stood there, cradled by a male I hated—no, loathed. And yet, I couldn't will myself to move. I didn't want to move, to pull away.

Night had truly fallen as the room was engulfed in shadows that somehow seemed bright even through their darkness. Mardi cleared his throat and stopped his comforting strokes on my back. "So, Fletch is in fact dead then." A statement and not a question.

"Don't act like you care. *You* did this to him!" I didn't care that I was being irrational, craving his touch yet loathing the male. Didn't care that moments ago I found comfort in his touch. The mere sound of Fletch's name on his lips released a new wave of anger.

I dug my fingers into his throat, but just as before, he didn't pull back. Blood began to pool there, oddly colored. It was deep red with swirls of gold.

"You should have notified us the moment you found him." His eyes held a certain sorrow to them. Was he serious?

"You don't even care! You just wanted to use him. He said so himself! He was just your informant." I squeezed tighter, but his hand came up and grabbed my wrist this time.

"Enough. What's done is done." He jerked my hand from his throat.

Fire rose in my belly.

I screamed as I threw myself at him, kicking out his knee from under him and sending him toppling over. I used my forearm to pin him to the ground. Within a second, he was out of my grasp and had my left arm yanked behind my back, my belly pinned to the floor.

"First off, your fighting skills are shit." Any tenderness had left his voice, replaced by the steel of a leader, an anax. "Secondly, his loss is a tragedy. A sacrifice and one that I will not squander. Now tell me exactly what happened."

I couldn't move, I couldn't breathe. This was my fault. My presence ushered in Fletch's death.

"You wouldn't have done anything! He was already being interrogated and mutilated!" I bucked and tried to break his grip on my left forearm, but he leaned into me, his weight compressing my lungs.

"Tate. What happened?"

"They killed him! Because of you and your stupid leader's quest for knowledge, they killed him and left him like he was..." My voice began to break as my vision blurred. "Like he was nothing." No. I would not give him the satisfaction of my tears.

"What did he say, word for word?" His voice softened a bit as his grip loosened.

I didn't want to talk. The memory, the pressure was too painful. It seeped through me, consumed my soul.

Mardi flipped me over and locked eyes with me.

Known.

My sorrow began to overwhelm my senses and words just started to pour out.

"I came back to my home completely trashed. I was taken in for questioning, and then witnessed them torture Fletch until they decided to use me as additional motivation to get him to speak." A sob broke from my lips. I hated that he was seeing me like this.

Anger coursed through his face. He yanked up my sleeve. My skin was still pink from healing, scratch marks covered my arm. The scars I'd created.

"Tell me exactly what happened, don't skip a single word."

Hours later, I sat across from Mardi in an overstuffed armchair. At least I had that comfort. Two glasses of blood were in front of us, no wine because according to the controlling jackass in front of me, I'd had enough.

"Again. I need you to try to remember."

"I told you already! I was in and out of consciousness. I didn't even know it was Fletch once the gas started."

"That's what you think, Tate, but you're smarter than you think. You have better abilities than you know. Your subconscious is capable of so much more than you're aware. So please, try to focus."

"I was being gassed. I heard his voice and agonizing cries. It's just..." I rubbed my temples with my fingers. "It's all a blur."

Mardi sighed and ran his hand down his face, mirroring my own actions.

"This may surprise you, Mardi, but this is exhausting for me too. Living it was hell and now you're asking me to *relive* it again and again."

He stared at me, his face once again an unreadable mask. "What did it smell like when the gas was on?"

"What?"

"Focus on one of your senses and block everything else out. What did it smell like?"

"I don't know."

"Close your eyes and try."

I sighed; he was truly agitating. Good news was that morning would be dawning soon and I'd finally be able to get out of this room and back in a tin can. Dear Blood, I couldn't believe I wished to be cooped up in that smelly thing again.

"Fine." I closed my eyes and tried to focus on the scent in the interrogation room. "It smelled like citrus and fire. I don't know, peppery?"

"Good. Now did it always smell like that?"

"No." I paused, trying to put my finger on the smell of the mist that came after the gas. "Black licorice. The mist smelled like candy."

"Perfect, now what did you hear? Not words, but sounds. What did the gas sound like?"

"It sounded like gas!" I shot him a glare. He just stared at me. Fine. "It sputtered and then sprayed and made a 'cshhhh' sound."

"Good. Now think back to the room, focus on those sounds."

I could recall the sound of the gas pumping into the room, the hum of the generator, the clicking of the nozzle, the buzzing sensation on the floor. I felt a swirling pressure around me, pulling at my mind. My eyes flew open to see Mardi's index finger extended at me, his eyes closed. *Magic*, he was using magic.

"Focus on *that* room Tate, not this one."

"But you're using magic."

"Yes, I am and you're wasting it. Fletch died to give us some information, he risked his life for it, for us and for you. So please, try to focus on that room."

I hated that he was right. I wouldn't let Fletch's death be in vain. I wanted to remember what he said. At the time, it felt important. I didn't give two craps about Mardi or his mission, but *I* wanted to remember Fletch's last message to me.

"Fine."

I recalled the room again and everything became heightened. I could hear the hum of electricity, the gentle clicking of the nozzle letting the gas in the room, the way the window felt under my fingers when I pressed against it. The feeling of the cool floor, the agonizing sizzle on my skin. The sounds of my screams escalating in sound and then...Fletch's scream. Agonizing. It surrounded me—his cries were everywhere.

"Enough, it's too much." My heart rate increased.

A gentle pressure surrounded me, comforting strokes up and down my back. "Block out the cries, focus on the sound of his breathing."

I tried. At first, I couldn't. All I could hear were his screams, but then a calm settled over me and muted his screams. I could *hear* the breaths in between. I could hear him panting. Drops of blood hitting the floor. I could hear it all.

"Good, now focus on what he said, let everything else fall away."

I inhaled and focused on Fletch's breaths. Inhale and exhale. Then his words. Tears pricked at my eyes. My Fletch had spoken words of love, words of my childhood. That was his final message to me. I sniffled.

"What, Tate? What did he say?" Mardi didn't deserve to know. It was none of his business.

"Nothing."

Suddenly the pleasant coaxing sensation heightening everything vanished and was replaced with a prodding pressure around my mind. My eyes flew open.

"Stop it." I shot daggers at him with my eyes.

"Tell me what he said."

"It won't matter to you, it was a message for me."

"It may be important." His eyes hooded and he seemed to be in conflict with himself. The comforting silence of the memory ended. Instead of Fletch's undiluted words of love, I could hear his screams, feel the gas. The burning. The pain. The screams were all around.

"It hurts!"

"It's all in your head, Tate, please just tell me what he said. It could be encrypted."

My senses were overwhelmed, no longer muted. I caved. "He said, *'Tate, no matter what, know that my love for you was true! You always were my firecracker in life. Shine bright from your heart, only it knows the truth!'*"

Fletch's voice echoed through my mind and heart. The painful sensation evaporated and was replaced with a warm fuzzy feeling across my skin. The screams were muted, the gas and its painful memory staunched.

"Thank you. I'm...sorry." He stood. "Fletch was a good male."

"I hate you." I shot daggers at him even through pain-filled eyes. It was the worst moment of my life, and I'd just relived it. Yes, I got answers and a memory that was buried, but I also had to experience the loss of him all over again.

He stood and left the room without another word.

The warm sensation still flitted and swarmed around me like an embrace.

I sat there, tears pricking at my eyes. Fletch wanted me to live even while he died. I don't remember if he said anything else to them, but they stopped gassing me and killed him instead. He was gone. I curled my arms around myself and began to rock back and forth.

I recalled the sound of his breath, the love in his words, the kindness in his tone. The image and scent of his remains assaulted my memory. Tears began to fall and stream down my face.

My head began to get heavy and fuzzy. The tingling around me deepened, calming my senses with a cloaking pressure.

I closed my eyes and tried to block all the memories out. Angry. I was angry. He left me and it was because of the work he was doing for Arithi. I would live to make her regret putting Fletch in danger.

I sat there rocking myself in comfort for hours or minutes, I didn't know. The pressure around me soothed my senses and reassured me that I was still alive—even while Fletch wasn't. His cries and screams were muted, I couldn't even remember what they sounded like, and for that I was grateful. The room of pain vanished from my mind and instead, I only saw Fletch. The love in his eyes as he spoke to me—gave me his final words.

I clung to that.

A bell sounded. It was time to board the circuit. I opened my eyes, wiped my face, and stood. Mardi would wish he'd never met me. I'd make sure of it. I began to make my way to the circuit, purpose in each step.

CHAPTER 41

CHANCE

Command Central was a literal mess. Files covered the entirety of the counters, desks, and even some of the control board. Paper files. Apparently, leadership here did not appreciate modern technology. Holland and I had been instructed to meet the head of the base here twenty minutes ago. I paced over to the board and picked up another file, browsing through it. They were all the same. Personnel files from all the staff on base.

"I suppose we can just commandeer the library and cart these files over there," Holland spoke as she lifted a stack of files in her arms.

"You've got to be kidding? We can access all this electronically." I looked at her like she'd grown two heads.

"Dale, leadership was using these paper files for a reason. With all the redacted information and missing or classified digitalized reports, I can't help but wonder if these paper files offer something that our electronic ones don't."

I just leveled a look at her. I was done having the same conversation.

"What if the attack wasn't just physical? We know they breached the lab and database in the Eastern Outpost. What if they contaminated our e-files?"

My jaw dropped. How had I not thought of this? It would explain so much—and it would prevent yet another argument.

"Gather as much as you can and let's go commandeer that library." I began scooping up files. This would take a while.

A knock on the door drew my attention. Anax Clark and Dux Carran entered the room, the latter looking just as confused as I must have at first.

"As you can see, the files are all here as promised. Our hunt has been going...slowly," Anax Clark said as she walked over to the whiteboard on the wall. It looked like something out of a murder mystery, red lines connecting to names and photos of evidence. Definitely old-school.

"Why did you choose to use paper instead of the electronic files?" Holland asked. Did Anax Clark suspect a cyber-attack as well?

"I personally believe you can't see the whole picture with just electronic files. It helps to visualize it. Believe it or not, we didn't always have electronic files and disks to project our data. It used to *all* be paper." Anax Clark huffed a sigh. Her light blonde hair was freckled with grey, and her shoulders held a certain slump to them—a tell-tale sign of age.

"So, you resorted to paper because it helps you see everything?" I asked, my voice held a bit of superiority, even I could admit that. But it had been a long day and if I was honest with myself, I was disappointed that she too hadn't drawn the same conclusion Holland and I had.

"Boy, I've told you once and I'll tell you again, seniority knows a thing or two. Anax Clark was my commanding officer when I first enlisted a century ago. Somethings are better old-school." The look on Carran's face softened as he gazed at Clark.

My shoulders involuntarily shook. The image of those two—

"What did you conclude?" Holland's voice interrupted my train of thought. Thank Mother Blood.

"Not much. I have listed three potential moles based on their whereabouts and possible motives. But honestly, I know these three and I have a hard time actually believing any one of them did this." Anax Clark pointed to the board where three photos of young-looking vampires were.

"Did you find any evidence of tampering with our database or research facility?" I asked.

"No. Not here at least. EO's research database was breached and their command center is where most casualties were found. However, I've been instructed to focus solely on this base's attack and none of the assailants made it past the inner courtyard. Nothing of value there. Not really sure why they even bothered." She pushed large, thick-framed glasses higher up her sharp nose. They say a nose never stops growing and dear blood, hers must've been growing for a century or two.

"What of intel value is there in the inner courtyard?" Holland asked, approaching a map in the corner of the room.

"Not much." Clark walked, or rather limped, over to the map to show Holland where they entered.

"They breached the wall here," she pointed to the far eastern side of the outpost, "then cut a path through the outer courtyard, past the dokimoses' lodging, and made their way here to the inner courtyard." She drew a path with her crooked finger.

"Is that a power frame?" I pointed to a box on the map near the inner courtyard.

"It is. But we never lost power," Clark answered, shaking her now crooked finger in a way that took way too much effort.

"You wouldn't have to lose power for them to siphon data," I said. It was all beginning to make more sense. The Southern Outpost was known to have the largest data stores of all four outposts due to the fact that it was the oldest. There are certain files here that aren't even housed at HQ and are still being uploaded to the cloud. This was purely an intel mission. It had to be.

"Who here has clearance to access the database?" Holland asked, walking back to the who-done-it board.

"Most of the staff. All arches and the majority of dokimoses. It's a part of their training. Although," Anax Clark paused, taking a deep breath, "in order to access anything of value, you'd need a higher clearance badge or be a hell of a coding genius."

"How many of ya' have upper-level clearance?" Dux Carran spoke from the corner of the room. Even from where he stood, his voice was far too loud for the tiny space.

"Well, I'd say all anaxes and duxes have higher clearance, but the only ones who can access the entirety of all classified files is myself, Dr. Webbler, and Dux Johns."

Interesting. I looked at Holland and she looked back at me. The board didn't list any of those three.

"Thank you for your time, Anax Clark, we know you must have a lot going on. Do you mind if we set up in the library?" Holland asked. I could feel a prickle in the air. Subtle, but powerful.

"Not at all. I have a lot to do. With you all rolling in like bats out of hell with tall tales of evil creatures, I'm swamped with enough paperwork for a lifetime." Clark looked at Carran. "Not that I mind, it's good to see you again." There was definitely history there.

My shoulders shook. Fuck, I didn't want to think about that.

"Great. We'll let you know when we hear back from HQ. We submitted our reports about four hours ago and are waiting to hear back." Holland scooped up her folders again and then started to head for the door. The tingling in the air stopped immediately.

Anax Clark and Dux Carran blinked several times before nodding in response. Gross, just gross. I picked up several files and followed Holland out the door and down a series of halls until we reached the library.

She set her stack down on the table and then looked to me. "This is going to take a while. Anyone you trust to help us sort through the basics?"

"I wouldn't trust anyone who was here for the security breach..." I paused, smiling as a thought occurred to me. "But I may have someone *new* in mind." A certain blue-haired pixie would be perfect for this.

After several hours, my phone buzzed. HQ had finally reviewed our files and I was informed we would have a meeting in forty-five minutes. Perfect. Enough time to finish organizing this utter chaos and then hopefully start getting some answers. If our enemies were willing to use dark magic and they breached our database, then we needed to act, and fast, or we would lose any upcoming battles. Knowledge was power. If my father taught me anything, it was that.

The smell of dusty books was beginning to make my nose itch. Shae was hunched over a stack, making a list of dokimoses, arches, duxes, and anaxes. She, of course, came up with the idea to sort the data based on rank, security clearance, and whereabouts during the attack. So far, we were merely filling out the first two columns while Holland was working on placing each person during the attack.

"This would go a lot faster if you'd just let me access the electronic files, I could run a program and—"

"Shae, we've been over this. For now, it's paper." I cracked my knuckles before opening another folder.

"I'm just saying, there's a lot of data here, Chance." Shae huffed, blowing a blue piece of hair out of her eyes.

"Yeah, well this is a heavily occupied base."

"Your mom is a heavily occupied base," Shae retorted, half grumbling.

"And just when I thought you'd grown up," I teased, elbowing her gently as I circled the table to grab the next stack of files.

Holland circled over from the other table and came over to where Shae was working.

"So, you two grew up together?" Holland didn't look up as she asked the question. Ever the focused dux.

"You could say that, although I'm not sure *that* one ever became an adult." Shae pointed a thumb at me and winked. "But yes, we went to school together, and used to hang out a fair share before this one got too cool for us and up and left for the guara five years back."

"So...there is a history," Holland stated casually, even though I could swear her cheeks were coloring. Was she jealous of Shae?

"I mean, I guess. Who doesn't have history?" Shae clearly wasn't picking up on Holland's line of thought.

I sucked my fang. "Would that bother you?" I asked Holland.

Her brown eyes snapped up to mine and for a minute she just stared. "Just making conversation, Dale."

I'm not sure *how* I felt about her jealousy. I mean, yes, we hooked up, but it was never a relationship. At least not a spoken one. Females, they were all the same. Too easily attached.

"Oh..." Shae's grey-blue eyes snapped up to Holland's honeyed eyes, widening as realization dawned on her. "You mean, you thought?" She bit her lips to stifle a chuckle. "No, blood no! We've never been that way." She giggled and covered her lips with her hand.

Apparently being intimate with me was funny.

"I mean Tate and Chance, now they were *always* the item, the couple everyone talked about, you know? But me, never. He's uh, not my type." Shae cleared her throat and walked to the next stack at the table behind me.

"Tate, huh?" Holland asked.

"Yep, they were like hot and heavy for a bit until...well, until they weren't."

"Hot and heavy?" Holland actually looked a little sick.

This was not good. I wasn't ready for the emotional entanglement a relationship brought. Perhaps it was best Holland thought of me as unavailable. Then again, she clearly couldn't focus on anything else. Pride swelled within me.

"I wouldn't say *'hot and heavy'*. But my romantic history is neither here nor there. How's your list coming, Holland?" I tried to redirect her to the task at hand. Even if I was secretly pleased, she couldn't get me out of her head.

"My list?" Holland's eyes bugged out. "Oh, my list. Right, uh I thought, well never mind what I thought." She shook her head. "It's coming. Slow but steady."

"Just like I've heard Chance likes it—"

"Shae, it's Dux Dale here."

"Right, should I salute you, or does your 'anax' have that one covered?" Shae smirked, clearly noting my aroused state. She was insatiable.

"You two sure sound like there's a history..." Holland let the accusation hang. Her pale cheeks flushed as she tucked some brown hair behind her ear while sucking on a fang.

Fuck me. How had I gotten here?

"Shae's not interested in me, or really any *male*." I rested my hand on her shoulders.

"Oh." Holland's eyes snapped to mine. "Oh! I just, I'm sorry, I don't know what's wrong with me. It's none of my business anyway. I just thought—"

"Girl, you are not the first one to be flustered over this one. His count has got to be miles long, but if he's into you, then he'll make sure you know it. But like Chance said, nothing to worry about here." Shae patted Holland on the back before swapping out stacks of files. "These have all been added to my list, they're ready for you now."

So much work. I looked around. The files would take at least a week to go through. If we had more help, maybe we could cut down the time, but who else could I trust here? I released Holland's shoulders and walked back to my clipboard.

"Anyone miss me?" a gruff unmistakable voice came from the entrance to the room. I could feel spit spraying. Rusty.

CHAPTER 42

TATE

I'd been one of the last to make it to the circuit. I took a seat in the back and sat there for about two hours. I would contact Chance as soon as we made it to the outpost. I'd reveal who Mardi was and then he'd be taken in for questioning. Maybe they'd catch Arithi and James before the week was over. They would never put another Fletch in danger again. I don't know why Fletch would ever betray the Glenn, not that I liked the Glenn. I hated President Dale, but I, like my mother, was loyal. That was one core trait she taught me: loyalty. Then again, Arithi claimed to have known her, so maybe she had defected. If she had, then they were responsible for her death too.

"There she is," Vala said.

Just perfect, I did not need her incessant chattering right now.

"Girl, what happened to you last night?" She took an empty seat in front of me, Jared sitting next to me.

"Mardi, that's what."

"Yeah, I mean when we left you in the vineyard with him, and I thought, 'Crap! We're in trouble,' but then he took you and I heard you two kissed?"

My eyes shot up to meet her chocolate ones.

"He kissed me."

"Mhmm. Tell me, how was it?" She leaned forward, putting her chin in her right palm.

"Vala," Jared admonished, but she just waved him off.

"It was wrong, that's how."

"Mmm, wrong like in a bad boy kind of way? Damn, *that's* hot and steamy!"

"Vala!" Jared's voice held embarrassed indignation.

"Wrong as in gross, not right, and completely inappropriate." I tried to shut out the memory of his touch, the craving that took over my senses, the way he tasted...

"Well, the look on your face says otherwise," Vala smirked.

I shot Vala a silencing glare. The circuit jerked violently and then the brakes screeched. I went flying forward, only for Jared to reach out and stop me from careening completely to the floor.

"What on earth?" Vala's voice was breathy. I righted myself and looked around. The train car's lights were flickering on, off, and then on again. The power then went out completely and a shrill metal sound filled the air. I shook off Jared's grip.

"That doesn't sound good." Jared's voice was close. Too close.

"Come with me, now." Mardi was there, whispering in my ear, grabbing my right arm. Where did he come from?

"What's going on?" Jared demanded.

"There's been an attack." Mardi pulled me, beckoning me to follow.

An attack? Was Arithi or another Vamp attacking The Glenn?

"Let go of me! I'm not going anywhere with you," I hissed. I became dead weight and my feet stopped moving.

"Tate, now's not the time for a grandstand." Vala's voice was the calmest I'd ever heard it—that alone had me questioning my stance.

"We're leaving now." Mardi released my arm and approached the door. He began to kick at it. Good luck with that. These doors were built with ten inches of steel. No vampire could break it with a few lousy kicks. Least of all, this jackass.

But to my shock, it slowly dented.

Loud bangs came from the front, along with screams followed by unnatural cries and snarls.

"What the hell is that?" No one answered me. Voices on the circuit rose; the other dokimoses were moving around, talking in panicked tones. With a thud, the door finally gave and Mardi stepped out into the darkness.

"Let's go. Now."

Animal cries and howls echoed in the tunnel. I hated underground travel.

"What about the rest of them, Aether?"

Aether? I'd forgotten that Arithi had called him that. I'd thought it was his first name, but now I wondered if Mardi was just a cover. Like an idiot, I'd been calling him Mardi and taking it at face value. I mentally kicked myself.

"Vala!" Jared tried to shut her up. I could feel his presence behind me pushing me out of the train car.

"We can't just leave them!" she insisted. Jared gave me a gentle push and I stepped out onto the loose stone ground. Musky air filled the cavern.

"Shut up, Vala." Jared was really beginning to annoy me.

"No, Vala's right! Something is very wrong here. We need to get the rest of them. Isn't that your job, *Aether*?" I couldn't keep the bite out of my tone.

Aether inhaled sharply. "Look, Tate, my job is whatever the hell I say it is, and in this moment, it means that you just follow me blindly or die. Understand?"

"But what about the..." Vala's voice cut off as loud crashing and screams came from just ahead.

"Dear blood, they're in the car." Jared sounded scared, actually scared.

"Who's they?" Again, no one answered.

"Now. Move it. We have to move now." Mardi, Aether, whatever his name was, yanked on my arm and we began walking blindly down the tunnel.

"Step up," Aether commanded as my foot stubbed part of the track.

I had good vision, but not night vision. How did they know where we were going?

"Careful, step over the beam ahead." Vala was guiding me like she could see everything.

"Door up ahead, you guys go through it." Aether pushed open a door and maneuvered me through, ducking my head with his hand, before Vala took over guiding me by the elbow. We were in a tunnel. It too was pitch black.

"Where are we going?" Vala's voice was strained.

"Jared, make sure they make it out. I'll be just behind." Aether's tone held no room for questions. Screams sounded, far too close for comfort, along with loud snapping and gurgling cries. This was a massacre.

"We have to help them!" I tried to turn around and find the door, but it was too dark. "How can you guys see anything!?"

"Later, Tate. We have to keep moving."

"Vala! They're dying, can't you hear it? We don't even know what's killing them, but they are people and need us."

"I'm sorry, Tate. Aether gave us an order," Vala spoke quietly, continuing to usher me forward.

I dug my heels in. If they wouldn't help, then I would.

"I admire your morals, but do you for a second think any of those vampires would stop long enough to save you? What about a human? Vampires are predators, we attack, and when we know we're outmatched, we flee." Jared placed two hands on my shoulders and pushed me forward, Vala still tugging on my elbow.

"He's right, Tate. We have a pretty good idea of what is attacking them, and we need to leave now, or we don't stand a chance."

My feet began to move, the obvious pieces finally falling in place. They were together. Aether, Jared, Vala. They were working me, lying to me. If they knew what was attacking us and were scared, should I just run toward the assailants? What if it was the guara searching for these traitors?

"Who are you?" My voice sounded vulnerable, and I hated it. I yanked my elbow free from Vala and dug it into Jared's abdomen. He grunted as I tried to step behind him. It was so damn dark.

"Tate! No!" Vala cried as I took a wrong step and began to tumble down a series of stairs. My left arm took most of the impact, pain screaming from the undoubtedly fractured bone.

"And you thought this would be a fun mission." Jared mocked before securing his hands around my waist and hoisting me up.

How the hell could they see?

A loud crash sounded from behind, along with heavy breaths and footsteps.

"See, Aether went back for them. He too has a strong moral code that values *all* life, Tate." Even though I couldn't see Vala's face, I could swear she was admonishing me.

"Hurry!" Jared and Vala both practically dragged me up the steps. I moved my feet, cooperating with them.

"GO!" Aether's voice echoed from further down the stairs. Several footsteps sounded behind me, whimpers and cries. We reached the top of the stairs, and I could finally make out the vague outline of a door. Jared approached it and kicked it open. Sunlight poured through it, filling the tunnel with a hazy warm glow.

"Out, now!" Vala darted for the door.

Behind me I could see several guaramen from the circuit racing blindly up the steps, tumbling and tripping over each other. A young male slipped and fell only to be buried by the steps of other panicked dokimoses clawing their way up the staircase.

No one bothered to help anyone.

Aether. He had gone back for them. Why?

Animalistic cries echoed louder than before. Whatever that was, they were in the tunnels, likely the very one we were in. I turned and passed through the door and into the forest. The pine needles covered the floor and crunched under my feet. Momentarily, I felt blinded. It was so bright.

"This way!" Vala instructed as she ran through the trees. "There should be a settlement just ahead."

How did they know where we were?

"Weapons ready!" Jared commanded as he unsheathed a dagger.

I ran after them, noting that the other dokimoses also followed. Several of them were bloody. They surpassed me, running like they could outrun death.

"Monsters! They're monsters!" a young dokimos cried. She had a nasty gouge on her arm where her pressed hand did little to staunch the bleeding.

I focused on her too long and didn't see the root ahead of me. My foot caught on it, and I couldn't catch myself as I stumbled, face-planting on the forest floor. Momentarily stunned, I lay there.

Was this really happening? *Monsters*? Impossible.

A scream filled the air, sending shivers down my spine and eliciting panicked cries from the dokimoses around me. Blurs of black and grey streamed through the air, exiting the tunnel. They were jumping, sprinting, attacking.

One was headed right for me. It had large talons at the end of each of its limbs. I pushed up on my elbows and tried to back away as it hurtled toward me on all fours. It gnashed its teeth, black foam dripping from its mouth, as its razor-sharp teeth cut the air. Its eyes were black pools circled by purple.

I sat there paralyzed by what I was seeing.

"Tate!" Vala screamed from ahead, but she was too far to help.

The creature lunged in the air, its trajectory straight toward me. I'd be dead in seconds.

I tried to get my feet under me but couldn't seem to remember how to properly use my legs.

The thing was five feet away, three feet, two—

It halted its path and was yanked backwards as a blade pierced its chest, lifting it in the air and splitting it apart. Black blood sprayed everywhere, like rain from the sky, coating the ground and covering my shins and feet.

"Up, now Tate!" Aether was there, covered in blood and gore, sword at the ready.

Aether had just killed the thing in front of me. He stood there, hand outstretched, waiting for me. "NOW!" His voice rang out, breaking through my momentary shock.

"Yeah, OK." I stumbled to my feet, ignoring his hand, and then began to flee from the creatures overwhelming the forest. They jumped and lunged, slashing and devouring the dokimoses who were too slow or had fallen. That could have been me. It should have been me.

I unsheathed a dagger, next time one of those things came for me, I'd be ready.

"This way!" Aether directed as he weaved through the heavily wooded forest at my side, keeping pace with me.

Up ahead was a cluster of pines and scrub oak, dense and hard to see through. It would provide temporary relief.

"If we make it through there, we should have some coverage and can hopefully make it to the village below," he stated the obvious. For once, I felt up to speed on the plan.

"What are those things?"

"You're asking me?"'

"No, Aether, I'm demanding. You know what they are." I was sick of the secrets and lies. Vala, Jared, and Aether all knew. It was purely infuriating.

"Later, Tate. Let's just survive this first."

"But—"

I was cut off by a creature landing just in front of me. It raised itself to a standing position and towered over me. It was at least eight feet tall. It swiped at me with its claws. I ducked and jumped back. It barely missed.

I struck at it with my dagger, once, twice, three times, but didn't make contact. The thing smiled at me, revealing sharp black teeth inside its mouth before roaring and taking a step toward me. Aether ripped his sword out of one creature he'd taken down and then swung for the one attacking me.

No way, I didn't need him saving me again. My pride wouldn't allow it. I pulled out my other dagger, the smaller, lighter one, and threw it at the thing. It was only three feet away, so aiming was easier, and my dagger struck true. Right between its eyes. It stood there, momentarily frozen, before screaming at me and reaching up to grab the blade. As its hand closed around the hilt of it, Aether was there, pushing the blade all the way through. A crunch sounded and the creature collapsed. Aether yanked my blade out of its skull, black blood covering it, and handed it to me.

"Move!" he commanded as he took off, not waiting to see if I responded.

Damn him. I had that thing. I shook my head and followed him through the brush, ducking under a branch. I tuned out the cries from behind, the sounds of bones snapping, the guttural cries. No more loss. I blocked it all out and focused on my breathing.

"Tate! Over here!" Vala stood just ahead, chest heaving and blade bloody. Several creatures' corpses lay scattered around her. Now that was what a badass looked like. I really should have taken more tactical courses in high school. "This way," she said as she motioned wildly toward the path.

I followed her, ignoring the sickening sounds from behind, forgetting the pain in my arm from when I'd fallen. I rejected the pain creeping up my left leg, the old bone beginning to throb, begging for relief. I would not break.

She weaved between large pine trees and skinny aspens. I focused on the way she moved, her braids flying behind her, steps sure. She avoided a fallen tree trunk, and I too sidestepped it. She jumped past a dented part in the forest floor, full of pine needles and cones, and I followed suit, wincing as I landed and my left leg began to cramp.

Finally, we were through the densest part of the forest and made it to the clearing. A valley, with green grass and wheat stalks. Peaceful almost.

I could see the settlement about ten miles ahead, and to my relief, Jared was running *toward* us, leading a small battalion of armed soldiers. We just needed to make it to them.

"Keep going! Everyone, just make it to the village, arm yourselves properly, and then get the hell back here to take these creatures back to the grave where they belong!" Anax Mardi, Aether, commanded all the dokimoses like it was second nature. They all obeyed, admiration in their eyes. He'd saved them. He was their leader, traitor or not.

His dark hair was spattered in red and black blood, and his muscles flexed as he lifted his sword and turned his back on the village, facing the grove we'd just run through. Dokimoses kept pouring through the trees in a stream, slowly dissipating, most had already made it to the valley. The ones who hadn't, well, they were likely dead.

Aether dug his feet in the ground. He was going to face those things by himself. I stopped moving and just stared at him. Several dokimoses ran past him toward the army approaching, none stopped to help. Through the pines, I could see blurs of grey and black. Dozens of those creatures were closing in. Too many for him alone. I didn't care how good a swordsman he was, he couldn't take them all. Damn it.

My feet began moving toward Aether, dagger in hand. I could feel a tug on my *being*, commanding me forward. He would not face this alone.

"Tate!" Vala screamed my name from behind, but I didn't stop.

Aether turned to see me, eyes widening as conflict warred in them. Was that admiration?

He cursed under his breath. "What do you think you're doing? Turn around and go to the village!" His eyes were full and...panicked? If I didn't know better, I'd say he was concerned for my safety. Wasn't this the same male who made me relive the worst night of my life just yesterday? Why did I care about him? My stupid confused heart.

"You need me!" I challenged him as I stopped moving and stood by him. Dagger ready.

He cursed under his breath as he reached for his other sword strapped to his back. "Use the pointy end on them. Slice through the heart up through their head, the head through the heart, cut the head off, or like before, sink it straight between their eyes." He handed me his sword.

"I know how to use a sword." I grabbed it, and it clunked to the ground. It was heavy, very heavy.

"Could have fooled me. Use your dagger if you have to." Aether didn't have time for more instruction as the first creature broke through the tree line, charging us.

Aether ran for it, sword at the ready. "Stay behind me."

Several others began to pour through the shrubs. Most were on all fours, but a few ran upright like we did.

My pulse quickened. No, I would not be afraid.

A calmness blanketed my senses along with a foreign strength.

I was not alone. I would not fail.

"Get ready!" Vala's voice at my side surprised me. Her dark braids had fallen from their pony and were now scattered across her shoulders. Several strands had broken free. She gripped her sword and raised it as one creature ran past Aether, straight for us.

"Ready," I replied as I picked up the sword, prepared for its weight this time, and swung it at the creature. I caught it in its shin, but only managed to swing halfway through it—the blade stuck in its leg. The creature crumpled and then tried to right itself. Vala swung her sword and managed to decapitate it.

"Nice! Just swing higher next time," she instructed as she turned, ready for the next one.

Steady. Power. Focus.

Aether was up ahead and was systematically taking them down one by one. He was graceful in his approach, and it looked more like dancing than it did fighting. He had managed to take down at least eight and was forging forward into the thick of it.

"Come on, you can do it. Just stay strong," Vala was murmuring under her breath, eyes fixed on Aether.

Aether sliced through two creatures at once before pivoting to face off with a third.

A roar came from the left. Vala turned, weapon poised. The beast lunged at her but she had her blade in its belly before it hit the ground. She yanked it free; the sickening sound of flesh and metal meeting made my stomach turn.

A blur from behind was moving quickly. I threw my dagger before I could even register how close the beast was. To my utter shock, it struck true. It landed straight into its left eye socket, the blade embedded a few inches. The creature shrieked and threw its head back and forth before taking a step toward me. And then, as if gravity itself had increased, the dagger began to move. It was pulled deeper and deeper until the blade fully disappeared into its skull. With a cry, the thing collapsed. I reached for my dagger, grunting as I freed it from the *thing's* now mutilated face.

The charge in the air intensified, the fire in my blood begging to be released. I could feel that old itch come alive, demanding I scratch it and embrace who I really was. But I could not, not in front of so many. Shifting here would be a death sentence.

Aether was fighting three at a time, but dozens more were swarming him. It would only be a moment before they overpowered him. He needed help.

"Damn it, just wield," Vala whispered, attention focused on Aether, who was about fifty yards ahead.

"Watch out!" I shouted as a creature landed just to the side of Vala. I charged it and swung my sword, higher this time, and lodged it in its gut. The damn thing just stood there and then began swiping at us. Its right claw caught my left forearm and broke my contact with it. I fell backward and landed on the grass. Vala screamed and black blood went flying along with the thing's head.

Panic. Rage. Power.

The air around me thickened, filled with a charge. A wind—almost unnatural—blew from where Aether was, kicking up dirt and blood, filling the air with a haze.   I forced myself back to my feet, ignoring the blood dripping down my arm, blinking through the dusty air. I tuned out the pain from the dirt in my eyes and focused on the pulsing of the air. Like a heartbeat I knew well.

The air cleared and Aether stood there, sword poised and feet apart. Around him, at least two dozen creatures lay dismembered, bodies bubbling in pools of black blood.

How did he take that many down in a moment?

Another creature shrieked as Vala removed its head with her blade. I stood there, chest heaving. There were no more creatures nearby, just movement in the brush, behind the tree line. Several black streaks broke through the pines, the brush teeming with those things. More were coming.

I pulled free a dagger with my good arm and stood. This was something I could easily maneuver.

Footsteps pounded behind, along with familiar shouts. The battalion, they'd finally arrived. Jared was at the head of the group, sword raised.

One of the upright creatures landed in the outskirts of the valley, focusing on Aether. It raised its head and let out a cry. The other things froze, and then as one unit, they turned and retreated *back* into the forest.

"Don't let them get away!" Jared commanded as he led the soldiers forward, following the now fleeing creatures.

I looked around. The ground was covered in bodies. Pools of blood were everywhere. For the first time, I noticed not the dozens of creatures' bodies dotting the valley's floor, but several dokimoses' corpses. They were lifeless, fallen in the once green, now black grass.

I had no idea how many we lost, but my guess was that more than half of the circuit's roster were now dead.

Aether turned, his gaze finding mine.

Power. Peace. Admiration. Lust.

The charge in the air surrounding me doubled, tickling my skin and caressing my mind. He began to stride toward me, wiping his sword on his muddy pants before sheathing it.

"When I give you a command, you damn well better listen to it!" He was angry, the skin at his eyes and mouth pulled tight. "You could have died." He flexed his hands, knuckles turning white when he curled his fingers inward.

"You needed help!" I was not about to be talked down to for helping. "A thank you would be nice!"

"A thank you?" His eyebrows shot up. "Tell me Tate, how many did you kill? Hmm?" He gestured around him.

"You're such a bastard."

"So you've said." He turned as Vala approached. "Vala, next time I give you a command, you follow it, no questions asked. If Tate had died, it would've been on your head. You would have paid for it with your life." He pointed a finger at her.

Seriously, what was his problem?

"Well, she's not exactly the type to listen and I didn't want to leave her, and really, she did help...even if she didn't exactly kill any by herself, she was close," Vala stated my failure like it was worthy of praise. Aether was right, I hadn't killed any—not on my own. I was a poor warrior and more of an exposure than an asset.

"She. Could. Have. Died." Aether glared at Vala.

"But she didn't. She's stubborn, like someone else I know."

"She's right *here*. I can hold my own and answer for my own actions." I was sick of them speaking of me like I was a child to be minded.

"Enough. I need to reach out to command and inform them of the situation." Aether stormed off toward the village, leaving a trail of bloody footprints.

I gritted my teeth. The charge in the air dissipated, but the tug on my soul did not relent. It followed Aether as he marched through the valley.

CHAPTER 43

CHANCE

The conference room was stuffy. I took my seat toward the head of the table, across from Rusty. Only Anax Clark's frame occupied the head of the table. Dux Carran stood against the wall, directly behind Rusty, the intensity of his gaze focused on Clark was unsettling. I definitely didn't want to know what was going on in his mind.

"Alright, everyone, let's begin," Anax Clark spoke, her voice holding a definite exhaustion to it. She tapped on her disk and a projection filled the second half of the table. Empty seats were now filled with blue holograms. HQ's leadership. I could make out the definite profile of Anax Graf, her bun impeccable as ever. There were several other anaxes filling the seats, a head scientist for HQ, and to my utter shock, my father's frame filled the seat at the opposite head of the table.

"Anax Clark, we were informed you have received the convoy of troops sent from HQ, among which Dux Dale and Dux Holland were a part of, yes?" President Dale spoke.

Anax Clark nodded in confirmation. Her face looked slacker than before. I wasn't the only one surprised by my father's presence.

"Dux Dale, it is my understanding that *you* requested this meeting, citing high security threats. Does this have to do with the mole hunt?" My father's voice was all president. Not a single note of any concern for what had occurred on our transport. Maybe he didn't know, but my money was on the fact that he simply didn't care. Not surprising.

"That is correct."

"Then by all means, please fill us in on your intel," Dux Graf spoke up, her voice soft but sharp as ever.

"Well," I cleared my throat, "see for yourself." I pulled out my disk and projected several photos I had snapped of the first incident: piles of goo, bloodied vampire bodies, total carnage. "As you can see, we encountered more than a mere rift in our transport at the Brookside and Bexley settlements. My entire team was cut in half and leadership barely escaped alive. At the first settlement, we were victorious and destroyed these creatures, but we had to evacuate the second. I fear they will continue to multiply and spread. They appeared highly intelligent and were lethal." I paused, looking each hologram in the face. "We believe dark magic is at play." A collective gasp gave me satisfaction. There, at least now maybe they'd take this threat seriously.

"What you speak of is highly criminal. How certain are you?" Anax Graf zoomed in on the images and then leveled a look at me.

"Certain."

"What evidence have you boy of such an accusation?" Rusty spoke up, spit flying across the table and landing just short of my fingers. He was as gross as he was annoying.

"The things we've seen can only be explained by dark magic," I responded, trying to keep calm.

"So you've said, but where I come from boy, we need more than just hearsay. What proof do you have?" Rusty pounded his fist on the table, glaring at me.

"Comatose humans. Hundreds of them. Unresponsive staff at the processing plant Dux Bole ran in the Brookside settlement. Creatures that are *intelligent* and yet, beastly," Holland spoke up, projecting her own photos. I hadn't even known she'd taken them. She projected pictures not only of the carnage but of the unresponsive humans, the staff looking at her but not focusing, and even a short video of me walking around trying to wake comatose vessels. "Not only was Dux Bole processing more than the allotted amount, but his settlement was also feeding on children. Several infractions occurred there; the least unsettling was Dux Bole's indifference to the attack. I do not personally believe it was the first time."

"This is all disturbing, but not enough to warrant an immediate meeting. I will further Rusty's question, what *evidence* do you have that dark magic is responsible for this?" My father spoke up, eyes shooting daggers at Holland.

To her credit, she lifted her chin and focused solely on my father. "What else could be responsible for this?" Holland projected a quick battle scene of the creatures attacking our men, sinking four sets of fangs into vampires, slicing with their claws, jumping so high they were practically flying before landing on dokimoses and devouring them. My stomach hollowed out at the sight. I had lived it, but seeing it replayed was nearly as traumatic.

"As you can see, they have a high level of intellect, and furthermore, Dux Dale recognized one as a previous arche from the Eastern Outpost. One of the arches who was listed as dead and missing," Holland voiced. Damn she was good.

"Doctor Worshah?" Anax Graf directed the question at the thin looking male wearing a lab coat and thick glasses.

"A number of things could have caused this. One of which, would be dark magic," he spoke as he removed a piece of lint from his coat. "I'd have to run several tests on the remains and the areas of attack to determine if it was dark magic."

"What else could create these things? What else could convert vampires into monsters?" Holland asked.

"Many things. You're young, dux. But I've been studying science my entire life. You weren't here for the Great War, but there are weapons our neighbors have that we do not. Some manifested from dark magic and then changed, evolved. They are a new species that we do not any longer consider dark magic due to their distance from the original source of magic, even if it was dark. And yet, given our truce, we do not have intel to determine if they still play with dark magic. What you witnessed could be an enemy more evolved than us," Doctor Worshah spoke as he swiped back his greasy black hair that was styled in a bad comb-over.

"But Dale recognized one as our own?" Holland pushed. I could see her point, but I could also feel the room's temperature drop.

"Dux Dale?" President Dale leveled the question at me.

"It is true. I recognized Arche Shultz. It was unmistakably him."

"Very well. Doctor Worshah, you will look into this and send a crew to extract samples from the settlements. Run your tests. In the meantime, what data do you have of the mole hunt?" Any relief from my father's response vanished upon his redirection. Normal strategy for him. I don't know why I'd expect anything less.

"Not much." I gritted my teeth.

"*Boy*, you called a meeting to tell us fairytales and share information about an attack from the enemy, but don't have any vital information about the mole lurking within our borders?" Rusty spat, pounding his fists on the table.

I leveled a look at him. Dark veins spread out from his eyes, branching toward his hairline and ears. He looked wrong. But then again, he'd always looked wrong.

"We are reviewing data now; however, we believe these creatures are an attack from the enemy, as you stated, and therefore, according to Article Two of the Glenn's Wartime Conduct, a meeting was in order," I spoke, smiling when I could see Rusty snarl. "But you don't seem surprised by any of this, so tell me, why are you here, Rusty, and what do you know?"

Rusty narrowed his eyes. "How dare you—"

"Answer the question, Dux Richards," Anax Graf interrupted him.

"We were rerouted here due to the attacks Dux Holland filed about. We also encountered a few of these creatures ourselves and Dux Philips didn't make it."

What? I couldn't believe he didn't make that known before. Philips was a good male. Rusty spoke of his death like he was casually reciting the weather.

"Unlike these children, I don't go crying dark magic. I do my damn job. It seemed the creatures were coming from the south, so we rerouted to this outpost in order to get a better understanding of our enemy's position. From what I witnessed, I'd say we're under attack," Rusty finished speaking.

"You're suggesting we are, in fact, at war?" Anax Graf asked, clarifying the situation.

"Yes. These attacks are not just happening with these kids. I too, was under attack on our way here. I'd say the enemy has landed and declared war with these weapons."

"Anax Clark?" Anax Graf leveled a look at her. Declaring war was as serious an accusation as declaring dark magic. Both were punishable by death if they proved to be maliciously spoken, or if you took part in instigating either.

"From the videos and photos Dux Holland shared, along with Dux Dale and Dux Richards testimony, it would appear that we may be under attack. Our base has not personally seen any of these creatures, and I have yet to witness any enemy activity apart from the attack a week ago. Dux Carran, what is your stance?" She turned and looked at the giant who was leaning, arms crossed, against the wall.

"I say something is goin' on. Dark magic or not, we are under attack. So yes, I believe we are at war. Mother Blood help us," he raised his voice and fist in the air.

"I see. I will take this information to the council. We will keep you apprised," President Dale spoke, ready to end the meeting.

Shit, we could be officially at war and with an enemy we didn't understand.

"President Dale," Anax Graf spoke, voice tight. "I just received a transmission. Our Eastern Outpost is under attack and the circuit has been compromised."

CHAPTER 44

TATE

I sat on a couch outside under the stars. Loud music from the pub sounded from behind. Apparently, death only made these doki-moses crave blood and sex. I couldn't bring myself to partake in the live feeds like the rest of the vampires, but the bartender had brought me a pitcher of blood and I'd downed it and then got a refill.

"Slow down or you'll throw it up," Vala's voice was soft as she approached.

"What, you don't feel like joining in a live feed?" I asked as I looked across the courtyard. Several couples engaged in intimate feeding with their vessels perched on chairs or chaises. Two vampires were partaking from one male vessel as he lay on a couch, offering his wrist to each of them. They drank deeply, red dripping from the sides of their mouths. Moans filled the air.

"Oh, I'm like you. I prefer to drink the drained stuff. Live feeding is just not my cup of tea." She laughed, but it fell flat. I hadn't forgotten about her lies, her betrayal. She sat down next to me.

"You don't strike me as the type to be shy."

"Well, not with those I *want* to be intimate with, I just don't like the blood haze clouding my judgment from a live feed. Let's just say

I've quenched more than just my physical thirst from a vessel before and the feeling afterwards when I sobered up…" She shivered. "It's just not me." She cleared her throat. "Thank you for today."

"For what? I, as you pointed out, didn't do anything." I toed the table in front of me.

"No, but you tried and that's more than most do."

"Vala, what's going on?" I was sick of the code and everyone speaking in hushed tones. Tired of them acting like I was stupid and like they could just nudge me this way and that.

"Soon. You'll find out soon. I promise." She sighed as she leaned forward, cradling her midsection with her folded arms.

"What aren't you telling me?"

Before she could respond, Aether entered the courtyard and made his way to the podium. "Everyone, please pause for a moment." He cleared his voice before surveying the room. To my surprise, the doki-moses disengaged from their feedings and turned their attention to him. Respect, these recruits respected him. Impressive.

"We suffered a large loss last night. The transmission I just received from HQ is that our Eastern Outpost was also attacked, and they no longer deem it safe for us to continue our journey there. We are to reroute to the Southern Outpost and leave first thing in the morning. At dawn." He paused. "Be prepared to hike and be ready for anything. It's likely we will have to fight again. We will not be taking the circuit. However, cutting through the forest will be more direct, so it should only take two days to make it to the SO." He took a moment and surveyed the crowd. His eyes landed on me. I could have sworn the air behind him was darkening slightly and thickening. "Thank you for your bravery and continued cooperation." His eyes didn't leave mine. Not for several moments until cheers erupted from the crowd and Aether left the stage, striding straight for us.

Vala nodded and then reached for my hand. "Come with us." Her eyes pleaded with me.

"No." I didn't trust them. For all I knew, they were behind the attack, or the *reason* for the attack.

"You want answers? Come with us." She extended her hand in invitation as she stood, facing me, and waiting to see what I'd do.

Damn my curiosity.

I took her hand and stood following her and Aether as they left the courtyard. They walked out past the village buildings to the outskirts, where a large fire was burning. Too bright considering the kindling was that of the corpses of the fallen. Piles of bodies we'd recovered from the forest were gathered near the fire, waiting to be burned. Puddles of black goo dotted the field and reeked an awful odor. Vala and Aether dodged the piles and stepped over them without another thought.

Jared stood by the fire, tossing another corpse into the flames. He spotted us and motioned for us to continue out further past the fire into a ring on the ground composed of rocks and sticks in the sand.

Aether and Vala followed him, stepping inside the circle. I hesitated. The stench from the black goo was nearly unbearable. My nerves were sensitive, senses heightened. Perhaps nearly dying did that to a person.

Pop! I jumped at the sound of the fire crackling as it absorbed the most recent corpse. I was tired of being scared. Straightening my back, I stepped into the circle. All eyes landed on me.

"Well, start talking." I motioned with my hand before crossing my arms. I may be out here, and they may know I'm curious, but it was time for them to spill their guts—not me.

Aether flat-out ignored me and turned his attention to Jared. "Is it warded?"

"Naturally. No one will be able to hear what we say, but visuals are still open," Jared responded.

"Tate, has some, uh, questions," Vala started, looking between Aether and Jared.

"Damn right I do. Let's start with, what were those *things*?"

"We don't really know," Aether responded. "We call them seethings, but it's just a term as we don't have the genetic workup yet determined. We're still trying to learn *how* they were made."

"What do you mean how? Isn't Arithi responsible for them?" I was done with their bullshit. They all exchanged a look.

"Tate," Aether sighed. "We believe President Dale is creating them."

"What?" Did they really think I was that gullible?

"Why do you think Fletcher was working with us?"

"How dare you bring him up? He's dead because of you!" I stepped forward and dug my finger into Aether's chest. Rage, pure and deep, began to seep everywhere. I had every right to be angry, but my emotions were dominating, taking over my nervous system. I began to shake with their force. This emotional energy was something I'd never experienced before.

"Aether, maybe we should—" Vala started.

"Aether?" I interrupted. "Let's start there. You *lied* about your name. Why should I believe you're not lying now? That you didn't spread these same lies to Fletch?"

"We never lied to Fletch. He knew exactly who we were and what our purpose was and still is. A purpose that he believed in," Aether spoke, grabbing my hand gently in his. My skin burned from his touch.

"No. You don't get to invoke Fletch as a means to get me to trust you." I yanked my hand back, immediately mourning the absence of his touch. Every nerve ending was heightened, hell, *everything* felt heightened. Perhaps he was using magic on me again?

"It's not magic," Aether spoke.

Had I voiced my thoughts out loud? I truly was unraveling. I cupped my head in my hands. Those creatures, seethings, as Mardino, Aether—referred to them, had infiltrated the Glenn. Fletch would have fought them, and apparently had been doing so. But his involvement led to his death...this was too much.

I uncovered my face and locked eyes with Aether who was still just a foot away.

Remorse. Pain. Mine.

Emotions began to overwhelm me.

"Stop it!" I shouted, shielding my ears. The movement only amplified what I heard. Aether's breaths, warm and heavy. Vala's sharp inhale. Jared grinding his teeth. Too much.

"It's too much."

"Later. This can wait," Aether spoke, placing a hand on my shoulder. "Clear out."

"Aether, this can't wait," Jared challenged.

"Enough. She's overstimulated. This is a sensitive time for her."

"I don't give a damn. We've all risked a lot for her and it's time we have an honest conversation."

Aether turned, back to me and squared off with Jared.

"Jared, this isn't helping anyone," Vala tried to soothe the situation. A situation I didn't understand in the least.

"He's acting as if he's—" Jared's voice trailed off, sniffing in my direction. "You bastard." His eyes flared with anger; jaw set in challenge.

"Stop," Aether's tone held a deadly calm.

"It's against our laws. Our code. She's *changing*. How dare you—"

Aether's fist split Jared's lips. Blood sprayed as Jared stumbled back.

"You're dead!" Jared flung himself at Aether before halting, as if the air itself prevented him from getting any closer.

"Enough!" Vala shouted, stepping between the two. "Enough." She leveled a look at Jared and then turned pleading eyes to Aether.

Aether's chest heaved and the charge to the air dissipated, releasing Jared.

I could still *feel* the energy in the air. It called to me, tingling, even as Aether's shoulders released some tension, slumping slightly.

"Aether, we need to know what she told HQ about us. Why else would they attack their own transport?" Jared spoke, his eyes landing on mine, distrust shown in them.

Was he seriously accusing me of causing the attack?

"Later."

"That's it? Later?" Jared waved his hands, still covered in his blood.

"Yes," Aether spoke, heading for the circle's edge. "She's pulsing with unleashed energy. We should wait to do this."

My heart rate quickened as my emotional energy began to double; now anger and sadness coursed through my veins, mixed with righteous indignation.

"I did nothing. I said nothing. If you're looking to blame someone, blame your precious Arithi," I spat the words at Jared.

He took a step toward me, eyes wild.

"That's close enough," Aether intercepted him.

His scent of ash and salt became all-consuming—all I could think of, see, and feel. I felt my blood flowing, pulling in his direction, if that were even possible.

"How did they know we were in the circuit, Aether?" Jared pointed to me.

"She said she didn't say anything."

Were my ears failing me? It sounded like Aether was *defending* me.

"She can speak for herself." I stepped past Aether, approaching Jared. "I swear, I said nothing to them about Aether, Arithi, or your group. Honestly, I knew little to nothing." I huffed, blowing out too hot air. "I *know* little to nothing."

Sweat dripped down my forehead. Jared sneered at me. From here, I could see the fine lines tightening at his eyes, the disgust pulling at his mouth, the vein bulging at his neck. He didn't believe me.

My chest shook as I struggled to control my breaths. After everything I'd been through, I was having to *prove* myself—to him? To this male who *lied* to me and pretended to be my friend just the night before?

"I don't buy it." Jared glared at me. "You expect me to believe that you're really *that* naïve? That you didn't know about us? You want me to believe you are just another vampirical girl, a victim to the seethings, lied to by all you love? And to think, Arithi believes we *need* you." His nostrils flared.

I struggled to stay composed.

Death. Anger. Patience.

Aether's hands cupped my shoulders, swallowing them whole. It was idly comforting.

I took a deep breath. "Who is 'we' exactly? Are you an enemy Vamp who's attacking the Glenn? Are you behind the attack on the Eastern Outpost?"

Jared stepped closer before yet again being halted mid-step, the air suspending him. I could feel the charge surrounding me, the manipulation of molecules, and a foreign energy I couldn't place.

"Wow." Jared scoffed and shook his head. "Arithi thinks you will be an asset, thinks *you're* important, worth risking our lives. You know what I think?" He looked past me to Aether. "I think you're just another pretty face with nothing in your—" His words were cut off as he began to choke, desperately clawing at the air around him.

"Aether. Stop it," Vala commanded, but it was in vain. Jared just continued to claw at the air.

Aether released my shoulders and took a step back as he ran his hands through his hair. He was unfazed by Jared's gurgling and the red pallor spreading across his skin.

My veins pulsed, and I could feel my power building...the itch to shift more intense than ever. I couldn't shift now—I couldn't reveal that card. That required trust in them that I didn't have.

"Aether, look at her," Vala said, eyes wide and wholly focused on me.

I looked down, following Vala's queue, and could see my arms glowing. Shining with untapped power. Perhaps I could shift, perhaps I could kill. I wasn't stupid. I wasn't useless. And I wasn't powerless.

Yes, this felt right. I stepped closer to Jared. I could feel the charge surrounding him, feel the air manipulating his every breath. I reached out and caressed it, moving it with my sheer will. To my shock, the air responded. It released its grip on Jared, and he dropped to his knees, panting like a dog.

Power.

"Understand one thing, Jared," I spoke, the confidence in my tone foreign to me, "I did not expose you in the least. Furthermore, as for the suggested stupidity on my part, how would you fare if everyone in your life *lied* to you? How am I supposed to offer *you* answers when no one will offer me honesty?" I let my anger get the better of me. I lifted my wrapped forearm. Light began pouring out from under the bandage. "Do you really think I'd set myself up to be attacked by *things* I didn't even know existed eight hours ago?"

Jared didn't respond. He just stared at me, shock and disbelief filling his eyes.

I liked the way this power tasted. Sweet. "Answer my damn questions or I'll start asking elsewhere."

Energy began crackling through my veins, my vision becoming encompassed by a pink halo. The air around me swirled, lifting Vala's braids and Jared's shirt. I began to shake, any control I toted over my own physicality was slipping.

"Aether," there was a warning in Vala's voice.

The dome in which we stood swirled, the dirt was being picked up by the wind, whipping around and spattering in my face. The rocks began to shake, the sticks lifted and joined the cyclone now spinning around us.

Control.

I could sense air pressing around me, blanketing my senses. Calming.

"What do you want to know?" Vala was approaching me like I was a skittish kitten. It was purely infuriating.

"How about you start with Fletch's involvement? What did he have to do with your group?" I raised my brows. My breaths became rapid as my anger intensified. The pink halo was now a lens I could see out of—coloring the world around me. The wind increased and Jared's shirt began to rip from his body; his eyes squinted to keep the debris out.

"Tate," Aether spoke my name slowly, quietly, like it was a prayer. He began to stroke my shoulders, slow massaging circles, easing the tension.

I blinked. Vala's face looked scared. Like *I* was the monster. Control, I could control whatever this was. I closed my eyes.

Breathe. This is yours.

The wind slowed, and the rocks dropped and plummeted to the ground. Inhales, exhales, the distant popping of the fire. I grounded myself, one sense at a time. Warmth from the body behind mine; soft soothing circles being drawn on my back. I opened my eyes. The wind had stopped. Vala's braids were no longer floating, but now lay still in a tangled mess. Jared's shirt was half torn, dirt clinging to the blood dripping from his mouth.

"Tell me about Fletch," I commanded, each breath a challenge to force through my lips. Exhaustion was gnawing at me.

"He has been working with us, and for security purposes, just consider 'us' a rogue group." Vala cleared her throat, looking past me to Aether, who was still massaging my shoulders. His breath was warm against my neck. "We are not representative of any Vamp. We keep the peace and ensure justice. We are keepers of balance. Fletcher believed in our cause, was a *member* of our group, and upon the discovery of nature's laws being violated by the seething's creation, he took measures to help."

Fletch was a member of their group.

The realization began to quiet every other thought. If what she said was true, then Fletch wasn't *used* by Arithi, he worked with her to fulfill his own cause. My nerve endings began to cool, the intensity releasing slowly.

"And the seethings?" I questioned.

"It's our belief President Dale is creating them," Vala spoke, stepping in front of Jared and looking into my eyes earnestly.

The warm sensation around me further caressed my skin.

Incredible. Comfort. Pride.

"What was Fletch searching for?" I asked, my power further dissipating.

"Fletcher volunteered to locate information on the creation of the seethings. Things like how much dark magic was being projected, what organic matter was being used as a starting point, and the criteria for those *things'* creation. He wanted what we all want. To stop

President Dale." Vala's chest was heaving. Relief began to show as the tightness in her face faded and her eyes returned to their comforting brown tone. The friend I thought I'd had.

I stood there processing. It did sound like Fletch. He always had his own moral code and he often spoke of nature's balance. He instilled it in me.

I closed my eyes. "Why? Why would anyone create those things, those 'seethings' as you call them?" I couldn't fathom creating something that evil.

"We believe President Dale intends on starting another Great War. I think these are supposed to be his soldiers, his weapons," Aether answered, his voice calm and hot on my neck. My skin pebbled in response to the gentle tickle of his breath. It wasn't lost on me that his hands still held my shoulders, and that the air was thick around me like a security blanket.

"And how do I know you didn't create them? Huh? How do I know you didn't trick Fletch into helping?"

"You *know*," Aether whispered in my ear.

In my heart, I did know. I knew Fletch, trusted him. My skin began to brighten, arms lighting up as a peace settled into the core of my being.

"Shine bright from your heart, only it knows the truth!"

Fletch's last words now guided me. He was a good male. One who believed in valuing all life forms. One who supported my way of life, of feeding. He was, in many ways, a pacifist and often the first voice to condemn violence. If what Vala said about her group was true, then Fletch was—by his own standards—a member.

I nodded at Vala.

My vision cleared and the glow again faded as a steady welcome buzz began to hum through my body. I was hungry, inexplicably hungry. What was wrong with me?

"Tate, you need to get back to camp and feed. Vala," Aether commanded, releasing my shoulders. He stepped away, the airy assuagement following him.

"Right." She nodded at him and reached for my hand.

I hesitated. Every movement suddenly felt like too much. Weak, I felt weak. Gone was the heady power I'd felt moments before. In its place was a twinge of pain followed by the purest form of exhaustion. I'd only experienced this once before, and that was when I was transitioning into a vampire nearly five years before.

"Jared, get a message to Arithi that either President Dale released the seethings in the tunnels or that he doesn't have control over them. This could be posturing to support a declaration of war." Aether's words struck terror in my heart and snapped my attention from Vala's extended hand.

Images assaulted my mind. Those *things* attacking my fellow vampires in the forest, the one looming over me, smiling. I could see them being set free on the Glenn, attacking any and all in their path. Injuring the vamplings. Breaking through the veil, devouring the human realm. Dark magic was evil and destructive.

This is why Fletch gave his life. Tears began to collect in my eyes. I could still see him sitting on the couch, wine bottle in his hand, laughing. The relaxed way he was that night when he let all decorum fall. Happy. That was how I'd remember him, the way he was in life and not in death.

He hadn't failed me, I'd failed him. I should've been more aware, listened more. I was gone veil side too much. But wasn't that what he encouraged? For me to spend time *outside* the veil? To pursue justice? I may not have been there for him when he tried to tell me the truth, but I would not let his final words be in vain. My heart *did* know the truth. Fletch was a good male and had good values. If he thought this cause was worth dying for, then so would I.

I took Vala's hand and stepped forward, limping from the throbbing in my left leg.

"I'll send it. But Aether, we need to get back. Leadership is approaching," Jared voiced, nodding past the fire. He glared at me, and wiped the bloodied dirt from his mouth, spitting some on the ground. "Tate, try not to look so sick."

He definitely didn't like me.

Two village duxes were approaching the fire. They'd soon be close enough to see us huddled together.

"Disperse. Prepare for departure. Plan is the same," Aether ordered.

Vala tentatively led me toward the fire. Jared immediately headed for the woods.

We walked to the perimeter of the circle where Vala kicked several stones and sticks to break the pattern—a pattern that had somehow returned even after my breezy outburst.

I raised a questioning brow.

"Can't give all our secrets away." She winked at me.

Aether strode confidently toward the approaching duxes, his back straight and posture non-threatening. Ever the wolf in sheep's clothing.

CHAPTER 45

CHANCE

S hit. Holy shit. The Eastern Outpost had *another* attack. This one was, of course, classified and details were on a need-to-know basis. Apparently, leadership worried that any information about the attack would sway our search here.

"It doesn't sit right with my gut. Information is power, why withhold it?" Holland asked, massaging her temples. We'd been sent away hours ago, once the meeting had been adjourned by my father and Anax Graf.

"I don't have an answer." I sucked on my fang. Exhaustion was beginning to set in. That, combined with concern for the arches at the EO I had worked with last spring, had my head throbbing. How many had been killed in this most recent attack? Was it by those creatures? Were they evolving further than we'd seen?

"It smells. That's what I think." Holland stretched out her back. She was hunched over the desk poring through files while I combed through surveillance footage—footage that was disturbingly destroyed or missing, go figure—from the week leading up to the attack.

"Meaning?" I was too tired to have this fight again. My father was many things, but a dark magic wielder? That, he was not.

"Meaning there is information leadership is *intentionally* withholding. I don't like it."

"I don't either, but it is technically within the realm of protocol. I mean, when searching for a mole or suspected traitor, it is standard procedure to withhold new evidence from a separate outpost if it is suspected to contaminate the existing evidence or sway the opinion of the council." It was weak reasoning. Even I knew that we weren't councilmen, *and* we were working on an attack that had simultaneously occurred at the Eastern Outpost—not to mention, dealing with an enemy we didn't understand. All information *should* be shared with us.

"Really?" Holland leveled a stare at me. "We both know that doesn't really apply here. I know you want to believe that everything is on the up and up, and maybe it is, but there are several red flags here."

"Red flags? Did you guys make progress?" Shae's voice was a welcome interruption. I didn't feel like arguing this point with Holland —again. Maybe I was willfully ignorant or naive, but I wasn't willing to part with my firm belief in the good of the guara based on a few mishandled events and classified files.

"No, it's above your pay grade," I responded.

"It's above all our pay grades," Holland muttered under her breath.

"What is?" Shae asked, circling around with a completed roster. "I've finished filling out the first few sections, but you know it would be helpful if you told me what to look for in a little more detail—and if I could dig in *digital* files, you know the modern way we store, collect, and access information."

"Shae," I reprimanded.

"I know, we're not at that point yet," Shae mimicked my voice from earlier. "But a little more detail would be helpful."

"It goes against protocol and—"

"We're searching for a mole," Holland interrupted me.

"Holland," I snapped. Was she being serious?

"Look, we're in over our heads and have limited resources. If the Eastern Outpost is under attack, it's only a matter of time before this outpost may be attacked again. And since you don't want to let Shae do her thing..." Holland's reasoning was out of line.

"I thought better of you." I couldn't stop the words from spilling out or the widening of Holland's eyes. Shit. I was too tired for this, all of it.

"The Eastern Outpost is under attack? Are we at war?" Shae's grey-blue eyes nearly popped out of her head.

"We don't know." Holland closed her eyes. We were both mentally exhausted and it had been too long since our last feed. The blood bags we'd received three hours ago had worn off and, in reality, was really just a snack.

"How do you not know?" Shae circled the desk and put a hand on my shoulder. "Chance, what's going on?" Her eyes were pleading. I wanted to answer, but what could I safely tell her?

"Oh for fuck's sake, Dale, she's a brand-new *dokimos* and your oldest friend. If you can't trust her with a few details that could help us speed up our investigation, then who can you trust?" Holland's meaning was clear. This wasn't about Shae.

"Look, Shae, you know I trust you. It's why I brought you in to help in the first place. It's just, involving you and your *expertise* can have consequences."

"As if I haven't been taking risks my whole life. Besides, I know how to cover my tracks. Put me in coach." Shae puffed up her chest and tilted her chin back. Sometimes I swear she's still that seventeen-year-old kid who hacked into the high school mainframe to change her grades. "Chance, I can handle myself. I want to help. Let me."

I sighed and threw up my hands. "I guess you could help comb through the surveillance and look for—"

"Shit," Holland interrupted, disk in hand. "The council is ready to meet with us in twenty minutes. And Dale, the stretch of the circuit that was compromised has been identified. It's the eastern track, the one the new recruits were on. The entire circuit has been cited as destroyed just two clicks north of the last settlement to the EO."

Time slowed as I pieced together what she was saying. If the circuit was compromised, then there would be casualties. Dozens. One in particular had my blood running cold. How had I not thought of this before?

"Tate," Shae and Holland said at the same time, the first a plea, the second a curse word.

"What do we know?" I asked, yanking my disk out of my pocket.

"The file is remarkably short. It lists the stretch as unusable, unknown casualties, and that coms are down with the duxes and anaxes leading the new recruits," Holland's voice was monotone. I could see the conflict warring on her face.

"Was Tate on that circuit?" Shae's questions mirrored my internal one.

"Looking at the roster now." I scrolled quickly, thank blood her last name started with an 'A'. I froze. There was her name, clear as day: Tatealia Kaitlyn Aaralyn. "Shit."

"You have to help her! We have to do something! Send a convoy to intercept or something!" Shae was beginning to shake. "Chance, she deserves *your* help, you can't just leave her. She needs you."

Those three words shook my core. I could see Tate's mahogany eyes, all-consuming, the wrinkle between her brows when she scrunched her nose, her honey lily scent that always left a haunting feeling. I swallowed. Tate could very well be dead.

"We have to wait for the council meeting. They'll inform us of any new plans," Holland spoke slowly as she approached Shae. "But we'll do everything we can to help *all* remaining dokimoses." She rested her small hands on Shae's broad shoulders.

I stood there frozen as images of those monsters on four legs charging Tate and gutting her flooded my mind. Their black saliva dripping all over her, around her; four sets of fangs sinking into her flesh, tearing, sucking, devouring. The leader of those beasts on two legs howling before ripping Tate's limbs from her one by one. I could hear her cries, see her tears as her eyes slowly faded until the fire in them was gone and just mere shells remained.

We didn't know nearly enough about those things to defeat them. I barely escaped alive; the wound at my stomach was freshly healed and still twinged with pain from time to time. I had years of combat experience and personal military training even before I joined the guara; I was an excellent shot and decent swordsman.

Tate was not.

Fear gripped me as the possibilities continued to assault my mind. There was a very good chance Tate didn't make it. I needed to do more, know more, to stop these things. I should have already made progress in understanding their origins. I knew shamefully little about dark magic.

"Meeting starts soon, Holland, let's go. Shae, dig and dig deep. Search the database and research archives for anything on 'dark magic'. Cover your tracks. And...check the research lab here on base for ongoing projects. I want to know what leadership knows about those things." I clenched my jaw. "And Shae, you better damn well be as good as you boast. Getting caught can lead to a Disciplinary Hearing and execution. You don't have to—"

"Stop. I said I want to help, and you're insulting my intellect."

"This isn't high school, and I won't be able to—"

"I said I'll be fine. Now go." Shae swatted at me to leave as she pulled out a coder's disk I didn't even see her carrying.

"Shae," I started as I grabbed my coat from the chair back. "Get Arche Damaris in here and have him start combing through the rest of the surveillance. Have him look for anything out of the ordinary, unauthorized personnel entries, changes in patterns of workflow, arches going where they shouldn't, more visits to the research center by the wrong personnel, you get the point. Fuck protocol." I never thought I'd hear those words coming from my own mouth, but time became invaluable. "And Shae, this goes without saying, but don't tell him why or what you're doing."

I followed Holland through the door and into the large arched hallway. I could see the smirk on her face even from this angle. Holland and I may disagree as to who was manufacturing those things, but I was certain we had data on dark magic and historical references that could help us better understand these things that were infesting our borders.

"So, this has you skipping protocol, boy scout?" Holland whispered.

"Not now, Holland. Lives are at stake." With that, I brushed past her, heading for the conference room. I had more on my mind than Holland's ego. I had lives on the line. I could ignore the wrath of a female for now. Right now, I needed to try to hold on to all the pieces before my entire world imploded.

CHAPTER 46
TATE

We had been traveling since sun-up. It had been about ten hours and we were, allegedly, an hour out from the next settlement. Tomorrow. Tomorrow we would finish our trek to the Southern Outpost where I would finally be able to corner Chance for some answers. Shae too. I missed my pixie-haired friend. She was full of endless wisdom, and I found myself grateful that I'd soon be with her, if even as a part of the guara.

A pinecone crunched underfoot, and I looked up. These trees were ancient, bigger than the ones near HQ. They filled the air with a warm pine scent and offered pleasant patches of shade. The sun would go down soon and the sweat on my back would then turn to ice. My feet ached, my left leg throbbed with each step, and I was pretty sure my entire person was covered with dirt. I hated traveling like this.

"Hey, want some company?" Vala's voice sounded as she approached slowly from behind.

"Pass."

"Oh, come on, Tate. It's far too boring to be traveling all this way without a decent conversation. I'm so bored!" She was acting like nothing happened. Like we weren't just attacked, like I hadn't just learned Fletch was a part of her rogue group.

"Stop it!" I hissed, moving closer. "Stop acting like my friend and stop acting like nothing is going on."

"Tate, if I act like something's up, we'll all die."

Her words stung. Even though her statement was simple and serious, it took me back. This was the other side of the otherwise perky Vala. The serious, traitorous side.

"Well then, go talk to someone else. I don't have anything to say to you."

"You don't have to say anything at all. I'll do all the talking." She giggled, actually giggled. "Jared says I do way too much of it, so I'm sure he'll be relieved to hear I've unloaded some of it on you."

I clenched my jaw. This was going to be a long walk.

She continued to ramble on about the forest, the beautiful colors, and Jared's eyes. All normal stuff. All teenage stuff for a twenty-year-old, assuming she actually was twenty, to be focused on. It was completely at odds with the mission and the rogue group she served.

"How old are you?" I interrupted her soliloquy on tree lifespans.

"Me? I'm twenty, just a little younger than everyone else."

"Seriously, Vala. How old are you?"

"I'm," she looked around to see that no one was within earshot, "I'm really twenty, OK? That's part of why *I* was sent on this mission rather than more experienced operatives. But don't tell Jared I told you that."

Right, like that was the biggest secret I was keeping.

"Is anything else about you true? Any of that stuff you said on the circuit or the ramblings in the pub?"

"Yes, actually, just not in the same lens as you assumed."

Her response made no sense. "What?"

"Tate, what am I going to do with you?" She sighed and then pulled me into a side embrace and continued marching forward. "Ok, listen up. First off, I never lied to you. Not really. My family is in the military," she lowered her voice and whispered in my ear. "They just don't serve the Glenn," with every word, her voice grew even quieter.

"Where do they serve?" If she wanted to talk then fine, but I wasn't going to make it easy. I would get some *real* information.

"Uh-uh, no specifics. Let's just say they serve the rogue group." She winked at me before continuing. "My mother is in research. She's been trying to figure out the science behind the creation of those *things*. That part is completely true. She also is super strict and wanted me to follow her path and become a researcher, a scientist. Pshh." She swatted the air in front of her. "But, yeah, she believes dark magic is involved and that these creatures are not made from scratch." She was speaking so quietly I was surprised I could even make out what she was saying.

"Meaning?" I pried.

I'd learned from my mother that asking questions and short replies was often the best way of listening and learning. I wonder if she ever thought I'd end up here, using her advice to betray my country by having this very conversation.

"Meaning, they are starting with organic material and transforming it. We just don't know how yet." She swatted at the air again.

Charged. I could feel it buzzing, the electricity to the air current shifted and increased ever so slightly. He was near.

She picked up her step and actually began skipping down a hill, dragging me behind her. I gritted my teeth as I almost fell when my foot caught on a tree stump.

"For the love of blood, Vala, please slow down."

"Sorry!" She looked a little sheepish. "Jared says I walk too fast as well. I guess I just like to move at a quick pace. I know most vampires are gifted with speed, it's a common trait, but I like to move with style." She wagged her brows before letting go of my hand and sprinting forward to perform a cartwheel. What did she do for the group before this mission? She acted like she'd never been set free before.

The charge increased a tad, as if the source was getting closer. I squinted. There, I could see it. The glimmer of a thin shield in the air, of the air, hovering just a few feet in front of me. A sound shield.

"Show off." Jared's voice startled me.

"How long have you been there?"

He was standing just behind me, Aether to his left. I looked to Aether, he wielded no apparent effort in the forming of the shield, and yet from what I'd seen earlier, he was the one manipulating the air. He had to be.

"Not long. But long enough to know Vala was doing most of the talking. Per the norm," Aether grumbled under his breath as Jared focused his eyes dead ahead. Still not talking to me.

"Yeah, she's something else."

I saw it then. The barely noticeable dip in Jared's chin. The twinkle in his eyes, the pure admiration. He really cared for her, it wasn't just an act or a cover.

"You love her." Some of the ice around my heart began to thaw. They had been somewhat truthful. Perhaps the perky and serious version of Vala was just that, a variation of a real person and not an act or projected persona.

"You know nothing," Jared snarled before passing me, bumping my shoulder, and jogging down the hill.

Ice walls back in place. He may like Vala, but it was clear he didn't like me. Fine. I wasn't a fan of that boring male either.

Vala was back-springing down the hill, showing off her fantastic physique. Jared caught up to her and continued forward walking next to her backward steps. Ever the odd couple.

"There's a history there, in case you guessed it. But you're best to leave it be. Just a word of advice," Aether said.

"You're still there." I wished he would leave me alone. I didn't understand my body's response to his proximity, and I certainly didn't understand what had occurred within the warded circle earlier this morning. I'd never done *anything* like that before. Never felt that emotionally charged.

"Yep. I'll be sticking to you like a fly on honey."

"Seriously? Gross." His analogies could use some work. "If you're going to be there, then how about you tell me who you are."

"You know who I am."

"No, tell me your full name." I stared at him, noting the way some of his dark hair fell over his forehead in loose waves. The ends appeared a bit darker than the roots, but it could just be from sweat. Even with the scar across the right side of his face, he was magnificent to behold.

"I'll bite. My name is Aether. Just...Aether for now."

I shook my head from my stupor. I didn't need to be fixated on his face, no matter how appealing he was to look at. "No Mardi?"

He laughed and it was such a humbling sound coming from him. It made his eyes light up, changing from the black shade to that of a dark chocolate. The smile on his face softened his features and gave him a youthful appearance. And yet, it didn't diminish his masculinity, instead it oddly increased his sex factor.

"Nope. Mardi was something I made up just for Gari. And it uh, carried over." He winked at me, the smile not leaving his face. It drew my full attention to his lips. They were full, and even now I could recall the taste of them.

My heart rate sped up along with the fire in my blood. I could feel it sparking.

Desire.

"Tate Aaralyn." He cleared his throat, tearing his now deepening eyes from my face to focus ahead. "What else do you want to know?"

What? Was he seriously being nice to me and opening up?

"Why were you working for Gari?"

Stupid question! I should ask more about Fletch...and yet, I couldn't bring myself to say his name or think about him. I'd been trying to avoid that this whole trek.

"Intel."

Gee, that was helpful.

"Such as?" I was trying to recall his interrogation from the warehouse. Was that really just a few days ago? I shook my head. Life had really derailed.

"We became aware of President Dale's—"

"Collin, please, he doesn't deserve his title. Never has," I interrupted.

"Collin's." He smiled at me, and I couldn't place the look in his eyes. "Partnership with Gari. He was having Gari smuggle humans to him, specific individuals and bloodlines. We were trying to ascertain the criteria for human selection and the use of them once attained."

Tim's missing person's research came to mind. All those files, all those missing families. I had suspected a serial feeder, but I had never thought Collin would be behind it.

"To what end? Does Collin just have an acquired taste?" It wouldn't be the most disturbing thing about the male. Images of the most recent missing girl, Allie, came to mind. She may only be human, but she had a right to life, didn't she?

"Something like that."

Ah, that was the end of his openness. I should've guessed.

"You ever notice this trend or suspect Gari's involvement with the Glenn?" he asked the question as he bent down and retrieved a stick, fiddling with it between his fingers.

I wasn't about to answer him. We *both* would be open, or we both would not.

"See, James said you didn't, but I thought maybe you did. Maybe that's why you were attacking Gari?" He was fishing, I knew it, but still I *wanted* to answer. "Jared thinks we may have overestimated you."

"I had an idea but didn't know Collin was behind it."

"Mmm." He continued to fiddle with his stick.

"So, do you know what became of the missing humans?"

He didn't respond, just focused on peeling the bark off the wood with his thumbnail.

"I see," I grunted, increasing my pace. No company was better than his silent company.

"The seethings. I believe they were once humans...or that the human blood-magic was used to create them. Just a theory," his voice was quiet and stopped me in my tracks.

Did he really just *give* me information?

"No." If what he said was true, then those humans were not only dead, but they'd also been defiled.

"You're a lot like him, you know. He got that same puzzled expression on his face, all concentrated and simultaneously revolted."

"Fletch did?"

"He was a good male. I am sorry for your loss."

I didn't respond, didn't know what to say. I felt like Aether and Mardi were two very different people and I'd only dealt with Mardi before. This Aether was too different from the male I originally met. Or was he? Was I being deceived, again?

My hands began to jitter with energy. I really needed to figure out what was going on; maybe it was just adrenaline, but whatever it was, it needed to stop. I felt crazy.

"Thank you. See you at the settlement."

Without waiting for him to respond, I jogged forward and pressed through the air shield. At first, it resisted but then it just vanished, and I was free of the charged air.

Vala and Jared were walking hand-in-hand up ahead, Vala chatting constantly to the ever-silent Jared. I rolled my eyes. Perhaps they were predictable.

Aether's words affected me more than I'd like. Fletch was not a blood relative, and yet, the thought that I have a similar trait to that male made my heart warm. I would not let Fletch down. Not again.

CHAPTER 47

CHANCE

There was only one question I could think of: where was the death roster? We'd been sitting around the table for the past fifteen minutes before leadership finally arrived. Anax Clark looked disheveled; her grey bob was a staticky mess, and her pores were huge, sweat pouring from them. Sometimes super vision sucked.

"We have heard back and can confirm there are survivors. Of them, Anax Mardi informed me about two hundred of the five hundred dokimoses made it out alive. All experienced staff was accounted for with the exception of Dux Housha, may he rest in peace," Anax Graf started the meeting. My father's chair next to hers was glaringly absent. Where the hell was he?

"They are traveling on foot and have been rerouted to your location," she continued, "we expect them to arrive in about forty-eight to seventy-two hours. There are settlements on the way to house them."

Was she serious? They were just attacked and now they were exposed and traveling on foot through woods that were possibly infested?

"Excuse me," I interrupted. Today, apparently, was a day for breaking all kinds of protocol. A slippery slope. "Will we be discharging a team to bring them back? Surely, they'll have injured among them, and we don't know where those things have gone."

"Dux Dale." Anax Graf leveled her gaze at me. Fine, let her be pissed, just answer the damn question. "We will not."

"What?" The word came out a half-whisper. How could we not help our own?

"Leadership has deemed the woods an unsafe space and as such, they're on their own until we can better understand our enemy and how to stop them. From your very own report, it appears they are evolving. We don't know who will make it through the night, let alone who will be standing by the time any team reaches them."

"So, you've sentenced them to death?" Unbelievable. I stood up; if they wouldn't help, I sure as hell would.

"Sit down, boy!" Rusty spat, saliva landing on my hands. Black veins webbed from around his eyes that were now haloed in deep purple. Worse than earlier today.

I leveled a glare at Rusty and straightened my back to my full height.

"Enough. Both of you stand down," my father's voice barreled through the room.

I glanced to the head of the table. Sure enough, his hologram was there and was more terrifying than in person. I swallowed. I needed answers. Leaving our men to die, *that* is exactly the opposite of what I stood for, why I enlisted.

"Now," my father's voice had a cold monotone key to it. *TAP!*

Hands gripped my shoulders and slammed me back into my seat. I rocked back before finding my balance and the grip on my shoulders vanished. Across from me, Rusty looked just as perplexed as he rocked in his chair. He was a new shade of red, embarrassed. At least I could appreciate that.

"Dux Dale, we understand your stance," Anax Graf's voice drew both mine and Rusty's attention. "It's a horrible situation, but the fact is that sending more recruits out there is merely increasing the death toll risk. They won't make it back any faster if we send aid, we'd merely be increasing our exposure. Surely you recall your combat and strategy training?"

"It's true, lad. Much as I hate to admit it, we were outnumbered back there and barely escaped. I mean, you were a sack of potatoes on me shoulders," Dux Carran let out a dry chuckle. "Any chance they have is in their own hands," he finished, his tone softer than usual.

"But surely there's something we can—"

"Dux Holland, we've addressed that at length. Time to move on to more pressing matters," my father's voice interrupted her.

More pressing matters? Was he serious?

"The council has voted, and the Glenn is now at war."

The entire room fell silent. War. Something we had fought hard to avoid in the last century. War. Unimagined carnage, loss of life, and for what? Why were we going to war?

"With whom?" Anax Clark voiced, her eyebrows raised, forming a rather unattractive unibrow.

"That is the question, isn't it. Anax Graf?" My father turned to the anax sitting at his right.

"Our enemy has proven elusive. However, based on the intel we've received from Dux Richards and from the Eastern Outpost's ongoing investigation, it would appear The Fern and possibly Wataedge are involved."

I gasped. She was speaking of an all-out war, not with just one vamp, but two and possibly all three?

"What intel?" Holland asked, her honey-brown eyes clear and searching the holograms.

"We intercepted some transmissions that point to the Fern's involvement. Additionally, the data breach at the Eastern Outpost had Fern markers all over it. Our technical team followed the trail, and it is believed the hack originated in two parts: one in-person with a device to override our security system from the base itself and the other originating from the south, from the Fern. They followed it as far as they could before they hit resistance from the Fern's own intelligence team. Furthermore, the hardware recovered from EO has been traced back to the Fern," she spoke slowly and folded her hands before straightening her spine. "Given this data, we are inclined to believe they are also responsible for the attacks on the EO and SO, though the SO search has yet to yield anything helpful." Anax Graf raised a brow at Holland and me.

Like we hadn't been trying. Like we weren't attacked by creatures, and like I wasn't just gutted alive.

"What other evidence is there connecting Wataedge or Yates?" I voiced. Like hell I was going to have the conversation derail to my apparent misgivings.

"Good question," Anax Graf started before looking to my father. To my shock, he looked *proud?*

"Sources have confirmed that both The Fern and Wataedge are stacking their borders and centralizing their troops. Furthermore, when our internal intelligence team sent feelers out, they were unanimously banned by a shield that has components from both Wataedge and the Fern. In addition to some foreign markers that of Mydant..."

The land of the Fae? They hadn't involved themselves with our realm since the last Great War. Even their embassy base here was barely manned. Dear blood. This could turn into another dimensional war. Just like the last.

I began to massage my temples. No wonder they were denying a rescue convoy. If we were indeed at war, they would need every soldier we had—and more.

"So, nothing solid connecting Yates?" Anax Clark spoke up. She pushed her thick-framed glasses further up her elongated nose. "You suggested they were involved?"

"Nothing solid connecting them to the recent attacks," Anax Graf answered. "However, upon our ambassador's request for a meeting to gain an alliance if a realm war does ensue, he was denied and his quarters were ransacked. He barely made it out alive."

"So, this is it then?" Dux Carran spoke as he stood. "My generation's nightmare has become reality."

CHAPTER 48

TATE

We made it to the settlement, Oak Shire, just as it got dark. Thankfully, the trip was uneventful. I didn't speak to any of the dirty trio, my new nickname for them, the rest of the day. Since I'd gotten here, I'd managed to hide away and remain blissfully unnoticed by most. This was a retirement settlement with a small plant. They manufactured glass bottles and managed a small, but stable farm. No human vessels. The thought had upset most of the dokimoses and caused a near riot. To make things worse, the settlement was not prepared to host a group of soldiers. Even with our platoon being cut down to less than half our original size after the last attack, we were too much for them to handle. We'd be sleeping outside.

Additionally, the blood supply was low, which meant we were being rationed. I was given one small blood bag, a snack, and not nearly enough after the long trek.

My hands were shaking, they had been for the past two hours. Too much exertion, I supposed. I took a deep breath and tried to steady them. My vision began to double.

I felt sick.

Pulling up a blanket, I buried my hands in it and closed my eyes. I needed the dizziness to subside before we left again tomorrow morning. I tried to relax on the small bedroll I had found, but it proved nearly impossible with my new nausea and pounding headache; sitting was the best option.

I tried to think about the scenery, focus on nature like Fletch had once taught me after a particular grueling training session. I was tucked into the corner of a building that overlooked the valley below. It was peaceful here. Unprotected, but peaceful. The settlement had only one hundred fifteen vampires staffing it. I couldn't help but notice that most of these vampires were maimed. Several were missing limbs and had prosthetics in their place. The one who handed me the blood bag didn't speak and another was missing an eye. So, this is where they sent the injured or those who couldn't serve the guara's military might.

It felt wrong to see them here, wasting away. They were all very thin and their skin held a sickly pallor. Given how I felt, I wondered how far off my complexion was.

Footsteps approached, but I was too tired to look up. Hopefully whoever it was would just keep going.

"You look like shit."

Apparently, I wasn't that lucky. I looked up and met Aether's eyes, trying to focus on him but failing epically with my new double vision.

"Just keeping pace with you," I tried to add swagger to my tone, but it fell flat.

"Here. Drink this, it will help." He extended a pint glass full of scarlet liquid. It was darker than bloodwine usually was and had a strange golden glow to it. That is, assuming it wasn't my vision acting up on me again.

"No thanks." I turned my head and closed my eyes. I didn't have verbal sparring in my arsenal at the moment.

"One truth. I'll give you one truth if you take this and drink it."

Was he really trying to bribe me into drinking the bloodwine? I mean, I sure as hell wanted it, but I didn't need charity or to be more vulnerable to him. Still…I could get some answers this way, if I could focus long enough to ask a question.

"One truth."

I looked at him. His leathers were clean; apparently, he'd brought a change with him—where the hell he kept it, I'd never know. They fit him perfectly. Highlighted each curve and muscle. His black shirt was unbuttoned and the leather vest he wore held daggers in it.

He was ever the dark angel.

"How do you manipulate the air?" It had been bothering me since I first witnessed it. Since I'd *felt* it and had reached out to the power. I'd never known such magical giftings existed. "What type of magic-wielding is it?"

The right side of his lips tipped up in a smile.

Pride.

"Magic, my dear." He winked at me.

"No shit, what type of magic? I never knew that air manipulation was possible."

"It's hard to explain but think of it like a charge. Lightning responds when negative ions build up and are met by positive ones. It's a striking force of power. Like responding to like." He sat down, back resting on the wall behind us.

Close, he was so close. I became engulfed in his scent: ash and salt.

"Honestly, it's shocking how little the Glenn focuses on magic education. They'd have you believe it's rare, that aside from normal giftings, magic doesn't exist. They lie. To you and to every citizen. Your very being is composed of magic, the ground we sit on is rich with it."

I could feel the air around me tightening to a pleasant pressure. Comforting my aching body, almost to the point of massaging it. Delightful.

"But to answer your question," he cleared his throat—his voice suddenly deeper and breathy. "Consider it a manipulation of air pressure. I can feel the weak spots and feed it, making it stronger, or yank it away altogether." He moved his hand, and the air in front of my face swirled and danced, blowing wisps of my hair around in its breeze.

"And that's not accounting for the moisture in the air or the electrical charge it holds. They are all elements that respond to me—to my power. Energy manipulation." He flexed his fist and a small burst of light appeared in front of me along with a sizzling. The charge in the air strengthened, making the hair on my arms stand and my blood tingle. Then he relaxed, dropped his hand back to the glass he still held in the other. The charge dissipated, but the welcoming comfort from the air pressure did not. "Power you too hold, Tate."

His eyes locked with mine. I hadn't noticed before, but he had flecks of gold in them that circled his irises. The scar that jutted from his forehead was jagged and about a quarter inch thick.

"What caused that?" I reached out and touched the scar with my fingers. It was soft and tight. Old then. The air around me sparked and a gentle wind began to caress my face.

"I said one truth." He grabbed my hand with his, stopping me from caressing his face.

What was wrong with me? I yanked my hand away, red creeping up my cheeks.

"I don't have magic." Lie. I knew it, and from his look, so did he. They may think they need me, and they may be open about *their* use of magic, but shifting was punishable by death in the guara. Who knew what kind of stand Arithi had on shifting? Perhaps, she and Aether would also consider it a violation of natural law and be disgusted by me.

No more rejection.

"You have so much more raw magic than you know."

"I know myself. I know what I'm capable of, and what I'm not. And right now, it's about to all come flying out of my mouth in the form of stomach bile." I pulled the blanket up higher, willing my stomach to calm.

"It's normal, you know." He gestured to my hands. "It's called Starving Nervous Breakdown Syndrome. Many of us experience it when going through the Changing."

Changing.

"Are you seriously diagnosing me? I'm just tired and hungry. That's it."

"We both know there is more to it than just that. You've probably never felt like this before, and believe it or not, I *can* relate to how you feel."

I leveled a look at him, grateful that even though I couldn't focus, I could still glare at both of his outlines.

"Don't believe me? Let me guess then," he relaxed his shoulders as he spoke. "You are seeing double, have a splitting headache, and are nauseous. You're starving and exhausted and I've already seen your hands shake. This blood will help." He swirled it in the glass, the gold mixing with the red. "You're end of the deal." He winked at me as he set the glass down and stood up, the warmth from his body fleeing with him.

I stared at the liquid. I must be really sick because the gold in it was now swirling into a patterned shape. Part of me *knew* that shape with its large talons, wings, and fire-lit throat. Impossible.

"I'll leave you to it then." He walked away, each footstep carrying the sharp air with him until the comforting pressure ceased and I was left to the cold, dull air.

The wine beckoned me. I wanted to drink it, my body was craving it, and yet I didn't fully trust Aether. Logically, I know he saved my ass back in the tunnels and that Arithi wanted me, though I wasn't sure why. Could my sickness be brought on by his magic? Could this all be an elaborate game to gain my trust?

I grabbed the cup and sniffed it lightly. It smelled divine, better than any bloodwine I'd ever smelt. The glass was warm, which was odd considering this settlement's lack of vessels. Perhaps he heated it up? Or maybe I was just *that* cold and hallucinating.

Rustling in the valley below drew my attention. Panic seized me as I saw two figures emerge. I exhaled a breath of relief. It was just the scouts. Or scout, with my double vision I really wasn't sure. If that had been a seething, would I have survived? No, not with how I'm feeling now. Like it or not, I needed food and for whatever reason, Aether brought me some. I lifted it to my lips, spilling a little because my hands wouldn't stop shaking, and drank.

The moment the liquid hit my tongue, sparks fired throughout my whole system. I felt amazing. The wine slid down my throat and my very being responded to it, welcoming the thick iron like it was an old friend I'd missed and never even knew. I became hyperaware as I took another sip.

My vision cleared almost instantaneously. What type of blood was this? The flavor had berry notes to it that were covered with something heavier, something ashy, and almost molten tasting. It was divine.

I continued to drink and my whole body warmed, my hands stopped shaking, and my mind became clear. I could hear the crackling of pine needles and cones falling in the forest far below; the swaying of the grass was a melody riding the notes on the slight breeze that wove through the aspens and pines, into the valley where it seemed to twirl and dance. I could hear conversations from several different people all at once; I could see the details on the scout, singular, below and noted it was one of the newer dokimoses. He was aboard the circuit with us. His name was Louie. I took one last deep drag and to my utter disappointment, the glass was drained. My arm was tingling, and I looked down to see it glowing slightly under the wrap.

I pulled at the fabric and saw my skin mending itself in real-time from the bite I'd sustained. My flesh was glowing as it melted over the exposed, blistered parts and began to fuse. Small scales lit up in a pink hue over the wound and then disappeared, like they were never there. The pain I'd felt since the bite was gone and the skin looked completely healed, unbroken.

My head no longer hurt either. I ran my fingers through my hair and noticed the ends looked different. They were tinted rose pink. What the hell? I stood and the amount of energy I felt was amazing. I bounced from one foot to the other, unable to stop moving. It was like I'd just downed three energy drinks, fed from a live vessel, and had a full night's sleep. I was amped.

I began walking, but it felt too slow. I needed to run, I needed to move. Each step was sure, confident. My left leg no longer throbbed, instead I felt glaringly *nothing* from it. A smile tugged at my lips. I could get used to this.

I was warm. Really, really warm. There was a stream not too far back, just a short walk down the path from the village. The water was cool when I'd crossed it earlier. It was miserable then, but now? Now, it sounded like heaven. I began to walk that way without hesitating. Seethings? If they came, I was confident I could fight them or, at the very least, outrun them. Is this what drugs felt like? The thought of Aether drugging me didn't bother me nearly as much as it should.

I weaved past several couples making out, some were intimate while others fought. It sounded like they were arguing over food, big surprise there. But I didn't care. I continued until I reached the edge of the village and then down the path. I was drunk on power. The raw feeling in my nerves was something I'd never experienced at this level before. It was as if my entire being was composed of energy, raw power waiting to be tapped. When I'd shifted before, I'd feel some energy, but nothing compared to this.

Perhaps this is what I've been missing all along. The missing notes to my soul's unfinished song.

My temperature continued to spike, sweat dribbled at the side of my forehead, my arms, and my chest. I breathed heavily and the airway to my lungs was scalding, each breath began to burn. I needed water and I needed it now.

I could hear the stream up ahead and began to unbutton my jacket. I tossed it off, careless of where it landed. Too hot, I was too hot. Inhaling again, I could feel the air heating up as it entered my lungs. It seared upon exhale and the air around me fogged up like it does in the middle of winter. But it wasn't winter, it was fall. And much too warm for night.

I pulled my tank off next and abandoned it too. The ground was getting moist, the reeds and grass thicker. I was on the riverbank a moment later. I unzipped my pants and stepped out of them, letting them fall to the shore. Stepping into the water, steam rose. The water sizzled. I stepped further in and was engulfed in a cloud of steam. The clear night became foggy, and the further in I walked, the denser the air became. I could see only a foot in any direction, nestled in a blanket of privacy of my own creation.

I took a deep breath, still far too hot, and dunked myself under water. The current gently pulled at me, beckoning me to follow its flow. I rooted my right foot against a few loose rocks on the bottom and stopped myself. My left foot couldn't quite reach, but what did it matter?

The current was a blessing. The water surrounding me began to boil, but was soon washed away and replaced with refreshing, new, cool water. I sprang up from the bottom and breached the surface, wet hair blocking my vision.

I swam a few feet to the left until both feet could touch and find purchase to hold me still. I closed my eyes and focused on one sense at a time. The sizzle of the air, like when water is poured onto flames. The sound of rushing water, beginning to boil. The reeds swaying in the distance.

The cool liquid coated my skin up to just below my armpits. It felt absolutely amazing. I opened my eyes, the mist thicker now. Steam. I gulped oxygen greedily, but even the air here was no longer cool; while it no longer scalded as it rushed into my lungs, it felt warm and muggy, like a hot humid night in July.

My entire body was reacting in a way that was foreign to me. For my internal temperature to be *this* warm, I should be dead. I was a vampire and fire could kill. And yet, I was alive and felt gloriously deadly.

The air shifted, filled with a charge, a tell-tale sign. He was near.

"I wondered if I'd find you down here," Aether's voice cut through my stupor.

I turned around, the steam so thick that it took a moment to realize he was only a few feet away. He was bare-chested, his tattoos crawling up both shoulders and peaking at his neck. They scrolled in an elegant design away from his collarbone, dipping slightly onto the right pec, before pulling back and disappearing behind his neck. The tattoo on his left arm scrolled further down in an intricate pattern I couldn't quite make out.

I instantly became *very* aware of my light pink thong and matching bra.

"It's dangerous to experience the first heat alone. I needed to make sure you didn't overheat."

His words weren't registering. All I could see were his lips moving, beckoning me forward.

"Dangerous, how?" I took a step closer, slipping slightly until my foot found a new stone to anchor onto.

I could make out a vague raising of his chest, the way the water lowered with his inhale, getting gloriously close to his hip bones… revealing the V that started to form just above the surface of the water. His exhale had the water rising, just enough to cover the teasing curves.

The sizzling sound coming from the water near me continued and more steam rose from all around me.

"Tate?" His eyes deepened in question. "How do you feel?" He stepped closer to me.

"Did you drug me?" I wasn't about to confide in him that I felt fucking amazing.

He extended his hand toward me, and I leaned back, just enough to cause my right foot to lose purchase. I was slipping, being pulled by the current.

His hands reached out and gripped my waist, holding me still in the water. "I won't hurt you." The sincerity in his brown eyes caught me off guard. "I just want to make sure you're okay. This is…" He cleared his throat as his gaze dipped to my breasts just hovering above the water in the pink lace bra. "A very delicate time for a Untishee."

Did he just say what I thought he did?

Words completely escaped me as I tried to conceive what he was telling me. He lifted one hand out of the water and touched my forehead.

Searing heat pulsed through me at his touch. The steam in the air hissed as the water around me began to *boil* on the surface. And yet, he didn't remove his hand. His eyes locked on mine, and for the first time, I could see the gold rings circling the black. Not just gold flecks, but golden rings. He was absolutely gorgeous. My breath caught.

"Breathe, just breathe." His other hand pulled me closer to him, my waist barely grazing his chest, the water a barrier growing thinner by the moment.

I could feel my core heating up, aching. I wanted him. Logic seemed to be failing me because all I could think of was how badly I wanted to reach out and caress his skin. Trace his tattoo with my fingers, pull at the hair tie holding his hair in a bun.

I reached up and grabbed the leather strap binding his hair with one hand. Here in the water, we didn't have such a large height difference. Here, with him holding me out slightly and his standing in a lower space, we were practically equals. I tugged on the leather strap, releasing it from its hold.

I hadn't noticed before now, but the ends of his hair were, in fact, black fading to brown at his roots. His eyes hooded and deepened as his jaw ticked back.

Desire. Beauty. Wrong.

I was acutely aware of his touch at my forehead as his other hand tightened on my waist, closing the distance between us so that my chest now pressed against his own. I wanted more. I looped my hands around his neck and played with his hair at the back of his skull.

This felt so right. My body acted on its own accord, with little to no thought from me. I could feel a pull within me, a tug like that of my shifting string, but this one didn't hide in murkiness. No, this one pulled outward, toward him.

I followed that string and allowed my left hand to search his tattoo. To trace it idly with my finger.

A moan escaped his lips as my chest pressed tighter against his. My skin was hyperaware. I intricately felt every nerve ending, every atom that pressed against his chest. He was delightfully warm, even in my current heated state, his warmth was welcoming. And his ash scent? Intoxicating.

"You smell like..." Home. He smelled like home. It was one thing to think it, another to say it aloud. That was a whole new level of vulnerability.

"It's just the transformation. You'll feel like this until it's complete." His lips were so close to my head. I angled up to look him in the eye and felt frighteningly small. Even so much closer to his height, I was still small. He gulped as his eyes filled with lust.

He wanted me. Just as I did him.

The air charged further; I could hear it sizzle and *pop!*. The mist thickened and pulsed with living energy.

Want. Wrong. Control.

"Don't tell me you're scared now. You can feel it. I know you can. I can...sense you." It was the most truthful I'd ever been with him and myself.

I could deny it further, pretend that I wasn't sensing him and his emotions, but I was tired of being afraid. Perhaps I really was drugged, but regardless, right now this *felt* right.

He moved his hand, now cupping the side of my head to the back of my skull before he leaned down and was just a mere breath away.

Slipping. Mistake. Need.

"You need me. I need you." It was so simple. Why was he resisting?

He pulled back, just enough so I could see his whole face.

"Tate, you hate me, remember?" He swallowed again as his eyes lowered to my heaving chest, then back to my lips, which were now wet and ready. "Trust me, you'll hate me for this."

"I decide what I want, who I want, and when. But you? I never pegged you for a coward."

His eyes flared. I got him. I slowly slid a hand down his abs, touching each muscle's outline until I reached the glorious 'V' leading to just beneath his boxers. Disappointment filled me, I'd hoped he'd be unencumbered.

My heat was building and the water around me boiled even

further. I remembered the way he tasted, the ancient flavor of him was fresh in my memory. I wanted more. I placed one hand flat on his chest and moved my other one lower, barely grazing the tip of his manhood. He wanted me. Of that I was certain.

I smiled.

He shuddered as I palmed the outline of *him*. He was ready and firm. "Your flagpole tells all. It's like that with all you males, no use denying attraction when it's physically evident." I smirked. I felt like I was in control again.

His hand on my back tightened and then moved lower to the dip in my back. His grip tightened, crushing me against him. I could see the warring in his eyes.

"You don't understand. This," he whispered as he tipped my chin up and looked me fully in the eyes. "This is a gift. One I...I don't deserve. You're too young to get it, but trust me, when this heat is over, you will hate me. If not then, when you complete your Changing."

"I am *not* a child." I tightened my grip on his cock, eliciting a moan.

"This is a mistake," he whispered, even as I could feel him thrust against my now pinned hand.

"Only your brain thinks so, your body has other ideas." With that, I squeezed him firmly as I sealed my lips with his. Gently.

I pulled back. "Tell me again. Tell me to stop," I whispered, challenging.

He didn't move. Didn't speak. He just breathed, the air around me tightened. I felt the air's current, its energy in my very core; a string wrapped in power. I pulled on it further and the air around me began to spin, lifting my wet hair from my chest and water droplets with it. We were now encased in a water cyclone, beauty and mist all around.

Incredible. Powerful.

"You're too much," his voice was barely audible before he leaned down and took my lips in his.

The kiss was consuming. Unlike the first time where it was full of ire and anger, a resentful capture of my lips, this was hot, wild, and desperate. I parted my lips further and made room for his tongue to slip in.

He explored my mouth as I tasted him slowly. My temperature spiked and the air around me hissed wildly. The wind increased as water droplets now began to pelt us both, slicking the movement of our unsubmerged bodies.

I never wanted anything so much. Anyone so much. Every stroke of his tongue, his hands, felt *right*. I began to contract at my center and slipped my legs around his waist. Removing my hand from his length, I dug both of them into his hair as he adjusted his grip on my lower back to now cup my butt. His hands were so large that an entire cheek was swallowed by his grip.

He tilted me back further. The kiss was claiming. Engrossing. It was everything that mattered.

I moaned as his hand stroked my inner thigh. Electricity filled me, my entire body hummed as he began to thrust, rocking us back and forth. He was hard and ready. Even in the water, I could feel my own wetness spreading and begging for more.

"I want you," I whispered as he pulled back and began to kiss my jawline, making his way down my neck to my collarbone.

Over the scar—the lover's mark—he hesitated.

I could feel a shift in the air as it began to screech like a teapot left on the stove for too long. Pressure from all angles began to consume me. He claimed that spot on my neck with his mouth and began to suck and then lick and then kiss until the skin felt raw. I arched into him as he made his way past that spot further down my neck to the top of my chest. He slipped his free hand to my shoulder, moved the bra strap down, and then continued the journey with his mouth.

Nothing had ever felt so right, so perfect, so intended. I felt like I'd found my missing piece.

With a snap, my bra came undone, and I shrugged it off before tossing it into the river. A glow enveloped us, it was hazy and black but also tinted pink, like a sunset in the aftermath of a fire.

"Yes," I could barely moan as his mouth found my peaked nipple.

He claimed it like he had my mouth and teased its peak with his tongue. He sucked deeply and my entire body exploded. I'd never felt this way without my clit being heavily stimulated, and hell, he hadn't even ventured down there. But as my body spasmed against him, I saw stars.

I was acutely aware of each gentle pass of his tongue, the graze of his fangs against my breast, and the way my body responded as he pulled me deeper into his mouth. Pressure was building within my core, demanding I release. The air around us began to twirl faster, hazy and pink; mysterious and beautiful. I threw my head back, letting the water tug at my hair while his grip tightened on my waist, all the while he licked and teased with his mouth.

More.

He adjusted his grip, freeing one hand that then began to graze the inside of my thigh. He worked his way up with his hand as he released my nipple from his mouth and licked the column of skin up to the old fang marks near my neck. He reached for my center with his hand and circled around the sensitive bud with his thumb, teasing even through my thong. I moaned as I rocked against him. He sucked on the old fang mark as his fingers teased me. The tension was nearly too much.

With a single stroke, he flicked my clit and I climaxed. My body seized as he shuddered against me, pleasure erupting and the pressure dismantling. The air stilled, and the charge reduced to a comforting caress, cradling my body. My hair lowered to my back, the only cover I had for my upper body. He released me from his mouth, and I sagged against him. The water quieted and was no longer boiling. I could feel his breath, mimicking mine in perfect time as we both held one another and simply breathed. I rested my head against his chest and closed my eyes.

The heady feeling I'd felt a moment ago was beginning to clear. I still felt every nerve and fiber of my body firing, but my breath no longer burned. I no longer was causing steam to form or the water to boil. This may not be right, perhaps it was in the heat of the moment like he'd said, but I didn't care. A content sigh escaped my lips.

"This was—"

"A mistake," he finished for me, releasing me from his grasp and letting my body fall into the water. I slipped, but the air around me held me steady until my foot touched the ground.

Hurt flooded my system at his rejection.

"I see you're feeling better. Your temperature is back to normal. I need to get back." He began to turn and leave.

How dare he? How dare he make me *feel* this way?

"No." Power surged from me and stopped him in his tracks, the air crackling as it constricted around him. "You don't get to do this. You don't get to make *me* a regret." I gritted my teeth, willing the air to turn his body so I could see his face.

His eyes locked onto mine. Wide. Surprised.

Good, the jackass didn't deserve to think he *knew* it all. He knew nothing.

"What happened here? You wanted it just as much as I did. I could sense it."

He said nothing, just stared at me. He didn't fight as I tightened the air around him. I didn't understand how I controlled it as instinct took over.

"Fine. Reshape these events in your own mind. But be honest with me about this; you said something earlier that struck me as odd..." I needed to voice the question I'd avoided. The one word I tried to tune out whenever I heard it uttered. "Untishee," I whispered the name.

"And?" He began to pull from the air's grip on him, easily slicing through the hold like it was nothing. Like my power was that of a child's. "You have much to learn, Tate."

I could feel the air around me respond to his call, his command. It left me, fleeing, and I could do nothing to stop it. Nothing to stop the comforting pressure from evaporating.

I felt naked without his body pressed against mine, without the air pressure cradling me. I was vulnerable. I crossed my arms across my chest and leveled a look at him.

I tried to mask the hurt, how small I felt. Logically, I knew it shouldn't feel this way. I didn't like him, right? I didn't *know* him or trust him. And yet, I felt drawn to him, as though there was an inexplicable electricity between us; a connection I'd never felt before. It was more than just chemistry, far more. It was as if we shared the very same energy. As if he was somehow an extension of me.

"I said Untishee earlier, because no, they're not mythical, and we both should know that because we both *are* Untish."

War. We were at war and I still didn't even know who all the players were. I filed out of the conference room following Holland.

"We need to refuel. I'll meet you back in the library in an hour." Without another word, she turned and headed down the hallway. I guess that was one mystery solved, she was upset. A hunch told me it had to do with Tate, but I didn't have time to concern myself with Holland's feelings.

It was just sex; she should know that.

Did I think she was an impressive female? Absolutely. Was she smoking hot? Damn straight. But was she Tate? No.

Shaking my head, I broke free from the group of leadership and headed for the kitchen. I needed a quick feed, a bottle of bloodwine, and then I needed to get back to the library. The meeting had lasted three hours. It could have been enough time for Shae to discover something. Maybe.

Heading through a dusty hallway, I turned left and went down three flights of stairs until, at last, the corridor opened to the outdoor courtyard. I strode across the stone floor, breathing in the fresh air. It was nearly morning. Odd how time means little to nothing when you're in meetings and locked inside all day. I took one more deep breath and then entered the arched hallway at the opposite end, noting how it was lit with torches. Funny how fire can kill us and yet we see it everywhere. I used to think it was poetic, the choice of using fire over electricity, that it kept us humble. Now I couldn't help but wonder if it was stupid or egotistical to have weapons lining the hallways throughout this entire fortress.

I walked by one patrol squad and then finally made it to the mess hall. Just a little further and I'd be in the wine reserves. The hall was buzzing, the first place I'd seen more arches than just the four in the squad. They were setting the tables, filling wine mugs, and then, of course, pouring blood into goblets at each seat. It was customary for vessel feeding to occur only for high-ranking officers or as a reward earned by dokimoses or arches. Otherwise, they got blood bags. If they were lucky, it would have wine in it. I definitely didn't miss this about prasinos.

Passing several dokimoses and arches who looked like they'd rather be sleeping or drowning themselves in blood, I made it to the kitchen and then continued back to the VIP room. The door was guarded, as I expected, by a squad of rather hungry looking arches.

"Credentials," one of the arches asked me as he approached, hand outstretched.

"Dux Dale." I pulled out my ID badge and he scanned it.

"Continue. Good day, Dux Dale." The guard motioned for me to move forward through the thick iron door. Some things never changed. I pushed the heavy door open and allowed my eyes to adjust. Inside, there were candles lining the walls, chaises throughout with sheer drapes from the ceiling, offering an intimate setting despite minimal privacy. I spotted several vessels already in use.

Weaving through the large room, I continued to the back. A male vessel lounged on a chaise, a glass of merlot in his hand. His red hair was wild and ruddy. Not my type.

I passed a set of doe-eyed twins; blonde and perky. Too much energy. I needed a pure feed and then I had to get back to Shae. In the back corner, I spotted a plump-looking brunette woman with a plate of cheese and chocolate. From the size of her, I'd bet she's been a vessel for a while. Perfect.

I approached her and she raised a brow. "Thirsty?"

I tried to ignore the gap in her teeth as she spoke, or the way spit hung between her lips. This one would be perfect. No trouble, no 'anax' rising, nothing more than a quick feed.

"Very," I spoke as I pulled up a stool close to the chaise.

She extended a plump arm to me, wrist up. "Enjoy."

Before I could second-guess my choice in vessel, I sank my fangs deep into her wrist. Immediately, my senses heightened. Sweet, rich, undiluted iron swelled on my tongue and then coated my throat. I pulled again, and again, deeper each time, allowing her blood to numb all other senses and heighten only my hunger. I gripped her wrist with both hands and gently squeezed her plump flesh.

She began to jerk a bit. I slowed my draw and injected some venom. Thank blood for the vampirical gift of venom. I could sense her relax immediately, enjoying the endorphins currently flooding her system. Good. I drew some more and was rewarded by an unhindered flow of blood. I could feel my stomach warming and my strength returning. The old wound at my stomach began to twitch, the skin no doubt healing itself. Yes, I'd chosen the right vessel.

Mahogany eyes. Tate was looking up at me, defiantly in the forest, darkness a halo around her.

I could still imagine the taste of her on my tongue, the way her hips felt in my hands. I wanted her. Damn it. Even if I didn't deserve her, I sure as hell missed her. I continued to drink, not caring if the blood was making me hallucinate my old lover. I could hear Tate's moans as she came, feel her fingers digging into my back. Blood, I could taste my own blood after she bit me in those woods. Old memories and recent ones mixed and overwhelmed my senses as I devoured the vessel and rode my emotional high.

Soft, red silk sheets in my bedroom at HQ. Her blonde hair draped over her tan back, nearly reaching the delicate curve of her spine just before her lush hips. Her hands splayed out over my chest as she mounted me, her eyes staring into my soul. Eyes that held so many secrets, intelligence, and passion. Eyes that swiftly turned heated, anger and hate filling them.

The way I held her in my arms moments before she was informed of her mother's death. The moment she discovered I'd withheld information; that I knew Irene was being interrogated and that execution could occur while we were together. Guilt stabbed my stomach as I recalled the way I held her close, kissed her, fucked her, all while her mother was having a Disciplinary Hearing—one that resulted in her immediate death. Regret tasted bitter.

I withdrew my fangs from the vessel and released her arm. She moaned as she lay splayed on the chaise. I stood, wiped my mouth, and shook my head. I didn't want to dwell on the past, on what was and what could have been with Tate.

I began pacing toward the back wall and the whole room started to spin. I forgot about the powerful effect of feeding from a vessel and releasing too much venom. Normally, I'd have someone to express the energy with, like last time with Holland, but this time it was overwhelming my system. I placed a steadying hand on the wall and leaned my forehead against it. It was cool to the touch and shocking to my system. Life was nothing if not full of regret.

Tate wasn't dead. She couldn't be. There had to be a way to help her, maybe I could go out with a small team and borrow a transporter. There had to be a way to have minimal exposure and yet still give her some aid. I just needed a few minutes to let this high fade and then I could head back to Shae with my head screwed on right.

I'd come up with a plan.

Whispered voices came from the corner. Great, I wasn't alone for this class-A spin-out. I took a breath and tried to focus on my breathing.

"Shhh," a female voice sounded. Snickering ensued.

"No, you shhh," a male responded, laughing as he spoke. Blood help me, was I hearing the aftereffects of a blood-high?

"Mmm, yeah right there..." the female commanded followed by male and female moans.

"You have no idea how good you are," the male rolled his 'r's.

I needed to move but my head wouldn't stop spinning.

"Hmp. *You* really don't. If you only knew what I knew—" the female spoke, cutting herself off with a moan. Nothing like a blood-high to cloud judgment and loosen the tongue.

"What'd ya mean?" That low timber was jogging my memory. Was that Dux Carran?

"Dark magic. We've been researching it for the past year," the female responded with breathiness.

What the hell? If that was true, then leadership kept this from me. Or was this female in on the recent attacks? Was I witnessing the mole in action? I shook my head, I needed to focus and the dizziness to stop.

"Off the record, eh?" Dux Carran responded.

"Ach, you know me, everything's above board. There's a classified site that I haven't been privy to, but that I see incoming transmissions from. Dark magic has been mentioned more than once in the unredacted information," Anax Clark, it had to be her, responded.

I blinked.

"Of course, ya are 'bove board," Dux Carran responded, grunting.

A classified site? Dark magic research? Why were we researching dark magic and why had Anax Graf and my father acted baffled by my suggestion about its role in those creatures? I needed a clear head.

"That's enough talking, focus," Anax Clark commanded. A slap on skin sounded, followed by pleasured noises. I needed no further encouragement to slip away. The whole thing with them was just gross.

I stepped past the brunette on the chaise, currently still reveling in the post-feed vessel high I'd given her, and made my way through the room. I ignored the stares, the moans, the spurting sound of blood. I ignored it all and continued through the iron door into the unwelcoming bright lights outside it. I had learned nothing from my time in the guara if not self-restraint.

Passing the guards, I headed through the mess hall to the kitchen. I swiped three blood bags and a bottle of bloodwine. Time to see Shae and have her narrow her research. I wanted to know all there was about this classified site on dark magic research.

CHAPTER 50
TATE

My breath caught in my lungs. Did he really just insinuate that not only is the Untish Tribe real, but also that I am in fact one of them? Impossible. It had to be, right?

"Steady there, Tate." The steam in the air was gone and I could now make out every detail and feature on Aether's face. His eyes held a certain intensity I couldn't place and his jaw was set. His full lips were pursed, almost in a grimace, but it contrasted with the rest of his expression. The scar appeared tighter than I'd thought before—the pale white of it still held a tint of pink. Perhaps not as old as I'd thought then.

"I know this is a lot. And I will answer your questions, but it's important that right now you understand one thing: *I* am the only one who can keep you alive."

"Excuse me?" He was incredulous.

"You're in a very delicate season for the Untish. You're transforming, evolving, stepping into your own. However you put it, things are changing for you. They have been for a while, but that burning we did back in the warehouse did more than just free you from the guara's magic inked in your flesh, it was your initiation. It will either kill you or transform you, depending on how pure your Untish blood is." His words weren't resonating with me. That whole interrogation was some bullshit initiation in which I wasn't given a choice.

"Are you fucking kidding me?" Anger rose within me. The water around me began to bubble and then sizzle, and once again, steam rose in waves. "You fucking lit me on fire to start some sort of transformation without so much as giving me a heads-up, let alone seeking my opinion, no, my *approval* on the issue? Who the hell do you think you are!"

"That's a loaded question." He smirked and looked away, almost as if he were uncomfortable.

"So, what? I'm just supposed to take your word for it? I'm supposed to believe that a tribe of shifters who can turn into dragons isn't the folklore I've always been taught? That what I was told my entire life was an impossibility, a fairytale, is in fact a reality? That *I'm* actually one of those said individuals? How can you expect me to believe that, let alone trust you when you have already lied to me and forced me into some *Changing* without so much as asking!"

"I knew it was a mistake," his voice was barely above a whisper. "But whether or not I think you should have been initiated, which by the way, my vote was against, I do believe you are smart enough to decipher truth from lie. Look at yourself as proof." He gestured to the now boiling water surrounding me, the steam in the air that was getting so thick that I could barely see past Aether, who was now only a foot away.

"Tell me you're not so stubborn that you refuse to see the facts. Tell me you're not too cowardly to acknowledge the truth. Tell me that you haven't felt this Change coming for the past couple of months, heightened within the past week?"

I hated that his words resonated. I was not a coward, and I was not stupid. I knew he was manipulating me, trying to work me, but I also knew that he had a point: things had been different recently. I thought back to the fire when I killed that child-murdering bastard. My clothes had burnt, but I hadn't. The peace that had surrounded me confused me at the time...I had attributed it to a high, but maybe it was more. The last flight I'd had where I shifted into my raven form felt different... the blackout had never happened before, and neither had the animalistic roar or fire imagined—possibly released. I sucked on my fang. I had been hungrier lately. And...I had done not one, but three life drains in the past week.

That had never happened before.

"I can see that at least I am right about your intelligence. We need to get back to camp, so let's get you dried off. It's almost time to depart." He began wading through the water toward the riverbank, leaving me stewing in the middle of gurgling water that I apparently manifested.

"I—"

An animalistic screech cut me off, and screams filled the air along with roars.

The settlement was under attack.

Aether cursed under his breath before jumping out of the water and throwing his shirt on, stepping into his pants, and strapping his sword across his back. Daggers were strapped to his side before I'd even exited the river.

"Stay close and whatever you do, ignore the sparking sensation to turn. You're not ready and premature shifting can kill you."

"Excuse me?" I barely registered his words when screams from the village ahead enveloped me, overpowering my senses. Normally I had *good* hearing, but this was different...this was infinitely more all at once. I could hear individual pants, the sound of teeth sinking into flesh, the spurts of blood hitting the ground. I could hear pain like never before and not just from one source, but from everywhere. The sensation was too much. My head began to spin, the screams were debilitating. I crumbled to the ground at the riverbank, cupping my ears.

"Tate," Aether's voice was stern. He gripped my shoulders and shook me. "Tune it out. Block it out. Just focus on a core memory and recall the sounds from it. Something calming."

"I can't, it's too much. They're everywhere!"

A young female cried as I heard the slash of claws against flesh, the flow of blood coating the ground. A male's shrieks blended with battle cries as metal clanging against flesh, cutting through bone, rang out. Gunshots sounded, a drum to the melody of pain.

"You can. Think about your mother. What did she look like? What did she sound like? Did she ever sing to you?"

Energy pulsed around me. My pressure points began to respond to the tightening of the air. Steadying.

My mother. Her green eyes, dark blonde hair, the smile that *only* I saw. Her soft voice calling my name, telling me I did good. My pulse slowed down, and the noises began to fade.

"Good. Now focus on a specific memory and let it play through your mind." He lifted my chin to meet his golden-black eyes. "Focus."

Energy surrounded me as a favorite childhood memory surfaced.

"But why, Mommy?" four-year-old me asked.

"Because we must always be prepared," my mother spoke to me in that hushed, soft voice she reserved for only me.

"I don't want to approach the edge."

My mother's face filled my vision, her green eyes shrewd as she tipped my chin up to hers.

"Firecracker, you need to be brave. It is our fear that holds us captive. Trust me and trust yourself." She extended her hand and beckoned me to step forward.

I took a step gingerly, gripping her hand tightly. Then another. Finally, my feet brushed the cliff's edge and pebbles fell below.

"Good girl. Now look out, Tate. What do you see?"

I lifted my eyes to the cavern below, but I also saw the sea turning and foaming. Waves crashed against the cliff's edge and then rolled back only to be swallowed again by the sea.

"It's freedom. Smell the salt? See the horizon? That's freedom. This airspace is unoccupied and completely ours. This," she gestured out at the sea and the sky, "this has no limit. It's yours." She placed her hand on my chest. "Feel this?"

My heart pounded rapidly in response.

"This is the truth. It's within you. It's responding to the open horizon. It's beckoning for freedom. This Tate," she tapped my chest with her index finger. "This is your truth meter. Your heart knows even when the mind doesn't."

The cool night air assaulted my face as the memory faded. Aether was saying something, but I wasn't sure what.

"Tate?"

I focused on him.

"Good, you're calmer. Now just keep that memory playing through your mind and stay close. And do me a favor, don't die." He lifted me to my feet and threw a jacket around me, reminding me I was only in my underwear. I threw my boots on, hopping on the ground trying to find my balance, before loosely lacing them and then zipping the jacket up. I wrapped my arms around my midsection. At least the jacket was large enough to cover my butt and drape down to my mid-thigh.

"Here, take this." He pushed a dagger in my palm and then grabbed my other hand and began sprinting toward the village, my body in tow. A village that was now on fire. Smoke began to fill my vision. Black ash floated through the air, dancing in the firelight.

"Duck!" Aether shouted as a creature lunged for us. He let go of my hand and cut the thing in half before I could even fully stop moving with incredible speed.

He barely paused before grabbing my hand again and hauling off toward the center of the village. The buildings were all on fire. Bodies were scattered everywhere, covering the ground. Pools of blood, both black and red, stained the once neat cobblestone paths.

"Shit." Aether desperately turned around, trying to spot the assailants through the thick smoke.

As far as I could tell, we were the only ones moving. The whole place fell eerily silent for a moment.

Through the haze, I could make out the forms of figures clashing against each other. Fighting. Their screams rang out, overwhelming my system.

The guttural cries of the dead all around me began to sound, to moan. It was too much. The tingle in my system heightened, demanding I shift. The energy was building up. My arms began to *glow*, and I could feel my nerves firing rapidly; pain shot up and down my body. The string ending in the murky pool was growing taut, and the urge to shift felt nearly suffocating. Perhaps I could. Mentally I reached out to the string, just to touch it—

"No!" Aether's voice silenced my thoughts. He grabbed my face in both hands for the briefest moment. "Tate, focus on your mother. Tell me about her." And then he released me, gripping his sword and aiming it at a seething who was running on all fours toward us.

I opened my mouth to answer him, but the air pressure dropped and then increased, suspending the seething in mid-air. He manipulated it like it was nothing, slicing through its head and then releasing its body, allowing it to crumple to the ground. It twitched, even headless, and wiggled. Pure evil.

The pressure from the air shifting was too much, and the internal string was now glowing, just as the string leading out of me toward Aether was glowing. They both yearned to be connected. I just needed to—

"Tell. Me. About. Irene!"

The use of my mother's name from his lips jarred me from my thoughts.

Right, I could do this. Focus.

"Feel this? This is the truth." My mother's voice calmed my system.

Aether threw a dagger at a seething running upright toward me, sinking it right between the eyes before pivoting and slicing the head from another one about to attack him. The energy in me responding to every manipulation of the air. It devoured me, crashing through my system, demanding an outlet.

No, I would not shift.

"This is your truth meter. Your heart knows even when the mind doesn't."

My pulse slowed and commanded the energy coursing through me. It simmered to a slow hum. The pain subsided a bit and my glow diminished. Did she know? Suspect I'd wind up here without her guidance? Could she also shift into a dragon? She claimed she couldn't shift, but since she clearly was working with—

"This way!" Aether commanded as he once again grabbed the crook of my arm and steered me through a maze of corpses, some seething and some vampirical.

Screams from ahead sounded; cries, flesh being torn. Too much sensory input.

I took a deep breath, focusing on only the sound of my inhales and exhales, willing everything else to mute.

My mother's green eyes. Eyes I'd always envied. Eyes I didn't have.

"Thank Mother Blood! Tate, where the hell *were* you!" Vala's voice cut through my thoughts. She was covered in blood and soot, her own sword bloodied. Jared was just behind her, gripping his arm as blood gushed through what appeared to be an ugly bite. The sound of battle engulfed me: the clang of swords against claws, the screams, the tearing of flesh. Rapid firing of weapons...bodies hitting the ground.

Tingling, such intense tingling began to claim me as the energy inside swirled.

"Control it, Tate!"

The air around me constricted, trying to calm the storm building within.

"Oh my gosh, is she reforming, like in the Changing?! Holy shit, how is this happening *now*?!" Vala leveled eyed Aether. Her eyes were brown, solid chocolate now as the gold and black swirled, mixing in harmony. Not green like my mother. Irene.

"Irene," I whispered it to myself, her name an anchor against the assaulting noises coming from absolutely everywhere. The crackling from the fire heightened. "Irene, Irene, Irene," I said her name like a chant, focusing on it, picturing her and the sea.

"Good, just keep focusing on her, Tate. I promise I'll get us all through this."

A monstrous screech from ahead shook my core. It was louder than the rest of the noises, fiercer, and it became *numerous*.

Shadows began to form behind the flames and walls of smoke. Large frames, eight feet tall at least. They walked upright and held *weapons.* Their talons were at least a foot long, and still, they carried swords and rifles. The one leading the pack leveled its weapon at us before raising its head and howling. It was a command.

The whole ground shook as dozens of seethings poured out of buildings and debris in the distance, beginning to surround us. They ran on twos and fours. They snapped their teeth and snarled. It would only be a moment before they were upon us.

With another monstrous howl, the lead thing began to run in our direction. As it moved, at least eight other shadows moved with it. All tall, not quite as tall, but almost. They stalked and the ground shook with every unanimous step.

Aether pulled at the air and forced it in the direction of the large creatures. It was strong enough to knock them all over, but not enough to keep them down.

"Vala! Guard her with your life! Use whatever is needed. No restraints!" he commanded as he stepped in front of us, Jared following suit, to face off against the largest seething, now on its feet, marching toward us. It was taller than I'd initially guessed, at least ten feet tall and covered in black scales. It sported two wings out of its shoulders that were tucked in.

A blast of air blew out from just behind the monstrous beast and the screeches from several seethings sounded. Aether had knocked them over and managed to kill a few. A nice delay, but not enough. Not nearly enough as the howls sounded from all around, the vibration in the ground increasing. We'd soon be overrun.

"This way!" Vala grabbed my arm and tugged me back to a building about a hundred feet behind. I could see several seethings charging us on all fours, vengeance in their eyes. Vala tucked me in an alcove with her and then outstretched her hands. A shimmering projected forth and surrounded us in a dome. The noise suddenly quieted, and my senses begin to dull.

"A noise dome?" This would never hold.

"As if," she smirked, "they won't get through. This is more like a forcefield." She straightened her back and then pushed at the air. The shimmering stopped and the shield solidified. "We should be safe in here. And this one mutes the noise and brings it down to a more bearable level, especially for someone like you." She winked at me.

Did they all possess magic?

The ground shook as several blurs ran past our dome, headed straight for Aether and Jared. Aether threw one of his hands back, keeping his attention on the giant seething stalking toward him, but still projected another blast backwards that knocked the smaller seethings off their feet. They whined as the pressure seemed to keep them down.

Jared charged the small ones with his weapon extended and began stabbing and slashing. If he didn't kill, he maimed. I could see Vala biting her lip, hopping from foot to foot. She wanted to fight.

The large seething was only fifteen yards away from Aether now, a pack of several large seethings upright behind it. We were too far in the smoky air to tell if they too sprouted wings, but even from here, I could tell they were big. Bigger than Aether—even at nearly six and a half feet tall.

They were at least three feet taller and their claws, five to a hand, were the equivalent of four daggers. How would they take them? Jared stabbed yet another seething and then backtracked to where Aether now stood, poised, ready to fight.

It swung at Aether with its sword and missed. Aether expertly pivoted and landed a strike to its abdomen, eliciting a roar from the beast. He extended his free hand and suspended the other two large monstrosities who were closing in. They froze midair. Perhaps they could take them.

But then the seething swung again at Aether with its sword, then its taloned hand. It barely missed him. Aether ducked, avoiding the seething's swing, and simultaneously attacked its leg with his sword. The creature roared and then swung at Aether, even as it fell on its knees. Jared snuck up behind it and buried his blade in its back until it protruded through its chest. The howl it released was deafening, even from within the shield.

Jared freed the sword and then, with one stroke, decapitated it. One down.

The beasts Aether had held down began to move, inching forward as dozens more appeared to creep within the smoke. They were small, but numerous. A large seething broke free from Aether's hold and closed the distance between them, swinging with its talons and throwing its sword at Aether. He dropped and rolled, prepared to strike it again when the beast did the same and used its taloned foot to kick out Aether's feet from under him. He lost hold of his sword and went flying backwards into a burning building. The thing stalked after him, pausing just on the other side of the flames—as if the fire repelled it.

The smaller seethings were released from Aether's hold and ran toward us; they reached our shield and began clawing and pounding on it. The shield shook but held.

"Told you," Vala murmured. But the concern in her voice would not be masked by her bravado. She was worried. Her eyes were locked on Jared, who was throwing daggers at the beasts approaching him, taking them down one by one. He pulled his sword from across his back and pivoted to strike at a large seething who was now within ten feet. It too had black wings and scales. He struck at it, but it deflected and counter-struck, barely missing Jared's core and shredding his jacket.

Close, too damn close.

Jared yanked the dagger free from his leg and began stabbing the beast as he ran circles around him. Jared was fast, but he missed the beast's head and heart. His strikes fell short. He impaled the seething's shoulders with his blade, just below the collarbone. It roared and then dipped its head, swinging its upper body right into Jared, who became airborne, landing on the ground mere feet away. Before he could find his footing, the seething was atop him, digging its talons into Jared's shoulder as it leaned its head closer.

"No!" Vala screamed. She lunged forward and then stopped.

The seethings on the other side of the dome paused, lifting their heads in the direction of Jared. His blood called to them. They sniffed before backing up and moving toward Jared, who was now being gutted by the monster seething.

"Go help him! I'll be fine in the shield. Go!"

I really hoped I was right.

"I can't. I was ordered to stay here with you." Vala set her jaw, even as her eyes filled with worry, and she bounced from foot to foot.

A loud screech shook the dome as the other large seethings, six at least, stopped about ten yards from Jared, who was battling a monster-sized seething. He held another dagger and repeatedly struck the thing's chest, digging it in every time the beast leaned closer. Still, it did not release him.

It turned and roared at the small seethings and the large ones alike, like it was claiming its prey, and they all stopped in their tracks. The large seething began to twitch, to jerk, as its claw was forced out of Jared's chest.

Aether.

He appeared through the shadows and stepped over the corpse of the first giant seething, now dead at his feet. He was here. He could rescue Jared. As he manipulated the thing away from Jared, he threw his daggers at the beast, landing them in a straight row, impaling its chest right around the heart. He unleashed his other sword strapped at his back and sliced its legs off, one at a time. He wasn't just defeating it—he was making a point, putting on a show. A bolster meant to scare the others away. He cut its arm off, then with a large swipe, he cut the entire creature in half, from its head to its stump. It fell, split in two with sickening thumps, black blood oozing everywhere.

The other creatures broke from the hold and, as one, charged him. The bluff didn't work...too much blood in the air. Aether released a blast at the small ones, and they not only fell, but they were thrown backwards about twenty feet. The large seethings paused but were unfazed. Two of them reached Aether, one leveled its rifle at him and began firing. Its aiming, thank blood, sucked and bullets dotted the ground around Aether's feet.

The charge in the air increased, even from within the shield I sensed Aether wielding more power.

The other seething attacked Aether with a series of swipes and strikes. Aether countered each one, beautifully dancing around it. The thing just kept striking and swiping. The four remaining large ones entered the sparring ring. Two headed straight for Jared, still lying on the ground, deep red blood blooming everywhere.

Aether pressed more energy into the air, and the beasts aiming for Jared stalled, momentarily, but the distraction cost Aether. The large seething swiped at him and sent him flying backwards. He landed and fumbled for his footing while the seething stalked toward him. Aether raised a blade and swiped at it, meeting its talons in midair. The creature smiled and then squeezed its talons together over the blade, snapping it in half before backhanding Aether, sending him tumbling back to the ground.

"Shit!" Vala took several steps toward the barrier and then stopped. Resolve straightened her shoulders.

Jared screamed as two seethings jumped him, digging their claws deeper into his shoulders and his leg. Aether stood, finding his footing, and yanked at the creatures attacking Jared—they flew backwards and were knocked off their feet. The other seething raised Aether's broken blade and aimed it straight for Aether's heart.

Time stopped.

I held my breath as I saw the seething push the blade toward Aether. Aether shouted as he tried to keep the thing back with an air shield. The two charging Jared took a step forward, Aether's strength was faltering.

The blade pierced the air shield and began to sink into Aether's chest. I screamed, the golden thread in me tightened, demanding I reach for it.

"Do not shift." Aether had said. But his warning faded as the blade began to sink into his chest.

I wouldn't shift, but I *could* reach out and take control. The energy in me built, seared, and begged for an outlet. I reached for that thread and pulled.

Power. I was power. Pure energy, unrelenting. It coursed around me, through me. I could feel the air as if it were a second skin. I whipped my hand toward the large seething and willed it to stop.

It did.

I pulled at the blade and demanded it to turn in on itself. The thing fought, threw its head back and forth as foam flew from its mouth along with its cries. Still, the blade began to turn, toward the seething's own heart.

Awe.

I could swear I sensed Aether's heartbeat increase, the energy in the air sparked and grew.

The seething was resisting my control, but I pushed further, releasing a scream. I threw all the adrenaline, all the energy, everything I had into my effort.

Through sheer will and force, the jagged blade plunged into the seething's chest, and it toppled backwards, dead.

Aether dropped to his knees. His jaw slackened as he stared at me from across the space. Even from thirty yards away, I could tell his focus was solely on me.

I began to shake, my temperature spiking. The other seethings attacking Jared stood, suspended by my will or Aether's—which I didn't know—and didn't attack Jared further.

The shaking worsened and my eyes haloed, I couldn't see through the light—I'd used too much energy. I needed to cool down.

Irene. I remembered my mother, her soft voice and cool touch. I closed my eyes. One breath at a time. "Irene," I whispered.

I willed the excess energy in my system to flee, to release into the air. To go anywhere but in me. I released the thread, even as it begged me to give it more, to pull harder.

"Irene." Her name was a prayer on my lips.

My breath slowed and my temperature began to drop. My head

stopped pulsing. I would be alright. I opened my eyes to see Vala staring at me, eyes wide with uncertainty painted across her face.

"What?" I shrugged, trying to act nonchalant.

"You weren't supposed to be *that* powerful."

I didn't understand. What was she saying?

The shield shook and I peeled my eyes from Vala's nearly scared ones to see small seethings once again attacking our dome, pawing at it and slashing with their claws. It shuddered but did not give.

Jared shouted. He'd somehow found his feet again but was facing off with the remaining *three* large seethings—one hand at his abdomen trying to staunch the bleeding. Where had Aether gone?

Jared swung at the one closest to him, but the blade faltered. He could barely use his left shoulder, he was deeply wounded.

"Go. Now!" I commanded Vala. Jared needed help. He needed *her*.

She looked at me and then back at Jared. He evaded one swipe, countered another, but was caught off guard from behind. The seething dug its talons into Jared's back and lifted him in the air, roaring as it did so. It flung its arm back and sent Jared flying into the remains of a destroyed building. He landed in a cloud of ash.

Vala's resolve broke. She twirled back to me. "As long as I'm standing, nothing can get in and you won't be able to get out, but just in case." She pressed another dagger to my other hand and then ran through the shield, it shimmered as she shoved through its hold. The small seethings on the other side were dead before she'd even made it ten feet from the dome. Daggers protruded from each of their heads.

I watched helplessly as Vala ran straight toward the monsters. Toward the cloud of ash that encased Jared.

Vala leveled her sword and threw it toward the largest beast stalking toward Jared, blocking her path. It rotated through the air, hilt over end, until it found its target in the creature's back. The beast fell to the ground in a heap.

Vala jumped over its body, ignoring the other two seethings mere yards away, and reached the now settling cloud of ash and charcoal. She lifted her hands in a series of motions before pulsing them. Even from my shield, I could see the glimmer. It set just as the two giant seethings reached the dome's perimeter.

One beast crouched and then lunged, attempting to get through. It impacted the shield and went careening back into the other one, knocking them both down.

The reprieve was short. Several shrieks filled the air as black and grey blurs swarmed everywhere. They rose in the buildings of ash, from the path that led to the river, from the other end of the settlement...

It was as if they were beckoned here. There must be at least a hundred, all directed toward the center. Toward both domes.

The air began to pulse. I could feel it pulling, dragging, requesting. My body responded as my energy stores began to rapidly fire. The pressure under my skin built, the thread was now glowing bright. It demanded release.

Let go.

I didn't understand how or why, but I released the power into the air and sent the energy away. It was being siphoned from me, taken, but I freely gave. The source felt familiar, not threatening—helpful almost. The burning in my chest began to ease as I released more and more power, until at last, I dropped to my knees and released the thread entirely. I had nothing left to give.

The air pulsed, the shield shuddered, and the ground shook. Energy had been expended.

CHAPTER 51
TATE

The ground continued to shake as the air charged. My nerves were firing rapidly, this energy was *familiar*. I pressed my palms to the earth. I could feel the dirt seeping under my fingernails, but more than that, there was a pulsing beneath my palm.

Wings beat. The sound was unmistakable. I smiled as the murky pond within became translucent, revealing horns, sharp teeth, and *fire*.

An earth-shattering cry shook the entire ground, the domes, and my very being. Building remains toppled to the ground as the unmistakable roar of a dragon filled the night sky. Streams of fire lit up the otherwise dark sky as another dragon's outcry dominated the entirety of the village. The seethings swarming the village only paused a moment before they began to charge each dome, almost in a panic.

The beat of wings became louder along with the dragon's roar, fury filling the night sky. I could feel the shimmer of heat a moment before I saw the flames. Fire rained down from above and coated the shield. The heat was intense, even from within the shield—yet it did not break its protective barrier. I looked up to see the dragon flying overhead, lighting everything up. It breathed fire on the rubble, on the throngs of seethings now scrambling away, seeking shelter. A moment later, its enormous body passed over the village, releasing yet another bellow.

An internal tug in my soul *followed* the dragon, its path, its trajectory. I sat there unable to move. It was the most magnificent thing I'd ever beheld. It was at least fifty feet long and black as midnight. Its scales appeared impenetrable, and its tail was barbed with spikes. Nothing fiercer existed.

Power. Death. Vengeance.

It banked left and then turned around, approaching the settlement from the other direction. I could see its throat light up, *glow black*, moments before black-white flames poured from its mouth, engulfing the other end of the village, and swallowing the remaining seethings whole. The fire was an endless stream, decimating all in its path. Where the fire had been, charred earth now remained. The seethings ran from the fire, but it devoured them all, leaving only smoking ash behind.

The remaining giant seethings pounded on Vala's shield, attempting to break in. But they would not.

Fire engulfed them and ended their shrieks. They were no more.

Only one remained, a small one on all fours. The dragon roared at it as the seething fled the burning buildings and charred ground. It made it to the perimeter of the village and the dragon watched it go, allowing it to escape.

With a roar, the dragon slowly lowered itself into the heart of the village, perching its legs on the buildings' rubble. They crumbled further under its weight, stones crashing to the ground, releasing new clouds of ash.

It swung its tail around, curling it in on itself before raising its head into the night sky and releasing a roar that shook my very bones.

It huffed and steam filled the air, even from inside my shield, I could tell the external temperature had risen.

Vala stumbled out of her dome, stabilizing Jared as they walked toward the dragon. What the hell? Had they lost their minds?

"About damn time!" Jared's voice was severe even though his face looked relieved, slack even.

"Yeah, you cut that pretty close," Vala added. She looked worn and tired; her steps uneven as she wobbled from carrying Jared's weight.

The dragon lowered its head and huffed at them, lightly this time, just a puff. The force from it still blew Vala's braids around and nearly knocked Jared over—again.

The dragon's horns jutted out from its head. Some were practically the entire length of my body. Smaller ones bulged out behind the bigger ones, covering the back of its head like a crown—a very primal, deadly crown. All were gold at the base and faded to black. Uncertainty claimed me. I rocked back on my butt and cradled my knees to my chest, grateful now more than ever for this dome of protection.

"Yeah, yeah. You're a badass, we get it." Jared rolled his eyes, or at least I thought he did. It was hard to see from seventy feet away, even with my increased eyesight, through the smoke-filled air.

"What now?" Vala asked, gesturing in my direction.

The dragon swiveled its head toward me. Its face was suddenly mere feet from my shield. It was easily the same size as the dome, if not bigger.

I sank back a bit. I'd never seen anything more intimidating. The scales on it weren't just scales, they were intricately crafted armor, black with swirls of gold. It lowered its head further, huffing at the dome. Its back was ridged with spikes plating up along its spine. Its wings were tucked in as it kneeled on its front legs, barbed tail in the air, adjusting so it was as close to eye level as it could get.

Intelligence lit the dragon's eyes. Eyes that squinted at me, pure gold. It had a jagged scar that started at the top of its head near its horns and cut down through its eye to its jaw.

My fingers tingled, recalling the sensation of tracing that very scar pattern on a male not long ago. The dragon's eyes hooded in a gesture I've seen more than once before, tilting its head.

I see you.

Aether.

The shield around me dissipated as the air began to swirl, gently pulling at me. Willing me forward. The unmistakable scent of ash and salt surrounded me, filled my lungs and left its mark. This was the male I'd been scenting. The pull in my blood yanked me forward, causing my feet to move of their own accord.

I was mere feet in front of a head that could end me in one bite or puff of fire. My mind began to swim as energy pulsed through me and harmonized with that of the air. A song that I unwittingly knew the notes to. The thread within—one that was often hard to locate or manipulate—begged to be freed, to finally be *seen*. The murky pool inside me cleared. A female beast with sharp claws and horns of her own. She smiled.

Hello.

I lifted a hand and reached out toward the dragon's snout. Aether lowered his head just enough so I could touch a small horn jutting out from under his jaw. I wrapped my hand around it, not even able to close my fingers due to its girth.

Magic roiled up within me, begging for release. The air began to spark, the charge was tangible.

There she is.

I threw back my head and screamed. Energy poured from me rapidly as I thrusted my chest forward, allowing the power to pulse from me in a bright light. Lightheaded, I tilted toward the ground only to be caught by the air's resistance until it laid me down, gently. The sky above was full of ash and smoke, but my view was solely that of a dragon. Aether.

My eyes became heavy, so very heavy. I closed them and savored the consuming scent of ash and salt.

CHAPTER 52

CHANCE

Shae was where I expected, tucked away in an alcove in the library. I'd passed Arche Damaris on the way in and informed him I'd need a briefing in fifteen minutes. The library smelt of dust and disuse, a true shame and yet not surprising. When I was in prasinos, I certainly didn't spend much time here. And once I was out? I was much more interested in the revelry to be found at settlements— not ancient words scrolled on papyrus.

"How'd the meeting go?" Shae asked, immediately swiping at the air, closing her browser. A few perks of having a technical team member as your hacker, she had all the fun gadgets.

"Not great. We're at war."

"Shit," Shae responded. "And Tate, any word?"

"Nope." I clenched my jaw. "Leadership denied a rescue convoy."

"What?" Shae was already standing.

"I know, don't worry, we'll come up with something, but first I need to know if you found anything?"

Her chest was heaving; I could see her muscles tightening as her dragon tattoo danced across her back behind her black tank top. "I have. But it seems irrelevant when Tate is out there and *needs* us."

"I understand, I swear to you Shae, I will help. But first, I need to know what you've found."

"You'd better." She blew hair out of her face before nodding at me and pulling out a device. A shield formed around us and then frosted white. "A privacy shield, we can't use it for long without raising suspicion and I'll have to delete surveillance footage as these are supposed to only be used on authorized tasks, but it's necessary."

She flicked her disk out and projected a screen for me to see. Code filled several lines. After a few swipes, the numbers turned to letters, and I could understand what I was seeing. Documents, briefs, research notes, and files filled the screen. They all had the same two words: dark magic.

"As you can see, my search proved profitable." Shae gestured. "Not only did I find all these files, but there are incoming transmissions from an undisclosed location that mention 'dark magic' in coded updates. I've managed to decode the terms they use for 'dark magic' but I'm still working on cracking the rest of the encrypted messages."

"Undisclosed location. Can you geo-locate them?"

"What do you think?" Shae smirked. "I should have it by the end of the day."

"You're the best." I patted her on the back as I scrolled through dozens and dozens of transmissions and files. "Can you send them to me securely once they're readable?"

"You bet. But I will warn you, internal intelligence pays attention to all disks, leadership included. Not me, but the higher-level team members do. So..."

"So, there's a chance I'll be flagged with this data." That would be problematic if I wanted to continue to operate under the radar.

"It *would* be, but I wasn't first in my class for nothing." She winked at me and then tossed a device to me. "Just open this up, enter the code I wrote on it, then enter your disk's IP number and you'll be shielded for thirty minutes at a time. I wish it were longer, but if you're noticed to be online but inaccessible, it defeats the whole purpose. So, thirty-minute increments."

"Thirty minutes. Got it. How long until I should have the first file?"

"I have several being decrypted as we speak. Depending on file length, you could have some as soon as ten minutes. But I also have to re-encrypt them to send to you. I developed the device I gave you so it will read my encryption and translate it for you." She raised her brows and gave me a mock bow. "I know, I'm the best. Now what are *you* doing for Tate?"

"What indeed." I ran my hand over my face. "Here." I handed her the blood bags and then uncorked the bottle of bloodwine with my teeth. Fangs were good for more than siphoning blood.

"Thanks." She copied suit, ripping the top of the blood bag with her teeth, and began drinking, blood trailing down the sides of her mouth. She never was one for etiquette. Blood trails looked fierce on most vampires, but with Shae, the lines just looked comical on her narrow, pale face. Like she was too young and innocent to be a threat.

"Well?" She braced a hand on a hip, widening her eyes.

"I'm going to trace the path they'd take from the circuit, get an update on any incoming transmissions from their leadership, and then see about commandeering a vehicle. Then, I'll assemble a small team and leave as soon as I can. Hopefully within two hours." I hated that I couldn't leave now, but I needed to know where to go and have a plan in place, or it would all be pointless.

"Need help with that?"

"No, you just focus on those files. The sooner I know what we are up against, the better. And Shae, you've been digging into the research lab files as well, right?""

"Naturally."

"Good, make those priority with the decryption."

"Will do." She nodded. The shield vanished and the rest of the library appeared.

I strode out and took a swig from the bottle. Liquid courage. Arche Damaris was still bent over the desk, combing through footage. I needed to check in with him and then do my own research into convoys.

"Damaris, you have that update?" I asked, putting the bottle down.

"Hell yeah." He reached for the bottle, but I swiped it out of his way.

"Talk first."

"You would," he grumbled. "I've combed through the day of the attack multiple times and honestly, I haven't seen anything. I mean *nothing*."

"So, you're useless."

"No, what I mean is I didn't even see anyone breach the borders. No one approached the data box you had me focus on. Not even the squad making rounds. NO ONE. NOTHING. Someone doctored the video footage."

That would explain a lot.

"How can you be sure? I started watching the footage and didn't notice anything."

"Well, my gift for sensing magic doesn't only work in person. I can sense a residual effect, even from footage. There's a split second when the film glitches, the torches flare just a bit, and the flags here," he pointed to the screen, "are moving. But in the next second the torches aren't waving, the flag isn't blowing, it's completely silent. It's like this for thirty minutes and then the flags resumed blowing and the torches dance once more."

I studied the screen.

"Good work. Get this to Shae and tell her what you told me, she'll take it from there." I set the bottle down in front of him. "Keep combing through the week before and after, focus on those areas, and also, I want you to comb through footage of the research lab entrance and Anax Clark's office."

"You're asking me to spy on leadership."

"I am." A moment passed. Damaris looked at me. He could easily tell Anax Clark, and I could be court-martialed. So much was at stake.

"Didn't think you had it in you." Damaris smiled and then nodded before swigging from the bottle. "But...I want another bottle and access to the VIP lounge. The blood bags here suck."

"Done." If that's all it took to buy his silence, I could handle it. I just hoped his loyalty wasn't as easily purchased. "Keep this between us. If someone asks, you're a part of a task force to investigate the recent attack and are combing through footage of the perimeter."

Damaris nodded before putting his earbuds in and drinking deeply from the bottle. It would be gone within minutes. Good luck to him.

I left the library and headed down the stone corridor. I wasn't sure what time it was, but from the windows I could see daylight. A familiar frame filled the hallway before me, sauntering down, hips swaying. If it weren't for the short bob and squared shoulders, I may have mistaken Holland for someone else.

"There you are," her last word was spoken slowly.

I approached her steadily until her facial features were crystal clear: her eyes were dilated, and her pale skin was flushed. She'd just fed.

"Holland, maybe you should go sleep it—"

"Shh." She placed a finger to my lips before snuggling her body against mine. "I've been thinking," she spoke slowly as she traced her finger down my jaw and neck to my shirt collar. "I still haven't seen *all* you're capable of." She popped a button and bit her lip at the same time.

"Holland, I'd like to explore this with you, it sounds fucking nice, but I—"

Her lips closed over mine before I could finish the sentence. Cherry and honey notes filled my mouth as she swept her tongue inside, gliding over my own, exploring. A groan escaped me as she cupped my ass in her free hand while her left one dug into the back of my neck. She deepened the kiss and pressed her body even closer to mine.

I cupped the back of her neck and pushed her against a nearby wall. She lifted her legs around my hip, trapping me. Normally, I would enjoy playing the role of hostage, but the part of my brain that was still working told me I didn't have time for this. Life was hanging in the balance, a special one with mahogany eyes.

I broke the kiss and rested my forehead against hers. "We need to talk."

"Do we?" she asked as she began to rock against me, grinding in the most sensual way. Fuck.

"Holland, I've found some—"

Her mouth clamped over mine in a claiming motion, devouring me and momentarily stealing my senses. She deepened the kiss and simultaneously moaned into my mouth.

"Now." She pulled back and pierced my eyes with her own. "What have you found?"

"Found?" Right. I cleared my throat and set her down. "I believe leadership here is withholding sensitive information regarding 'dark magic' and I've learned of a concealed facility that I believe is conducting research. This could be—"

"What the attackers were looking for and possibly also connected to the creatures," Holland finished my thought. She pushed off my chest and took a step back, adjusting her shirt. Her lips were still deliciously swollen.

"You're as hot as you are brilliant," I said as I traced her collarbone with my index finger.

"Naturally." She winked at me, but it lacked cockiness. Pink began to spread across her cheeks as she looked around and noticed where we were: a public hallway. The high was wearing off quickly, a feeling I was all too familiar with.

"So, what's the plan?" she asked me, tucking a lock of stray honey-brown hair behind her slightly pointed ear.

"We need a transport and a team."

CHAPTER 53
TATE

The air was blissfully cold. I opened my eyes and noticed the snow in the sky. No, not snow, ash. Its grey and white flakes danced through the air with bits of black charcoal.

"She's up," Vala's voice registered along with its taxed tone.

"Thank blood," Aether responded.

Aether.

The hellish scene I'd just witnessed played before me. Aether was a dragon. A DRAGON. I sat up and suddenly wished I hadn't. The whole world was spinning.

"Woah, take it slow, Tate." Aether's face came into view. He steadied my shoulders, shoulders that were wearing his jacket and nothing else. I didn't just see a dragon—I'd also made out with him in his other form. Shit, I climaxed in that river. Clearly, I'd lost my mind.

"Who would've thought you have a gentle touch." Vala smirked at Aether.

He shot her a glare before slowly letting go. I pulled my knees to my chest under the jacket, cause yes, it's that big, and then wrapped my arms around myself. My whole life I'd been taught that dragons were mythical, that the Untish Tribe was pure fiction. And yet, here I was sitting right in front of one that I'd just witnessed in his dragon form.

I could *feel* him. His breath seemed to echo my own. My inner pool of truth had awakened. I knew if I looked there, I'd see a fierce creature. I wasn't ready. Not yet.

"How is any of this possible?" My voice was hoarse and dry.

"It's a lot, I know, but you've spent enough time in the human realm to know they think vampires are a myth and absurd, and yet, here we are." Vala gestured to the village, the ruins, and then us before she dramatically spun. She looked better, much better. The fatigue I noted before was mostly gone and she appeared to be her perky self once again.

"It will all make sense in time. Meanwhile, how do you feel?" Aether asked, extending a blood bag to me.

"Is this more of that *good* stuff, you know, the blood you gave me earlier?" I ripped the top of the bag and began to drink it before he even answered. Nope. Boring, human blood.

"You gave her 'good' stuff?" Vala's eyes sharpened, and the air charged. Unlike the usual charge, this one felt hostile.

"I made necessary choices. I'm head of this unit."

"Aether, if she had *dragon* blood, then you...and she's...this is not okay..." She couldn't finish a thought. "What will Arithi say? I mean Tate is positively not ready for that—"

"Enough."

"Not to mention the bonding effects," Vala ignored Aether's command, clearly finding her words again. "You *know* there's a reason that blood sharing is outlawed until they've completed the reformation, the Changing!" Vala raised her voice at the end. She was clearly upset.

Aether just clenched his jaw. He said nothing.

He let Vala admonish him?

"Mother Blood, what were you thinking?" Vala's hands flexed.

Her words from earlier registered: dragon blood?

"Hold up." I tore my lips from the bag. "Are you telling me *he* gave me dragon blood earlier?"

Aether glared at Vala. "Now who is breaking protocol by giving out classified Untish Tribal info?"

"Ooops," Vala responded sarcastically. "Well, it's not like I started it. I mean, look at her, it's clear you've crossed many lines *and* barriers with her tonight."

"As the leader of this group, you will stand down and let this go." The tension in the air increased as Aether took a step toward Vala.

"Fine. But Jared saw it too. You'll need to address this with him as well." Vala huffed before looking at me. "Sorry, Tate. I mean no disrespect to you. I'm all for a girl getting hers, it's just—"

"Vala!" Aether cut her off, violence radiating from him in waves of heat.

My nakedness. How had I forgotten? I needed to find some clothes.

"Go get her some clothes."

"I will, but have you seen what you did to the place?" Vala gestured to the decimated village. "Tell me where she lost hers and I'll go hunt it down and see what else I find."

"Enough. Go," Aether commanded.

She mock-saluted him before turning and leaving, anger simmering on her normally peaceful face.

"Thanks," I mumbled before putting the bag back to my lips. I was starving.

"You'll be hungrier than normal for the next couple of months until the Changing is complete." Fan-freaking-tastic.

"So..." I broached the topic. "Where uh, did you get dragon's blood?" I averted my eyes. For some reason, I couldn't focus on his now dark chocolate ones. Ironic considering what we did in the river, and yet he felt like a completely different person.

"It was mine."

I choked on the blood.

"What?"

"Don't look so surprised. It used to be common to have dragon's blood when going through the Changing. It steadies you when your body is craving more nutrients than human blood alone can provide. Ideally, you'd be on the Changing grounds for this, and able to draw magic from the rich land itself to sustain you and supplement, but as you can see, we don't have that here."

"Changing grounds? You've lost me." Pulling magic? That was yet another foreign concept. As far as I knew, some of us had magical gifts, but that was it: gifts, given through hereditary lines. Drawing magic from the ground? That sounded whacked.

"How are your senses? You seemed overloaded last night."

"I was. But things are..." I searched for the right word. "Quiet."

"Good. It's common to have heightened senses during the initial Changing surge, the reformation, usually when absorbing magic, like from the blood, and then it lessens as your body changes on a cellular level, and you master control. It will likely happen again until the Changing is complete."

"Fan-freaking-tastic," I grumbled before downing the rest of the blood.

He'd seen me last night. Hell, I *saw* me. Who—what I really was. I didn't want to face it, not yet.

Instead, I scanned the village. Fire was still burning in places, but most of it was just embers. Bodies littered the ground along with black puddles and piles of ash and bone fragments. The village was destroyed.

"Did anyone survive?" I thought back to the elderly man who'd handed me my bedroll, he was missing his left arm. How could he have survived those things when Aether and Jared had their asses handed to them?

"A few. About a dozen villagers survived by hiding in an underground bunker when the attack started. We have about eight doki-moses left as well."

That's it?. We had twenty left from our original party of two hundred. It was a slaughter. It was...

Now I understood.

"Fletch was trying to stop this."

"He was." Smoky air burned my lungs as ash coated my hair, my jacket, and the ground around me.

"He was a good male. He would never want this. He told me stories of the Great War and feared another one. If he'd known this could happen, I don't think he would've stopped at anything to stop this evil from permeating," I spoke softly as I started to draw his name in the ashes.

"You sound like him." Aether's eyes filled with thoughtfulness as he squatted down so he wasn't towering over me. Equal.

"You knew him well?" This was the second time he'd compared me to Fletch.

"Not well, but I'd been working with him for months. He was a huge help to the effort, and if he'd been able to finish getting us the data, we would have been even closer to stopping them. They're evolving, have you noticed?"

Months. Fletch had been working with Aether for months. So many secrets. If Fletch had told me the truth, would I have listened?

"Seeing as I didn't know seethings existed more than two days ago, no, I did not notice them evolving," I spoke through clenched teeth. I had been left out of critical info, not just by Fletch, but by Arithi, Aether, and likely my mother. Hell, was this why she died?

"Is this why they killed her? Irene?"

Aether averted his eyes as he drew in the ash.

"I don't know. Irene's death was before I started working on the front lines with Arithi."

"Ah." Another dead-end or lie, which, I didn't know.

"But from what I've heard about your mother, she was an incredible female and an asset to the cause. Arithi depended on her a lot. From what I know, they worked together closely at the end, and her death...it set Arithi's plans back, by a lot."

"Just a cog on a wheel." My mother's death was *inconvenient* for Arithi. It cost me my world.

"I'm sorry," he spoke with such sincerity and his tone held no bite.

I looked into his eyes. Truth. Perhaps he really was offering me the truth. More than anyone had, Fletch included.

He brushed his hands on his pants. "We leave in twenty. I'll see to it that Vala gets you some clothes." Ash covered his black pants. "If you feel lightheaded," he continued, "start seeing double, begin shaking, or feel heightened senses that are overwhelming, let me know immediately. This is a very delicate time for you."

He turned on his heel and left before I could even respond. I glanced at the ground where he'd been drawing. Two interlaced circles were drawn in the ash.

WE HAD BEEN HIKING for about two hours. Vala had secured me a change of clothes that were two sizes too big, but I wasn't complaining. I still had no idea where she'd even found them. I'd rolled the pant legs up twice and cinched the pants to my waist with a belt. Not perfect, but I could walk in them. Thankfully, I'd put my boots on before leaving the river, so at least my shoes fit correctly, and I could walk evenly.

Rain pelted the forest floor as we trekked through it. The smell of smoke still clung to the air and the surviving vampires in our party were silent; no one wanted to talk. Trauma. We'd all been through the impossible. Seethings, dragons, total destruction? All of it wasn't supposed to exist and the bloodshed should never have happened.

I inhaled, searching for the deep pine scent. It was barely there, mingled with that of smoke. But the rain was cleansing. Rinsing the air. If only it could wash my very soul. Fletch had known. He'd tried to tell me, and I dismissed it as a drunken episode. What was it he had said?

"Knowledge is power."

So why did he leave me powerless? Why did my mother not teach me the truth? I thought back to that fond memory of the female I trusted teaching the girl of freedom.

Our space.

That's what she had called it. She could shift too. She'd lied.

I kicked a pinecone and savored the crunch of it as I crushed it with my other foot. At least some things were still the same.

I'd *beheld* a dragon. Touched it with my hand. I should be terrified, shaking in my boots, vomiting my guts out, and yet, I felt oddly at peace with this revelation. Somehow, it felt like a puzzle piece had clicked into place for me, something I'd been missing my whole life.

Nervously anxious. That's what I felt. I still wouldn't look within. I didn't want to see *that* part of myself. Some truths were still too scary to accept.

I needed to be logical. I may not know much, but I did my fair share of reading, thanks to Fletch. What did I know about the not-so-mythical Untish Tribe? They were rumored to support nature's laws and fight for justice. That lined up closely with the values that both Fletch and my mother instilled in me from a young age.

They were the most feared warriors in mythology, and they were real. *Are* real. I exhaled, and the air around me puffed from the heat of my breath. My nerves began bouncing. Even if I accepted the Untish as real, how was I supposed to reconcile that I was one of them? I was Changing, I could sense it, but my mind was lagging. These facts seemed impossible.

We turned around a bend and Aether stopped the somber procession by holding a fist to the air. I nearly slammed into the dokimos in front of me. Shaking my head, I tried to focus on what Aether was saying.

"We'll rest here for a half hour while we scout ahead. If we keep this pace up, we should reach the SO by this evening, or tomorrow morning at the latest."

Scout ahead?

The group nodded as several elderly vampires found seats by leaning against the trees or on various boulders scattered across the forest floor. Vala and Jared approached Aether who was discreetly stepping into the brush away from prying ears, away from me.

Uh-uh. I'd had enough of secrets. Aether wanted me to believe I was the same as him? Fine. Then I'd be privy to *all* their plotting.

I followed their movements and cut through some bushes until I was just behind Jared, with only some thick scrub oak between us. Squatting down, I could just make out their shapes, well within earshot.

"You sure this is a good idea?" Jared asked.

"We know where they're gathering, and it's close. If we can get eyes on the plant, we may be able to gain some valuable intel," Aether replied.

"But Aether, what about the group? If we leave them here and go scouting, there is a very real chance they could, you know, be attacked and not make it." Vala's voice sounded genuinely worried. She brought up a good point. Surely, they wouldn't leave these defenseless vampires to themselves, would they?

"Natural selection will play its role. We won't stop it."

I guess they would.

"I can't believe you, Aether. I thought you had a high moral code and all. What would Arithi say?" Vala's voice was incredulous.

"Arithi?" Aether released a bitter chuckle. "She'd have already disposed of them as a potential risk to the cause. Tell me, did Arithi ever tell you what protocol *she* established for a member who was seen using magic in front of non-tribal individuals? If I had to transform and be exposed?"

No one responded.

"Let me enlighten you then. *Your* loving Arithi instructed they be terminated. And while I don't believe these vampires are any threat to us, the knowledge they have definitely is. If they saw me transform yesterday, our secret is out. So yes, according to protocol, we leave them here and go scout."

I couldn't believe my ears. I pushed back from the ground and a twig snapped. Damn it! Aether and Vala's eyes turned in my direction.

"What about her? She's not an active tribal member until she's passed her assessments and completed her Changing. Do we eliminate her?" Vala's voice dripped with sarcasm, but the hairs on the back of my neck stood up. I'd seen a lot. Too much really.

"That's different and you know it." Aether jabbed a finger at Vala. "All Untish blood is given a chance to become an active member, and so will she. Not to mention, Arithi has a vested interest in her."

"Okay, look I'm all for keeping her alive. I like her, maybe not as much as *you* do, given her utter lack of clothes last night and the fact that she still smells like you..."

What the hell, Vala.

"But," she continued, "what if any of those dokimoses or elderly vampires wanted to join the cause? What if they have the gene?"

"Vala, you know that's highly unlikely, and even if they did, it's too late to vet them. We're in enemy territory," it was Jared's calm voice that did it for me.

"Excuse me, hi, yeah, over here." I stood up out of the brush. Lightning filled my veins and I felt oddly powerful. "Yeah, so...I have a say in all of this. I am not going to be killed or used by some stranger who claims to have known my mother and Fletch. So, this is how it's going to go." I approached the group and leveled my gaze at each of them, one at a time. "First," I held up a finger, focusing on Aether, "I will be going on this scouting mission; I refuse to be left in the dark, again. Secondly," I glared at Vala, "you will refrain from any mention of last night's *supposed* dalliance with that one." I jabbed a finger in Aether's direction. "Lastly, you will stay back and guard these innocents, or so help me, I will be a whistleblower, and believe me, you don't want to see that."

"I bet she's quite the blower. Tell me, Aether, did you have your whistle—"

"Vala!" I interrupted her. Unbelievable.

"What?" She winked at me, actually winked.

"Pretty impressive that you think you can march in here and give orders." Jared snarled. Clearly, he was pissed, but at least he was taking me seriously, unlike Vala.

Aether took a step toward me. His face was unreadable. "Why do you think we'd listen to you?"

"Because you need me." I gulped but refused to back down.

"I need you?"

"I bet you did last night," Vala snickered.

"For the love of blood, Vala, shut up." Jared rolled his eyes as he grabbed her elbow and pulled her further away from Aether who was currently circling me like I was his prey.

I looked into his eyes. Eyes that somehow were more golden now than black. Had they changed...or had I?

I saw you.

My jaw tightened. It was only in my head, it had to be. And yet, I swore his eyes *knew* what I'd heard.

I reached out to the air and pressed gently against it, willing my energy to fill it. I could be threatening, I was last night. But nothing happened.

"You'll get there." Aether took a step forward, his voice lowering. "Tell me though, what would happen if *we* didn't listen to your requests?"

"Demands," I clarified.

"Sure." He grinned.

The bastard.

I tried to reach for the air, to demand it close around Aether, to suspend him, but it didn't respond.

"Tell me, if we leave Jared and Vala behind to protect them and they *die* trying, would you be okay with that? With risking everything our cause is working toward for a few unimportant lives?"

"Screw you." I dug my finger into his chest while holding a hand up to Vala. Now was not the time for her jokes. "I believe in protecting all —no matter what they offer or if they can be useful. I thought that's what your group stood for too?"

"And what if doing as you suggest, we protect them, and it costs us two lives of our *members* and puts you in grave danger? What if we are unable to fulfill our mission because of this and let the tribe down, let Fletch down?" He grabbed my hand that was poking in his chest.

"Not that you'd understand, but Fletch believed in protecting the vulnerable, those who can't protect themselves. I grew up believing this. It's in the very core of who I am. So yes, I will stay back and protect them if no one else will." I yanked at my hand, but his grip tightened. "And so help me, I will not help a movement that slaughters innocents."

Anger exploded within me. He would not use Fletch to justify murder. My blood sparked and I could feel fire racing in my veins.

Aether's nostrils flared as his eyes deepened.

There she is.

"You heard her." He let go of my hand and turned to Jared and Vala. "You two stay here. I'll be doing a solo mission with this one." The look in his eyes heated my blood. What had I gotten myself into?

CHAPTER 54

CHANCE

The transport was secured. I strapped two pistols to my hip, an assault rifle across my back and I held a club, thanks to Carran's tip from the last settlement. I hoped if we encountered any creatures that they'd be less developed and go down with a bullet—but still, I'd be prepared either way.

"So, why is the team so small?" Damaris asked as he strapped on his own weapons.

"Shut up, Damaris." Shae nudged him with her elbow and then put a band over her hair to keep any short wisps out of her face. It was her idea to bring him and begrudgingly, I agreed.

"This is a small, classified mission, Damaris. Strictly need to know," I spoke with my words clipped. There would only be four of us heading out. I glanced at Holland. She hadn't said much as we prepped for the last two hours.

I looked at my disk and projected the route in front of us. The circuit went down about a hundred miles northeast of our location. They'd notified the outpost they had made it to a settlement about fifteen miles south of where the circuit was compromised. We still hadn't received a list of casualties, but I wanted to believe that Tate was alive. She was too annoying in life to be gone.

"So how long until you expect us to intercept them?" Shae asked, approaching me.

"Last transmission from their leadership was last night from a base about fifty miles from here. It was mostly used for harvesting crops and processing labels, etc. A retirement community really." I looked around. We were all ready, the transport was running. It was time.

"Load up."

One by one, we filed in. Shae and Damaris in the back, Holland and I in the front. I drove the truck through the garage and back to the service road gate.

"Shae?" Holland was staring at the large fifty-foot iron rod gate.

Shae punched a few buttons, and the gate began to buzz as it slowly swung open. My breath caught as I waited. If we could get out of this base without anyone noticing, there wouldn't be much they could do to stop us. It just needed to move a few more feet and then the truck would be able to pass through. A large figure appeared on the other side of the gate. The rain bounced off his tan trench coat. He jumped and landed in front of the transport in a crouch and then rose with his shoulders hunched.

"Going somewhere?" Rusty's eyes were haloed completely by purple and the venom in them was palpable.

What happened to this male?

"Yes, now step aside," I spoke, trying to force strength into the command.

Rusty instead approached the transport and put a hand on it. He began to push, and the transport went squeaking backwards. What the hell?

"Step aside, you're out of your jurisdiction."

But Rusty didn't stop, the vehicle began to slide backwards faster. I pumped the brakes, momentarily halting the momentum. Rusty's eyes flared. Water landed on his face and streaked down.

"She's not worth it. You are supposed to be hunting for our mole, not running to save your booty call."

I got out of the transport and slammed the door. Rusty removed his hand from the vehicle and looked at me, eyeing the weapons.

"Think that will make you male enough?" He snorted.

"Dux Richards, you need to move. Now."

"No." Rusty took a step toward me and palmed a dagger.

Was he serious?

"Not to pull the nepotism card, but any idea what would happen to you if my father found out you attacked me while I'm conducting an authorized investigation? One that I oversee, and you don't." I stepped closer to him, allowing the tip of the knife to brush against my vest. Water glistened as it coated the blade.

"Brat," Rusty cursed under his breath. I could see his restraint slipping, the knife beginning to press deeper into my vest as his hand shook violently. "You don't deserve to share breath with me, boy."

"Dale," Holland called out. From my peripheral, I could see her weapon trained on Rusty as she leaned out of the transport, across the windshield.

I shook my head at her, negative. Rusty needed to back down and I needed to be the one to do it.

"You're old, Rusty, maybe it's time you hung up your cape and stopped beating poor dokimoses and simply retire. I hear there's a lovely village just fifty miles from here. The perfect place for you. Well, that is assuming you're not senile, and judging from your pallor, you're not well."

The tip of Rusty's blade dug deeper, and I could feel it prick my skin. I could see black veins webbing from his eyes to his forehead and ears. His black eyes were fully dilated, and I smelt...fear?

"Enough." Anax Clark appeared with Dux Carran. They strode out from the side and stopped just short of the transport. The headlights shining in all our faces made it hard to see, but I was fairly certain they had weapons drawn. "Stand down, Dux Richards," Clark commanded.

"He is sneaking out of here, violating the council's decision." Rusty glared at me, releasing some pressure on the knife but not retracting it completely.

"I will address what I need to. But I run this base, not you. I command you to stand down. Now," Clark spoke with an eerie calmness.

Rusty didn't move.

The whole world went white for a moment and then my vision returned as the brightness faded—Rusty lay convulsing on the ground, static dancing over his skin. Clark lowered her hands and then strode toward Rusty. Fuck. She was a magic wielder. Things began to click into place. *That* was why she ran this base, even in her old age.

"When I give a command, you listen." She kicked him with her boots, and he stopped shaking. Carran bent over and picked him up, wearing rubber gloves, I noted for the first time, and threw him over his shoulder.

"Now, where are you going, Dux Dale?" Anax Clark turned, shoulders squared, and addressed me.

"I believe I have a lead on the mole hunt and what the intruders were searching for. It's just a hunch, but I need to evaluate the outside of the compound and visit a nearby base to gather additional intel."

"Hunch?" She looked past me into the transport. How she could see past the lights and rain was beyond me. "Taking an arche and an internal intelligence trainee?"

"Yes, just a hunch, but I believe their skills could be of use if it pans out."

"Very well." She looked at Holland. "You both should be aware that we just received word an hour ago that the base the convoy was reportedly at last night has been leveled and nothing remains. Not sure what you will be able to gather from that intel."

I inhaled. No, we were too late.

"Any survivors?" Holland asked.

"We aren't certain, intel was gathered from a flyover." She returned her gaze to mine. "Do not mistake me for a fool, Dux Dale. Should you encounter Dokimos Aaralyn and her convoy, I do expect you to see them back safely."

"Of course." I nodded.

She held my gaze for a moment longer before stalking off, Dux Carran trailing behind with an unconscious Rusty hanging limply across his back.

I climbed back in the transport, as did Holland, and then drove through the gate. We should have left hours ago.

CHAPTER 55

TATE

We'd hiked about seven miles, and I, for one, was hot. My blood felt unnaturally warm and I was pretty sure my face was flushed.

The trees around us were black, they had been for the past several miles. At first, they merely looked black, but the further we went, the eerier they appeared. Many of the trees had white goo dripping from them. The grass didn't exist up here, and the dirt was no longer brown but grey with black veins webbing from between the trees.

"Almost there. Just try to avoid making any other noise," Aether spoke lightly, not at all winded. Prick.

"I haven't 'made any noise' since we first started out. I didn't see the branch lying there. Not all of us have super sight." Every word came out softer than the last. I thought I was in shape, but this? This was ridiculous. And I was so, so warm. Sweat had pooled at the front of my shirt. I was grateful it was black, hopefully it made the sweat ring less noticeable.

"You'll cool off soon, I promise. Going through the Changing, espe-

401

cially in the beginning, the reformation, usually causes a spike in internal temperature."

"But it goes away?" We hadn't spoken much on this hike. I wasn't sure what to ask, and honestly, I didn't even know if I could process any new details.

"Yes, just need to fully adjust. Your molecular level is rapidly changing. You're a *dragon*, Tate, but that gene was dormant until recent events."

I huffed. That was a *mild* way of putting it. "You mean like when you burned me?"

"That and when I gave you my blood. But you would have noticed some changes before the burning. The blood sample we collected from the clinic—"

"You mean the blood Ferrari stole," I interrupted. Way too much shit had gone down and I was tired of the sugarcoating and side-stepping.

He chuckled. "That blood sample," he continued, ignoring my jab, "confirmed you had the gene marker and that some changes had already started naturally. Usually, those things include an increase of hunger bordering on bloodlust, external glowing when the cells are becoming active, and unpredictable behavior are some of the common ones."

I wasn't about to admit that I was pretty sure I experienced all of those. Bitterness swelled within me. Fletch and my mother had to have known I had the gene. Yet, neither one prepared me. Neither helped me through this, they abandoned me to go through this *alone*.

The stench in the air grew. It no longer smelled like sour mold, now it felt like the air itself had been corrupted, drained.

"It's unstable," Aether confirmed my thoughts. "You can sense it too?"

I nodded. We both fell silent as we crested the top of the hill. He stopped and signaled for me to follow. Down below lay a network of large warehouses. I couldn't see any movement outside, but smoke plumed from the exhaust outlets of each building.

"This is it."

The ground near the warehouses was pure black, with an unnatural-looking mud swirling across the ground.

"How can you be so sure? I don't see anything." It screamed *wrong,* but I didn't see any seethings.

Aether rolled his eyes at me. "Just when I thought you'd honed your skills a bit. You have other senses than just sight. Use them. What do you hear, Tate?"

What did I hear? Nothing. No, that wasn't quite true. I closed my eyes and focused. I could hear the wind blowing through the brittle trees, the cracking of mud under my feet, a buzzing that I couldn't quite place. Distant crunching of pine needles from something small, a rabbit perhaps?

I could hear the hum of a generator and...there! I could hear voices. Grunts would be a better explanation, but I heard languages being spoken that I didn't understand. I heard cries along with roars and I knew Aether was right. It was the unmistakable sound of seethings.

"I hear them."

"Of course you do." There was a look of pride in his eyes and it completely weirded me out. "Ok, so you stay here, and I'll be—"

"No way. You are NOT leaving me here, alone." I wasn't about to be benched, again. I might not have the greatest fighting skills, the sword may be too heavy, and I may be in a vulnerable state of 'the Changing,' but I had my wits and determination. I could be an asset. I would be.

"Fine," he responded way too quickly. I was a little shocked. "Stay close, Tate. And stay quiet."

I nodded in confirmation, and we began working our way down the hill. We crept along the tree line to the closest warehouse and then around the back. There was a ladder attached to the building on the side, a typical escape route in case of fire. We climbed it, and I held my breath as I inched up one rung at a time. Finally, we made it to the top.

We walked softly. Aether, to my chagrin, was light-footed and better at sneaking than I was. Why Arithi wanted me, I'd never know. As far as I could tell, I was useless and clueless. Or was I? Why had they taken so much of my blood and given me so much attention? Was it a deal with Fletch?

Aether motioned for me to follow as we approached a skylight. We moved slowly and then lowered to our bellies, heads just popping over the windowpane.

My breath caught at the sight below. Hundreds of seethings were gathered in a large cage that occupied half the room. It was composed of iron bars on all sides, even covering the floor and ceiling. The seethings restlessly prowled about the cage. Every seething moved on all fours, none were upright like we saw before, and none had wings. They all appeared to be like the smaller seethings we encountered in the circuit and forest initially; nothing like the large monstrosities I witnessed just the night before.

There were several scuffles going on, but the ones not involved didn't stop the brawling. Not even when sickly snaps occurred and bodies went limp. Just beyond the sea of grey, I spotted another cage. This one held a single individual in it. From here I could just make out a shock of red hair. It appeared to be a small male, human perhaps. He was shirtless and covered in scars and barely scabbed wounds. He gripped the bar tightly with two hands and screamed before pressing his face between the bars and weeping. Freckles, he had so many freckles.

Holy shit.

"Aether, when did you start your undercover work with Gari?"

"What?" He looked at me like I'd lost my mind.

"When?"

"I don't know…about six months ago. Why?" He motioned below, clearly signaling we had more important things to focus on at the moment.

"Because I'm pretty sure that's Carter Johnstain, one of the missing persons Gari was trafficking."

Aether eyed the cage holding the lone figure. "How sure are you?"

I studied the male. He was much thinner than he was in the picture in Tim's folder; his body bore many wounds—some fresh and some old. His face looked sickly with a purple hue, but those freckles. Those common eyes. It had to be him.

"I'm like ninety percent sure."

He nodded. "This is good. We never clearly ascertained where they'd taken the humans or why. This could—"

His hushed voice was interrupted by the screeching of the warehouse door. Figures dressed in black and blue entered. Uniforms. I could make out the Glenn's standard-issue uniforms from here. My stomach dropped. This was undeniably Collin's doing. All other means and reasons had just been eliminated as dozens of guaramen poured through the door. All armed.

They had guns strapped over their backs, daggers at their sides, and several carried a strange weapon I'd never seen before. It almost looked like a fire torch? I couldn't be sure from here, but it was *not* standard-issue.

The figure in the middle was tall, female from her stance, with black hair coiled into a bun. She was too far to make out her face, but I'd never forget that rigid form...the cruelty in her posture. Luina.

My heart raced as images from that glass interrogation room flooded my mind. The smell of burning flesh, the screams, Luina's cool voice—

Calm. Comfort. Over.

Peace blanketed my soul and my senses; I was brought back to the present. The warehouse, seethings, that evil female. I didn't look at Aether, even though I could feel his eyes on me, and instead focused below—I'd been too vulnerable with that male for a lifetime.

Luina's lips were moving, she was speaking. Closing my eyes, I tried to focus on the sounds. Too many began to flood my system. The grunts of the seethings, their heavy breaths, the crunch of dirt under their paws, and the clang of metal as several ran stubbornly into the bars.

Focus, I just needed to focus on one thing.

I heard breathing, the rapid pants of the seethings. Not what I was looking for. I kept sifting through the sounds until I heard only evenly-paced, natural breaths. A rhythm. Bingo. I could hear words and the hum of a voice box.

"These are ahead of schedule," a high-pitched, nasally voice said.

"Not good enough. After last night, we need to move faster. We need to do this now. Why aren't they walking upright? Where are their wings?" Luina's pitchy voice replied.

"The more *evolved* ones are in the other warehouse. We've been dividing them based on batches. This batch is older and didn't have certain markers in their blood, so it's unlikely they'll ever walk upright, and they won't produce wings. Perhaps if their maker was helpful, they could evolve further, but it's unlikely," the nasal voice continued, his hands nervously ringing each other as he stood just to the side of the tall female.

"Mmm." Luina, clearly the leader, turned and approached the caged male. "And you. Has this time with *your* failures helped you realize why we need you? What the importance of your cooperation is?" She tsked as she ran her fingers across the metal bars.

The male didn't respond.

"Still not talking I see." She huffed. "Very well, leave him for another ten hours. No food. No water. And uh, to make things interesting, let one of the creatures out. Perhaps it can convince him." She turned on her heel.

"Yes ma'am," the squeaky male responded before gesturing to the guaramen at his side to follow him.

"Oh, and Carter, dear. You should *see* how helpful your sister has been. Her creations are truly something to gawk at. They've sprouted wings." The female laughed and chills ran down my spine. It was full of anything but mirth.

They left the warehouse as the skinny male slowly opened the first cage door that led to a chamber before a second door that opened into the cage. Several guaramen entered the chamber, their weapons at the ready. Sparks and fire erupted from the ends of the sticks they carried and scared all the seethings back from the door. They opened the second.

Carter's head swung up and looked at the beasts. He cupped his ears with his hands, but the whole room was silent. The beasts stopped any noise and froze, as if terrified by the little fire and light coming from the guaramen's weapons. One large guaraman entered the cage with a stick holding a metal ring at the end. It was about six feet long and he maneuvered it just far enough to drop it around the neck of one of the beasts. It bucked and with it several seethings ran at the male holding the stick. Fire whipped out in a burst of sparks and pops from the other guards' weapons and struck the beasts. They dropped to the ground with a unified scream, convulsing.

Carter's cries rang out as he too fell to his knees and was holding his chest.

What the hell? I looked at Aether, he too appeared to be focused on Carter, only he wore an expression of disgust.

They led the collared beast into the chamber and shut the door, leaving all the other creatures roaring.

Aether tapped my shoulder; it was time to go.

I followed him to the edge of the roof, where we stopped. The door to the warehouse across the yard screeched open and I could see the figures filing into it. Moans filled the air, some sounded oddly *human*.

I surveyed the yard. Dozens of buildings were scattered across the muddy ground. This place was a huge maze, it would take hours to explore it all.

Unnatural smoke filled the air and the whole place smelled rotten, wrong. The moans and cries and shrieks filling the air began to conjoin and become one ominous sound. It was overwhelming.

The figures disappeared into another warehouse and closed the door, and then, waiting no further, Aether began to climb down the ladder. I followed. The metal was cold to my touch. In fact, the whole world seemed to be freezing. My heightened hearing failed me as everything went from overwhelming to underwhelming. I felt deaf. I couldn't hear the rustling of feet or the growling of the seethings anymore. I couldn't even hear my own breaths.

Panic welled up as I quickened my pace. I still had at least a hundred feet to go. I stepped down for the next rung and missed it. Slipping, my feet fought for purchase while my hands dug in deeper to the metal rung. I kicked out with my left foot and found a footing on the icy rung. Taking a deep breath to steady myself, I removed my forehead from the cold bar I'd pressed it to and opened my eyes.

Calmness began to surround me, and my nerve endings didn't feel so sensitive to the cold anymore. The panic in my chest subsided as my pulse slowed back down. I wasn't going to fall. I was fine. Slowly, this time, I stepped down to the next rung and continued until my feet were on the blessed ground.

Aether nodded at me and then gestured for me to lead the way back to the charred tree line. I led us past the trees and up the hill, amazed at the serenity of my thoughts. The anxiety was gone; I felt at peace. I walked slowly, unrushed, and took careful steps to avoid the moldy pinecones, black pine needles, and dead branches that littered the path. I almost felt like humming. When was the last time I felt this good?

Cresting the hill, we began our descent and then reached a thick swatch of trees that were still alive, but black.

"Nicely done." Was that a compliment, from Aether, of all people?

"Child's play," I responded, enjoying this high. I felt good, I felt... the look in his eyes was pure amusement. He was messing with me. "What are you doing?" I growled.

"Just helping you calm down," he admitted. To my utter horror, I realized *he* was influencing my emotions.

"That is a total violation of my person. How dare you?" The warm fuzzy feeling dissipated and the anxiety returned. My nerves began rapidly firing and my chest hurt with every breath.

"Happy?" He looked disappointed as he laced his hands behind his back in some act of restraint.

No, I wasn't happy in the least, but I sure as hell wouldn't admit that to him.

"Let's go, we need to get back soon unless we want to just head to the Southern Outpost as a party of two."

I sucked on my fang and blew past him on the trail back. He was unbelievable. Not only could he transform into the fiercest thing I've ever seen, a badass dragon, but he could influence my emotions? Has he—

"Wait." I stopped abruptly, and he bumped into me, bracing my shoulders with his hands. Hands that completely swallowed my small shoulders in a suggestive way. Shaking my head, I tried to regain my train of thought. Violation, yes, that was what I was upset about. "Have you ever messed with my emotions before?"

He didn't answer, but his thumbs began to caress lazy circles on each scapula. The sensation was a distraction, but not *that* distracting. Not going to work.

"Answer me, Aether," I demanded.

His fingers stopped circling my shoulder. "Yes."

"Last night?" The horror of the prospect threatened to overwhelm me. Did he heighten my sexual drive?

"No. Never, I'm not that type of male." His voice was serious, earnest almost. He tried to turn me to face him, but I resisted. I did not need to melt in those dark eyes.

"Then when?"

"Only one other time. I used emotional manipulation in that duxes' quarters when I needed you to recall what happened to you and Fletch."

When he'd made me recall one of the worst days of my life. I swallowed back bile at the scene that filled my head: Fletch limp in a metal chair, blood everywhere—

"Don't mess with my emotions." I yanked free of his grasp and continued down the path. I couldn't get away from his body heat fast enough. He'd influenced me to relive one of the most horrific and vulnerable states I'd ever been in. Tears began to blur my vision. How did this too feel like a betrayal?

I knew he was using magic in that room, but to alter the way I felt? To heighten my anxiety or calm my nerves, to influence my emotions? I didn't even know such a thing was possible. Stupid, I was so very stupid.

We continued down the path in silence, with me leading, until we were about a quarter mile out. Aether grabbed my shoulders and jumped in front of me. Ever the predator.

Screams. I could hear screams and grunts, animalistic shrieks filling the air. We both broke out into a sprint, Aether's sword drawn. I pulled out my dagger, it felt pathetic by comparison, but at least it was something. I was in control of my emotions; I would *not* feel inadequate.

We reached the end of the path, right where we'd left the group, but they weren't there. Shouts came from around the bend.

As one we followed their cries and found the first sign of slaughter. Several dead corpses lay face down in the mud. Four to my count, along with two seethings, the latter already decomposing into black goo.

"Hold!" I could hear Vala command.

She was just ahead, in a small dome with Jared. To her right, closer to us, was a larger dome that held half a dozen vampires from our group, only a few of which were standing. Dozens of seethings, small ones, thank blood, were pounding on the shields Vala had created. They were holding, but beginning to splinter, and Vala was being physically propped up by Jared. I didn't know much about her magic, or any magic really, but I knew these fields drained her.

"Damn it! Stay back." Aether flew in front of me, faster than I've ever seen, and withdrew his sword. He pulsed at the air and the seethings went flying in every direction but ours. With his blade, he sliced through two seethings who had been blown in his direction. The remaining beasts regrouped and charged Aether. At least two dozen from my count. They lifted their heads as one and called out into the night. Their cry was unnatural and wrong at its very core. I stood there frozen. Aether would need to shift. We were dead if he didn't.

But instead, Aether pulsed the air again, and this time, they flew back a bit further, only to recover quickly. Aether stabbed a couple close to him and continued fighting his way toward the rest of the seethings, some of which continued to attack the dome. The splinters fractured further—deep cuts that I could see from here as the shield pulsed in response. Vala cried out and dropped to her knees, even Jared couldn't support her. The shields shimmered and blinked; she wouldn't be able to hold for long.

"Hold it, Vala!" Aether commanded. And then, to my horror, he dropped his sword. It sank into the mud at his feet.

The seethings noticed and left the dome. They began inching toward Aether on all fours. Closer, closer, and closer.

Still, Aether did not move. No way, no way he was sacrificing himself.

I tried to step forward, but the air surrounding me gripped my feet. I couldn't move. Anger filled my veins. *How dare he.* I tried again, willing the air to move, but it wouldn't respond. I was stuck. Damn it!

Howls from the woods sounded and several new grey and black blurs began to pour through the forest. They charged both Aether and Vala. Upon impacting the shield, Vala cried out and collapsed, both domes vanishing the moment her head hit the muddied ground.

I yanked again at the air and this time it budged—a little. I forced a step forward, using all my strength to fight the resistance.

Aether glanced at me. "Stop," he commanded. The beasts were nearly on him. They were mere feet from Vala and Jared. "Now, Jared!" Aether outstretched his hands and black fire erupted from them in a liquid stream. The moment it touched the beasts, they were incinerated, leaving nothing but charred remains where they once were. He directed the fire toward Jared and Vala. Jared's hands were outstretched, and even from here, I could see the faint form of a shield, about four feet in diameter and circular. Nothing compared to what Vala could wield, and yet it would be enough. The fire swallowed the seethings and bounced off the shield Jared bore. Incredible.

Four more seethings lunged at Aether, all at once, from different directions. He blasted two in midair with liquid lava; they didn't even make a sound as their ashes floated through the air. Turning to the other two, he pulled free a dagger and stabbed one in the eye just as it was about to land on his back before sidestepping and swallowing the remaining one in black flames. It was the most graceful dance I'd seen yet, absolutely mesmerizing.

Cries came from the remaining vampires as seethings began to attack them. Several were being dragged off into the woods by beasts while a few attempted to fight back. They needed help.

I willed my left foot forward, but I couldn't move it. I focused on the air, the bindings holding me still, and tried to remove them.

Several blurs raced through the trees right toward Jared, Vala, and Aether. They were being swarmed.

The vampires screamed as two of the three who were fighting fell. I palmed my dagger and aimed, throwing it toward the group a hundred feet away. Too far. I reached out and felt the air around the blade and pushed on it, willing it forward. The blade continued its flight, level until it sank into the brain of a beast about to devour a now unarmed vampire.

Aether looked at me, even as he fought, and *smiled* before swallowing the remaining seethings attacking the vampires in his flames.

I took a step toward him, relieved that the air gave and allowed a small step. I could do this. I could fight.

The beasts racing through the trees were howling and grunting, increasing in volume. More were coming. I reached for the other dagger at my side.

Crunch! A scream escaped me as pain exploded from my shoulder. I was thrown to my side, the whole world spinning, as a blur of grey assaulted my vision with black, razor-sharp teeth.

The seething sunk its fangs into my left arm next as it pulled back its talons and swiped at my stomach. I twisted away, barely missing its talons, but its mouth was embedded in my arm. Stabbing pain began to shoot through my veins as the monster pulled on my arm with its fangs—drawing. I could feel my nerves coming alive, practically boiling, and energy coursing through me. It was demanding a release. I shrieked as I forced my energy into the beast trying to consume me. I jolted, but its jaw remained locked.

My energy was being drawn, almost yanked out of my control, as it began to flow from me into the seething. It was draining me. I hadn't stopped it...I had *fed* it. I withdrew a dagger and began plunging it into the seething's side, its neck, and the back of its skull. I tried to control the air, but my focus was fractured. It growled even as it kept its fangs in my flesh before whipping its head side to side, throwing me around like a rag doll.

Another scream escaped my lips as my arm snapped and the bone broke. I began to see circles filling my vision before the seething flipped me onto my stomach and swiped at me with its claws, cutting across my back and digging into my shoulder, where it then paused and pressed down. I yanked my face up from the mud, gasping for breath. The whole world was spinning.

You will not die.

I refused to die, especially like this.

I could hear distant cries, Aether's voice along with Jared's, but their words held no meaning. Aether screamed and the fangs and claws impaling me gloriously disappeared as the seething fled a moment before heat raced across my back.

Panic. Pain. Regret.

I couldn't focus on anything as the entire world began to spin. Vomit escaped my mouth as I rolled to my side. A face filled my vision, concerned eyes hooded by dark, bloodied hair.

The forest began to dance overhead, and the rain started falling once more. I could see the trees swaying and was aware of movement with no sound.

Someone's warm body was pressed against mine and the steady sway of my body was that of being moved, gently.

"Wha—" I couldn't even form words to voice what I was thinking. My vision blurred again as water hit my face in droplets.

Anger. Dominance. Vowed protection.

"Shh, just rest. You will be okay. I promise."

CHAPTER 56

CHANCE

We had been driving for an hour. We just had about thirty miles to go to the settlement that had been leveled. So far, no sign of any convoy. Shae launched a drone about twenty minutes ago and sent it ahead of us, searching either side of the road for life. There was a good chance they were taking a trail and not the road.

Holland sighed and kept her focus forward. No one had said much since we'd left.

"Anyone here know about the anax's magic-wielding?" Damaris asked, trying to sound casual.

"Nope," I answered. "But I expect you could sense it?"

"I did sense magic, but it doesn't tell me what kind."

"Well, do better than that in the future. I want to know if someone so much as smells weird to you." If he'd given me a heads-up, I'd have at least been prepared and not dumbfounded.

"Yes, your excellence. Perhaps I can even—"

"Stop!" Shae interrupted, her face focused on her screen. "I see movement, hard to tell what exactly, but about a mile inland and three miles up the road. Could be the convoy, hard to tell through the trees."

"Can you track their route?" Holland asked.

"Trying to follow. If this is them, then there's a big problem." Shae didn't finish the thought.

"And that is?" Damaris pressed her to continue.

"It's a very, very small convoy."

Shit. I drove up two more miles and then parked the transport on the side of the road. The rig was big enough to fit thirty, I'd hoped we'd at least fill it and then have some following us. That didn't sound like it would be the case.

"Alright, everyone out. Stay tight. Any sign of those creatures?" I got out of the transport and shut the door, my feet sinking into the mud.

"Hard to say, but the movement appears methodical, so I'd say, no," Shae responded, adjusting the strap of the rifle I'd given her before we left.

"Damaris, anything?" I asked.

He lifted his face to the grey sky and wrinkled his nose. Then he sniffed again, obnoxiously loud. "I sense magic. Foreign magic."

"Like those creatures?" Holland asked, coming around the vehicle, weapon trained on the forest. She was always at the ready.

"Yes and no. There are traces of dark magic, but also something else I can't place."

"Like with Anax Clark?"

"No, not quite. This is stronger, but again, it's hard to tell."

I nodded.

"Shae, where is the group now?" Holland asked, not taking her eyes off the thick tree line. The rain had stopped and was a mere mist now, fog rolling through the pines, most of which held an unnatural grey color to their bark. What once was a glorious redwood forest, was now washed by death and left corpses for trees.

"I can't tell, low visibility. But last movement had them southeast of here. Maybe guard dog here can sniff them out as we get closer." She winked at Damaris, nudging past him.

"Right, because that is my sole purpose in life." He rolled his eyes.

"Move out. Stay close, stay quiet," I ordered as I took the lead position and entered the brush. The scrub oak appeared dead, no leaves, just bare grey branches covered in a white powder. Odd.

The fog only thickened as I began to pass into the dark forest. The mist was beginning to paw at my nose, it was cool but somehow still murky in a way that reminded me of a swamp and not the crisp air that was common in this southern forest.

A large tree had fallen, snapped at the base. White pus oozed out of it. I didn't need Damaris to tell me he sensed dark magic. This place reeked of it.

I stepped over a large fallen trunk and then continued to scan ahead. Visibility was bad, I could see maybe thirty feet in front of me at a time.

"Anyone else feel like this is a scene from a horror movie?" Damaris asked.

"What, you scared?" Shae prodded him as she walked alongside Holland, who was directly to my right.

"Nope, just feel like if I were watching this on TV, I'd be shouting at the characters to turn back. Nothing ever good comes from fog, forests, and weird magic."

"Shut it, Damaris," I commanded. We didn't need everyone getting easily spooked.

Holland walked up closer to me, her pistol aimed at the trees, scanning behind each one that came into view.

"He's right though," she whispered so only I could hear. "Those creatures would blend into this fog far too easily."

"We keep moving."

She nodded in response, even as her jaw ticked. She didn't have to like it, but we were moving forward. I did not shy back at the first sign of trouble.

I listened for any sounds of life beyond the horizon. Any signs of those creatures or of Tate's convoy. They were small, that could work to their advantage.

"Stop!" Damaris gripped my shoulder. "*That* magic. It's strong, very strong. Just ahead." He nodded beyond the large grey wood tree trunks.

"Stay here. Holland, hold this line." I walked slowly toward the brush just ahead and then past the large trees. Trees that have been here for hundreds of years, ones that were normally comforting, were now ominous—bad omens.

"Good boy." Shae's teasing was beginning to fade as I continued forward. The mist got thicker, and my arms were slick with the moisture. A twig snapped under my foot; I froze. No sound, no motion.

I inhaled and continued forward. I just needed to keep moving—

I was thrown to the side and landed on my back. A large hand was squeezing my throat. I opened my eyes and saw a ruddy buzz cut. A large male pinned me to the ground with his body.

"Who are you?" he demanded, but his grip only tightened, constricting my airway. I tried bucking him off, but his weight was expertly placed.

"Du...Dux Dale," I choked out, barely able to form the words.

"Guara." The male wrinkled his nose but released the pressure on my throat. "Are you one of them?"

What was he asking? Was I member of the guara? Yes, but the look in his eyes warned that the wrong answer could result in death. I remained silent.

"Answer me!"

"Freeze, or the next breath you take will be your last," Holland demanded. Thank blood for her. She stood behind a tree, weapon trained on the male atop me. "Roll off him, now."

Before the male could respond, I bucked out from under him and rolled on top, trading places. From this angle, I could see the standard-issue dokimos uniform. He appeared younger than I'd originally thought and had bruising across his face. The convoy.

"Arms up, shortie," a female voice came from behind me. I twirled around, still keeping the dokimos pinned underneath me, but enough to get a visual. Fuck. A tall female with chocolate eyes came out. She had a rifle trained on Holland. Black braids were thrown around her shoulders, disheveled and yet feminine. "You," she snorted at the male below me, "get off him. Now." She didn't take her eyes from Holland, but a twitch in her wrist told me she could change her aim and take both Holland and I down in a single moment.

"Look, we're on the same side. We're the rescue transport sent to intercept your convoy," I spoke slowly as I moved from the male beneath me.

"You two, that's a rescue party?" The female arched her brow. She didn't lower her weapon.

"Pathetic, right Vala," the male spoke as he stood and walked toward the female. "Then again, are we surprised?"

"Alright now, you two. I see you. Come out from behind the tree line, throw your weapons down," the female, Vala I surmised, commanded. "Don't and—" She scrunched her nose and I swore she found some sick humor in this. "Don't and I'll blow 'em brains out!" she said the last few words in an accent while giving the male next to her a wink, before whispering, "Always wanted to say that."

What the actual hell?

Shae and Damaris both walked out from behind the pines and held their hands up. Damaris had a weapon, though it was raised, while Shae held a disk. Her blue eyes wide.

"Good, now drop your weapons," Vala commanded.

Damaris dropped it and kicked it toward her, Holland following suit.

"Like I said, we're on the same side here. This is all unnecessary."

Movement behind Vala drew my attention. I could see a figure peeking through the fog. He was large and appeared to be carrying something. No, not something, someone.

She was limp, hanging from his arms. Almost lifeless.

"Tate!" Shae started forward, forgetting about Vala and her gun.

To my utter surprise, Vala lowered her weapon. She exchanged a glance with the male and then looked to the shadowed figure. He nodded and then continued toward us. Blood covered the limp tan arms that dangled from his hold, along with golden hair that was muddied and clumped together.

"Is she..." I couldn't finish the thought. Tate's head was nestled against his shoulder, eyes closed. Blood and mud covered her uniform, and I could see a makeshift bandage on her shoulder, wrapping her back, and on her arm.

"Alive," the male carrying her spoke.

"What the hell happened?" I stood up and began to approach him. Tate was injured under his watch.

"You know what happened, Dale."

I instantly hated this male. He knew who I was and spoke to me as if I were beneath him.

"Move, we need to get to your transport. Tate needs medical attention." He brushed past me, and I didn't miss the protective tightening of his arms or the way his scent was mingled with Tate's.

"Will she be okay?" Shae asked, blocking the male's path as she placed a hand to Tate's forehead. "She's burning up."

"We need to get her medical attention," he repeated, sidestepping Shae.

"You heard him, move out and take us to your convoy," Vala spoke, placing her weapon in its holster. Away but with easy access. Clearly, she had tactical training. The male next to her herded Shae toward the tree line we'd just come from.

"Where is the rest of your convoy, dux?" Holland spoke, eyeing the large male holding Tate.

"Anax Mardi. And this is it. Now move."

WE WERE ABOUT fifteen minutes from the outpost. I was driving with Dokimos Vala next to me. Holland was in the back with the male, a Dokimos Jared. Shae sat next to Damaris across from Anax Mardi who refused to place Tate down. The way he held her was proprietary. I sucked on my fang. I didn't like it and I didn't trust him. The road jostled as I hit a rut and then swerved to avoid another.

"Easy," Mardi commanded. I glanced in the rearview mirror to see him cradling Tate's body. Possessive asshole.

"Damaris, how's it smelling?" I asked, not wanting to be obvious but also needing to know if this anax also had magic.

"Wrong and strong," he responded.

Vala gave me an incredulous look and then looked back to Dokimos Jared. "I smell sweat and B.O."

"I can only imagine what it was like for you. We are investigating these creatures but need more intel. Can you tell us what they looked like?" Holland asked, pulling out a recording device.

"Big, black and grey, some upright and some on all fours," Jared responded.

"So, you encountered both as well?"

"We did. You too?" he countered Holland.

She nodded in response. I focused my gaze ahead of me. The outpost's lights came into view.

"How did you survive?" Holland prodded. We needed to know if they had evolved further or still could be killed with a blow to the head.

"Swords," Vala responded. "I drew mine, and well, Jared *always* has his drawn."

Was that a euphemism?

"Ok, so you just stabbed them, or did you have to decapitate them?"

"Decapitation killed them, stabbing and cutting limbs off maimed them enough to get away," Vala answered.

"So—"

"Enough. We're here," Anax Mardi interrupted Holland as he gestured to the gate in front of us.

"Shae," I said, but didn't even need to ask, the door was already opening. I waited for the gate to fully open and then pulled through.

CHAPTER 57

TATE

Scratchy sheets rubbed against my skin. I opened my eyes and saw an unremarkable, white ceiling. Watermarks formed in scattered spots. It was cast in a warm, red glow from the open window nearby. I pulled my hands out from under the blanket and paused. An IV was connected to my arm and I could see blood in it. Was I seriously being tube-fed? I tried jolting upright but was met with instant pain. I turned over the side of the bed and retched.

"Here." A bucket appeared, and I puked into it without question. After several heaves, my stomach was empty.

"Take it slow, TK." TK?

My eyes snapped up and I focused on a swatch of blue hair and steel-grey eyes.

"Shae." My heart rate slowed, comforted by her mere presence. "What—" My voice was so dry.

"Drink this. It's doused with medicine, so it probably tastes gross, but it will soothe your throat." Shae lifted a cup of murky water to my lips.

I drank, at first slowly, and then greedily. It did taste gross, sour even, but soon my throat went blissfully numb, and I didn't even notice the taste.

She pulled the cup back from my lips. "Blood Tate, I thought you were dead when Anax Mardi brought you in here."

I closed my eyes. It wasn't all a bad dream.

"What happened?" My voice was still hoarse from disuse, but the painful sandpaper sensation was gone.

"I was hoping you could tell me that. All I was told was that you were attacked en route and that most of your party didn't make it." Her steel eyes searched mine. "You can trust me, you know? I've seen some pretty crazy shit this past week." She moved and her new dragon tattoo danced with her. Did she know? Was she aware of the Untish Tribe?

What could I safely disclose? Shae was my oldest friend, if I couldn't trust her, who could I trust? And yet, the very knowledge I held could place her in danger...

"Creatures. We were overwhelmed by these grey monsters," I began. That was safe, in the very least, it should be common knowledge based on the attacks and reports Aether allegedly filed.

Shae nodded, not fazed.

"You experienced it too?"

"Yup. A couple of times. Scary shit. But nothing compared to when I saw that anax carrying you; I thought you were dead," her voice dropped to a whisper. "That was the scariest thing."

Before I could respond, the door opened, and a familiar set of chocolate eyes came into view.

"You're up! I knew one bite wouldn't keep you down. How's she doing, Shae?"

Vala knew Shae? She walked over and touched my forehead, scrunching her nose as she noted the bowl of vomit sitting next to the bed.

"Good, she just woke," Shae responded, moving the bowl of vomit from the end table to the floor.

"Yeah, I figured. Girl," Vala started as she sat on the bed next to me.

"When I saw you after Anax Mardi cleared the field, I thought you were a goner. I mean, you were coated in mud and blood and vomit." She wrinkled her nose on the last word.

"So, vomit is where your stomach gives out," I teased. She wasn't afraid of dragons, seethings, and knew so much about magic that I couldn't begin to guess how. But she wasn't invincible. Apparently, normal bodily fluids were too much for her to handle.

"Yeah," Vala giggled, "I may not like vomit, but I can handle my own. Anyway, when you opened your eyes and started blinking, I knew you'd make it. Not that Anax Mardi listened. He was soo worried that we moved double time. He was set on reaching the outpost by dark."

The outpost. We made it.

"We're here?" my voice broke on the last word. I was a mess. I didn't want to be here, serving the guara, and yet I was deeply relieved to be within the safety of its walls.

"Where else?" Vala teased.

"You're here. You're safe." Shae grabbed my hand and squeezed. She was always so reassuring and softer than her appearance would suggest.

"How many?" I leveled my gaze at Vala. "How many made it?"

She averted her gaze and walked over to the window. "This is my first time here at the SO. I was all prepared for life in the Eastern Outpost, but this forest is much nicer. Who knew we'd get lucky and end up here."

"Vala." I locked eyes with hers. "How many?"

A sigh escaped her lips as she came back over standing behind Shae. "Anax Mardi will want to know you're up and debrief you on any *classified* intel from those horrific events. I'll go let him know." Her message was clear: I wasn't supposed to talk to Shae.

I watched as Vala exited the room, swaying her hips as she sauntered out.

"She's a character," Shae said, biting her lower, now pierced, lip. "Tell me she didn't get the best friend spot?" While there was teasing in her tone, there was also concern. We hadn't left things good upon our last interaction.

"Never." I squeezed her hand to reassure. "So, as fate has it, I ended up being forced to enlist."

"Yeah, how the hell did that happen?" Shae's eyes widened in her characteristic way as she released my hand and leaned back in her seat.

"I broke the no-kill law and was caught."

"You what?" Shae said, disbelief across her face. "You, the one who taught me the value of human life, the one with a moral compass to where she can barely feed on vessels, killed someone? I don't believe it."

If she only knew how many I'd killed recently.

"Yeah, I got a little overzealous, but believe me, the guy had it coming."

"Mobster?"

"Something like that. But I got clumsy with his corpse and Collin was delivered his head. Soo...yeah. Disciplinary hearing and, well, here I am."

"Here you are. Metamorphosis at its finest."

"Metamorphosis?"

"Yup. We're evolving."

Indeed, we were. We were also together. That's what mattered. Even if she volunteered to be here and I was forced, we both ended up in the same place, serving the same crappy government, fighting dark magic of all things.

"You know, Shae. I'm glad you're here too. I—" The door opened, cutting me off. Aether entered.

My stupid traitorous heart paused a moment. The room's air charged, and I could feel my skin pebble.

"Glad to see you up. Dokimos Drew, if you don't mind." He gestured at the door. Shae stood, winking at me in reassurance before exiting.

"We need to talk." Aether sat across from me, his eyes intense and darkening as he looked me over. I gulped, something had changed between us, and I wasn't sure when it had happened, but the heat between my thighs told me that Aether and I had started down a different path.

What if this is more emotional manipulation? This male was not to be trusted, no matter *how* my body responded.

I tilted my chin up. "Well, I hope you're happy."

"Excuse me?" His eyebrows shot up as the right side of his mouth curved up in a smile.

"Yeah, you tried to incapacitate me. You tried to restrain me and what did it get me? Attacked, bait on a fishhook, you left me there, a statue to be mauled to death."

I wasn't fully serious, but I was angry. He had restrained me, and yet, hadn't he also been the one to step in when I needed assistance?

"My deepest apologies." The mirth in his eyes was angering.

"This is funny to you?" I questioned, lifting my arm that had tubes coming from it.

"Not in the least." He sighed, gingerly reaching for my wrist. "This was never supposed to happen. So much of what happened wasn't..." He stopped, gently rubbing my wrist with his thumb.

Never again.

The air bounced with electricity. I could feel it caressing my back, the nape of my neck. I wanted to lean into it, to embrace it.

"Enough." I shook my shoulders and withdrew my wrist. I was done with the mind fuckery. Done being used. Done being lied to.

"Right." He nodded. The sensation ended, leaving me cold and full of regret. I was a mess.

"We need to talk."

CHAPTER 58
CHANCE

Shae found me in the library. She stalked in, a smirk plastered across her face, and approached me as I studied my disk.

"I'm surprised you're not talking Tate's ear off."

"Oh, I started to. I mean, I had to fill her in on my new viewpoint of metamorphosis as I feel it really applies here, not to mention you and Holland—and this outpost—but uh...we got interrupted."

She shouldn't be talking about Holland and me. We weren't even a *thing*.

"Interrupted?" I prodded, not taking my eyes from the screen.

"Yup. Anax Mardi wanted a moment with her."

"Alone?" My eyes snapped to hers. So much for self-control.

"I guess. I mean, it was just the two of them. But what do you care, I mean you and Tate haven't been a thing in a *while*, Chance. I thought you'd *both* moved on." Shae nodded toward Holland who was approaching the table I'd commandeered as my desk. Her face looked tired, worn even. It had been a long week.

"I may have found something," Holland started, clearly missing the current energy—thank blood for that.

"What?" I rubbed my hands across my face. I'd been reviewing the decrypted files for the past ten hours, in thirty-minute increments, and hadn't found much of anything beyond confirming my suspicion that the outpost research lab was indeed studying dark magic. Beyond a few ominous remarks, the reports were glaringly bare.

"This. It's one of the last reports Shae sent outlining communication from the unknown location to this outpost's Research Lab, not command." She projected the screen for us to see as Shae simultaneously enacted a shield around us.

"Here. Look for yourself." Holland pointed to a specific bit of text that was highlighted for Shae and me to study.

"DMC Round Eight: success. More movement and intelligence rendered. Moving on to round nine. Awaiting candidates," I read aloud.

"DMC?"

"Yeah, I wasn't sure what that was either. But I noticed several transmissions coming from a blocked location directly to the lab, dodging command, which is against code and regulation."

"Which would be why it wasn't flagged higher up in my algorithm," Shae mumbled, shaking her head.

"Right. After reading several coded transmissions, one references 'magic' and another 'creation', so I think DMC could stand for 'Dark Magic Creation'. Either way, it's concerning. And even if it doesn't have to do with those things," Holland paused and looked pointedly at me. "It could concern the data and motivation for the recent attack on this Outpost."

"I can't believe I didn't think of this with the algorithm. I should have had these at the top of the decryption list." Shae studied the screen like it was holy.

Holland shrugged and leaned across me, her lavender scent filling my nostrils, as she closed the file and opened another. "See this?" She pointed to a location. "Shae, could you locate the transmission's location if you follow the response sent *from* the research lab to the location?"

"That's brilliant." Shae looked at Holland with newfound respect. I knew the feeling well.

"Well, you're not the only one who went to Coders Cottage as a kid." Holland winked at Shae, red creeping in her cheeks in the adorable way it did when she was embarrassed. She was cute and good in bed, a great soldier, but still...we weren't a thing. Not yet at least.

"This is good. I can work with this. Give me an hour or two." Without another word, Shae closed the shield, grabbed her bag, and left.

Holland and I stood there in silence for minutes.

"So, uh, did you find anything out?" Holland asked, playing with a stray lock of hair peeking out from her ponytail.

"Not really, vague mentions of dark magic and then, of course, our reports of the incidents. I did find three other reports sent to leadership here concerning the creatures, but the oldest one dates back two months ago. Then there's a gap until three weeks ago, then the week of the attack on the SO and EO, and, of course, our reports." Saying it aloud helped, but still, I felt like I was looking at the picture upside down. I had several facts, but couldn't place them together.

"Dale, if the first attack happened *before* the attack on this outpost, then..." Holland left it unsaid.

"And we're back again." I let out a frustrated sigh. "Holland, I don't want to have this argument." Why did she always circle back to blaming my father and our nation? This, this right here, is *why* we weren't a good idea, not as an item. Working with her could be so infuriating.

"Dale, you're being stupid and stubborn. Willfully ignorant." She took a step back, disgust coloring her face.

"I'll admit that, perhaps, I was wrong about leadership's knowledge of dark magic. It's obvious they've been studying it, but to insinuate that *we* are responsible for those things? *Things* that attacked *our* men, *our* outposts. To believe that my father knowingly sent me into harm's way, not just once but twice, that's just—" I couldn't finish the thought.

I wanted to believe my father had a heart, that his only son would be valued, but who was I kidding? He never really cared for me. As soon as my magic screening showed low results, he basically forgot I existed until I made dux last year.

"Look, I know you want to believe in the goodness of the guara, but I think you're not viewing this like you would if we were investigating a foreign party."

"We are investigating a foreign party. Three, in fact, in case you missed that in briefing."

"Dale. Look at this." Holland pulled out her disk and then a similar cloaking device. "Here. This is the report I was referencing with Shae, look at the date it was sent."

I looked where she pointed. "April fifteenth," I whispered aloud. The whole room felt too warm.

"Exactly," she paused, "and here, it mentions 'round eight' insinuating this has been going on before that. Want to know how long between this transmission and one I located that mentioned round ten?"

No, I really didn't.

"Six weeks." She grabbed my chin to direct my gaze to her eyes. "Six weeks, Dale. That means that it takes at least three weeks per round, if it's consistent, and if round eight happened in mid-April, then—"

"Then our government has been conducting dark magic experiments since last year," I finished for her.

Closing my eyes, I tried to separate myself from the facts. Holland had a point. Clearly, the Glenn knew more about dark magic than they admitted during the meeting. They were conducting experiments at an off-the-grid facility since last year. The first documentation of these creatures was a month before our borders were breached. How could a foreign enemy infiltrate us without notice for a month and then be caught breaching our borders? The attack on this outpost wasn't that sophisticated, just minor hacking and doctored security footage.

"Only one way to find out, Holland. You up for a field trip?"

"Look who found his backbone." She smirked.

I prayed to blood that we wouldn't find those creatures there.

CHAPTER 59
TATE

"You look different," Aether spoke.

"As opposed to being muddy and bloody? Gee, thanks." I rolled my eyes.

"How are you feeling?" he asked. It felt uncharacteristic of him to show genuine concern. Like he actually cared, not just looking after me for Arithi as he so often reminded me.

"Fine," I lied. I felt like complete garbage.

"Mhmm." He eyed the bowl of vomit on the floor. "When one is going through the Changing, it can be common to experience intense side effects. We've already discussed some, but overheating and vomiting can unfortunately be common when expressing magic. And when trying to recover from severe wounds—"

"What?"

"Your wounds were bad, I wish—"

"No, you said magic." I didn't understand much about magic, but I knew I had larger stores of it than I'd originally thought. I could shift and manipulate air, or whatever it was, and I knew if I'd searched within to that now clear pool, I'd have to confront another truth...

"I wish I could explain more, but not here. There are a few things we need to go over."

He sat on the edge of the bed and folded his hands inward, his eyes darkening. "Tate, you can't tell Shae or anyone here about the Untish Tribe or your connection to it. And you certainly can't tell them about us."

"I know." I looked down. I hated keeping Shae in the dark, but after what happened to Fletch, I couldn't stomach the thought of getting Shae involved.

"Good. I just got word from Arithi. We have a mission."

"A mission?" My eyes bugged out. I was hooked up to an IV, could barely move, and *I* was supposed to complete a mission?

"Yes, as soon as you're able, we're going to destroy that base creating the seethings, and then get the hell out of here."

I was silent. We needed to kill those creatures; I knew that. But I'd nearly died the last time I encountered one. And I could barely move at the moment. My pulse quickened as panic began to settle in.

"Where will we go?" I asked, focusing instead on the male in front of me. Tattoos peeked out from his black jacket and crawled up his neck. His dark hair was pulled back in a bun just above the nape of his neck and I swore the ends of it looked a little different, darker somehow.

"Classified."

Of course it was. I looked away and gazed out the window. I didn't want to be at the Southern Outpost. I didn't want to be caught up in a war. But the guara needed to be dealt with, more specifically, President Dale needed to be handled. He was involved in the creation of those creatures and was responsible for Fletch's death.

"I'll go with you. But I need to know that Shae will be safe. I want to take her with us."

"Not an option."

"I say it is," I challenged him, lifting my chin and feigning defiance I simply didn't feel. The movement itself was incredibly draining.

"Tate." He let out a heavy sigh. "I know you care for her. And because you do, trust me when I say, she's safer here."

Was he serious? Safer with the evil responsible for the seethings? Serving the guara?

"Then I won't leave."

It was a bluff. From the way he smirked, the asshole knew it.

"I'm serious. She's the only family I have left, and I won't leave her to be swallowed whole by the guara."

The air in the room thickened. Pacifying. Soothing, he was soothing me.

"Stop. I'm not a child who needs to be coddled. I am an adult who is making a reasonable demand." I wiggled in the bed, the sensations surrounding me didn't relent. To my chagrin, it *was* calming.

"Tate, everyone who knows about the Untish is in danger, they are a threat both to the Glenn and to the Untish Tribe."

"But *I* know about you guys. Fletch did and—"

"Tate." His eyes deepened. I knew what he was getting at. Fletch was gone because of his involvement with the Untish Tribe and the Glenn's discovery of it.

"That's exactly what I'm concerned about, Aether. If they discover I'm involved with *you guys,* they may come after Shae. I can't risk exposing her to harm."

"If Shae comes with us, Arithi will kill her."

My blood stilled in my veins, the fire I felt building a moment ago fell silent. Extinguished.

Aether's jaw ticked. "She's safer here. The sooner we leave, the better."

I looked away, down at the sheet, thin and low-thread count—a worn white. I couldn't protect Shae. Leaving her here meant leaving her to be attacked by those *things* again. Leaving her to the protection of the guara and Chance. But taking her? Death. Neither option was acceptable. I ran my hands over my face, they trembled from the movement. I was weak. In so many ways, I was pathetically weak.

"The sooner we leave, the less contact you have with her, the better. We need to get you on your feet."

I didn't respond. What would Shae do? I exhaled.

"I need you to get full strength, but since you're Changing, you need to feed."

"I thought that's what the tubes were for." I lifted my arm, wincing as the cannulas dug in at an uncomfortable angle in the crook of my elbow.

"Not that kind of blood." He took off his jacket, revealing a navy tank underneath that highlighted his well-formed chest.

Ah. His blood.

"I thought Vala insinuated it was a 'no-no' to give me your blood."

"You may one day hate me for it. But I'm willing to deal with it when that day comes." His lips tensed.

I didn't move, didn't reach out for him, I just sat there. Unsure.

"And if I don't..." I left the question hanging. Better to let him reveal his hand.

"You won't make it through the next day if you don't have blood with richer magic to restore your depletion."

I bit my lip. "Then why would I despise you for this? For offering to help me."

He didn't answer, just looked away. I could *feel* his energy surrounding me, pulsing, begging to claim me, and yet, it remained just beyond my reach.

I glanced at his pulsing veins. Easy to puncture. The arm was less intimate...

And yet, I didn't want to drink, at least not in the way he offered. I'd only fed from vessels when they *deserved* it. My mind reasoned that perhaps he did deserve it. He was a liar, a manipulator. But...he had saved my ass.

A part of me was *drawn* to him in a way I didn't comprehend.

He pulled his arm back as if sensing my hesitancy. "You don't have to direct feed." He stalked over to the cabinet and retrieved an IV kit. With expert movements, he dug the needle into his vein and then turned on the flow, allowing it to enter the cannula he'd attached. Blood, deep maroon and golden, filled the tube and began dripping on the floor. He ignored it as he turned back to the cabinet, rummaging through the drawers.

"Damn it."

"What?" I asked, my focus wholly on the blood coating the floor. I could feel its call, the beckon of its magic.

Drink.

"No cups. Sorry." He stalked back to me, sat on the edge of the bed, and extended the end of the cannula to me.

I didn't hesitate. I grabbed it and put it to my lips. The flavor was exquisite, just as I'd recalled.

I adjusted my grip on the tube and pulled him closer. My whole body felt alive. I could feel energy flowing in me, through me, to me. I felt alive. I drank again, deeper this time. A buzz began to settle over my mind and my senses were suddenly heightened, then dulled. Powerful, I felt strong.

Aether's other arm came around me and steadied me as I wavered from this new wave of vibrancy. I was close to him and yet so very far. A mere foot was between us, but it felt like an ocean.

I began to hum. Or at least I did in my head. His blood was a symphony, the missing notes to my song. I scooted closer to him so that my knees were pressed against his thigh. His hand on my back stilled its motions but kept contact. I wanted more.

I moved again and this time I was sitting on his lap.

"Tate. You should really just—" His words broke with a moan as I adjusted on him, his length growing beneath me.

I drew more blood into my mouth, my throat, my being. This. This is what I'd needed, what I'd begged for. I could feel the room's energy again, sense the air molecules, a force I didn't understand but recognized.

"Just eat, a little more," his voice was low, husky.

I continued to feed, my mind falling blissfully unaware as the high took over. I could taste notes of cherry.

Passion.

Drops of honey.

Longing.

My nerve endings pulsed and every part where our bodies met was on fire. I let go of the tube with one hand and gripped his shoulder, while biting down on the cannula, the high making me feel dizzy.

"Tate, you need to release now," Aether was speaking, but I didn't want to let go. I wanted more, needed more.

"Tate," he commanded and pinched the tube, stopping the blood flow. I reached for his hand, but he lifted it higher and met my eyes with his.

His eyes were dark and full of promise—gone were the golden flecks. No, these eyes were purely sensual. I wanted more of him, his blood, his flavor, his being. He pulled the IV out, blood spurting across the bed and my lap before he threw a bandage I hadn't noticed before onto his wound. Closed for business. Or was he?

"Kiss me," I spoke as I leaned toward him.

"Tate," his voice was both a plea and a reprimand. I could see the way he stared at my lips, the way he swallowed, the heat and wanting in his eyes. Maybe this was just a blood-high, but I didn't care. If I couldn't have his blood in me, I could at least taste his mouth.

"Kiss me?" I leaned in and gently brushed my lips over his and then pulled back. Waiting. Wanting.

He moaned and then swallowed my mouth with his as his hands tightened around my waist. He reached up and dug one hand into my hair at the base of my neck as the other pressed my body closer to his. I began to grind against him as I swept my tongue inside his mouth. Mother Blood, he tasted so good. So right.

He stood up and flipped me over, so I was lying on my back on the bed, never breaking contact as his tongue was dancing inside my mouth. I trapped him with my legs and pulled him closer to me. I could feel the hard length of him at my core. I wanted this. I was ready.

His hand slipped up the medical gown to my breast and gently squeezed, teasing. I moaned and he broke the kiss before claiming my clavicle. I could feel his fangs graze the soft spot at my neck. The lover's mark.

He growled deeply, pressing his fangs to the mark but not puncturing, before savagely taking the tender skin above my clavicle in his mouth in a deep kiss. More, I wanted more. I reached down and grabbed the length of him. He bucked at my touch.

He released my neck and then licked a slow path up to just behind my ear.

Pleasure. Pure bliss. I moaned and moved my left hand under his shirt, sinking my fingers into his back, not caring that I could feel blood blooming from where my fingers dug.

He paused and then pulled back, cradling my face in one hand.

"Not now, not this way."

What?

Bleary-eyed, I tried to comprehend his denial. He moved away from me and stood out of reach, just in front of me.

"It's just…not right. Not now." Then he turned and walked over to the chair before dropping into it.

Had he seriously just denied me? Red crept up my cheeks. Rejection was new.

My blood fired within me, sparked, and sang. I could still feel the ache in my core. He may not be willing to satisfy me, but I'd be damned if I was left wanting.

I locked eyes with him as I lowered my hand to my gown that was crumpled up around my thighs. Slowly, I placed one hand inside, brushing the entrance to my core. The sensation elicited a moan from me.

Aether's eyes widened and I could scent his desire from across the room. Good, he deserved to burn with unreciprocated passion.

I grazed my thumb against the sensitive bud, back and forth. My nerve endings rapidly buzzed, the pleasure radiating through my core. I dropped my head onto the bed and closed my eyes, focusing on the pleasure.

Slowly, I inserted one finger, and then a second, and began pumping, the motion smooth from my wetness. I moved faster and then slower, building the friction and feeling the pressure build in my core.

I opened my eyes. Aether's focus was entirely mine. The look on his face was pure lust. I focused on his pupils, they dilated with my attention. The air around me tightened, like I was being held, stroked even.

I continued to pump, savoring each motion and the flick of my knuckles against the bud of my sex. The tension around us built; pure vibrancy, one I was beginning to become familiar with, filled the room.

Aether reached down to his engorged crotch, pulling at his zipper.

"Uh-uh." I shook my head. "You can watch. But no participation of any kind."

His eyes flared with the challenge.

Desire. Sex. Pure, undiluted attraction.

I smirked as I picked up my motion and widened my legs. I released a teasing moan, Aether's hands flexed in response.

I reached out to the air from within and touched the energy buzzing. Aether's moan was audible, as was the fisting of his hands. Interesting.

I continued to tease myself before finally, digging in deeper to find the perfect spot, to stroke the ache. Satisfaction ruptured through me as the force in the room intensified, my blood sparking, and my body seizing around my fingers. Release coursed through me as I threw back my head and groaned. The tension around my base tensed with each of my movements before dissipating, the room's atmosphere returning to natural levels. Gone was the external pressure, the hold on my body that was but wasn't there. The air was neutral again. I relaxed as my core stopped seizing, and I pulled out my fingers, one by one, locking eyes once again with Aether.

He sat perched on the chair, barely restrained. His groin was still growing, not satisfied.

I smirked.

"Happy?" I asked.

He didn't respond, but his hooded expression suggested I'd merely awoken his inner beast.

Mine.

My pulse quickened and I swore I could feel the fire within the room dance around me in a claiming protective wave.

Possibly.

The message erupted from me. His eyes widened as his crotch pulsed loudly in response. I'd never sent a message like that before. I was apparently more capable than I knew.

"So much more, my dear," Aether's words jarred me from my thoughts. The sex haze began to clear my head and I realized I was still on the bed, legs spread. I closed them and pulled at my hair.

"When do we leave?"

CHAPTER 60

CHANCE

"This is incredible, Shae. In case I don't say it enough, you're amazing." I patted her on the back as I looked at the screen. She'd narrowed the off-site location down to a two-mile radius. This was fucking awesome. It gave us a good chance of locating the facility.

"You don't really say it enough. And yes, I am a pretty damn amazing female."

"A real badass," Holland confirmed, smiling at Shae.

"So, what now?" Shae voiced the one question we all were thinking.

"I say we raid the center and see what's really going on. Find out what leadership is hiding," Holland said.

"I don't know. It could be risky. I think it may be best to do a small intel mission...sneak in, sneak out," I spoke, hoping Holland would see the logic in my suggestion.

"Dale, if this is what we think it is, we'll need to do more than observe. We'll need hard evidence."

"Holland, I'm not about to risk the lives of other guaramen on a hunch. Besides, we don't know what we'll find. Hence, reconnaissance." Why were we always having the same argument?

"Hold up, why don't we do both?" Shae placed one hand on both of our shoulders. "But first, everyone needs to take a deep breath." She inhaled and motioned for us to follow suit.

Was she serious?

"Dale. Come on now, you're not too big and bad for some meditative breathing." Shae gave me a pointed look as Holland inhaled, but I stubbornly refused.

"Good, Holland. Now exhale with me." Shae exhaled with force.

I hated the sound of forced breath. It sounded wrong and reminded me too much of yoga. Go figure, Shae would like it.

"Good. Now, what if we have a reconnaissance mission that *also* obtains hard data? We can prepare for the worst, have a small team, and hopefully avoid bloodshed."

"How?" I demanded.

"With me of course." She gave me a cocky smirk and then turned to Holland. "And her. If she's able to help with some basic coding, I believe that the three of us can sneak close enough to the base and, with my toys and mad skills, we should be able to get the data *while* having eyes on what's going on."

"What if you can't?" I asked. I knew she was good at hacking, but I also knew it took her twenty-four hours to decrypt some basic messages due to the high level security and firewalls she had to break through.

"Please, I'll be able to. But if it is too challenging to do from afar, I'll just need access to the mainframe. There should be main hubs at each building, powering everything. Each box has a hard line connected to the heart, as I like to call it. I'd just need to tap that, leave my mindscrambler, and then I can finish the hack from afar." She snapped her fingers. "Child's play."

"No—"

"Alright—"

Holland spoke over me, our answers—naturally—were very different. This was getting old. It would be a 'no' for me on the relationship front with this one. No matter how good she could fuck, she was beginning to be a headache to work with—a true tell-tale of a complex, dramatic female who would require far too much effort.

"Why in blood's name not?" Holland demanded.

She was ready to square off with me. Fine.

"Because it's too dangerous. If we get caught, if Shae gets caught, it could be death. We could receive a disciplinary hearing that doesn't go our way. Any one of us could be executed. I say we approach; I get in closer with a drone and launch it. Then Shae and you can receive the data from a safe distance. Once we know what we're dealing with, we can reevaluate."

"Absolutely NOT." Holland stepped toward me, lifting her chin.

She looked adorable from this angle. All five feet of her.

"Holland, I know you're—"

"Uh-uh. My turn to monologue." She snapped at my fingers with her teeth as I reached for her. Damn it if it wasn't a turn-on.

"I am joint leadership," Holland continued, "your equal. And like it or not, I'm coming. I am not some flower that will wilt, so don't you dare tell me what I can or cannot do."

"Amen sister." Shae slapped her on the back and stood behind her.

Females.

"It has nothing to do with you being female, I just think—"

"Allow me to think for myself. Or don't. But either way, I'm coming as *I've* made up my mind." Holland stepped closer, raised her chin, and lowered her voice. "And guess what? I have an advantage. It turns out, not having a phallus means I can focus on multiple things at once and don't go saluting every female with two legs." She raised up on her tiptoes and pecked my chin before turning on her heels. "Let's go, Shae. We have planning to do."

"Love it." Shae stared after Holland, watching her walk away. The sway of Holland's hips emphasized her figure. Apparently, I wasn't the only one to notice. "Alrighty then, if you screw up with her Dale, I can't promise you my loyalty." Shae wagged her brows and then strode off toward Holland, her steps much more athletic and less graceful than Holland's.

I didn't for a second like her insinuation. I was a male after all, we were known to be territorial, even if I *didn't* want a relationship with Holland.

Patience. I closed my eyes and exhaled.

I needed to catch up with them before they went off half-cocked on their own to do reconnaissance, but first I needed to do one thing.

TATE WAS FULLY DRESSED in black, staring out the window. She had a bandage wrapped around her shoulder and arm, marks from where she'd been bitten. I hated that she experienced even an ounce of pain.

She swayed slightly. I could see the beginning of sweat rings forming on her shirt; it was hot here, but not *that* hot. Even with her perspiration, her figure from here was jaw-dropping. I could feel myself preparing to salute and immediately focused on something else, noting the bowl of vomit by the bed. Perfect.

I looked at the chunky green goo floating in the bowl as I strode in before raising my eyes back to Tate and her glorious ass.

"I suppose I'd have to deal with you eventually." Tate sighed as she turned, meeting me with familiar mahogany eyes. Her dark blonde hair hung loosely around her shoulders, framing her face a bit. It was clean now, unlike when I found her in the forest, and even from here I could smell the scent of lilacs from her shampoo.

The ends of her hair were rose pink. Shae must be wearing off on her.

"Tate, I just wanted to see how you were doing." I hated how my voice wobbled. This female drove the senses and confidence out of me.

"How am I doing?" She huffed, taking a slender step toward me with her gloriously curved thigh. The movement caused the leather to flow with her and showcased her lush hips and swelling chest. Fuck I loved the guara's black leather combat suits. Tighter than the pants and shirts entry-level were given.

"Let's see." She held up a finger as she bit her lip. "First, I'm forced to join the blood-damned guara." She took another step. Her skin glistened from sweat. Her scent had changed since I'd seen her last. It now also held a smoky hue—hot.

"Second, I am attacked by creatures that reek of evil and a vile use of magic, and third, but certainly not least, I'm stuck here with *you*." She waved a delicate, but bruised, hand around the room. "But you know what is absolutely worst of all?" The look in her eyes was lethal.

"Tate—"

Before I could move, she lunged. Stronger than before and with a new grace that knocked me on my ass. She straddled me and had a blade at my throat. Fuck, that was new.

"You killed him, you son of a bitch. You tell me here, right now. Did. You. Know?" Her voice dropped to barely a whisper as she dug the tip of the blade into my throat, drawing blood.

"Know what?" Females. They'd all lost it today.

"Did you know they planned to kill him? Fletch. Were you part of his death?"

"Fletch is dead?" The blood drained from my face.

From the look in her eyes, she saw the truth there. I wished I could wipe the pain from those pools of red-brown. "Fuck, Tate. I swear, this is the first I've heard of it. Why? How—"

"Get out." She got off me and stood, giving me her back as she walked to the window. I'd been dismissed.

"Tate, I'm so sorry. I had no idea. I swear if I did, I'd—"

"You'd what? Tell me, prepare me, try to stop it?" She laughed. The sound was purely feral. "No, wait. That's not your style, you'd just make love to me, like you did while my mother was being executed." She locked eyes with mine.

What could I say to that? I could tell her how sorry I was, how I regretted that one thing more than anything, but it wouldn't bring her mother back.

I just stood there.

"Get! Out!"

I took a step toward her, but a hand gripped my shoulder and spun me around. A large male stood in front of me. Anax Mardi. He may be a bit taller and more built, but he sure as hell didn't have the right to grab me.

"She said get out. Do as she commands. Now," he ordered.

"Like hell I will." I shook his hand from my shoulder.

"You really are the pain in the ass I've heard about."

What was that supposed to mean?

"Tate, you look well. You ready?" Mardi's question drew my attention back to Tate. She was dressed in all leathers, fighting leathers. Her chest was wrapped with a battle vest, daggers were sheathed at her sides, hips, and shoulders. She was prepared for battle. How the fuck had I not noticed it sooner?

I glanced at her feet and felt stupid for not seeing it sooner. She wore her combat boots, one heel much thicker than the other to accommodate for the one flaw this female had. A duffle bag lay next to her.

"Where do you think you're taking her?" I demanded.

"Careful, Dale. I am her commanding officer and I outrank you."

I hated that he had a point. "She needs to be cleared by medical before relocating, let alone training." Dear blood I hoped that was all they were planning. Training I could handle, actual combat? Tate didn't know the first thing about fighting vampires, let alone those creatures.

"She has been cleared. We're ordered to head for the Eastern Outpost. We leave in twenty. Thanks for the hospitality. And..." he paused, eyes heating, "you may want to wash the sheets." He winked at me before placing a hand on Tate's back and gently guiding her out of the room.

CHAPTER 61

TATE

"You may want to wash the sheets?" I couldn't believe my own ears. "Really, Aether, you had to go there?"

Males were all the same. Maybe I should swear them all off like Shae had.

"He needed to be distracted in order to stop questioning things. We have to go, and as much as I'd rather kick his ass, we don't have time for that or the headache that would ensue." Aether guided me down several flights of stairs and into a dimly lit hallway. "Besides, the look on his face, tell me you didn't enjoy the way his jaw dropped and red spread across his cheeks." Aether snorted.

"Males," I muttered.

It was dark out. We'd wasted an entire day on my healing and extracurricular activities. Even as we moved through the hallway, his hand still hadn't left my back. I liked it and I didn't at the same time. My body was responding in ways I'd never responded to any male before. I could feel my core heating, aching, wanting. But my head? Nope. My head was clear and told me this was a bad idea, that I didn't know him, couldn't trust him. His people got Fletch killed. Even if

449

Fletch had believed in the cause and volunteered, his work with them was what the guara killed him for.

Was I really supposed to just throw caution to the wind to please my increasingly horny self? Not a chance.

"You can move your hand," I spoke as I shook from his grasp.

"As you wish." His voice was cool, and I didn't miss the narrowing of his eyes or the way he glared at every guaraman we passed.

The spot on my back where his hand had rested was suddenly chilled, and my body betrayed me by *missing* his physical touch.

"Just ahead," he spoke to me as he nodded to a door.

Four guaramen were on the other side. They stopped us before we could continue into the large warehouse full of trucks, rigs, and transports.

"Name and order number," a young male asked, looking from Aether to me. His eyes sparked as he noted my leathers, and I could see him sniffing. Was he really smelling me?

Aether growled. Actually growled. What was wrong with him?

"Tate Aaralyn and this is Anax Mardi," I spoke. If Aether was just going to go primal and stare the poor male down, then at least I could expedite this process.

"That's a pretty name. Dokimos Aaralyn, I see you on the roster as a guest. You're leaving so soon?" He made a point of eyeing my figure. This male really wasn't the brightest. Before I could respond, Aether had the arche by his throat and threw him against the wall. The other three guaramen raised their weapons, but Aether had each one dismantled before they could even land a strike.

"I am Anax Mardi. I will not be questioned, and Dokimos Aaralyn will be treated with respect," he spat at them before motioning for me to continue.

This day just kept getting weirder. I adjusted the strap to my rifle, heavy on my back, as we walked past two guaramen heading toward the door, I motioned for them to stop.

"Would you be a dear and get this to Shae Drew for me?" I

extended a letter toward the male. His eyes widened and I swore his frame shook a bit.

"She asked you a question," Aether growled from behind me.

"Ye...yess," the arche stuttered as he reached for the envelope and then pulled his hand back quickly, as if he'd been burned or bitten.

"Thank you," I chirped as I passed them and walked further into the warehouse.

I knew the guara had resources, but this was pure egotistical. Rows upon rows of transports lined the walls. Smaller rigs were in front with a few trucks here and there. The larger transports were in the back, and there were hundreds of them. There had to be at least enough to transport a large convoy of ten thousand or more.

"Just ahead," Aether spoke softly to me as he pointed.

I spotted Vala's frost-tipped hair as she waved at us. That was new. She'd cut her braids off and now sported an adorable pixie cut. Her curls bounced off in every direction, all of which were tinted white at the ends. When did she have time for that? Jared stood beside her. Arms crossed. I smirked, those two *had* grown on me. Even if Jared was insufferable.

"Good, we're all here. Time to go," Aether spoke.

"All the gear has been loaded. We are ready. You sure *she* is?" Jared motioned toward me.

Ok, maybe he hadn't grown on me that much. I didn't appreciate the insinuation.

"She'll be fine." Aether nodded. The air around me circulated in a delightful breeze.

I could see his hand reach for me and then pull back. My heart rate increased.

Just breathe.

Sweat began to pool at the back of my neck and lower back. I felt ungodly warm.

"Ready." I nodded at Vala who raised her brow. A smirk covered her face, like *somehow* she knew just how close Aether and I had gotten.

"Let's go then," Jared spoke as he jumped into the small, ten-person transport.

Aether followed, taking the driver's seat with Vala up front in passenger. I climbed into the back and strapped into the five-point harness. I supposed if the thing rolled, I'd be glad to have this even if it felt cumbersome. The transport jolted forward and then pulled out of the garage. No one spoke as we left the outpost behind. A sour taste filled my mouth as I thought of Shae and her grey eyes and fairy-blue hair. What would she think when she got my note? Would she be OK? I closed my eyes. I'd never hated myself like I did right now. I just had to hope she listened to what I said and got the hell out of the guara. My head was pounding.

"So, what's the plan?" I asked. A moment passed and no one responded. "Come on guys, I think I've more than earned enough trust in this regard. How are we going to destroy the warehouse?"

"Blow it up," Aether answered.

Was he serious? Just blow the damn thing up? Wouldn't that raise some red flags with the guara?

"What about the innocent guards?"

"Can't save everyone, Tate." Vala looked at me with compassion. "Besides, if they're in the guara working at an off-site warehouse full of monsters, how innocent are they?"

"Not everyone can choose where they get assigned." Was I really defending guaramen? I began to massage my aching temples, moisture collecting at my fingertips.

"We can only control so much," Vala spoke softly.

Aether pulled through the gate, and we left the outpost behind. I couldn't shake the feeling that I'd never see this place again.

CHAPTER 62

CHANCE

Walking outside in the cool night air did nothing to lower my temperature. I was radiating steam. Who the hell did Mardi think he was? I mean, her commanding officer fine, but to insinuate that he and Tate—

I couldn't finish the thought. I unclenched my hands and tried to steady my breath. Tate was no longer my concern. She was safe. She was on her way to the EO. She wasn't mine, not anymore. Accept it. I had to, or I'd go absolutely insane.

"Everything alright?" Holland asked, approaching me from the courtyard to my left.

"Peachy."

"Ah." She nodded, as if understanding. "Shae and I are ready. We've added Damaris to the transport manifest, and I assigned us as the night patrol squad at the border. We leave in ten."

I nodded. I couldn't swallow the bitter taste filling my senses.

"Also, Shae made a discovery while I was sorting through the red tape to get us assigned to patrol," Holland spoke, but I had a hard time focusing. All I could see was red-brown eyes, blonde hair, lush hips being claimed by Mardi. That damn male.

"Dale, you with me?" Holland placed a hand on my back.

"Yes." I exhaled and shook my head. "What did Shae find?"

Holland looked around, the courtyard was empty, but she stepped closer anyway and lowered her voice so it was barely audible. "The footage Damaris mentioned that had been doctored, it has markers all over it. Shae traced it back to here. It was altered from here, this compound, by our mole."

"Shit." It was definitely an inside job. Someone here was skilled and knew about dark magic. That made them very, very dangerous.

"Shae's waiting for us." Holland began walking away. "Dale, on a personal note, I understand we all have our history. But I don't want to be involved with someone who's stuck in their past and whose history is still present." She nodded and then strode off back through the courtyard and into the compound.

Double shit. Apparently, my internal turmoil was palpable. I ran a hand over my face and followed her inside. I needed a fucking fix.

SHAE WAS SITTING in the rig next to Damaris as Holland and I took the commanding seats. I drove, circling further out. We had just finished our first lap of the outpost's exterior and were now headed to do the perimeter sweep of the grounds. Or at least, that's what the outpost leadership expected from us.

"Alright, we should be out of earshot of any devices." Shae nodded at the road behind us. "I already told Holland, but Dale, I recovered part of the deleted footage from the night of the attack."

"You're just now telling me this?" I nearly hit the brakes.

"We didn't exactly have time back there." Shae rolled her eyes. "It doesn't show much. I see a team of three breaching the courtyard. One stalks off to the box and plugs something in while the other two stand guard. They're gone within forty-five seconds."

"Could you make out their faces? Recognize any of them?"

"Nope. They're wearing black masks. I am running their movements through my profiler to see if it matches any on base, but I won't have those back for another day or so."

I nodded. "Keep me posted," I spoke, hands gripping the wheel. "Are we all clear on what needs to happen?" We'd been over the plan already, but I needed to make sure we were all on board.

I glanced around, everyone nodded. Focused. Good, that's what we needed to be.

"I'll park us three miles from the border of the radius Shae identified. Then we hike in, and Shae will use her drone while Damaris and I sneak in closer to connect the device—"

"The mindscrambler," Shae clarified.

Her and her stupid thing for naming her creations.

"Fine, the mindscrambler, to the server so Shae can connect."

"I still think we should all four get in closer. At least to be within a short jog in the event you need backup," Holland grumbled. It was unlike her to complain, but then again, we were all on edge.

"We've discussed this. Tactically, two is easier than four. Safer too. If we get caught and killed, you can continue the search and claim no knowledge of our actions, thereby avoiding disciplinary hearings."

It made sense. The plan had been calculated, we just had to get there now. We could pull this off. We would survive. I continued up the road and then stopped when we reached about three and a half miles out.

Time to hike.

CHAPTER 63

TATE

We had split up into two teams. Vala and Jared took the west side of the compound, while Aether and I took the east side. We were to circle around the buildings and place the charges. Apparently, Jared was a computer science and security team member, or CSST, and he planned to secure their data prior to the detonation.

"You ready for this?" Aether's question had so many layers.

Was I ready to blow up those vile things? Absolutely. Was I ready for this life-altering path? I wasn't sure, but I nodded anyway.

Aether led the way behind a building, the one we had approached before, and set several charges, spacing them apart in eight-foot increments. My grip on the shoulder bag I carried tightened. I was, essentially, dead weight. The packhorse.

I took a steadying breath. I hated that I allowed myself this role, but at the same time, I wasn't sure I wanted a bigger one. Coward, that's what I was. My vision became a bit hazy, and I shook my head. I was sick, that much I knew.

"Is it common for there to be prolonged heat strokes when going through the Changing?" I whispered as Aether placed another charge.

"It is, but not too hot." He turned and placed the back of his hand to my forehead. The electricity from the contact was startling. He pursed his lips. "Normal, a bit on the high end, but I've seen worse. Let me know if you have any trouble with basic motor skills, that would be indicative of something—"

Footsteps sounded ahead, instinctively I backed close to the building and flattened myself against it. Aether did the same, blocking my view. The steps sounded numerous, at least half a dozen. Good news was that they were getting quieter—they were moving away.

"Vala, Jared, come in," Aether whispered into his com.

"Here," Vala responded, her voice a bit more strained than normal.

"Movement outside, eastern building. Squad of eight from my count. Anax at front. All guara."

"Copy. Finished with the first two buildings, heading for the server at the third," Jared responded.

"Stay alert." Aether stepped forward and reached the front of the building. He poked his head around the corner of the metal side and motioned for me to stay put. Like a damn guard dog. I approached the edge and rested my head against the rusty side. Cool. Calming almost. Or perhaps that was Aether. This whole place felt off, not just physically, but on a magical level; I intuitively knew something was wrong. Not that I understood how I knew that. I was essentially an uneducated buffoon when it came to magic. Thank you, mother, Fletch, and the Glenn. I bit down on my lip.

The breeze around me picked up, cooling and tickling, catching my senses. Aether. I should be upset that he was, once again, manipulating me, and yet, I was grateful for the cool air. If he started messing with my emotions though, that would be another story. Claws out.

I could hear the growls and grunts from within the warehouse. This was a different building than the one we climbed a couple of afternoons ago. That one was just up ahead, next on our list. My skin was literally crawling. My breaths became shallow. They would not get me, not this time. I palmed my blade; I'd be damned if a seething tried to catch me off guard.

"Charges placed. Time to head to the next building. We'll be exposed for about twenty seconds, you ready?" Aether looked at the blade, his eyes filling with emotion. Was that pride?

"Ready." I nodded.

"Jared, do we have control of video, are we good to go?"

"Can't hack it from here. Tried. But I do have a scrambler enacted. In ten, I'll activate it. They'll know something's up but won't be able to see anything but static."

"In ten," Aether confirmed.

In eight seconds, I'd be running. In seven seconds, my whole world would change. They'd know we were here. There was a very good chance we'd have to fight. In five seconds, my head had better clear, or I could very well die. In three seconds, I'd force myself further into this irreversible course.

"Now," Aether spoke and then took off in a sprint. I followed him, envious of his long strides and speed. I was fast, getting faster with each day, thanks to what I assumed was the Changing, but not *nearly* as fast as Aether. He was practically jogging while I was sprinting and huffing, barely keeping up.

The edge of the next building was just a few feet ahead. My feet sank into the mud with each step, but I kept going, ignoring the sounds I was making. At last, we reached the building and ducked behind it, secure in its shadow.

"Good. Catch your breath," Aether commanded as he began placing charges. Not even winded. The eerie feeling in the air deepened. It felt wrong, like my magic was pulling and recoiling at the same time.

The energy around me calmed, pressed against me like a weighted blanket. Comfort. I gritted my teeth. Aether was really beginning to get on my nerves.

I took a few steps forward, following him, but my breaths were ragged. I gripped my black backpack straps and bent over, trying to clear my focus. I was seeing stars, and my temperature was barely tolerable. I wanted to take my boots off, get rid of the pack, and just strip.

"Ok, let's move." Aether surveyed the ground and then continued down the side of the worn building. He placed charge after charge, looking at me after each one to ensure I was still there. I placed my hands on the side of the building, the coolness a welcome relief.

"Almost done here. Three more buildings to go. Status?" Aether spoke into the com. I hated how sexy his voice sounded coming so close to me, as if in me. I logically knew he was ten feet away, but the nearness of his voice and the husky tone had my toes curling in my boots. I was definitely delusional.

"At the server now. Just need a minute or less and then I'm set," Jared said.

"Good. I'm setting the charges on the last exterior building now. Aether, are you going to be able to hit the central one or do we need to?" Vala's voice came through. It sounded winded; at least I wasn't the only one feeling the impacts from this cardio workout.

"I can, tentatively." Aether looked to me, the question in his eyes.

"We can do it," I spoke more confidently than I felt, hoping like hell it didn't show.

"Copy." Vala's voice paused. "Aether, we have encountered a few patrols which have been taken care of. But this place is *swarming* with them. If you can't reach the central box, we can try, but we may need to cut—"

"We'll reach it."

"Okay, it's just you know you *can't* shift, right?"

"Over and out." Aether placed another charge and all voices ceased.

Can't shift? What the hell?

"What does she mean, 'you can't shift'?" I asked, heart pounding as I watched Aether attach the last several charges.

"Alright, almost time to head to the central building. You ready?" he asked, ignoring my question.

"Aether."

He locked eyes with me. Neither of us spoke, we just stared at each other, chests heaving. The energy coursing around me doubled, matching my heart rate.

"I've expended an enormous amount of energy and haven't taken the proper steps to restore my levels. I will once we're back."

"Proper steps?" Why was everything a code?

"Let it go."

"No. I'm not going to walk into the center of this complex with you when you can't shift and save our asses if those things get loose. Not unless you tell me *why*." I placed a sweaty hand on my hip, these leathers were insufferable. I could barely breathe, every movement felt restricted. I hated leather *almost* as much as secrets.

"I need to feed or siphon an enormous amount of energy, magic if you will, and neither can happen here."

"Why the fuck not?" I huffed. He'd fed *me*.

"Because I need pure Untish blood and it's a personal thing. This ground here has been contaminated and it's not rich enough for me to draw from. It would require being close to the heart of Untish territory to restore my levels without feeding. It's a balance, everything in nature is. Just trust me, okay?"

"Trust you." I gave him a dead look.

"I've kept you alive, haven't I? Besides, I like to think I'm lethal even in this form." He winked at me.

I clenched my jaw.

"Tate?" The pleading in his eyes was my undoing.

I've got you.

"Fine. Let's go."

His lips tilted in a sad smile before he nodded and placed the last charge. Once Jared was done, we'd make the biggest dash yet: into the heart of the enemy.

CHAPTER 64
CHANCE

"The building is just ahead, Chance," Shae's voice guided Damaris and me as we hiked up the last bluff. We had traveled in silence, other than Shae's direction. I could hear the slight buzz of the drone overhead. Soon, we'd have answers. One good thing about adrenaline, it blocked out all other annoying distractions. Including egotistical males and attractive blondes with haunting eyes.

I avoided a tree branch and motioned for Damaris to do the same, shining my light on the base of it. Black. The closer we got, the more preternatural the trees became. They weren't just grey anymore; no, they were black with moldy white spots oozing pus. Dark magic. We were close.

Damaris avoided the branch but stepped on another. *Snap!* We both froze. Nothing, no one, no movement. Thank fucking blood. Hiking in the dark was difficult for many reasons, but remaining quiet and tactical was priority. I had crunched a few pinecones early on and decided we needed to slow our speed down if we wanted to remain as stealthy as possible.

"Ok, you should be coming into view any minute now," Shae spoke.

We crested a hill and paused. Buildings filled the valley below. Dozens of large warehouses. It looked like an old barracks site or distribution plant. I'd never heard of it, but from the looks of the buildings and the wiring on the lampposts, it had been here for a while. The perfect place for off-the-books research.

"Spotted. Can you get a visual on any movement?" I asked.

"Mapping it now," Shae spoke, her voice low.

I didn't see much from here. The few lampposts that occupied the valley below were few and far apart. I scanned the yard, and in the corner, I spotted motion.

"I've got movement at the western corner."

"Got it. Zooming in now," Shae said. "It looks like two guaramen?"

"Any other movement?" Damaris asked from beside me.

"I see a squad in the northern corner and possible movement in the eastern quadrant."

I scanned the yard. I couldn't see the eastern half well from here, but the movement to the west caught my eye. It appeared to be one individual, not a squad, which was odd.

"Any idea where the main server is?" Damaris pulled out his binoculars and began searching the yard.

"Yeah, and it's not great. It's right where I'm picking up on movement in the western quadrant, the third building to your left, two in." Shae paused. "Guys, from what I'm picking up on—" Her voice cut out.

I tapped my com but could only hear static. Shit.

"Shae?" I spoke into my com. Nothing, no response. I called her name again but was met with only static. "Looks like we're on our own." I started down the hill toward the server with Damaris close behind.

We reached the outskirts and I tried to reach Shae again. Still, nothing. I could hear the drone from above, but our coms were down. I approached the third building, as instructed, and then paused. Peering around the corner, I could make out the one that held the server.

The ground was muddy, and my boots suctioned in with each step. Not great for covertness.

"Ok, we're going to have to be quick. You ready?" I looked to Damaris. He was young, but he had balls, I'd give him that.

"Ready."

"Picking up on anything?"

"You mean other than the creepy magic I picked up on at the settlement during the attack?"

I sighed. He couldn't just answer like a normal person.

"Stay close." I pulled out my pistol in one hand and gripped my club with the other. I looked in his eyes to ensure he heard me and then turned and rounded the building. It was about thirty yards to the building that held the server. Each step squished loudly in the mud. I kept peering around, expecting to see a creature at any moment. Nothing. We approached the building and sank into it as close as we could. Damaris checked his weapons before scanning our surroundings. I didn't see anything, no box or access point from this side. Just perfect.

We crept alongside the building.

"Hey, boss. Check it." Damaris shined his light on a small device attached to the building's side. I paused and approached it. It was stuck to the metal wall with magnets and was blinking. A charge. Shit. Either the base had this as a contingency plan, or we weren't the only players here. I exhaled through my teeth. We needed Shae and insight. I tapped my com again. Zilch. It still just buzzed with static. Shae was not an option.

"Any chance you can disarm these?" It would be a miracle if he knew how. I never did well with that part of training.

"As a matter of fact, I might."

"I'll be a monkey's uncle." I slapped him on the back. "Stay here and see what you can do, I'm heading for the server." I scanned the length of the building. Several other charges were spaced evenly apart. If this building had it, it was likely the others did too.

Damaris nodded at me while placing the flashlight between his teeth. I began to trot down the side of the building. The cool night air I was accustomed to was now murky, warm, and unpleasant. Odd. This whole place felt unnatural.

At the corner, I scanned the yard with my light and froze. In front of me was a large aluminum box, just like Shae had suggested. But that wasn't what gave me pause. Squatting in front of the box was a large male. He was hunched over and actively typing into a device. He slammed the box shut.

"All set," he called out. He turned and I got my first glance at the ruddy buzz cut. Arche O'Connel.

CHAPTER 65

TATE

"All set," Jared spoke into the coms. "Now," Aether's voice commanded as we both broke into a trot from the outer building to the center. I kept up with his strides, though it was likely from him slowing his pace rather than me magically becoming quicker. We had about twenty more yards until we reached the building.

My heart was pounding with the exertion, and my vision began to spot with black dots. Not good. I shook my head and focused on the warm night air. The fog was building all across the ground, hiding the muddy spots. Not unlike my vision currently.

We reached the edge of the building and Aether pulled me in tight to him. I could feel his chest pounding against mine. The tension in the air built as a breeze whipped across my face, cooling me down. He placed his lips to my forehead.

"You're warm."

Not what I wanted to hear. What was wrong with me?

He released me and stepped back. The atmosphere's static didn't diminish as he surveyed me and then the yard. We had a mission to do.

We were close, we'd made it to the central building. We just needed to set the charges and then get the hell out of here.

I hopped from foot to foot, trying to release the tingling that was overcoming my senses.

Anxiety. Stress.

Desire.

"I can help—"

"Don't you dare." I was done with him manipulating my emotions, even if it was to help me. If that wasn't backwards shit, I wasn't sure what was. Aether's jaw ticked.

"We have a problem," it was Jared's tone that immediately altered my thoughts and captured my full attention.

I glanced around, expecting to see seethings pouring out of the buildings, teeth gnashing.

"What's the situation?" Aether asked. He unstrapped his sword from his back.

"We have company," Jared's voice broke at the end in a grunt. His com stayed on, and I could hear the shuffling of feet, grunts, and a few sick thuds.

"Should we—"

Before I could finish my question, eerie screams broke the silent night. They filled the air, coming from everywhere. I knew instantly what they were: seethings. My hands began to shake a bit, the grip on my dagger loosening with the excess sweat I couldn't seem to control. I glanced up in the direction of the cry and my fears were confirmed.

"Tate, place the charges." Aether nodded to my backpack then stepped forward and placed his hands gently around my face. "Shit." He lifted my chin, so my eyes locked with his. "I'm sorry this is happening now, I was hoping it was just a precursory heat flash, but you're peaking much quicker than normal for a standard Changing. Stay close to me, try to focus on one of your senses, and stay away from anyone outside our squad—especially if you care for them."

What the hell did that mean? I didn't care for *anyone* here. A calming sensation began to take over. I could sense Aether's magic blanketing me.

"Aether—"

Screeches sounded nearer. Damn it. Aether searched my eyes, not looking behind him or anywhere but me, even with the sounds of mud squishing and feet charging.

"Fine."

He nodded in response, the calming sensation doubled. This time I accepted it, and the reprieve from the intensity of all my senses allowed me to take my first deep breath since we'd left the SO. The heat that was eating me from the inside out became mere background noise.

He released my face and turned toward the cries. Just a hundred yards out, a warehouse door was open and seethings were pouring out by the dozens. There had to be hundreds of grey and black streaks pounding the ground, gnashing their teeth, trampling over other seethings attempting to flee containment. Their movement was chaotic, unfocused.

A lone figure walking upright emerged from the building, the seethings giving him a wide berth. His red hair was a beacon, and even from three hundred feet away, I could see the unnatural purple tint to his skin. Carter. He locked eyes with me and then raised his head in the air and screamed. He lifted his left hand and pointed toward Aether and I. The once chaotic swarm of beasts paused, and then as one they turned, fixating on us. With another cry from Carter, the seethings began to run toward us.

They were rushing on all fours. Aether gripped his sword with both hands and stalked toward them, certainty in every step. I watched in awe as his sword *lit up* with fire. Badass. The first group of twelve reached him, but before they could even lunge, they were on the ground in clumps that were smoldering, disintegrating into piles of goo. He took down one beast after another in graceful measures, like he'd choreographed and perfected this very fight. Envy clawed through me along with a feeling of longing.

"The charges, darling," Aether's voice cut through the mental fog.

I shook my head. "Darling?"

"Had to break your stupor."

I could swear Aether was winking at me even as he took down a beast of a seething.

Shrugging off my backpack, I unzipped it and stared at the contents. There were at least a dozen charges in here. Vala had showed me how to activate them. I could do this.

I placed the first charge on the building and then jogged down about eight feet and reached for another in the bag. My temperature was spiking, even with the calming effect from Aether, I could feel my senses heightening. Screams and screeches were coming from everywhere. The wall shook as I placed a charge. It shook again and this time I could hear grunts from within. Seethings were trying to claw their way *out*.

I looked back at Aether. Piles of burning flesh surrounded him, but still more assailed. He projected one hand and liquid black flames shot out, engulfing any that tried to race past him toward me. I was safe— for now.

The screeching of another door sliding open filled the night. The sound that followed was one of nightmares. I dropped the charge and it sank in the mud. To my left another warehouse door was opening. Seethings began to file out, but this time they were on two feet instead of four. Still not the giants we'd encountered at the recoup settlement, but frightening nonetheless.

The pressure in the air built and I began to shake, I could feel my internal temperature increasing. I needed to place the charges. I tore my eyes from the seethings across the yard and searched for the dropped charge. I wiped my sweaty palms on my pants, my vision beginning to blur, and picked up the block. The device was filthy, hopefully with the mud wiped off, it would still work. I stuck it to the building and sighed with relief when it suctioned in place. Thank blood for magnets.

"Aether, we've got two warehouses on this side that are opening and releasing. Making my way to you, you'll be swarmed without help. May need to go to plan B," Vala's voice cut in. She was panting and sounded like she was running.

I kept moving along the building, ignoring the mud sloshing everywhere, or the way it seemed to be liquefying underneath my feet. I grunted as I pushed the heat *from* me, ignoring how the side of the warehouse began to whine from my increasing temperature. I wasn't even touching the wall...this couldn't be good.

A blissful breeze surrounded me, and I inhaled the scent of musky ash. Aether. Calming me in every way possible. I swallowed the mild irritability at his efforts to manipulate my environment, I could be mad about that tomorrow. For now, I needed the cool air. Needed his presence even from afar.

"Not yet, Vala. Work your way over here. Jared?" Aether grunted.

I glanced in his direction. Eight seethings lunged at him at once. He lifted a hand in their direction and before they even got within eight feet of him, they crumbled to the ground in piles of ash. The ground around Aether was steaming and bubbling.

"Cool down there, darling." Was he talking to me?

"What?"

"Eyes on the task. Just breathe. Your heat transferring is powerful. Helpful but frying." He swung his sword and sliced the head from an upright seething who was swiping at him. Duck, slice, project. His movements were liquid.

"Heat transferring?" Vala's voice rang out, panic lacing it. "Aether, she can't be *peaking* yet. Here of all places would not be—" Vala's voice was drowned out by an unholy scream.

A purple form emerged from the warehouse ahead with the upright seethings. It was bald, muscles bulging from it, even from its scalp. The fact that I could see that from here, hundreds of yards away, was concerning—even with my increased eyesight. With every step it took, a black aura ate at the air, the land turning black and white under its feet and in an outward circumference of ten feet. The upright seethings turned and looked at the lone figure emerging from the darkness. It pointed its hands in *my* direction and screamed. The seethings changed course from Aether and began to run toward me.

What the hell?

The lone figure threw back its head and pulled at the air with its hands. No, not the air, it pulled at *me* with its hands. I could feel my magic spiking within me, rebuffing its pull, recoiling within. Pain blossomed in my chest, shooting up and down my legs. I felt icepicks hacking into my mind as my ears rang. I cupped my hands to my head and doubled over, clenching myself, willing the pain to stop. My magic protested the prodding, the pulling of that *thing*, but the wall I tried to build around myself wasn't strong enough. It began flowing from me.

I pulled back against it.

"Block it, Tate!" Aether commanded.

I tried to form a mental wall, but I couldn't. I could feel the energy being taken from me. I was being drained. My temperature was spiking from the force of it being yanked from my very being. My nerves screamed out as the flow of magic from me increased, like my very skin was being peeled from my flesh.

I screamed and stumbled forward.

I will not fail.

I willed the air around me to block it. I could feel it buffering, protesting, before bending to my will. *There!* I'd formed a shield, small and not big enough to stop the pull, but it slowed the flow. I straightened and took a step forward, all while the world spun.

The pull on me ceased instantly. I glanced up and saw a shimmer encasing the figure who was now enraged.

Aether. His concentration was fully on trapping that figure in a shield, a glass closet. The seethings noticed and changed route, ambushing Aether. Even blocking their path with fire, they were swarming him, passing him to surround me—it was only a matter of time.

"Vala," Aether called, grunting with the force.

You will not fail.

Aether would succeed. He had to, I felt it in my soul.

Two upright seethings managed to get around him, one landing a slice on his back. Blood sprayed out from everywhere and Aether screamed as he dropped to his knees. He pivoted and sliced one in half, but the other seething evaded and landed another strike. Aether readied his weapon, but not fast enough as the seething lashed out, knocking the blade from his grip before backhanding him. Aether flew backwards, toward incoming seethings, and rolled in the mud before stopping himself. The seething stalked toward him, talons raised and ready.

"No!" I stretched out my hand and the seething attacking him froze, suspended a moment before I forced it backwards through the air. I threw out all my energy toward the oncoming herd of seethings now upon Aether, and to my utter delight, the air around them seized them, and then ignited with pink flames. They burned, flesh submitting to the flames, and disintegrated within a moment, their screeches filling the air and then falling silent.

Any euphoria I felt was short-lived. My temperature climaxed and my control vanished. The flames died out as I remained doubled over on my knees in the now boiling mud. I grunted as I tried and failed to stand.

Several seethings were bypassing him now, heading for me. The shield around the lone figure was fading, flickering, and I could feel the creature's pull growing stronger, reaching for me. It had tasted me and wanted me. Malice laced its eyes.

Placing a hand on the building, I tried to brace myself and stand. The metal instantly whistled with my contact and turned bright red. Warm, I was so very warm.

"Tate!" Aether's voice was a distant cry, muffled by the fog enveloping my brain.

The entire side of the building began to hum and glow. *BOOM!* The charges blew.

CHAPTER 66
CHANCE

Arche O'Connel stood and squared his shoulders, meeting my gaze with challenge.

"What are you doing?" I asked, aiming my weapon at his chest.

He smiled at me. Who did he think he was?

"I am your superior. Answer me, arche," I spat the last word, daring a step closer to him.

He just stood there unfazed by my weapon. I understood that bullets didn't necessarily kill a vampire, but they sure as hell could hurt and debilitate. Too much blood loss and he'd be unrevivable—the dagger at my side, now that could kill. Just one slice into the chest, plunged deep in the heart or through his neck, severing his spinal column, and he'd be dead.

"We have company," he spoke into his shoulder and then lunged for me.

I fired my weapon and completely missed him. He was fast, far faster than most vampires were and before I knew it, he was behind me, reaching for my weapon. I twirled and spun, elbowing him in the gut and kicking his feet out from under him. He landed in the mud.

I reached for him but grasped nothing but foul dirt. A hand pressed in on my skull, sinking my face into the ground. I tried to get out of his grip, but couldn't even fill my lungs with air. Mud began to seep into my nose, my eyes. My lungs burned, screaming for air. The dirt had an acidic quality to it that began to scald my skin.

I reached for the dagger sheathed at my calf. Feeling the hilt of it, I yanked it free and plunged it blindly into the male atop me. A cry sounded and the pressure released. I used the moment and rolled, continuing my attack with the blade. Stabbing. Sinking. Gutting.

Air, sweet and warm, met my lungs. I inhaled it greedily as I continued to get up on all fours. Wiping mud from my eyes, I blinked, trying to focus and ignoring the burn of my skin.

The buzzcut was gone. I could see a trail of blood. Like hell I'd let him get away.

Screeches and screams filled the yard along with the most unnatural cry I'd ever heard. Those things were here. Set free. The building across the yard was opening, releasing dozens of them. They ran toward the central building on all fours. Whatever they were after, I didn't care so long as it wasn't me.

Bending over, I pulled my pistol from the ground and wiped it off on my pants before following the trail of blood. Arche O'Connel headed west, toward the central building, but off to the side.

"Damaris?" I spoke into my com, nothing but static. Damn it. I was alone.

The air began to warm, heat even. The ground was starting to hum. The door beside me, on the building with the circuit box, jerked open and beasts began to pour out. They were mostly upright, but some hobbled on three legs at a time.

I leveled my weapon and began to fire. One shot, two, three. Before I knew it, they were falling and then rising again, some altering their trajectory toward me. They were pouring out randomly, in every direction. I couldn't take them all down on my own. Several began to assault me.

I pulled my club from my back and readied myself. Those bastards were about to have their skulls crushed in. The first one reached me, hobbling on three legs, and I swung for it, catching the side of its head. Black blood sprayed everywhere, covering my face with an odious scent. The next one was already upon me. I swung again and broke its arm. Its other claw swiped at me, I ducked and dug my dagger into its chest before kicking the hilt of it deeper and burying it inside.

Claws swiped at me from my right, and I barely had time to evade them before swinging blindly with my club. A sickening thump was all the confirmation I needed before turning my attention to another three creatures rushing me on two feet. Where the hell were the guaramen who were patrolling this base?

Another large warehouse door whined open. Shit. I couldn't turn to look, not as the three were approaching me rapidly, but the vibrating ground confirmed my fears. More were flooding the yard. I was as good as dead.

"Anyone!" I called into the com. Silence.

The air spiked and sweat began to drip from my forehead into my eyes, bringing with it remnants of mud. I could barely see as my eyes began to water.

The first of the three swiped at me while the other two lunged. I dodged the first's claws and swung my club, meeting nothing but air. I pivoted just as claws sank into my side from behind and flung me into the building. The whole world blurred and then twirled. I could feel liquid running down my temple, into my eyes, more than just drops of sweat. Blood.

A two-headed creature was stalking toward me. No, it had three heads, and they were wavering. I reached for my club, but it was gone. I'd lost it when I was struck. My pistol was still at my side. I unstrapped it and tried to aim, but the creature was doing an unnatural dance as it approached me.

The energy around me pulsed. A foreign roar echoed throughout the yard as pain shot up my spine. I could feel magic swarming me, inquiring as to my being, before being yanked away. My blood was firing within and the small amount of magic I possessed was jolting up and down my nerves. Something was wrong.

My body felt like it was being dissected. The monster approaching was within mere feet of my body. This was it.

"Dale!" a female screamed my name. Holland? No, she wasn't supposed to be here.

I fired my weapon at the thing, but it continued toward me, unfazed. It raised its hands into the air.

"Dale, don't you dare give up!" Holland screamed. Were the coms working?

The creature swiped at me with three hands. It froze mid-swing and then collapsed forward, its talons brushing my boots. Three blades were sticking out of its back, right into his chest and heart. Honey-brown hair waved in front of me as a delicate hand touched my forehead.

"You're hurt, but not too bad. Can you walk?" Holland's concerned brown eyes locked on mine.

"I think so."

She wiped the blood from my forehead and face with the back of her sleeve and my vision improved immensely, but the burning remained.

"This will help." She pulled out a syringe and plunged it into my thigh without warning. Liquid fire filled my veins, and everything burned before going blissfully numb. Immediately, my head cleared; I saw two eyes instead of four, one head instead of two, and it wasn't swaying anymore. Holland was crouched in front of me. Behind her, chaos reigned. Creatures everywhere, Damaris fighting several off, blood oozing from his leg in a makeshift wrap. And Shae, dear blood, that was Shae standing near Damaris and rapidly typing into some device. The drone overhead was shooting at the creatures, injuring but not killing; it was a distraction at least.

"Better?"

"Much. We need to move, now." I stood up, accepting Holland's hand. The entire place was crawling with those things, they were everywhere.

"Behind this building, now." I nodded to the one behind me, it was close to the outskirts of the complex and so far, the doors had remained closed.

Holland whistled and Shae nodded. Slowly, she and Damaris backed up until the drone ahead fired a few bombs into the throng of creatures swarming. They were spreading out in every direction, some coming at us, but most toward the central building.

The bombs landed and the whole area lit up. Limbs lay everywhere. Good, that bought us time, but not much.

"Now!" I shouted.

Damaris lowered his rifle and took Shae's shoulder, guiding her through the muddy ground that now boiled, and past severed limbs. Her focus was still on the disk in front of her. She continued to type like a mad female, commanding the drone that was once again firing at the newly released creatures rushing from the eastern side. The four of us headed for the back of the building. We made it behind.

"What the hell are you doing?" I demanded.

"Saving your ass. You're welcome by the way." Holland glared at me.

"You were supposed to stay near the rig. Not rush into danger!" I surveyed the landscape behind. The forest was quiet. Eerily so. Thumps came from the wall behind us, those things were crashing into it. We needed to leave, now.

"Enough! We have bigger problems," Shae's voice cut in. She held up the disk's screen and then projected it so we could all see what she was showing us. Huddled against the side of a building was a familiar small frame with sandy blonde hair. Tate.

Even from drone coverage, I could tell it was her.

I closed my eyes. How had I forgotten about Anax Mardi? Naturally, they left with Tate. That meant Mardi was here, he brought *her* here into this throng of danger. I would kill him. I refocused on Tate, mentally calculating how to reach her. Those things were everywhere, they were trying to rush her but being held off by Mardi who was on the ground, fighting a large two-legged creature with…was that fire? Suddenly, dozens were suspended in air and then lit in *pink flames*?

Magic.

Thump! The door behind me crashed and dented. We didn't have time for this.

"Dale, don't even think about it. Shae got the data and we need to leave. Now." Holland reached for my arm, but I stepped out of her grasp. Leave Tate? I looked at the screen again, Tate crumpled to the ground. The warehouse began to steam and turn red. The ground around her was roiling.

I looked up and met Holland's eyes. If I didn't leave now, there was a very good chance we would all die. I'd be risking Holland and Shae's lives for someone who rejected me. Hated me. Someone I'd let down before.

"You know I'm right. We need to leave now, or we won't leave at all." Holland nodded to the warehouse wall behind us. It shuttered again. It wouldn't hold for long. I hated it, but she was *right*. We needed to get the data back to the outpost so we could stop these things. My father needed to be apprised of what was going on. We needed answers and a way of ending these creatures.

Shae deserved to live. Holland deserved to live.

I nodded at Holland, hating myself for it. Tate had been right. I would only let her down, time after time.

"Screw that. Tate needs us. She's one of *us*." Shae glared at me. "I can't believe you!"

Before I could respond, she darted out, rushing into the heart of chaos.

"Shae!" I shouted, but it was drowned out by a resounding boom as the whole yard shook and fire erupted.

CHAPTER 67

TATE

It was snowing black and red flakes. They landed everywhere—around me, on my skin, my hair, my eyelashes. I blinked. The sky was grey and speckled. Ash continued to accumulate on me. I didn't move for a moment. The night air was blissfully cool. Like the fire in my veins had finally extinguished. My ears were ringing as I tried to sit up and find my balance.

I'd set off the charges. Numbly, I looked around. The place where the warehouse had been was now nothing but charred remains. I had been shot back about fifty yards to the far eastern edge of the compound and was lying in a boiling puddle of muddy water. The whole yard was moving.

Aether was holding his ground, fighting three giant seethings at once while simultaneously destroying smaller ones on four legs. Behind him, Jared fought with skill, even as blood dripped down his form, signaling a deep injury, but he still took down several smaller seethings that charged him and tried to get to Aether.

Snarling sounded from behind me.

I whipped my head and spotted three seethings on two legs stalking toward me. They toed the boiling mud and winced before immediately retreating, heading for a figure far off to my right in a dome. Vala. She was in the northern central position, about a hundred yards out, fighting several seethings who were attempting to break her shield. She fired, her shots going through the dome and hitting the small seethings on all fours. They dropped instantly. The large two-legged seethings took a hit but continued toward her. They refused to go down. Instead, they approached the shield and pounded against it. With each hit and swipe of their talons, they were projected back several feet. But they returned and struck again. The shield was fracturing. I could see it spiderwebbing in veins that shimmered. She needed help.

I stood, flexing my legs and arms. My whole body was on pins and needles, everything hurt and simultaneously tingled. I reached for my daggers, but the sheaths were empty. I'd lost them. Scanning the ground, I spotted a club. Perfect. I walked for it, losing my balance for a moment, before recovering. Sweat dripped into my eyes.

Each movement felt like friction, my limbs swelling and my temperature once again beginning to climb. The moment my hand closed around the club's hilt, it glowed bright gold with a pink tint. My hands lit up and I was encased in a rose gold halo. What was happening?

"Tate, you with us?" Aether's voice came through my com. The ringing in my ears subsided a bit.

"Tate? Make your way to Vala. I'll be," he grunted, "right there. We need to leave now—" The large seething he was fighting had Aether rolling and pivoting to avoid the claws swiping at him.

I could feel the tug on my power, my control slipping a bit. The bald purple figure stood across the yard, seethings' corpses surrounding it. It locked eyes with me and smiled. Black saliva dripped from its mouth, steaming as it snarled at me. Its eyes were pools of black and its naked body was covered in muscles. Every square inch. Muscles upon muscles, all purple with angry black veins.

It raised its hand toward me and grunted, pulling at my power. I felt a gentle tug, and nothing more. It raised its head and screamed in frustration, swiping at a shimmering shield around it.

"Aether, I can't hold him forever. Running," Vala panted, "very low." Her voice was strained, like she was actively holding a large weight suspended in air. It was her shield holding that *thing* back. Preventing it from ripping my soul, my magic, my very essence from me.

I stood with my back straight. I needed to help Vala, rid her of the seethings tearing at her shield.

The whole yard was on fire. Several buildings had been leveled, piles of black goo littered the ground along with limbs, some vampirical and some appeared *human*. I tried not to think about what I'd done.

Several buildings still stood, there must have been a short in the wiring or the connection between charges. Perhaps I blew them too soon.

Vala cried out as seethings attacked her shield in sequence. The dome flickered out for a moment, the purple monster pulled at me, but then the shield was reinforced.

I cursed myself under my breath.

Vala, I could make it to her. I could take down those beasts and help her. Power thumped through my veins. I felt cocky—invincible even. It was as if the blood-high from a kill was coursing through me. A smile tugged at my lips and the left side of my mouth raised.

"Cool down there, darling. Just get to Vala."

"I can help," I spoke, my voice hoarse and huskier than normal.

"Aether, she's gone full *Changeling*," Vala's voice was frail, soft even.

Had I? If so, it felt marvelous. I no longer felt nauseous, my vision had cleared, the headache I'd been sporting since we left SO had finally left and everything was transparent. My body tingled, but with aching awareness. My movements were fluid. The club balanced in my palm, shining like a beacon. Like it too had found its strength, renewed vigor.

I tossed it from one hand to the other, even with its spiked steel ends, it was so *light.*

A shrill screech sounded as two tall seethings charged Vala. Not today bitches—a laugh escaped my lips.

I ran, my feet practically flying across the yard. Everywhere my feet touched, the ground steamed, boiled, melted. The seethings whipped their heads at me, and if they could look shocked, they did. They began to retreat but I threw the club at a cluster of them, even from thirty yards away, and it landed with a sick smack in the skull of the big one and then knocked it back into three others. They crumpled to the ground.

A dozen other seethings turned and looked at me. They snapped their teeth and began to attack. I had no more weapons. A large beast was closing in, it moved swiftly on two feet—only twenty yards away. Talons swiped at the air, black saliva dripped from its serpent-like tongue, as it jumped toward me.

Peace filled me, calming my nerves. Everything else began to move in slow motion. But this was different than before. This was a blanket of comfort that silenced all fear. This wasn't Aether's magic, it was *mine.*

I sped up, charging the thing head-on. Ten yards away, it landed in front of me, its talons swiping in slow movements. Five yards away, and then I was behind it. I grabbed its head and twisted it. *Snap!* The thing fell to the ground. Dead.

Delight. Apprehension. Allure.

Aether was just ahead to my right, still fighting. Even from here, I could feel the gentle caress of his presence, the assuagement of his touch.

I smiled.

"Tate!" A familiar scream echoed through the yard, breaking my stupor.

Across the field toward the west side of the compound, a familiar swatch of blue hair was being held up in the air by the largest seething I'd seen yet. It was at least fifteen feet tall, and wings sprouted from its back. It had a tail that swayed on the ground with barbs coming from it. To its left was a small female, barely clothed in rags, a purple tint to her skin that clashed with her shocking red hair. Allie.

"That's the one," the giant spoke as it pointed at me, Allie twitching when it took a step closer.

A tall, slender female walked beside the beast. My gut clenched. Even from here, I knew it was Luina.

Anger flooded my system. How dare she threaten Shae.

The creature held Shae's waist in one hand, squeezing her abdomen. She swatted at its grip helplessly.

"Put her down. Now," I commanded as I stalked toward the thing. It was huge, at least three times my height. Its talons were at least two feet long and looked lethal as hell.

"No! Vala get Tate the hell out of here, now!" Aether's voice was a distant command in my com.

"Her? You're sure?" Luina asked the creature.

"Oh yes, I'll never forget what she *tastes* like." The seething extended its tongue and licked its lips while its eyes devoured me.

"Seize her," Luina commanded before turning around. "Kill the rest." She waved a hand and stalked off toward one of the unharmed buildings.

"Tate!" Shae shouted.

A buzz in the air sounded and rapid fire began to rain down on the beasts surrounding the mega seething holding Shae. The seethings all faltered for a moment.

The creature holding her roared and then threw Shae forward, toward me. She landed in the mud and rolled, head over ass. A loud snap told me that she must've broken something. She lay there, limp and unconscious. I watched in horror as seethings began to assault her, surround her, teeth gnashing and spit splattering as they rushed to end her.

Time slowed as I began to move. I ran, faster than ever, and approached her. The air began to hum, buzz even. My temperature increased, and my arms were glowing brightly even underneath my leathers. Pink haloed me.

I was a walking torch.

The creatures rushing Shae were about ten feet out, but they seemed to crawl.

I could hear voices in the distance, possibly Aether's or Vala's, but I couldn't focus on them. I could see the purple figure clawing at the shield, trying to break free, to siphon my life from me, but I paid him no focus.

Instead, I saw Shae when she was five years old sharing her teddy bear, Mr. Snuggles, with me. He was what got me through my first bad day of school.

My speed picked up, and my feet began lifting off the ground as I ran.

A pouty nose and round cheeks looked at me as we laughed together, getting over our first heartbreaks in middle school. We'd egged their homes as payback for the emotional pain. Even then, Shae stood with me.

It was high time I was there for her.

I pumped my arms as I ran, friction and energy warring in the space I occupied. My halo intensified as the air crackled from my energy. The first creatures closest to me melted the moment my aura reached them.

I recalled Shae's steel grey eyes as she told me she planned to leave, to join the guara. The sorrow in them was so akin to the look she gave me after my mother was killed. I would not lose another family member.

She held me when I fell apart, lost in grief, not judging when I cursed the world.

Those eyes snapped open as she awoke, screaming as she gripped her broken leg. She looked at me in awe and pain.

I would not let her down.

I will not fail.

You never have. Aether's voice was in my mind, my head, my heart.

It was as if even from dozens of yards away, I could read him, hear him in my very soul. Like his being spoke to mine, our energy connected and intricately intertwined.

I reached the perimeter of the beasts circling Shae and jumped, lunging into the center of the herd, rushing her. I locked eyes with silver ones, shadowed by blue hair that was covered in mud and blood.

"I love you," I whispered.

Planting my feet, I threw out my hands and screamed as energy poured through my fingertips. Blinding pink and white light swallowed and engulfed all the creatures surrounding me. I poured more of myself into the exertion, sending my force into the night. Firing my power, my heat, my energy. I willed it, controlled it. It was a flame ripping them apart, eating them whole, melting them on the spot. It was consuming.

They sizzled, convulsed, and collapsed instantly.

I released the force of my power and the flames and sparks stopped. The aura ended and I could see the aftermath. Total decimation of every seething within a hundred feet of me.

Every single beast in that circumference was gone except for the one monstrous seething. It was about a hundred feet out, hiding behind its scaled wings. I took a step toward it and then another. Sweat was running down my face, my arms, my legs.

I could feel the cool night air on my limbs and didn't have to look to know that my clothes had burned off and were likely gone altogether. The air around me thickened, stroking my bare skin.

Pure undiluted reverence. Fucking amazing.

Aether. I could *sense* his words, his emotions. I didn't know how, but they boosted my confidence. I was fucking amazing. Perhaps it was the high I was experiencing, but I felt potent—invincible.

Careful darling.

The air around me began to poke playfully at my skin in the most sensual way.

I flipped Aether off as I stalked toward the monster, the half dragon-like seething, now unfurling its wings as it stood. I would destroy it.

"Maker, meet your creation." It smiled at me and then lunged forward. Within a moment, it had traveled twenty feet and was swiping for me, barely missing.

I ducked, rolled, and then found my footing. I glanced in Shae's direction. She was inside a dome, Vala next to her with her weapon trained on the monster currently turning to meet me.

Energy tingled at my fingertips and demanded a release. I could feel the itch from within demanding I cave, calling for me to shift. It was greater than I'd ever felt before, raw power laced through my limbs and core, my very essence humming with unused reserves begging for release.

I braced my feet in the mud and willed some of the energy into my fingers. I wouldn't shift, not yet. I leveled my hands at it and prepared to let loose the storm within.

One moment, dear.

A figure landed in front of me. His shirt had melted off and his tattoos were actually swirling, moving in his skin, in streaks of black and gold. Aether stood there, gloriously sweaty and covered in blood. He was shielding me from the atrocity that was currently swiping at us with unholy claws.

What are you doing?

Couldn't let you have all the fun, now could I, darling?

Aether lifted his sword and met the beast's talons.

CHAPTER 68
CHANCE

My being vibrated; every nerve was rapidly firing. I could barely think straight. Moments of clarity came and went. Holland had fled with Damaris, helping him as he limped away, blood seeping from an ugly gash on his head. I'd made sure they'd run into the forest.

The look of hurt on Holland's face when I chose to run after Shae was something I would never forget.

I shook my head, willing it to stop ringing. For the red to stop dancing across my vision. My heart was squeezed by the internal pressure, and every breath felt labored. I threw out my hands in an attempt to cool the internal fire, the ground shook in response.

My eyes cleared in time to see a monstrous creature holding Shae. It was the thing of nightmares. Evil embodied. I crouched lower, hiding behind some debris from one of the blown buildings. I checked my pistol. It would be useless against the thing that held Shae hostage. If only I had my club. Even then, I wasn't sure what I could do to save her.

A tall female figure came out from beside the beast. Old weathered skin and an unmistakable grimace, with a neat black bun.

489

"Her? You're sure?" Luina asked.

From here, I could see her squinting her eyes, focusing on Tate who was far across the compound.

"Oh yes, I'll never forget what she tastes like." The seething's black tongue licked itself, wings rustling in excitement.

Luina nodded and then looked from Shae to Tate. I could see a female figure behind Tate, rushing toward her and Shae. Mardi was in the distance fighting seethings who were relentlessly charging him. Small compared to the atrocity that held Shae, but fierce nonetheless.

"Seize her," Luina commanded with a sway of the hand. "Kill the rest." She nodded toward Shae and then turned her back.

Anger brewed within me as the debris I hid behind whined and turned red-hot. Shae was one of our own. Rapid fire bullets rained down all around the ground, striking near my feet. The beast raised its wings, shielding it from the bullets, and then howled. The firing stopped, and it lifted Shae like a football and threw her forward. Time seemed to stop as I helplessly watched one of my best friends being projected through the air, into the heart of a herd of seethings. *Snap!* She landed on the ground at an unnatural angle and lay there limply, not moving.

"Shae!" I shouted her name, earning a glance from the monster, before darting out from behind the debris. I had to help her.

The whole ground began to shake and buzz, bright light enveloped us all. Before I could even move ten feet, Tate was there. Hovering mid-air. Her entire being was so bright I had to squint, and even then, it hurt to look. Her arms and legs, hell every part of her, was glowing gold with a pink tint. Her hair floated around her, light pouring from each strand. She looked nothing short of a goddess.

She dropped to the ground in a crouch, her leather leggings and body suit already sizzling away, revealing skin that now glowed golden pink with swirls of black dancing. The light dropped for a moment, and I could clearly see the female who had thoroughly wrecked me. The female whose body would forever be in my mind, whose laugh and deep eyes would haunt me even in death. The female I was ready to let down, again.

She outstretched her hands on either side of her, the seethings rushed her from all directions on two legs and four. She threw back her head, blonde hair that faded to pink, swaying with her movement, and she loosed a scream that shook the world. The entire compound lit up in a blinding light that sparked and burned.

CHAPTER 69
TATE

Aether fought the beast with surges of power as he projected energy at the thing. It came in spurts of sparks, streams of black fire, and manipulation that suspended the beast in midair. The monster roared and went flying back, impacting one of the building's remaining walls. Sparks lit up the night and a plume of smoke and ash filled the air, momentarily blocking our view of the seething.

"Tate, I know you want to shift, but doing so for your first time on this big of a scale without the power of the Changing grounds is dangerous," Aether spoke quickly, and quietly to me. He braced my shoulders and looked me over quickly, assessing.

Fucking perfect.

I smirked in response.

The smoke behind him began to clear and I could see the monster rising.

"I don't know how else to stop it." The admission hurt, but my pride could deal with it. The itching was growing unbearable, and my feet began to lift from the ground.

I locked eyes with dark chocolate ones. Pure admiration and trust.

I can't control it.

I won't let it happen.

Trust. He wanted me to trust him. Trust the male who had lied to me and manipulated my emotions. The male with whom Fletch's involvement cost his very life. The male who'd burnt me alive and served me up on a platter to Arithi.

His eyes deepened.

Regret.

Those same eyes that locked with mine that night in the river, the ones who watched me from the chair as I found pleasure. This was the same male who'd saved my ass multiple times and who had, unconsciously, captivated my soul and somehow had a direct path into my mind.

The energy was building, peaking, and I was hovering two feet off the ground. I could see steam forming in the air from the heat I was radiating. Panic seized me. The energy would be released.

"Channel it into me." Aether pressed his forehead to mine.

I lowered a bit and was now level with him. My hands began to shake, and my body brightened to brilliant rose gold. I could feel my hair rising from my back. Terror began to lace through me as the force I felt building was about to explode. I would hurt him. There was no way he could survive my temperature, the level of power demanding to be freed. Aether needed to get away from me. I didn't want to release with him this close.

"I can't. You need to get away, run. I can't hold this...I don't know what to do."

I was beginning to violently shudder as tears poured from my eyes. Even the emotional pull, the calmness that I now recognized as Aether, wouldn't dampen the hysteria building within.

Aether grabbed my hands in one of his and began to stroke them. He wrapped his other around my waist and pulled me close. We both began to lift in the air, higher and higher, enveloped in a cloud of gold. A cloud of my own making, one of pure power. The very air around me sizzled. I could sense it crackling and reaching out. Sparks bursting into fire.

"Just focus on me," Aether spoke slowly, drawing my chin up.

A calmness was knocking on my mind's door, asking to be let in.

I can take it.

Gently, he pried at the doors I had fused shut—the gate to the power that was overwhelming me.

"Just send it all to me. All the energy. Picture a river and just let it flow."

"I can't! I'll kill you!" My heart rate increased even as my temperature rose and grew. I couldn't hold it for long. Any moment and the power would erupt from me. Aether had to get away.

I wriggled in his arms, attempting to free myself from his touch.

I'm not safe! Save yourself.

There's no world in which I exist, and you don't. Aether's eyes pierced my very soul. *Trust me.*

I could do this. I could trust him. The pride I'd been feeling moments before was gone. Channel into him. How the hell do I do that?

"You can do this. You're more than capable."

Aether's words triggered images of Fletch. He had said that to me throughout my childhood. It was my mother's favorite thing to tell me when I whined that I couldn't do something.

The tugging at my mind increased, and yet, it remained gentle. I allowed it in and instantly felt a calming blanket arrest my nerves. It was soothing and quieting.

"Send it to me," Aether's request was met with a gentle guidance that I could feel in my energy. I closed my eyes as a mental image of a river dominated my senses. It was a river of light and life, from me to this male whom I now, somehow, trusted. I latched onto this image and opened the door, allowing a floodgate of energy to flow.

CHAPTER 70

CHANCE

The light faded and the crackle in the air dissipated. I stood up from behind the debris I used as cover and spotted Tate facing off with the monster. The entire field around her was bubbling. The seethings had been reduced to nothing but ashes and goo. The monster laughed as it stared at her.

"Maker," it spoke to her.

Maker? Was it insinuating Tate's magic was responsible for it? Impossible. And yet, I stared at the female who never so much as hinted at having magic and was dumbfounded. She had just leveled an entire field of at least a hundred seethings in one burst of power.

I clenched my jaw. It didn't matter. Her secrets, her betrayal, none of it mattered right now.

Where was Shae? I looked past Tate, who was now squaring her shoulders, ready to battle the beast of a creature until my eyes landed on Shae. She was inside a dome with one of Anax Mardi's dokimoses.

I could make it to Shae from here. Blood help me, but there was nothing I could do for Tate. I didn't even know *who* she was anymore. The amount of magic Tate was radiating was unnatural and undocumented.

I was close to a decimated building. The moment I left I'd be exposed. I moved forward quickly, but as quietly as possible. Thanks to Tate and what should have been impossible, the field was empty save for the beast she was currently facing off with.

I ducked behind a half-standing wall. Peering over it, I could see Anax Mardi blocking Tate from the monster. Good, let him die.

I took a breath and then ran, heading straight for Shae.

Her eyes widened as she saw me approaching. I ran across the yard, stepping in piles of goo and mud, unsure of what was what. Dokimos Eragon looked at me and raised her weapon. I didn't slow down, I could hear seethings beginning to stir, repopulating the field. Dokimos Eragon squeezed the trigger.

I winced, preparing to feel the bullet, but instead, I heard it wiz by and then a guttural cry came from behind. She'd taken down a seething. She fired several more times as I continued rushing toward them.

The dome Shae was in was solid, it wouldn't let me through.

"Drop the dome!" I commanded.

Dokimos Eragon simply raised an eyebrow at me. She spoke into her com before looking from Shae to me.

"All yours, buddy." She shrugged at me before looking to Shae. "Good luck, and uh, do me a favor girl, stay alive." With that, she touched the other side of the dome and then bolted through it, heading for the forest's edge about two hundred yards out.

I didn't hesitate before pressing through the shield and falling inside the dome. Pounding and screeching from the other side told me those *things* had been right behind.

"Dale!" Shae called out but didn't stand. Her left leg was at an unnatural angle. Broken.

"What the hell were you thinking?" I demanded, stalking toward her. The dome shuddered but held. I could see those things trying to get in. Thankfully, it appeared they couldn't.

"I was doing the *right* thing you bastard. You were just going to leave her!" Shae accused me, waving a hand to the scene playing out behind me.

"Yeah, well look where your *'rescue,'*" I air quoted the word, not caring how much of a jackass it made me, "got you."

A guttural roar came from behind, and I turned to see the monster being thrown backwards, landing in the crumpled remains of a warehouse. Anax Mardi was holding Tate, who looked at him. They were focused on each other as if the whole fucking world wasn't burning.

I turned away; I couldn't stomach the sight.

"We need to go. Now."

"What about Tate?"

"What about her?" I reached Shae and picked her up, holding her across my shoulder. I would carry her out of here.

"Dale, you're better than this. She needs us. She saved me."

"She's *not* on her own, and there is nothing I can do for her. Did you see the way Mardi threw that thing back? He's her best option and I'm yours." I looked through the dome.

I'd left Holland and Damaris at the west side of the compound—they made it to the trees in the initial chaos after the explosion. Judging by the amount of seethings I could see tearing into the remains of some guaramen —along with blood knew what—retreating the way we came was not an option. Dokimos Eragon had run for the forest. That was our best option.

My core shook as I could feel my ire awakening. Something foreign was taking root. Impossibilities replaced the known. The whole compound was destroyed, along with my beliefs.

"Can you use a pistol from there?" I asked, handing her one and not waiting for a response.

"What do you think?" she asked, firing and shooting the two seethings who were still trying to get through the shield.

"Good. Holland, do you come in?" I spoke into the com. Nothing, I couldn't hear anything but static. "Hold on Shae, we're going to make a run for it."

I glanced one last time in the direction of the half-clothed female who had wrecked my moral code so thoroughly. She was levitating, once again *floating* midair while being held by Mardi.

I could taste the magic and feel it pulsing all around me. I had no idea *what* Tate was, but I knew it couldn't be natural. The thought of her using dark magic made me sick. It made her an accomplice to those monsters—possibly even their creator. The whole sky turned from grey to golden white and I looked away, shielding my eyes. Red haloed them as I looked toward the tree line.

I swallowed the bitter sting of hate and ran through the shield. If I was going to make it to the tree line, now was the time.

CHAPTER 71
TATE

The release would have sent me to my knees if I had been standing. Instead, I could feel Aether's arms wrapped around me, pulling me close even as my energy force poured out of me and into him. He took it, every ounce I threw at him. I could hear him grunting and knew it had to be painful. But he didn't back down, he didn't slam his door shut and refuse me, instead he welcomed it. I hesitated, perhaps I should stop.

I can take it.

He was assuring me, and again, I trusted him. I pushed more of the energy drowning me into him.

I could feel my temperature dropping. The itch to shift was vanishing and the hyper-aware nerves were calming. My body was still tingling, but this time it wasn't frantic, it was soothing. My hair fell, brushing my shoulders, and I relished releasing so much potency. I'd never known such power, such force before.

I kept feeding Aether until the pressure lessened and I could feel myself think again. The high I'd felt moments ago was gone. The powerful invincible feeling had dissipated, and instead, I was exhausted, thoroughly tired.

I went numb.

Aether slammed his mental door shut and the energy stopped flowing. It pooled inside me, snuggling around itself.

"Hold on, Tate, I've got you," he whispered into my ear, brushing his lips ever so tenderly to my earlobe.

I looked into his eyes. I believed him.

Let's get the hell out of here, darling.

I could feel his grip on me tightening as his body began to shake, to buzz. He physically released me, but I remained suspended in air, cradled in his grasp. Aether threw back his head and a cloud of black engulfed him and crackled.

I went weightless. I couldn't see anything but black light swallowing me whole. I couldn't see Aether anywhere because I was *in* his shadows. The grip holding me released and I fell, plummeting toward the ground fifty feet below.

I screamed as I tried to find my internal thread, I would need to shift. If I could become a raven again, I could save myself. The thread hung limp like an empty glass and wouldn't do anything when I tugged on it.

Massive talons wrapped around my waist and stopped my fall. The air was knocked out of my lungs as I was being pulled upward. Black-scaled claws gently held me and then tucked me into the underside of a dragon's warm belly.

Aether.

I told you I had you.

He held me close to him, his heat keeping me warm as an odd sense of peace and coolness settled over me. I looked below to see the chaos and mass carnage. Three-quarters of the compound had been leveled. It was on fire, smoke and ash littered the air. Seethings crawled on all fours and some stalked on two legs as they looked up at Aether and shrieked before fleeing into the forest, seeking coverage.

The large, monstrous seething was nowhere to be found. Like it vanished.

Hold on, dear.

Before I could even respond, fire erupted. It swallowed the entire compound whole, one building at a time. The seethings all dropped the moment the fire hit them.

Aether circled his head around until he lit every single remaining building on fire.

Shae!

The thought was a plea. I scanned the ground. Just beyond the tree line in a small clearing, I could just make out the periwinkle blue of her head. She was alive, she was alive. He didn't fry her.

I resent the implication.

I wouldn't be surprised.

He chuckled—odd coming from a dragon, it sounded more like huffs and growls, and yet I *knew* it was a laugh.

Aether lifted his head and roared. The screech shook the ground, knocking the black leaves and pine needles from the trees, reducing all the structures to nothing but smoldering rubble. He released another roar, followed by a stream of black flames that lit the dark sky.

With mighty strokes, he flapped his massive wings and flew higher into the night air. His grip around me was tender, but secure. Both air and energy assured me I was safe.

I've got you.

Somehow, I believed him. Even after all the deception and betrayal I'd faced, the lies and power games he'd played, I trusted him. I *knew* him. This male, this dragon, was connected to me in ways I didn't understand. But that murky internal pool of power had been cleared, and with it came the clear realization that Aether was mine.

I lowered my inhibitions, sleep tugging at me as sheer exhaustion began to claim my essence. We continued our climb, and I watched the compound, along with the life I once knew, burn to the ground. It was now nothing but ash.

WANT TO KEEP READING?

Sink your *fangs* into a delicious bonus chapter starring two prime characters in a SPICY encounter...perhaps, it's even a bit of a prequel. Find where to read it today after an exclusive sneak peek at *Fangs of Fate's* sequel, *DAUGHTER OF DESTINY*.

DAUGHTER OF DESTINY

CHAPTER ONE: TATE

The air was cool, crisp even. We'd been traveling for blood knew how long with Aether clutching me tenderly in his talons. He was silent—had been since we left. Not much to say anyway, I supposed. The ground below me moved, flowing in wisps of white that slowly drifted down to coat the ground—snow. The air felt blissful given my extreme temperature shifts. Currently, I was still very hot...but cooler after having transferred my energy to Aether. Sweat pooled under my arms and threatened to cool in the night air. Perhaps it would freeze without Aether's body's proximity to mine.

Dragons were warm beasts.

Vala and Jared flew beside us. Vala, a much smaller white dragon, had Jared carefully held in her clutches. Somehow, the positioning simultaneously surprised me and was yet expected. Vala was clearly the alpha. But why wasn't Jared flying?

Aether banked, his talons tightening ever so slightly, before circling down toward a cliff with a cave carved into the mountainside. He landed, and a plume of snow filled the air...so similar to the scene we'd just left.

Ash. Blood. Smoke.

The entire base had exploded, leaving charred ground marred by violence and death. Those things, those seethings, were the embodiment of evil and I didn't regret my actions. I didn't regret setting the charges, didn't regret slaughtering them. And yet...I'd fled. I'd left Shae, the only family I have left, when I allowed Aether to scoop me up and flee. I—

No, I shook my head. *Too* soon. I would think about all that had happened, about the ones I'd *abandoned*, later. Much later. Once this splitting headache left me.

Hold on.

It was the first thing I'd heard from Aether since we'd left. A command. Perhaps he was reverting back to old ways, returning to his 'Mardi'-like state. Blinding darkness enveloped me, bright somehow, and full of energy as the air sizzled.

He was shifting.

A moment later, I was clutched in the capable arms of Aether's bare body, his feet rested on wet stone—the snow had melted, as if shrinking back from his mere presence. He looked down at me with dark eyes that were surrounded by blood and ash...

CONTINUE READING!

LOOKING FOR THE BONUS CHAPTER?

Want more of Tate and Chance?! You can find the bonus chapter here:

DID YOU ENJOY FANGS OF FATE?

Thank you again for sinking your 'fangs' into *Fangs of Fate*! I'd be honored if you shared your love for the book by reviewing it on various platforms, including Goodreads and Amazon! <3

THE UNTISH SERIES CONTINUES

Thank you for taking a Chance on *Fangs of Fate*. Tate's story continues in the second installment of the *Untish Series*, **Daughter of Destiny**!

MAGIC IS ITS OWN ENTITY. IT CAN BE AS RUTHLESS AS IT IS HELPFUL.

TATE AARALYN:

Dear blood, he was a dragon shifter. A male who was lethal in both forms, wielding *black* flames that were somehow light. And he wanted me... Claimed me. Desired me.

I never thought I'd find myself inside the Untish Embassy, masquerading as a Darkling... but then again, I never knew I was a rare vampire with a dragon shifting gift. And now, I'm haunted by my elusive past, while simultaneously hunted by my very own.

He says he can help me, wants to protect me, that it's *my* choice. But clothed in secrets, and leading a society that thrives on deceit, trusting Aether Brychan may be the one thing that gets me burned.

AETHER BRYCHAN:

She's exquisite. Everything I'm not. Everything I want to protect, honor, and worship... And they want to destroy her. Kill her.

Over my dead body.

I'm the embodiment of darkness, and I *will* protect my bonded from the monsters, scaled and not. Come what f*cking may.

CHANCE DALE:

My worst nightmare stalks on two feet; vile monsters crafted from dark magic.

With new power thrumming in my veins, the allure of it beckons, cleaving a way for me to control the dark magic. Only I can decide how far I'll go to defend those I'm sworn to protect.

Darkness and red warp everything. *Become* everything. Red lights the path to victory. Red strikes and destroys. This *RED* may just be my only saving grace...

In a world where half-truths and betrayals lurk in every shadow, three fates intertwine. A storm is coming—and when it breaks, only one will remain.

Daughter of Destiny is an epic fantasy centered in an urban, dragon-shifting world where the Chairs determine who you marry, and everyone must earn their place in this action-adventure romance! This paranormal romantasy boasts steamy spice with fated mates and banter that has readers devouring the pages, leaving them craving more. Step inside these morally grey characters' minds in this first-person, multi-POV, dark fantasy, where bloodwine is life and secrets are currency. But be forewarned, not everything is as it seems...

JOIN MY NEWSLETTER!

For further updates and to stay current on all *Untish Series* news, please join my newsletter! I look forward to sharing the rest of this story with you and delving into the deep intricacy of the Untish culture and magic system that we've just dipped our toes in.

Love has never tasted so good or cost so much...

Acknowledgments

Thank *you* for embarking on this journey with me. *Fangs of Fate* was a story that was burning inside of me, begging to be brought to life, and it has finally been realized. I cannot begin to express my gratitude to you for taking a chance on me. I truly hope you've fallen in love with this world and these characters; they are very dear to my heart.

Thank you also to my amazing team, and to every single person who has helped make this dream a reality. Thank you to my husband, John, who has been unconditionally supportive. To all my friends and family who supported me, thank you for everything.

The story isn't finished! This is only the beginning for Tate, Chance, and Aether—along with all the other delicious morally grey characters.

About the Author

I love all things fiction, specifically, fantasy. Add a little romance, or sometimes a whole heap, and you'll find my specialty: romantasy. As an avid reader and devourer of all things Fae, dragon, and magical, my work (as you may have guessed) is centered in that world. I love a strong female protagonist who defies the patriarchy while learning to love and trust.

I am one of the lucky ones; I married my high school sweetheart and am a mother of two adorable, rambunctious boys. As a Colorado native, I love the sunshine and crisp air while enjoying the outdoors with my guys...have I mentioned I'm outnumbered?

Stories have always held me captive—they are the air I breathe. It is my purest pleasure to share the tales that have been burning in my heart. To see a full list of my works, please visit my website: www.rebeccaparcha.com